# LYDIA R. OUTLAND

THE PAST AND PASSED BY | BOOK ONE

# THE
# STRANGEST
# WOMAN

Black Rose Writing | Texas

ISBN: 978-1-68433-526-8
PUBLISHED BY BLACK ROSE WRITING
www.blackrosewriting.com

Printed in the United States of America
Suggested Retail Price (SRP) $22.95

*The Strangest Woman* is printed in Andalus

*As a planet-friendly publisher, Black Rose Writing does its best to eliminate
unnecessary waste to reduce paper usage and energy costs, while never compromising
the reading experience. As a result, the final word count vs. page count may not meet
common expectations.

# ACKNOWLEDGMENTS

I want to thank my incredible family (my brothers Aaron and Luke, my sister Tessa, and my dad) for donating their time and effort into helping bring about this little dream of mine. I truly appreciate all your help and support.

And I would like to especially thank the wonderful woman who not only brought me into this world but made it possible to create my own. Without you, I would never have learned how to read, let alone love to write. You gave me that gift. You have given me so much, and I am so grateful.

Thank you, mom.

# THE
# STRANGEST
# WOMAN

"What a strange thing man is; and what a stranger thing woman."
~Lord Byron


'I don't believe in magic,' the young boy said.
The old man smiled.
'you will, when you see her.'
~Atticus

# PROLOGUE
## TIMES PASSED BY

Wind bellowed and buffeted a handful of citizens still brave enough to pick their way through the cobbled streets of their darkening kingdom. It was the worst storm in thirty years; they proclaimed to one another in anguished voices barely heard over the sound of wind whipping through the streets. Such rains never bode good things. It was the type of storm that tore crops out by their roots and sent dirt in streams of mud to seep into the stone roads. It sunk deep into the cracks, creating thick muddy traps which waited patiently for the misstep of a child or the unwary placement of a horse's hoof. Waiting to grab hold, trip, and snap bone. The citizens stepped with as much care allowed, holding tight to their cloaks, children, and items, trying to keep them from blowing away like so many helpless leaves which twirled in browns and reds through the air. They jerked and darted against the relentless pull of the wind. People fled into their homes, hiding in the warmth and safety of their walls. Parents tucked in squalling children, snuggling them deep into their beds. Mother's crooned to crying darlings while fathers made promises for brighter mornings. Promises, of course, they had no way of keeping.

Not far, in an ornate castle donned with statues of brave knights long dead, another father pulled the covers up to his young son's chin.

"It's alright," he assured the boy with large blue eyes which darted around in terror at the slightest change in the storm. The father smiled. They looked so much like his mother's eyes, he noticed, with equal parts pride and pain.

Out of the father's three beautiful children, his son was the only one to inherit his mother's brilliant blue eyes.

The window was fastened, and the curtains drawn tight, but the winds angry wail sounded something monstrous. Every wail brought the boy's eyes to the window, as if waiting for it to burst in and drown them both with pelting rain.

"Everything is fine," the father promised. "Everything is alright."

"Yes, sir," the young boy answered, straightening himself in bed and putting on that little boy type of bravery. Wishing with all his heart not to be scared… and yet still showing it. "It's not our place to be afraid."

The boy's father frowned. He knew his son's words, had said them plenty of times before, but he did not like hearing them repeated now. He suddenly cursed himself for saying them at all. It was easy to tell his boy not to be scared when he had no fear to hold back, but when he could see it welling up behind those large and determined eyes… those words sounded almost foolish. They were not, but his son was still a child. The time to be a man would come sooner than either of them would like, but for now, the boy deserved to be afraid of the wind if he wished.

The father sat down beside his son, running a rough hand over his bearded face. A face once so young, handsome and full of spirit. It was now wrinkled, grayed with age, and a spirit tempered by time.

"It's true… we do not get the luxury of normal men's fear," the father started slowly. "To everyone else, we must be unafraid, unshakable… unbreakable. But my son…" He leaned in and smiled as another heavy wind rattled at the shutters, and his boy jumped in his bed. "There is one 'someone' you don't have to be unshaken with… you and me… between you and me, we can allow for a little fear. Because fear does not disappear by desire, or by pretending it does not exist. Just like pain, or regret, we can't show them to others… but as long as you have one person… that one person who will see your fear, your pain, your regret… and never tell. Never use it against you. Never show it to anyone else. Just for the two of you. That one person who will never judge, never let it eat you alive. If you have that person, all will be alright. Because that happens to me sometimes you know… I am afraid." His son gave him a doubtful look, eyebrow cocking high above his eye in a way that looked so very much like his mother. His father's heart gave a desperate throb. But he also could not help a laugh, "It's true. I do. More often than I'd like to admit."

"Mamma…" the boy began, watching for his father's reaction. His father kept smiling, so he went on. "Was she that someone for you?"

"Yes… yes, my boy, she was… but now… will you help me now? Will you be that person for me?"

"Yes." His son smiled, bright blue eyes sparkling, the wind forgotten. "Yes, sir, I will. Of course, I will."

"Good. Then I will be that person for you. So, you can be afraid of the wind. Of anything. It's alright." He reached out and patted down his son's soft dark hair. That hair which had irked his wife so often. Hours she had spent trying to tame it in place. Brush in hand, eyebrow high on her beautiful thin face with just a speckling of freckles over her sweet nose. That nose he loved to kiss every night before watching her eyes slide closed, relinquishing reality to dreams. Those blue eyes. So many years. So much time. But he would always have her eyes. They watched him now, blinking and gleaming as he spoke the words his son so desperately needed to hear. "You can be afraid. Just know I'm here, and I won't let anything happen to you. Not wind. Not anything. Not my son." The boy lurched from his bed as another angry rattle came from the window. He buried his face in his father's cloak, and the man tried his best not to laugh as he soothed him.

"Here," he said, "How about a story? Something to distract us while we wait out this storm, eh?" His son nodded and laid back down. This father straightened his cloak and sat in the chair next to his son's bed, close enough to be reached if necessary. He fluffed the thick cushions around the boy before beginning.

"All right then," he cleared his throat and thought a moment. His gray beard split into a wide smile. "Have I told you about the First War? And Great King Lawrence II?"

"I've heard about King Lawrence," the boy said, frowning in thought.

"Well, this is the story of how he *became* great… but first I should tell you about the time before the First Peace."

"First Peace?"

"Yes, the time brought by the Four Kingdoms." The father nodded, and his voice slowly took on that low and far away tone that belongs only to fathers and their faraway stories of times long gone or ages that never were.

"Before that… before it all… In times long passed and passed by, there was strange quiet. A deep quiet over the entire land, a silence that hung thick overall, soft to the ear of all who lived within. Life, however, was far from soft.

There was no order, no laws. People roamed as they pleased, stole as they pleased, lived as they pleased, killed as they pleased. It was quiet, but it was quiet mayhem. Animals and men lived and slept side by side. Dark and light in equal measure. And the only ruler was chaos.

Into this world was born four siblings. The eldest, Carter, grew to be tall and strong. His mere appearance called attention and his booming voice like a trumpet calling for heed. He was a natural leader of men. The second, Lawrence, also grew strong but not as tall or striking as his elder brother. However, he had wisdom and wit to rival any other man. The third, Nannette, was born with an elegant beauty which only grew more intense with time. She too was wise, wiser than her elder brother, but she was also as quiet as the chaos itself and had a cold streak that concerned even her brothers at times. The youngest, Edwin, was born from the death of their mother and barely survived himself. He grew up thin, and prone to catching sickness at the slightest winter breeze, but his heart was the complete opposite. He had a love, a kindness, mercy and everlasting joy that followed him like an unstoppable wind. It would overcome all around him and could stay any storm."

The father watched his son's eyes growing glassy, not with sleep, not yet, but with imagination. He was being pulled into the world and characters his father was painting. Yet another similarity to his mother. His father had wondered, on more than one occasion, whether his beautiful son was a blessing from the gods or a curse. The boy was forever a part of his beautiful Elaine. A piece that would stay with him forever, but he was also a reminder of the one person he loved most. The one that was forever lost to him.

He paused only for a moment, cleared away the lump in his throat, and continued.

"They were as close as four siblings could be. They worked together, lived together, hunted together, and fought together. They lived alone in the mountains of the Caskcare where they mined for precious stones to trade with travelers.

One day they dug deep into the darkest corners of their mine and discovered something unbelievable. So deep and dark they might have missed. Somewhere old and forgotten by time itself, they came across five strange stones. Very strange stones. They were broad, rounded, and their surfaces seemed to flicker in the candlelight. The stones also gave off an intense heat."

"Heat?" the boy asked.

"Well, my boy... because they were not 'rocks' at all. The four siblings took one of them and spent days trying to break it open. They thought the stone might contain gems, or veins of silver to trade, but it did not. It held something far more precious. It took time, a long time, but when it finally broke open, something astounding emerged. You see, the siblings found, not five stones, but five eggs."

"Dragon eggs?" the boy asked, a wide grin spreading his face and crinkling the corners of his blue eyes.

"Right," the father answered, leaning in, his own grin widening. He was losing himself in his own story. "*Dragon* eggs. Remnants of an unknown era, long ago and forgotten. Inside the egg, they found a three headed baby dragon, with scales of the palest blue. It hadn't yet fully developed, however, and soon died. Being well-meaning people, the siblings did what must be done out of respect. To stave off bad luck, they gave the little foal a name. Iver. They buried it within the same cave they had found it. Out of fear for the four remaining eggs, the siblings carefully removed them from the icy mountain, each sibling taking charge of one egg. They brought the eggs to their home, warmed them in their stove fire for a solid year. They stoked the fire, day after day, taking turn after turn, keeping the fires hot, until one day, the eggs finally hatched. And four dragons were born.

"The egg belonging to Lawrence hatched first. The little two headed filly had blue scales as dark as midnight, deep chestnut eyes, and a calm temperament. Lawrence named her Aneira, and they bonded the instant she opened her pale eyes.

"Carter's dragon hatched next. He was larger than the rest, with sleek and silver scales that flashed white in the light of day. He named the foal Sterlyn and the two, although at odds at first, soon grew a fierce attachment to one another.

"Nannette took the dragon with shimmering oil black scales and dark green eyes. She called him Kyara. Kyara was loud, active, and led by his every emotional whim, the complete opposite of Nannette in every way. Despite this, the two would die for each other without hesitation, almost doing so on several occasions.

"The youngest sibling, Edwin, took care of the timid filly of pale gold, calling her Beryl. Beryl was sweet but shy. Afraid, but calm. Small, but powerful in ways that would be revealed in time. Beryl and Edwin would never leave the others side. Years down the road, after so much history had changed the sickly boy to a man, and the shy dragon to a warrior, the two would never falter. Beryl would be by his side through all. Even in death, the two went together. Side by side.

"This my son, this is how the Four Kingdoms were born. As the dragons grew, they grew in size, strength and sheer power. They soon revealed themselves to not only to be animals of incredible strength... but of magic. They possessed fire, a fire that could melt and burn anything but their own eggs. They could also fly. Soar for miles above meadows, lakes, and valleys. But each dragon had something more. Sterlyn had the ability to control not only fire but ice. Aneira seemed able to communicate and influence other animals, bend their will to hers. Kyara's intense green gaze could set an entire army falling to their knees... or even to insanity. And Beryl could breathe as easily in water as out.

"The dragons and their powers grew and grew, and with them, the sibling's ambition. Together they decided to end the lawlessness in the land. With their combined strength and their dragon's loyalties, they created the Four Kingdoms. They brought order to the land, and a great peace spread. The First Peace."

"What happened to the dragons?" his son asked, head tilting to one side. Now that, the father recognized, was his own habit in the boy.

"Well..." the father said, taking a long dramatic breath. "That is where the trouble began. The siblings were mortal and soon aged under their crowns. Their dragons, however, were things of magic. They aged far slower and were still in their early years when the siblings grew old. To the great despair of their kingdoms, and their dragons, the siblings began to die.

"Now the dragons were loyal creatures, very loyal, to their perspective sibling... but resentment festered as they were soon passed from father to son, mother to daughter, king to heir. Passed down through generations like the crown upon their heads, as if a simple object. Several generations later, the dragons were growing more restless, resentful, and angry. A few remained loyal to the kingdoms, but the dragons themselves also sired foals. Some of these dragons broke away from the kingdoms, creating their own clans. They developed among the forests, mountains, and outskirts of the cities.

This was a tense time across the realm. As the dragon's numbers began to grow, they broke away more easily from the kingdoms. They also developed their own followers. People that cared for them. Similar to how the Keepers once cared for the dragons belonging to the kingdoms. But it was more than that. These were curious people, interested in magic and devoted to a particular dragon or a specific family of dragons. They called themselves the Faithful. These Faithful seemed drawn to dragons, enchanted by the large magical beasts. Almost to worship them like second gods.

These clans grew strong and fast but were generally peaceful in nature. They mostly kept to themselves. However, fear began to grow among the kingdoms. These were creatures of incredible power and magic, and they were gathering more people to them now. They had even started teaching a few of their most prized humans the ways of magic. Magic had been unknown to these lands before the dragons were born, and the idea of humans wielding their powers was a terrifying concept to most. Dragons were things of magic, but humans were not, and never should be. As time passed their numbers grew larger and larger, and the citizens of the Four Kingdoms feared an uprising. Their fears were answered. An antagonistic clan began to develop. The dragons and their Faithful gathered under the title of "The First Dragon," and called themselves the Iver Faithful."

"The dragon foal who died?" the son asked, frowning, little nose crinkling with confusion.

"Exactly right."

"But why?"

"They believed the kingdoms were built upon the backs of dragons and that all the dragons, starting with Iver, had been abused. They believed that within the kingdoms, dragons were being disrespected, treated as mere pets and it was their duty to take the Four Kingdoms by force. They meant to cast out the kings and queens of the lands, uniting the four regions under a dragon's reign... 'By the name and blood of Iver,' was their chant, and with it they massacred millions. There were three powerful dragons in their clan, and all three went to war by the side of their humans, and they burned thrice that many cities to the ground."

"Wait," The boy's eyes widened in recognition. "This is the beginning of The First War, isn't it?"

"Yes, it is," the father said, head tilted to the side. "You know this story, don't you? I've told it to you before, haven't I?"

"I don't mind." The boy shrugged and smiled that smile which shattered his father's heart. "I like this story. Please don't stop now."

The father reached out and rumpled his son's hair, messing it up all the more.

"Humoring me are you, you little sneak? Well, I'll take it all the same. Yes, and so The First War had begun. Those monsters destroyed without hesitation, without regret, and without mercy. They spilled innocent, and royal blood alike, and burned towns to ash. Whoever or whatever stood in their way, they burned. They took control of Bryxton Castle in a matter of weeks, and killed most of King Carter's decedents, taking the rest captive. The dragons used their fire, and their Faithfuls used their adopted powers. They seemed unstoppable. Nothing in the kingdom's armories could hurt them, and the other clans and even the dragons within the kingdoms refused to fight their own kind. Not even in defense of their lords or their own lives. Nothing seemed able to hold the Iver Faithful at bay.

"It was then that Great King Lawrence II, made a discovery. At the time Lawrence II was a young prince who noticed how weak his people's weapons seemed against the ferocity of The First Dragon's powers. All the knight's arms were useless against the dragon's scales. Swords snapped in half. Arrows bent and fell before them, and as long as the dragons remained alive, their follower's adopted magic stayed unshakable."

"Well, what did he do?" His son was leaning forward now, eyes unblinking.

"He had an idea... he won the war... with an idea." The father smiled. "Lawrence II was in his study, admiring one of the shells which belonged to Aneira's first-born foal when he had his epiphany. He took the egg down to a trusted swords smith. Although fire could not burn the eggs, given enough time in the blistering furnaces, the eggshells began to liquify. The smith melted down the shell in manmade fire and had the swordsmith create a great long sword. It was an ugly thing. Dull colored blade, almost a dirt brown, with strips of black that slipped across its surface like spilled oil. Unpleasant as it was, it was strong and sharper than any blade known before. Lawrence II dubbed the sword Defier and took it with him into battle against The First Dragon clan at Bryxton. The blade proved invaluable and was the only thing able to pierce dragon scales. Lawrence II himself killed one of the three dragons and freed Bryxton, putting King Carter's decedents back on the throne.

"Lawrence II called for unity between the Four Kingdoms, a great bringing together of armies to once and for all hunt down the Iver Faithful and bring an end to The First Dragon clan. He and the other kings and queens commissioned three more blades to be made from dragon eggs, which was soon to be called dragon iron. A blade for each kingdom. All were scarred by the fire, unseemly, and utterly deadly. Every kingdom brought their armies, their dragon egg swords, and went to war."

"And all the dragons still refused to go," the boy said, saying the thing his father forgot.

"No matter how much it was begged of them." His father nodded. "Even when Lawrence II himself fell to his knees before the descendants of Aneria and begged for their aid in battle, they refused. No clan, nor kingdom born foal, would fight for us against their own. So, humans alone, side by side with Lawrence II as their leader, went to war. It took four long years, but the Iver Faithful and their dragons were finally defeated. The dragons were decapitated, and their remaining Faithful scattered to the wind. Without their dragons, the Iver Faithful's powers faded away. They hid, helpless, from the armies of the Four Kingdoms. It didn't come without cost. Many lost their lives. Lawrence II's father died before the end of the war, leaving Lawrence II to take his throne. Although Great King Lawrence II helped win the war... he knew it was not enough. They needed to prevent any further horror. Those creatures were too strong, too powerful. It took far too many, and far too long, to defeat only three dragons. And there were dozens of other clans with many dragons and many people. People drawn, seemingly helpless to these creatures, either by magic or the desire for the power that magic could bring. They came, and their numbers grew larger with every year that passed by. They were charmed. Seduced. They needed to be freed. Saved from these creatures. Saved from themselves.

"And there were also the dragons at the heart of every kingdom, who could turn against them... and easily burn it to the ground. There would always be a threat. One war had nearly burned down the kingdoms... one more may commit the entire world to flames. The kings and queen held secret counsel in the dead of night. A decision was made. With great sorrow, Lawrence II elected to be the first to give the sacrifice. He personally walked down to the dragon chambers with Defier. He went to the sleeping decedents of Aneira, who his ancestor Lawrence I had pulled from the mountainside. And while they slept, he executed them one by one. The rest of the kingdoms followed suit with their dragons on the same night, as had been decided during their counsel.

"After this execution, known now as The Sacrifice, the kingdoms set out to rid the world of these dangerous beasts. Eight more dragon egg swords were made and given to the most skilled and trusted knights among the kingdoms. These knights were dubbed Liberators and were burdened with a singular mission. They, along with their armies, scoured the forests, mountains, lakes, and valleys until they slayed every dragon. We, humans, pulled these creatures from the stone... and it was time we put them back. We cut out the monsters from this world, and we freed the Faithful's of their poisonous influences. It too came with a price.

"Great King Lawrence II died in the process, killed by one of the last decedents of Kyara. But we still honor him to this day because of his heroic and selfless actions and bravery against unquestionable power. His son took his place on the throne, and one of his first actions was to outlaw Faithful practices in this kingdom of Neira. Two of the other three kingdoms followed suit. The Faithful's soon had no dragons... but they still had their bones. The kingdoms tried to destroy them. They could remove the flesh, but the bones themselves stayed strong and full of magic. Breaking them was nearly impossible. Even in the few cases where they were able to shatter them, the pieces still clung to their magic. So, the kingdoms locked them away, deep in the caverns, and the Keepers had a new task. Keep the bones of creatures for which they had once cared.

"After fifteen long years, dragons were finally gone from the world. There was peace in the lands. The Second Peace. It was his job to keep that peace, just as it is ours now." The father patted his sleepy son's shoulder. He had begun to drift near the end of the story. The wind had calmed to a low whistle, and his son's fears were forgotten. These stories were ones of war, death and heroic battle... but they were just stories, and the hour was late. "We are here to protect that peace. At all costs."

"The Great King," his son yawned, eyes nearly closed. "Do you think he was afraid?"

"Yes, I believe he was."

"But he had a person, right?"

"Yes, I believe he did. His son. Just like I have you. Sleep now. All storms pass by. As all things must."

"Goodnight, sir."

"Goodnight Damian."

His son was already asleep before he closed the door. The father looked at his personal guard who had been waiting in the dark hallway, lit by nothing but a few sputtering lamps. Before he could say anything, the guard held up a large goblet. Lazy drifts of steam and a thick sweet smell wafted from its lip. He sighed with relief, and a broad smile broke the man's face.

"Gods bless you, Killian," he said, reaching out for the goblet and taking a drink. He reveled in the strong taste that slipped down the back of his tongue and the little flecks that dribbled through his beard. He had been waiting for this all day. It was just as sweet as ever. He wiped it away with the back of his hand and gave a wide grin. "What would I ever do without you?"

Killian said nothing at first. He was never one for many words. He had a quiet way about him, one that did not match his youth. Most young men of his age were loud, boisterous, with seemingly endless amounts of energy. It was one of the reasons his advisers had counseled against him having this young novice as his personal guard instead of one of his more seasoned men. Killian, however, had always been, and probably always would be, a steady, quiet and watchful companion. Killian also knew things, like how he would need a large glass of something hot and strong after tucking his beautiful, and so mother like, son into bed. He liked that. Screw seasoned.

"The prince alright your majesty?" Killian asked.

"Absolutely." The king smiled. "That's a good boy I have. A brave boy."

"Most children would fear such a storm." Killian nodded. "The prince is unique."

"Yes, I believe he is." The king smiled to himself. *Yes, my boy... I am your person as you are mine.* He then looked back at his guard. "How is Naomi?"

"Fast asleep, my lord."

The king chuckled. His baby daughter was such a mellow thing. She was never fussy. Never whined during storms or cried when she was hungry. In fact, the only time she had ever cried was directly after taking her first breath. She had opened her little mouth and had let fly the most ear-splitting sound her father had ever heard before or since. But that only lasted a moment. Her wails stopped with her twin brothers beating heart, as her mother's life's blood spilled across the bed. His baby girl had been silent ever since.

The king's chuckle died on his lips. He took another drink. "I think I will retire for the evening. Check on him in a few hours, won't you? For my sake more than his."

"Of course, your majesty." Killian bowed low and followed a few silent steps behind as King Lystad of Neira moved down the hall of Castle Lyist. His chestnut cloak billowed behind him and his shoes clicked against the stone floor. As he went, the king took another long swig from the goblet and glanced over at the shield that hung high on a far wall. He looked at the two headed blue dragon carved into its wooden surface, watching its paint shine and gleam in the erratic lamplight. Shadows fought for dominance against the light, twisting and swirling in an odd dance. Some strange fiery battle.

The king sighed. It was no easy thing, wearing that coat of arms, but his son would be just fine. In time. The boy had been sullen since his mother's passing a few months previous… but he had to admit, so had the king himself. So had they all. *Given time,* the king thought, taking another long drink, *all will be fine.* All things pass and pass by. As all things must.

# SIXTEEN YEARS LATER

# CHAPTER 1

She closed her long fingers tight around the rough branch of an old sprawling tree. The smell of dirt, rain, and grass clung to the wind that gently tugged her hair from her face. She leaned into that wind, breathing its sweetness, and watching the ground below. The forest was calm that day, only a few stray squirrels darted the floor, and a hand full of birds danced the treetops alongside her. It was lovely and soothing… but it meant difficult hunting. She crouched and moved down the branch, darting swiftly to another, and then another. She glided along the forest like a breeze, seeking something that might pass for dinner. Kyana had found little food over the past few days. She had begun picking though her reserves and they were getting woefully low. For one girl, she ate quite a bit.

A soft sound made her pause. Kyana leaned forward, rough bark cutting into her palms as she did so. A smile spread her small mouth. A large buck, with antlers that sprawled as wide as the trees he walked under, was picking his way around a berry bush. She pulled the bow from around her back and slipped an arrow from the quiver tied about her shoulder. The bow made a little creak as she pulled the end to her cheek. She was about to let the arrow fly when she noticed them. Four men, stalking the buck on the forest floor. They were crouched behind bushes and craning a peek from behind a wide trunk of a tree. They were out of view from the buck himself, but terribly visible at Kyana's vantage point. Kyana lowered her bow and scowled. She had hoped this would not happen. She rarely ventured this close to the outer edge of the forest. It was more likely to find other hunters this close to the open meadow which lead to towns, cities, and people in general. Unfortunately, Kyana's usual hunting spots had grown sparse over these past months, forcing her to stray from the comforts of the deeper forest.

Kyana frowned down at each of the men. One had thin, long limbs, and a face with a young, boyish nature. He wore simple clothes of brown and green, with a gray woolen cap pulled down low, almost covering his ears. The others, Kyana noticed, varied so comically in everything but their clothes. One was tall, the tallest man that Kyana had ever seen. He had long hair tied back in a low ponytail with a great beard braided down to his chest. Another was short for an average man but, in his place next to the tall man, he was dwarfed. This man was clean shaven, and far bulkier than the first. The muscles that strained under his shirt spoke of many nights and early morning obsessively tending to their growth. The last man was neither tall, nor short, but something in between. Unlike his fellows, who donned hair of browns in many shades and lengths, his hair was a thick mixture of black. It shone in the light that flitted between the leaves, giving it a unique liquid quality, something like spilled ink, or the tip of a raven's wing in the sunlight. Dark and yet somehow still able to shine.

All these men were dressed in browns and blues, but they also had swords at their sides, and a coat of arms decorated on their backs. Kyana peered closer, only to recoil. The crest was that of a two headed blue dragon against a light brown field... not good.

The dark-haired man pulled up a crossbow, paused, and let loose an arrow. The buck teetered a moment, giving a choked, bleating sound around the bolt that sunk deep below his chin. Then it fell motionless to the ground, legs splaying around its still body. The men stood up from their hiding places and hooted in their excitement. Kyana had to admit it was a smooth kill, but it also had been her meal plan for the upcoming week. She was ruefully slipping her bow back over her shoulder when something else caught her eye.

*Oh... well shit.*

Kyana wondered if she should warn the men with their coat of arms. They were no friends to her, why should she tell them they were about to be surrounded by bandits?

She could see ten or so dark figures creeping through the underbrush, taking position around the four men, who were obliviously celebrating their kill. The happy hunters were about to become the happily hunted... poetic, but completely none of her business. Before she could decide whether or not to warn them, the bandits attacked. From the shadows of the trees and around the bushes, eleven men in ragged black clothes emerged and surrounded the four hunters. Daggers gleamed in the bandits' hands, as the three men with their coat of arms pulled swords from loose hung scabbards on their hips. Kyana frowned as she noticed the man without a coat of arms made no such moves. Instead, he stayed close to the man with black hair as the bandits slunk nearer. Kyana was about to dart away through the trees when she paused. Four against eleven... one of the four without even a blade... how *cowardly*.

The men with coats of arms, knights of Castle Lyist Kyana guessed, stood back to back. Someone gave a loud yell, and everything went to shit. Swords clanged violently, and a bandit hit the ground never to get up. Kyana admired the knight's skill, but they could not win this fight. That became painfully evident when two of the knights were unarmed, and the third dark-haired knight was knocked to the ground with a blade pressed against his chest by a tall looming bandit.

"No!" screamed the fourth man, in a surprisingly high voice. He leaped forward to defend the fallen knight, but one of the bandits slammed him in the face with the butt of his sword. He crashed to the ground, dazed, blood beginning to pump from his damaged nose. The bandits laughed as the boy clutched his face and the thick redness oozed between his fingers. The dark-haired knight roared in anger and tried to stand. He was pushed back down by the tip of the bandit's blade.

"Well, well, well, what do we have here?" the bandit said, twisting the sword against the knight's chest. Kyana could see a gouge developing in the cloth, and a small stream of blood began to dye the edges.

"You will die for this," the dark-haired knight said. Kyana saw no fear on the knight's face. He was calm, reserved, and made no signs of pain as the bandit twisted the blade down deeper. A small smile twitched her lips, there and quickly gone.

"I'm afraid not, boy," the bandit said, grinning. The teeth that remained in his skull were dark and yellowed to the point of being brown. "I think I will pick myself up a nice ransom... and you? You get to see your parents today." The knight's eyes filled with fury, and he made another attempt to stand but was forced back once more. The bandit's laughter grew louder, and Kyana felt anger filling her empty stomach, striking and igniting like fire in a hearth.

3

*Playing with your kill? How… Gods damn cowardly.*

Before she knew what she was doing, she had pulled an arrow to her cheek and let it loose. It cut the air and caught the looming bandit in the side of his neck. Blood gushed from the wound as the bandit dropped his sword and clutched his throat. The others stood stunned for a moment, giving her plenty of time. Kyana unclipped her long dark buckskin cloak and let it fall over one of the bandits that stood below her tree, blinding him. She came down on top of it, pulling her dagger from her belt and stabbing it through her cloak. The bandit underneath groaned and stopped moving as she thrust again and turned the blade. She stood, dagger still in hand, blood slowly dripping from its tip.

"Who the hell are you?" asked one of the eight remaining bandits. His tone was furious, but his eyes were full of fear. Kyana could not hear him over the sound of blood rushing through her ears. It did not matter. The only thing that mattered were the three bandits circling around her back. She spun around and grabbed the nearest man by the wrist, planted her foot and used his momentum to swing him about as another bandit went at her with his sword. The blade plunged through his fellow and came out his back, missing Kyana by inches. Kyana shoved the impaled man-shield to the side, the sword still in him, and leaped at the now unarmed bandit. She rammed him in the chest and sent him stumbling into the third man. While they were trying to catch their balance, Kyana slashed her dagger across the throat of the first, and then the throat of the second. They both whimpered like dogs kicked by an unfair master, but soon slumped to their knees and went silent as their life's blood spilled out around them.

Kyana swung around, blood now spraying from her dagger, sending little red droplets in a grisly arch. She saw the dark- haired knight getting to his feet, the bandit's fallen sword in his hand.

"Ira! Are you alright?" he yelled to at the boy on the ground.

"Yes, I'm alright," the unarmed boy said through a stream of blood. The knight nodded and turned to the nearest bandits. The other two knights stood, picked back up their blades, and began to fight. Kyana stashed her dagger into her belt and loaded her bow as she stepped up beside the three knights and the unarmed boy. The five remaining bandits backed away.

"What?" the dark-haired knight asked, stepping forward. "You only like uneven battles?" They merely stood there and did not answer. "Who are you?"

the knight asked, taking another step, blade up. "Where are you from?" The bandits glanced at each other before turning to run. "Hey!" the dark-haired knight yelled and started after them. "Stop!"

Kyana aimed and let loose. The first arrow landed in one of the bandit's shoulders, but he kept running, so she let loose a second that hit another in the lower leg. This bandit let out a cry of pain, stumbled and fell forward next to the dead buck, his sword skidding across the ground out of reach. The knights darted after the rest, but the bandits knew the forest, and they vanished in seconds. The knights turned back and surrounded the downed bandit, hitting him around the head to knock him unconscious. They kicked his sword farther away, before breaking out into a loud whooping cheer that made Kyana cringe.

"Holy, shit!" one of the knights hooted. "That was unbelievable!"

"Yes, it was," the dark-haired knight stepped over to help the unarmed boy to his feet. "Gods Ira, are you okay? How's your nose?"

"Uh, well, not good," Ira said, fingering the bridge of his nose before groaning in pain.

"Ira, shit," the knight tried to pull back the boy's fingers to get a better look, but Ira moved away. "I shouldn't have dragged you along, I'm so sorry."

"It's okay." Ira waived one hand dismissively in his direction while the other tried to stem the flow of blood still oozing down his face. "Not your fault."

"Here, hold on." The dark-haired knight reached up and grabbed the woolen cap from the boy's head. A stream of bright gold came tumbling down from underneath its rim. It was not gold, of course, but a thick pile of hair. Waves fell around Ira's shoulders, and Kyana had a brief moment to take in his face framed by it, before the dark-haired knight put the cap over Ira's nose, and gently tipped his head back. "Now stay like that. We'll head back and find one of The Seven. Get you fixed up." Kyana watched this interaction with curiosity but soon turned her attention to the downed buck. Her stomach gave a violent throb that she mistook for hunger.

"Great…. Except now, I can't see anything," Ira laughed, looking up at the sky. Kyana started edging for the buck, her stomach really beginning to hurt.

"You sure you're alright?" the shorter knight also asked, only to receive an exasperated sigh.

"I'm not glass," Ira said. "I'm fine."

"Well, other than poor Ira, we made out rather well!" the tall knight exclaimed. "What luck! Speaking of which... wait, wait, wait, where is she?" They all turned, and Kyana froze halfway to the buck.

"There she is!" The shorter knight sheathed his sword and flashed her a wide grin. "Our angel from the treetops!" Kyana said nothing, her eyes darted from them, to the buck, and to the forest. Perhaps she should just leave the deer and go.

"I believe," said the dark-haired knight, brushing back his hair. "We owe you our thanks," He held out his hand. Kyana looked at it and then back at the coat of arms on his shirt. She took a step back and teetered on the edge of darting into the forest.

"Wait," the knight said, holding up his hands. "Don't be afraid. We're not going to hurt you." Kyana hesitated. She really wanted that buck. Perhaps they could let her take it for saving them... as long as she did not slip up... it would be fine. But as the dark-haired knight took a small step forward, she jumped back from him, fingers tapping a warning against her dagger.

"Wow, hold on, it's alright," the boy named Ira stepped up beside his dark-haired friend. It was then Kyana realized, that he was not a boy at all. The young boyish features were actually those of a freckled face girl in boy's hunting cloths. Blood smeared her face and hooked nose, but her eyes were a bright hazel and full of kindness. Her smile was wide and sincere, showing a long line of white teeth. "Uh, hi there," she said. "My name's Ira. May I ask your name?"

"... I... I be... no... I *am*... Kyana," she answered. She had not spoken in so long, her own voice sounded foreign to her. Her stomach was really hurting now... if she could just take the buck and go...

"Hello, Kyana," Ira said. "We just wanted to thank you for... you know..."

"Saving our asses," added the knight who was at least a head taller than the rest. "We would have been screwed. I mean, good gods, where did you learn to fight like that?"

Kyana opened her mouth to ask about the buck when the pain in her stomach gave a violent stab. She whimpered and clutched at it. When she drew her fingers back, they were wet and bright red.

*Oh...* She thought. *That makes sense.* Her knees buckled.

"She's hurt!" The dark-haired knight moved forward just in time to grab her arm as Kyana stumbled to her knees. Everything started to dim. Pain spread like ice down her legs and up her chest. She felt herself being lifted into the air. She was already weaving in and out of consciousness when she realized the knight was caring her towards a group of horses. The other knights swarmed around them like birds taking formation. Taking off towards home.

*No,* she thought, unable to find her voice. She could feel the blood slipping down her side, dripping away with her consciousness. *No, just leave me. I'd rather die. Leave me to die. Don't take me **there**.... I don't want to go **there**... evil is there, leave me here.*

All she could manage was another quiet whimper before she slipped into the darkness.

# CHAPTER 2

Kyana woke to a stabbing pain in her lower side. She groaned, opened her eyes and tried to orient herself. She felt warm. Very warm. Too warm. She lifted a hand to her forehead and felt sticky skin. A fever…. Wonderful. Her head hurt, and she was having trouble remembering where she was or how she got there. She tried to put it together. Images swirled in vague, disjointed spirals across her memory. She tried to catch them, but they kept skirting away like fish in a pond.

*Hunting… A knight with a crossbow poised… bandits in dark shadows… the blood on her fingertips… the dark-haired knight lifting her, taking her to… No!*

She jerked up on a bed covered in soft brown cushions. The room was large, with a high ceiling held up by thick, decoratively carved wooden beams. She could see a table in one corner and a small cabinet on the other. Both had been carved with the same skilled hand as the beams above. Spirals, flowers, and random forest animals donned every bit of the furniture that Kyana laid her eyes on. Every spare inch of wood was decorative. No beam, drawer, or bed frame was safe from the gaudy hand of the carver. A fire grumbled deep in the open mouth of the fireplace, filling the room with moist heat. Soft cloth draped around the bed in blue and brown hangings which served as a curtain for the sleeper.

Kyana pushed sticky auburn hair out of her face to look up at a flag which hung from the far wall. It was made from thick, fine cloth, and depicted a coat of arms. A dark two headed blue dragon mid-flight against a chestnut sky.

*Not good. Not at all good.*

She bolted out of bed, only to stagger and stumble to her knees on the hard-wooden floor. She hissed in pain, brushing hastily at her knees and watched as a small purple bruise blossomed beneath her skin. Her balance was thrown by the fever, and her head was swimming just from the effort of sitting back up. It did not matter, she needed to get out. She got to her feet and staggered to the door. Her fingers were inches from the doorknob when it turned before her touch. An older man, somewhere between his fortieth and fiftieth year, loomed before her, drawing her escape to a jutting halt. The man had a short beard, speckled with white. His pale eyes shot open wide at the sight of her up and about. His mouth dropped open into a small "o". Kyana might have found it funny if she had not been so close to puking all over his scuffed brown shoes.

"Oh, my dear, you're awake." She pushed passed him and headed out into the hall. "Wa-wait a moment, get back here!" Kyana did not pay attention. The man followed her down the large hallway, his dark black cloak flipped indignantly behind him. "Wait!" He called in a voice that came from somewhere deep in his chest. It rumbled up and out like far off thunder. "You're with a fever! You can't be up. You should be sleeping. Hold on, girl, get back here!"

"No," Kyana said, shaking off the man's gentle grip as he tried to stop her.

"Your wounds are still fresh. You keep moving around like that, you will open them again," the man tried to sooth in that deep voice, but Kyana ignored him and continued to stumble down the abandoned hall. She clutched at the cold stones swaying, feeling sick.

"Must leave now..." Her legs seemed to have other ideas. They kept tangling beneath her as she walked. She pushed herself forward with desperate determination. She needed to get out. They would surely kill her if she did not.

"Stop being ridiculous, you're going to hurt yourself," he barked, following close behind her. He reached for her several times, but she pushed him away. "Please slow down. You need to rest. You're delirious..." Kyana said nothing and staggered again. She caught herself on the stone wall which smelled unpleasantly of mold.

"Do you know where you are? This is Castle Lyist! You're safe here." His large but gentle hand tried to sneak around her elbow again, only to be shaken off once more.

"No, not safe." Kyana continued jerkily forward.

*I know exactly where I am... anywhere but safe.*

Kyana hesitated, as a wave of nausea, threatened the minimal contents of her stomach. She gritted her teeth and groaned.

"Guards!" the man called, rumbling voice echoing in the empty hall, "Everett, Neander, please, can I have some help over here!" Men in brown cloaks and gleaming armor had turned the corner. Kyana recognized them. They were two knights from the forest. Short-bulky and the tall-bearded. They were chatting, laughing, not noticing them at first. The short man had thick red-brown hair that fell in his face, and the tall man had to keep his long strides to a minimum to compensate for his friends' step. Both wore long chestnut cloaks. Both wore daggers. They hung off their hips in front of swords whose glint caught Kyana's blurred eyes. They both looked up at the man's insistent call.

"Hey! It's our treetop angel!" cried the shorter knight, catching sight of Kyana.

"Hello, Miss!" said the taller knight, a wide grin over his face. "What are you doing up?"

Kyana spun around them both, continuing to stumble down the hall.

"Oh, slow down, you don't look well." The shorter knight stepped in front of her and tried to catch her arm. Kyana instinctively pulled the dagger out of his belt and held it up.

"Wow," The men backed away, out of Kyana's reach. "Calm down... Augustine... what's wrong with her."

"It's the fever," the man named Augustine answered. "She is faint with fever... if she doesn't get rest and medicine, she'll get herself killed."

"Come now, angel," the short knight stepped forward, "let's nobody die today."

"Away..." Kyana stumbled backward, trying not to fall, "... They'll kill me."

"No one is here to hurt you..." the tall knight said, eyes darting from his fellows and back to her.

*That is all they do.* Kyana thought viciously as if the mere thought could strike out of her and cause pain of its own. *They hurt. They hunt, they convict, and they kill… that is all they do. They're demons of men.*

"Demons…" was all Kyana was able to say, dagger lowering to her side.

"Wait, what?" The shorter knight looked at the taller, who shrugged.

"She must be hallucinating," the older man said, sounding both fascinated and worried. "The fever… My dear, what are you seeing?" She did not answer. Instead, she continued to back away down the hall. The three men followed. The tallest knight slowly moved to place his hand on the hilt of his sword.

"Okay…. it's okay, angel… let's just all take a few breaths." The short knight's eyes darted behind her for half an instant before flicking back to her face. Kyana knew what that meant. She swung around and caught the arms which were meant to wrap around her. Kyana caught the would be sneak off guard and twisted one arm behind his back, forcing his fingertips up to touch shoulder blades. The sneak grunted in pain as she pressed the dagger against his throat.

"No, wait!" the taller knight yelped, taking his hands off his sword and holding them up. "No, it's okay, put down the knife."

Kyana frowned. *They send someone sneaking up behind me like a snake… and they say everything is okay?*

Kyana continued to back down the hall, the dagger still pressed to the person's throat. The sneak stumbled after her, swallowing fear, scrapping the skin of his neck against the blades sharp edge. They hit a flight of stairs, which made Kyana pause. She looked back at her pursuers.

"Leave me alone," she called, sweat rolling down the back of her neck, and hands trembling around the dagger in her hand.

"I'm afraid we can't do that," a calm voice spoke. Kyana recognized it. The dark-haired knight stepped out from around a corner to her right, sword in hand. His simple brown shirt was gone, replaced by a long-sleeved black shirt with what looked like golden rings on his fingers. His black hair fell haphazardly around bright blue eyes. She had not noticed before, but they were a mixture of dark and light blue. A yin-yang of day and night sky contrasted against deep olive skin.

"You've got a friend of ours," the dark-haired knight continued, taking a hunter's step forward. Silent. Smooth. Dangerous. "… and we'd like her back… Ira, you alright?"

"Oh, ya," said the sneak with the dagger against her neck. "I'm *perfect*."

"Ira?" Kyana asked. She remembered the girl without a coat of arms. Blood dripping leisurely down a wide grin, face framed in long golden hair.

"That's me," the girl said and raised her free hand to wave backward at her. "Hi, we met in the forest, remember?"

"Ira," she repeated, watching the other knights fall in behind the man. What was that chain around his neck? Was it made of gold as well? "Who is that?"

"The guy with black hair?" Ira asked, "That one, that's Damian. King Damian."

"King?" Kyana's eyes darted to the dark-haired man. *Damian...* His eyes were on her, blade up, flanked by his knights. She felt a flicker of fire in her chest. "Lystad? Damian Lystad?"

"Ya, that's him." Ira nodded. The blade brushed her throat again, and she stopped.

*No... no, not good. Very not good.*

Kyana pulled her blade away from Ira and pushed her forward. The king dropped his sword to catch the girl and Kyana turned to dashed down the staircase. She could hear the knights following close behind as a bell rang out in the distance, signaling an hour Kyana did not know. She flew down the steps, reaching the bottom and brushed passed a few serving girls as she made her way towards a door. Their shrieks were cut short as she slammed the creaking door behind her. The sun struck her like a wave as she made it to fresh air. It was sweet and wet with morning mist. She blinked up at the sky, which was splashed with soft blue and orange streaks. Even in her feverish delirium she recognized its beauty. It seemed as if painted there by lazy brush strokes while pink clouds floated in the subtle breeze.

Kyana tumbled out into the courtyard. The bell rang loud in her ears as she stumbled across the cobbles. Passersby going about their usual business watched her with curious eyes as she staggered to a standstill. Kyana scanned around, looking for a way out. She saw a large brick archway which opened out into the surrounding section of the city. Kyana headed straight for it. A yell came from behind her and six guards poured from behind the archway. The tall metal gates slammed closed before her eyes with a creak and thud. Her heart sank as she blinked fever sweat out of her eyes.

*They're going to kill me now. This is it. This is where I pass by.*

She flipped around to see her pursuers forming a circle around her. Kyana flipped her dagger and held it up, readying herself. Six knights at her back, four at her front, plus Ira who was standing off to the side... and the Lystad.

"I know you're afraid," the Lystad said, stepping forward. His eyes were wary, but his voice was strong and calm. His sword was away now that Ira was safe, and he held his empty hands out to her. "We aren't here to hurt you. We're only trying to help."

Kyana leaned forward on her toes, getting ready for a fight, but she was so unstable she almost fell on her face. She caught herself and wobbled back to a standing position. She noticed those around her glancing to one another rocking back and forth on their heels, unsure whether to come forward or stay where they were.

"No 'help'... not you... you do the hurting." Kyana stumbled again, words tripping over themselves.

"Augustine, what's wrong with her?" the Lystad asked over his shoulder to the older man. "Her balance..."

"And her color," Ira added.

"It's the fever," Augustine answered. "She shouldn't be awake, let alone moving around. She's very sick, my lord, delirious and hallucinating."

"She thinks she sees demons," the tall knight added.

"She looks so scared..." Ira mumbled just loud enough for Kyana to hear.

"How about we all take a breath, and calm down," the shorter knight said smiling. "And get you back to bed."

"Home," Kyana stumbled again and caught herself on a stack of barrels waiting for a horse and cart. Her voice broke as dark streaks crossed her eyes, consciousness waning. "Home... I want to go home." She sank, the blade slipping from her fingers and clattered against the cobbled street. She watched it fall in a time that seemed slower than reality. It gleamed in the morning light and clanked slowly to a halt. She reached for it, meaning to pick it up. Instead, she doubled over and vomited. After purging her stomach over the blade, Kyana tried to stand straight, only to stumble again.

"Catch her!" Augustine barked. A knight stepped forward and reached for her. Heat like fire shot lightning fast up her arm and down her throat. She dodged him, swung around, and planted her foot into his back. After knocking him to the ground, Kyana darted forward and slipped the sword from the knight's scabbard to the great cursing and discomfort of those around her. She backed away as the knight eased to his feet, eyes on his own blade, which was pointed at his face.

"Leave," was the only word she spoke and the only word he needed. The knight was more than eager to retreat into the safety of his fellows. All were whispering in incoherent rumblings that sounded to Kyana like a great beehive humming in her head. She turned to see the short knight with the shaggy hair, and the tall knight, standing with their swords drawn.

"Okay angel," said the shorter knight. "I'd rather not have to hurt you... seeing as you saved our lives and all..." Kyana flipped the sword, loosening her wrist, and said nothing.

"Damn it," the shorter knight grumbled, stepping forward. "You are a hard one to understand. You save us, then you try to kill us. Very, very, confusing you are." He was a chatty fellow.

"You look like you could be... what? In your twenty-fourth year? Twenty fifth? What is a girl like you doing in the woods on your own? Do you have family waiting for you?"

Kyana watched him warily. Why were they not coming at her? What was taking them so long? She was feeling fainter by the second. She wiped her soiled mouth on her sleeve, and her vision faded. She shook her head, blinked her glazed green eyes, trying to clear them. It did not work. The fever was taking its toll. She was going to lose consciousness, and she was going to lose it soon. She hoped they would attack before she fainted. If she was going to die, she wanted to die fighting.

"But you know," the short knight continued, "Your name... Kyana was it? Kyana doesn't sound like a local name. Where do you hail from?" Kyana frowned. Why the hell did he want to know? What did it matter what her name was, or where she came from? Especially now, with blades drawn and knights on the tips of their toes... unless of course, he was stalling? Kyana was suddenly aware that both Ira and the Lystad were out of sight. She looked drunkenly around but could not find either. She turned just in time to see the cloth before it covered her mouth. Kyana gasped without thinking and inhaled the chemicals they doused it in. She stumbled again, her vision fading, chased away by more than fever. She fell but was caught by arms she could no longer see. The dark streaks grew in her eyes, and she only caught a brief flash of golden hair before the world went black. In moments Kyana fell into another deep and unpleasant sleep.

# CHAPTER 3

Ira had to admit, even in a fevered sleep, the girl was lovely. Dark auburn hair lay in thick twines around her head and across her shoulders. The fever had made her face pale and sweaty, but it could not hide the elegance of sharp cheekbones, the fullness of small lips, or the thick curtain of lashes resting closed and hiding eyes that Ira knew were a dark and intense green.

Ira dunked the rag into a bowl of cold water and wrung it out. She wiped at the girl's face, trying to cool the warm skin of Kyana's forehead. The unfortunate thing had been fighting for three straight days, never waking. She had been in a deep and restless sleep since Ira had covered her mouth with a cloth doused in dream weed. The woman had dropped suddenly, which had terrified Ira. She had never used dream weed before and knew Augustine's reluctance with its use in any medical capacity because of the powerful effects. He only prescribed it for severe cases of insomnia. Just the other day Augustine had finally given into one of his patient's desires to try it, after four nights without sleep, and had sent for some.

The castle had a small amount placed under lock and key in the kitchen's cold closet. Dream weed was made for dark, damp, cold environments, and the cold closest was the best substitute available. Cabot had been more than happy to boil up a few leaves and send Ira to bring the little vile to Augustine. It was the only reason Ira had such a thing jingling around in her pocket when she ran into Everett and Neander trying to talk down a very ill and scared looking Kyana. But dream weed, although effective, could also be dangerous at high doses and Ira was no practitioner. She had simply spattered a cloth with a random amount of the green tinted liquid and had been shocked when Kyana instantly dropped. Her breathing had been so shallow that Ira was sure she had killed the girl. She had not, of course. With the infection and fever, Augustine did not know how Kyana had woken in the first place. As a matter of fact, he was not sure how she was *alive* at all. The cut to her side had bled a great deal on the way back from the forest. Ira had bandaged it up the best she could with the supplies she had in her bag. Unlike the dream weed, the bandages had been no lucky thing. Augustine, or any of The Seven, always sent bandages, ointments, and other such things when the king or any of his knights decided to go on a hunt or out to tourney. More than once, they came home with cuts and bruises of their own, and the practitioners found it better that they come with a little preparatory care. Ira, who had not wanted to go on the hunt, let alone kill anything they found, was charged with carrying them.

"Everyone needs to learn how to hunt!" Damian said after Ira had tried to back out for the fourth time the day leading up to their journey.

"I'm more of the, deal with them after their already dead kinda person," Ira had pressed, but Damian had only shaken his head. "Everyone should know how it's done. If you're going to eat it, then you should have the nerve to kill it. My father taught my sisters how, and today I'm going to teach you."

"Soooo, I'm playing your daughter in this little scenario?" Ira joked. Damian made a face.

"Ira, don't make this weird." So, they had gone. It did not matter that she did not want to hunt. It did not matter that she did not even eat meat. She cooked it, yes, that was her job, but she never liked the taste of animal flesh. It always felt off to her. Every bite felt strange. Almost wrong, and every time the cooked skin slipped from the muscle between her teeth, it made her want to gag. It gave her mother and father such grief when she had been a child. They had scolded her for turning her nose up at their dinners of chicken or goat.

"You will not grow strong on carrots alone Ira," her father had warned, but she seemed to have grown up just fine thank you very much.

However, Damian had made up his mind and could not be swayed. Ira had borrowed a young page's pants and shirt for the journey. She felt incredibly awkward in men's clothes, but she could not very well go hunting in her skirts and apron, now could she? She had also borrowed her father's thick wool cap to hold her long hair at bay. Dressed and ready, Damian had tried to teach Ira the ways of a hunter. Still, after several failed attempts (which they both new were purposeful blunders), Ira was freed from her obligation to hunt and was instead put in charge of any future catches (to make sure the meat was properly transported back to the kitchens) and the bag of practitioner supplies. Although they had not dreamed of how much they would need them.

Ira had done her best, but she was no healer or practitioner. The knights had talked her through Kyana's care. Most of them had tended to their own wounds from time to time, and knew the proper way to apply bandages and stem the flow of blood from Kyana's side. It had slowed, but it was a long ride back to the castle. By the time they had gotten Kyana to a practitioner, the gauze was soaked and leaking red. This was not a surprise to Augustine or any of The Seven. They seemed more surprised that she had not needed to change the dressing before reaching the castle. Kyana had bled, but gods be good, she had bled slow. Augustine told Ira that with such a wound, at such a depth, the girl should have been dead. Luckily, the blade had missed the most critical entrails, and she had kept her blood as well she could.

"The gods have plans for this one Ira, I'm sure of it," he had said, eyes narrowed as he threaded his needle and began to sow. "If she makes it through the night, that is."

She had made it through the night, and the next, but she had also developed a nasty infection. The infection was so complete that the woman trembled in her sleep despite the sweat that poured down her face. Augustine had assured Ira that it was no surprise the dream weed worked so quickly. She was half asleep on her feet already. Ira just helped her the rest of the way.

This gave Ira little comfort as the girl slept straight into the night and the next morning. Over that time, her fever had intensified. Red veins of infection had crept out from under the bandage on her side. They slithered threateningly up the pale skin of her ribs, little bloody fingers reaching for her heart.

Kyana gave a little groan, and her eyes flew back and forth beneath her lids. Ira wet the cloth, not bothering to wring it out this time. She let the ice-cold drops seep across the girl's face to pool under her head.

Yes, the poor thing had been fighting hard. But if the woman's skill set was any indication, she was no stranger to a fight. Ira remembered how she had swept across the bandits in the forest, like a wind, unseen, but strong enough to knock a grown man to the ground.

No, not *bandits* at all. Hirelings. The hireling they had captured, thanks to Kyana's incredible aim, broke within the day. He had spilled who had sent him, and what they had been planning. They were not an assassination attempt, or at least, they were not supposed to be. The small group of hirelings had been tasked as scouts. Their job was to seek out the outer guard stations, take inventory of those who maned it, account their patterns and retrieve that information for their employer. It had been mere chance that they had stumbled across Ira's party out hunting in the woods. All at once, relaxing day out turned into a bloody battle. As soon as the hirelings realized who they were and what kingdom they belonged, they knew the coin for their heads would be far more payment than their original mission.

They were wrong. Thanks to Kyana.

She churned in her sleep, a look of pain flashing across her face. It crinkled her thin brows and accentuated a light scar which cut down the hairline above her left eye. Ira dipped the towel once more. She glanced up at the window where the sky outside had grown very dark.

It was always dark when she finally got the chance to visit. Her duties had been keeping her later than usual. Ira worked in the east kitchen of the castle. She was not a main cook, merely an assistant. She cleaned, chopped up vegetables, did a few other odd jobs, and sometimes helped serve at meals and prep for feasts. That was where she had been earlier. The annual celebration of the Four Kingdoms was mere days away, and the kitchens were all in a panic. There was no end to the disasters. First, a nasty little bug infestation in the outer fields had torn to ruin a batch of corn and a few choice vegetables patches, leveling a large section before they were stopped. This cut dearly into the plans for the feast because the king insisted that there should be no food at his table that was short in supply. If it meant that his people had less, he would have none.

This was a beautiful gesture and only made his people love him more, if that was possible (which Ira doubted). This, however, turned upside down the head cook, Cabot's, original plans. He had been scrambling for other suitable alternatives ever since. When Cabot was stressed, the entire kitchen turned into a room full of heat, steam, yelling, clanking, dropping of pots, pans, and more yelling. It was not usually that way. The kitchen was generally a fun, and enjoyable place to work, and Ira counted herself very lucky to have a position there. It was just the large celebratory feasts that made life… let's say, *challenging.*

It did not help that Ira had gotten precious little sleep over the past few days. She always quit work and headed straight for this room. Augustine told her it was unnecessary, that he checked on Kyana often. Augustine had been the first of The Seven they found and had taken Kyana as his personal patient, which relived Ira. She knew the rest of The Seven, the high ranking practitioners of the city, were all competent in their work, but Ira knew Augustine best and trusted him. However, Augustine was only one man, with many patients, and could not be everywhere at once. Ira did not care if it was necessary or not. She felt it was. If she did not sit by Kyana's bed for a few hours, wiping away the sweat and fretting uselessly by her side, she would be left lying in bed, eyes wide and unable to sleep, imagining Kyana slipping into a dream weed delirium that she would never wake from. Ira had used too much of it, far too much, and she knew it.

Ira was also worried about what might happen if she **did** wake up. What sort of hallucinations might the fever have brought on? The last time she woke, she had tried to escape the castle half dead, under the impression they were all evil demons out for blood. Convinced they were there to kill her. Augustine had explained that the infection had already progressed extensively by that point, and she could have been *actually seeing* demons for all they knew. The poor thing was taking a sneak peek at what lies beyond.

If she did wake up seeing demons, Ira wanted to be there. Kyana had already seen plenty of demons in her life, this was clear. Ira glanced down at the scar in her hairline. That was not the only one. There were many to match it. Ira had caught a glance after they had carried Kyana in from the courtyard. Augustine had pulled back her shirt to check on the reopened wound, and she saw them. There were many other scars, some small, some large, crisscrossing her stomach and arms in irregular shapes like broken glass on the kitchen floor.

No, she was no stranger to a fight. But a fever was a whole other type of enemy. Even the most formidable of warriors could be defeated by a simple infection.

The door opened with a light creaking of rusty hinges and Ira looked up. Augustine stepped into the room.

"Here again?" Augustine asked, but he did not sound displeased. A faint smile pulled at the thin mouth between his beard. "Do you ever tire of sitting in that chair?"

"Not, really." Ira shrugged, dabbing the cold cloth down one of Kyana's sweating arms, and giving her bruised and battered knuckles a little attention. Kyana mumbled under her breath. Her words were not actually words at all, a jumble of letters that seemed to have no meaning, but they came out between mild whimpers and groans of pain. Ira looked up at Augustine who frowned.

"Her dreams are getting worse."

"For the last time Ira," Augustine said, dropping his large leather bag on a nearby table, causing its contents to clatter indignantly within. "The dream weed did not hurt her. It's the fever."

"I know… it's just…" Ira looked back at Kyana, who shifted, face contorting from unpleasant dreams. Augustine stepped over, resting a rough hand against her forehead. His frown deepened.

"She's getting worse," Ira said.

"All things get worse, just before they get better," Augustine answered, moving back to his bag to retrieve a few vials of medicine.

Augustine was not a religious man, but if he worshiped anything, it was that "all things get worse, just before they get better." It was his signpost, his eternal guide to life's troubles. Ira thought it was a massive piece of shit, and had half a mind to tell him so, but she never did. Augustine was a wise, kind man and Ira had great respect for him. He had been around only a few years before Ira and her family moved to Castle Lyist. Being the two fresh faces on the castles staff, Augustine had made it a point to be patient with her.

On one of her first days serving, Ira had dropped an entire pitcher of mead onto the table in front of him, spilling it all down the practitioner's lap. Everyone else, including the other servers, had laughed, and jeered, calling her an "idiot," and a "clumsy fool." Not Augustine. He had merely looked into the young girls petrified hazel eyes and smiled.

"Don't worry," he had said, reaching out and patting down her bright flyaway hair that was falling from its bun. "All things get worse… just before they get better."

So, Ira kept her mouth shut, and simply watched in useless worry as Kyana continued to sleep. Augustine brought over his vials, and Ira helped hold Kyana's head up as he shook a few drops of each into her mouth.

"You can go now," Augustine told Ira, replacing the rest of the medicine in his bag and pulling up another chair. "I'll stay with her for a while longer."

"Are you sure?" Ira asked. "I don't mind I could—"

"Go to sleep, Ira," Augustine ordered, but with a smile. "She'll be fine. And you need your rest. I hear Cabot is kicking up quite a fuss in the kitchens these days."

"You have no idea," Ira said, rubbing a sleepy eye with the back of her hand.

"Go on, girl. I've got her. Go to sleep. You need it." Augustine practically shooed her out the door. "Go on then, get!"

"Okay, okay," Ira said, yawning a little as she stood up. She really was tired. Ira glanced back at Augustine in his seat, a book pulled from his bag, feet kicked up on a stool, settling in for a long night. Ira looked over Kyana's face, which was still sweaty and pale, but for the time being, at rest. Not for the first time, Ira wondered what the woman's story might be. What was the history behind those closed eyes? Now was not the time to know, she supposed, but she could not stifle a strange feeling. A feeling that they had met before. She was sure they had not. There was no doubt in Ira's mind that they were indeed strangers. But there was still this feeling, this familiarity… Ira could not quite put her finger on it.

*Sleep well… strange lady.* She thought, before turning and pulling the door behind her. The bolt slid into place with a light creak and a soft click.

# CHAPTER 4

A calm settled over Castle Lyist. With the exceptions of the kitchens, which were a hectic haze of steam, smoke, and activity. Everywhere else was filled with calm. The type of peace which sank deep into the bones, lulling every citizen into an almost dozing state as they went about their business. News of the attack on their king had spread like fire, and just as quickly, extinguished. Of course, the king did not die. He was a master of combat, and he had his best knights by his side.

"Not to mention," whispered some, "The girl. Haven't you heard? She helped the knight's defeat the bandits. She saved King Damian's life! Yes! Well, she's in the castle now. They say she's dying... but Augustine took her under his charge, so she'll be alright. Yes, Augustine, love that man, wonderful practitioner. So glad he joined The Seven. Did you know he took care of my niece this one time..."

Day's passed. Kyana slept in fever dreams full of demons. The king ran his kingdom, the people went about their business, while a hireling continued to be interrogated in a damp stone-walled room beneath the castle. The calm days passed into sleepy nights. All was seemingly as it should be, the kingdom little knowing the strange and terrible things developing. Not knowing just how much danger would soon be brought down upon their peaceful kingdom, and how much was about to change.

# CHAPTER 5

Once again, Kyana was woken by pain. This time, it was a throbbing pain in her head. She groaned and clutched her face. It felt like someone was inside her ear, happily beating out some satanic rhythm against her skull.

"Yes," said a familiar, rumbling, voice to her right. "I suppose your head does hurt. Dream weed packs a nasty punch." Kyana opened her deep green eyes. She recognized the high decorative ceiling as soon as her vision came into focus. She was back in the large room, resting once more on soft brown sheets. She could hear the fire crackling off to the side. Kyana ran a hand across her face. Her head hurt, but there was no sweat. Her fever had broken. She sat up, wincing as a sliver of pain splintered up her side. She saw the man, Augustine, sitting in front of the table with bottles and papers spread out before him. He stood slowly. Kyana heard the popping of arthritic limbs as he moved. He came over to her. She shrank away, unnerved, but he did not demur. He smiled and held out a small bottle filled with a strange blue liquid.

"Here… It will help."

Kyana frowned at the bottle, unsure.

"I promise… it's for your head. I'd also like check that wound if you don't mind."

Kyana looked slowly up at the man. Her dark green eyes captured his gaze. Augustine had the oddest feeling, as if being drawn into that gaze. Like he was looking down into a deep tunnel filled with moss, vines, grass… and mold.

*One.* His eyes were a soft gray, but they had a brightness there. A kindness.

*Two.* He matched her look, but gently. Kyana noticed a spattering of pox scars that curved the side of his face and disappeared under the shortcut beard. His beard itself was streaked with that premature grayness that comes from caring for the sick, dying and dead. Responsibility made age come more quickly. His nose was oddly shaped, crooked, as if it had been broken one-to-many times by flailing arms.

*Three.* Augustine never broke her gaze, the little blue bottle in hand.

*Four.* He still did not look away, but Augustine's chest seemed oddly tight as if the air was thin. His hand trembled around the bottle, for reasons he could not understand. However, he did not look away, and Kyana noticed it all. Without breaking eye contact, she reached out and took the little bottle. She downed it in one swallow. Her headache began to subside. Kyana sighed in relief and closed her eyes.

"Better. Isn't it?" Augustine asked, taking a deep breath and a stepping back. The tightness in his chest disappeared. *Odd.* He thought, but he was no longer a young man and his body was always presenting new quirks as the years passed by. Perhaps this was just one more to add to the ever-growing list.

"Very much," Kyana opened her eyes, and a small smile broke her face. "Thank you... Augustine."

"You're welcome," Augustine answered, "You remember my name, I see."

"Yes."

"What else do you remember?"

"I...." Kyana thought. She remembered trying to run. She remembered being too sick to succeed... they had fought.... They had knocked her unconscious... but they did not kill her? Were they stupid? Or did they genuinely think the fever had addled her brain so intensely? She decided to find out.

"I was in the forest," she started slowly as if trying to remember some fuzzy memory. It was not. Every part was clear. "I was hurt."

"Yes... go on."

"I woke up... I... was afraid... I think.... Did I try to leave?"

"Yes, you did... rather insistently."

She paused for effect, before allowing her face to fall into surprise and concern.

"Did I... did I hurt anyone?"

24

"No," Augustine insisted resting a settling hand on her shoulder and shaking his head. "Everyone is alright. A few bumps and bruises, nothing more. I should know. I took care of them all."

"You're the practitioner?" Kyana asked, and he nodded.

"One of seven. There are many to care for here."

"Also... where is here?" Kyana asked, playing the innocent act.

"Oh, dear, that fever did a number on you, didn't it?" Augustine said, pressing three rough fingers against her head, a wrinkled crease developing between his thick brows. "That or the dream weed... Ira doused you rather more heavily than I would have suggested." The practitioner turned back to his table of books and bottles.

"You're in Castle Lyist. The heart of Neira kingdom." He lifted a few bottles to eye level and squinted at them thoughtfully before replacing them for another. Kyana moved to stand and felt something tighten around her ankle. She looked down to see a shackle around her ankle, and a short chain which locked it to one of the thick legs of the four-poster bed. Augustine looked over.

"Yes, sorry about that... you gave us quite a scare the other day... we thought it would be safest until you were more... lucid."

"The other day?" Kyana frowned, truly confused now. "How long have I been asleep?"

"It's been almost four days since you tried to leave the castle." Augustine took a step forward, holding another oddly colored bottle. He tilted the bottle and poured a clear sticky substance onto his fingers. He reached out, but hesitated.

"May I?" Kyana nodded, and he laid a hand against her forehead. He made slow circles with the transparent paste. It felt cold against her skin and gave off a sharp, minty scent.

"Your fever is gone, and your color is perfect." He stepped back, looking her over. "I suppose 'lucky' is not the proper word, but the blade did miss most of the more dangerous organs. Gods be praised, it only hit flesh. The most troubling thing was the blood loss and infection, but you're doing much better now. How's your side?"

"It's alright," she answered.

"Do you mind...?"

She shrugged. Augustine kneeled by her bed, and lifted the edge of her shirt, just enough to see a large white bandage winding her lower side. Kyana waited, as the practitioner unwrapped her bandage until the jagged scar with black stitching came into view. Augustine applied the same minty paste to her knife wound. It stung, but she did not flinch this time. She looked down to watch Augustine. His movements were practiced, trained, slow, and straightforward. Years of service had made such work as simple as breathing. It was quite lovely to watch his pale gray eyes intent on his work.

The large red gash that cut up her side, on the other hand, was anything but lovely. The bandit's knife had cut deep and long. It would take time to heal and would leave a scar. She could add it to her collection.

Kyana had been watching the man's hands move up and down her side, when she noticed a tattoo on the inside of his wrist. A small green dove rippled across blue veins.

"You're a medic."

"Hum?" Augustine looked up distracted.

She nodded towards his arm.

"You're a medic. The tattoo." She had seen it before. It was a tradition within the four main kingdoms. In times of war, they tattooed soldiers that were practitioners on the field. They were marked with a dove that denoted the color of whichever kingdom they belonged. In this way, if captured, their lives would be spared. Many times, they were even returned to their rightful kingdoms. Doctors, medics, practitioners, nurses were all very valuable, and regarded as an untouchable element of war.

"I was." Augustine shrugged, but Kyana saw the brief smile that crossed his face. There was pride in that smile. Men and their wars.

"It's green." Kyana pointed out.

"Yes."

"So, you aren't from Castle Lyist?" Castle Lyist medics had a flying dove with a blue tattoo to match their kingdoms color.

"No." Augustine shook his head and continued to work. "I'm originally from Kyar."

"Hence the green." Kyana nodded.

"Yes. When I was a young doctor… only in my eighteenth year, there was a short… and rather pathetic, revolution of several smaller towns and cities… nothing that Kyar couldn't bring under control."

"Why did you leave?" Generally, those willing to go to war for their kingdoms did not scurry off to the neighboring one without good reason.

"Well," Augustine said, gliding a hand down the stitches, prodding and pressing. Kyana winced at his touch. "We had a... difference of opinion, my kingdom and I."

"How so?" Kyana asked, curious.

"Well..." Augustine mused, grabbing another little vile out of his bag, and returning. The cork came off with a little pop and the smell of lavender filled the room. "I and my daughter... Liza is her name." Kyana saw another prideful smile cross his face. "We lived in one of the larger cities within Kyar... and oh, around sixteen or seventeen years passed... they started allowing sections of the city to be occupied."

"Occupied?"

"Yes. By Faithfuls."

"Oh..." Kyana's mouth went dry. She had heard murmurs of such before. Kyar, the kingdom to the west, had been considering allowing Faithfuls to live openly for the past hundred years or so. Not to use magic of course, that would always be forbidden. However, as years passed and dragon bones became more scarce, magic became less and less of a concern.

"Yes," Augustine frowned at a loose stitch. "'Oh.' Kyar had been debating on having segregated sections of the cities quartered off for a while, but I never thought they would follow through with it. The uproar that might result, you see, and they had just gotten out of their own revolutions. Allowing Faithfuls to live openly would just be begging for more trouble... but turns out they decided to go for it any way. Unfortunately, one of the cities they chose to test out their little experiment was my home." Augustine glanced up briefly before turning back to his work. "It... no longer felt safe for Liza and me. We decided it was time to go somewhere that held our values more closely."

"Right..." Kyana trailed off, "smart..."

She did not press the subject, just continued to watch the man at his work. She was distracted from her dark daydreaming when she noticed something else.

"What am I wearing?" she asked abruptly.

"Oh, yes," Augustine glanced up again. "Your clothes were rather... well... unsanitary. We sent them to the wash and found some underclothes that would serve for the time being. Your cloths are in there," he said and nodded to the cabinet.

"You changed my clothes?" Kyana should not have felt so uncomfortable with this information. He was a practitioner after all. He probably saw more naked men and women in his life than all the people in the city combined, but her eyes still averted in embarrassment. No man had ever seen her naked. If he had been a woman… or maybe a little older… maybe it would have been better. He looked old enough to be her father, but that had never stopped men from appreciating young girls before. Not that he had been leering over her as he stitched up her side, but a man was a man, and they had natures just like any other animal. In addition, he was a decent looking man. Despite the pox marks he had a sturdy frame, wide set shoulders, and lean muscles that wrapped his forearm and almost rippled as he worked. Kyana did not know why this made the idea of him seeing her unclothed worse, but it did.

"Actually, I simply cared for your wounds," Augustine said, noticing her uncomfortable expression. "A handmaid was nice enough to help change you."

"Oh," she answered, and winced as her wound gave a sharp pain. Augustine did not notice.

"There," he said, finishing re-wrapping her bandage and pulling down her nightshirt. "All set. You're healing well. The infection is gone now. Just down to getting plenty of rest."

"Good." Kyana nodded. "Healed enough to get up?"

Augustine considered. "Perhaps so. Maybe in a few hours, we could try going for a walk? See how your balance is coming along." Kyana opened her mouth to speak, but her stomach gave a loud growl. She placed a hand over her stomach and flinched again.

"Your wounds are healing, but they will take more time." Augustine looked up and smiled. "So, I would suggest not planning any more 'escapes' until you can run without pulling out your stitches. Would you like some food?" Kyana nodded. She liked this Augustine. He was blunt, straight forward, but mellow. She liked that a lot.

"Alright. Rest here, I'll have some food sent up."

"Where are you going?" Kyana asked, as he moved to the large wooden door.

"I have a few other patients that need my care. I'll be back in a few hours." Augustine pulled a gray bag over his shoulder while the contents jingled happily. He pulled another little vile of blue liquid out of his bag and handed it to her.

"Drink this if your headache returns. I'll be back soon." He gave her one last smile before disappearing out the door. Kyana glanced around the room. It was actually rather nice. The walls were large gray and brown stones that seemed to glow by the light of the fire. It gave everything a warm, flickering feel that Kyana quite liked. She pulled her legs up on the bed and wrapped her shoulders in the smooth sheets. She could not help a small smile. The room was warm. Kyana had not been in such comfortable shelter for a long time. It was a hard thing not to enjoy. She took a few slow sips out of the blue vile as she examined the dragon coat of arms on the wall. Its thick threads were bright and tightly woven. Very high quality, but Kyana would expect nothing less for where she was. She suddenly felt uneasy, and her long fingers trailed across the cold steel around her ankle.

*Warm... but not safe.*

She would play nice. They obviously did not know who or what she was, or they would have killed her the instant they had the chance. But she was alive and well taken care of. They thought she was an innocent little girl, one who saved their king. She would keep it that way until she was healed.

*And then... What?*

Kyana was at a significant advantage here, inside the castle. She heard stories as a child, the impenetrability of the walls, the skill of the guards, the strength of magnificent Castle Lyist... but she was already inside. She was cared for, even after her outburst the other day... but not fully trusted.

Her eyes fell to the shackle on her ankle. It sat dull and heavy against her skin. Then there was the wound which threatened to weep at any radical movement. No, better just to leave. Heal at home. Get out of this kingdom.

Kyana leaned back into the cushions, and despite herself, gave a great yawn. She was exhausted. Her eyes fluttered closed. Then she remembered.

*A handmaid was nice enough to help change you.*

Kyana's eyes flew open wide. She bolted up, pushing back the soft blankets.

*A handmaid was nice enough to help change you.*

Kyana's long fingers scrambled frantically at the edge of her left sleeve. The cloth was unfamiliar, soft, slippery, and difficult to grasp in her haste to peel it away.

*A handmaid was nice enough to help change you.*

Kyana pushed the sleeve, passed her elbow, and her eyes widened in surprise. Underneath, there was a soft white bandage wrapping the skin of her forearm. Kyana didn't remember being wounded there, and she doubted that she ever was. The bandage was too perfect, too precise, to be anything but purposefully covering the brand that marked her. Marked her in more ways than one. Marked her for death if anyone at this castle saw it... and yet...

*A handmaid was nice enough to help change you.*

Someone had covered it for her. Someone had protected her. She owed her life to some handmaid wandering somewhere in this massive castle. Why?

Kyana rolled down her sleeve and slowly eased back into the bed. She would ask Augustine about this later. For now, it seemed, her secret was safe. Besides, she thought as sleep weighed heavy, slowly dragging her eyelids down to her cheeks, and she gave another great yawn. She was very tired.

# CHAPTER 6

"Oh! And down it goes! How many does that make, Ira? Three?" Ira dropped to her knees, gathering up the bowl which had toppled from her hands moments ago, spilling carrots and beets in every direction. Ira glared up at the man now grinning and leaning against the door. He had appeared out of nowhere, nearly yelling Ira's name in her ear. Ira, who never did well with surprises, had shrieked and dropped everything in her hands.

"You could help, you know, Damian," Ira spoke up to her grinning king. "Instead of just standing there grinning like a—" A hard smack clapped against the back of her head before she could finish, sending a bolt of pain all the way through her eyes.

"That is our king you are speaking to *girl*," Cabot, the head cook, spoke in a voice that quivered in time with his ample belly. Cabot was a tall man, with a great girth that strained his shirt buttons to near bursting. He had a scruffy brown beard speckled with white, that commonly had a few stray crumbs lost within. He was usually a very mild-mannered man, quiet and playful, but when it came to feast time, he was an ass. And when King Damian decided to stop by for a visit, it only made things worse... so much worse.

"If you disrespect the king once more in my presence, I'll — and did you drop another bowl girl? Again!"

"It's alright Cabot," Damian said, taking a step forward. "This was my fault. I startled her, and she dropped it."

To Cabot's great horror, Damian got to his knees beside Ira and started helping gather up the spilled food.

"Your majesty please, you don't have to..." Cabot seemed about to keel over with shame and terror. He leaned against a counter as if he might faint from the horror of it all.

"You're going to give him a heart attack," Ira whispered, but she could not help a small grin as Cabot's large belly rose and fell with indignation.

"Oh, he just needs to relax," Damian answered, glancing up at the head cook who had been distracted from his shame by a loud clatter in another corner of the kitchen. They watched him bustle off in a huffing mass to deal with the new disaster, weaving in and out of the other kitchen help, who darted around the room like panicked bees in a steam-filled hive. "I'm here all the time. Gods, he's known me since I was a child."

"Yeees, but now you're 'King' Damian... not snot-nosed little prince Damian. Big difference."

"Not so big..." Damian mumbled, not even trying to convince himself anymore.

A great deal had changed over the years. When Damian's father began to fall ill three years passed, Damian quickly stepped up to help with the responsibilities. When his father suddenly died a year after this, he was already running the kingdom on his own. The people accepted the change. They had loved Damian as their little prince and still loved him as their new king, but it was not the smoothest of transitions. He was never born for the throne. Nor was his father. No, that honor was meant for Damian's uncle, Noah Lystad. Noah was the second born of the three sons sired by his grandfather, the noble Damian Lystad I and Damian's name sake. When the first son died in his nineteenth year after a hunting accident, Noah became heir to the throne. However, when elderly Damian Lystad I finally breathed his last, Noah promptly abdicated.

"I never wanted the damn thing!" Damian had heard his uncle say on many occasions when he and Damian's father shared a drink... or ten. It was such a scandal in the kingdom that Noah had been sent to live as an ambassador in Kyar kingdom to spare him the rippling agitation and unrest of the citizens of Castle Lyist. There Noah met, and was soon engaged to marry, the young princes Medea. This union soothed a rift between Neira and Kyar kingdoms, which had been developing over the past few years. It was a subtle rift, but one that had been building into minor squabbles in smaller townships and was gearing up to become something more lethal if something was not

LYDIA R. OUTLAND

done. With the engagement of Noah Lystad and the heir to the throne of Kyar Kingdom, dialogue between the two kingdoms began. Changes were enacted, deals were made, and all tensions faded until it was forgotten. As if it had never existed in the first place. Trade (which had been strangled off for the past two years) began to flow. The union was so successful, in fact, that all animosity towards Noah had vanished as quickly as it had grown.

Besides, there was still one son left of the Lystad line. Damian's father had eagerly stepped up to take the throne. Jeromy Lystad had always been an ambitious and charismatic man. He was an influential member of the court and held much respect throughout the kingdom, even though the throne had before seemed so out of his reach. When his brother openly denied his claim, Jeromy made no hesitation. Even then, Damian was not next in line. His elder sister Sophia, quiet and cunning Sophia, was meant to bare that burden. She, however, gave up her rights to rule only a year before Damian's father fell ill. She met, fell in love, and quickly wed the second prince of Sterlyn when he and a few other members of the Sterlyn court came on a political venture. In a blink of an eye, Sophia left to become royalty in another kingdom all together, and before Damian knew it, he was heir to the throne. He was not the only one to be taken aback, and it was only natural that attitudes would change.

Those that would be playful with a young prince, one who was far down the list of eligibility for a throne, were far more formal when that very prince was crowned king. Cabot was one. He used to give Damian a hard time over his clothes, studies, the little lisp he had when he was seven, but the instant he was crowned it all stopped. As if the crown had changed the boy he knew. It had not, of course. Ira knew that, but she was one of the few. Ira thought Damian appreciated this. It was why they were still friends. It was why she found him leaning against the kitchen door when she looked up. Because Ira did not change. Because Ira saw no difference. Because to her, Damian was the same boy, same man, no matter what clothes or crown. This being said, it was not always easy being friends with a king. Sometimes it made things downright difficult. It had been bad enough when he had been a mere prince. The rumors, the awkwardness, the odd nature of their opposing stations all made things tricky, and it only got worse after he took the throne. Now when he came to visit her at work, it was not just a slight inconvenience, it was a down right disaster. He knew it, too. Damian may not like that things had

33

changed so drastically so quickly... but he sometimes seemed to enjoy the chaos he could cause.

"For the love of the gods, get out of here," she whispered under her breath, tucking a loose strand of sweaty golden hair behind her ear. "I can't deal with your shit stirring right now. I've got to help keep this kitchen together."

"Me? Stir shit?" Damian asked, fluttering his blue eyes as if in shock. "Well, I never."

"Ya, ya, take your innocent baby blues and leave," Ira huffed, jerking to her feet and placing the bowl on the table.

Damian was about to say something else when Augustine suddenly appeared by his side.

"Oh, hello, your majesty." Augustine bowed his head.

"Hello, Augustine." Damian smiled. "How is our guest this morning?"

"That's why I'm here actually your majesty. She's awake."

Ira's head swung around, eyes wide and bright.

"Really? Is she alright? Is she still seeing things?"

"No, she is calm, and resting. The dream weed is completely out of her system, and her fever is broken."

"Thank the gods," Damian said, looking very pleased.

"Yes, she is lucid and very hungry. I thought, after all your worrying, you might like to see her up and about. Maybe bring her something to eat? Take her for a walk... a short walk, mind you, but a walk..." Augustine spoke to Ira.

"Oh, that's right...." Damian leaned back against the door jamb, grin back on his face. "You've been visiting her, haven't you?"

"Just checking on her is'll," Ira said, with a shrug.

"Yes.... Every night. Honestly, I couldn't get rid of her," Augustine said, giving Damian a sideways glance. Augustine was one of the few other people that treated Damian the same. Augustine had known Damian most of his life and had been present for every pivotal event. He had cared for every childish wound, every fall from a horse, his first tourney scars. Augustine had been the one to deliver his little sister Naomi into the world. He had also been the one to tell Damian of his mother's passing and had been the first to comfort him and soothe his sobs. Augustine had been the one Damian called when he thought his father had finally drunk himself too far into unconsciousness, and

Augustine was always the one to revive him. He knew Damian far too well, and was far too tired to change his ways now.

"Every night?" Damian asked, frowning. "Are you still feeling guilty?"

Without answering, Ira quickly darted around the kitchen, gathering a plateful of food. "Cabot, I'll be right back!" She called as she darted out the door.

"Oh, really? I thought you had to 'keep the kitchen together'?" Damian asked, following her. Augustine had stayed to gather a few things for other patients. When Ira ignored Damian's question, he asked another. "Do you truly still feel that bad? I thought you let the dream weed thing go."

"Damian… she… she barely had a heart beat!" Ira protested.

"Good gods woman, she also held a knife to your throat!" Damian said, laughing a little. "I think it is safe to say you are even."

"First off, you know I hate it when you call me 'woman.' I have a name Damian, for the sake of the gods, use it. And second…" Ira trailed off. She had no "second," in mind when she started her "first." She had been hoping it would come to her in a flash of eloquent epiphany like Damian's little sister had a habit of doing. Naomi had a way of launching into organized and moving speeches at the slightest provocation, and Damian 'provocated' quite a bit. She was younger than Ira by several years, and although Damian was quite quick-witted, his baby sister outstripped him by miles. She had a way about her, a quiet nature that was often mistaken for timidity, but when she had an opinion, she would voice it, voice it clear, voice it true. She was a sweet girl, but also a force to be reckoned with. Ira often wondered what the kingdom would have been like under her lead. Damian was a good leader, he truly was, but Ira could not help but wonder what his little sister might do if the crown was placed on her delicate and yet articulate person.

Ira, on the other hand, had never been good at off-the-cuff speeches, and her voice trailed off as they made their way further down the hall.

"Aaaaaaaaand second?" Damian prompted humorously, fully aware Ira had no "second." Sometimes Ira hated how much Damian knew her.

"And second, *go away."* Ira finished dully.

"Nah, think I'm good right here thanks," he said, continuing to follow her. "I'd actually like to check on her myself."

"Why?" Ira asked, frowning a little.

"Why?" Damian copied, eyebrows disappearing into his dark hair, "Why? Seriously? Come on! It's not every day you are saved by some strange woman in pants. I, for one, would love to hear her story. I'm curious. Aren't you?"

"That strange woman in pants *also* has a name you know."

Damian rolled his eyes and gave a huffy sigh.

"Besides," Ira padded down the hall. "We don't want to overwhelm her…"

"Why are you so against me coming along?" Damian wondered curiously, and then a smile slowly split his lips. It was a smile Ira recognized, and her eyes narrowed. "Are you jealous?"

"For the love of the gods." It was Ira's turn to roll her eyes. There was a long-running rumor that revolved around the king and Ira's relationship. It was insisted upon by all the courtiers, knights and even the serving staff, that Damian and Ira were secretly in love with one another. Or, at least, sleeping with one another. Of course, neither of these were true. They had never even entertained the idea. However, the rest of the castle enjoyed a good rumor, and there was no telling gossips to pipe down. Especially when the king himself found it utterly hilarious. He would always shut down any such discussions in public, but privately, he would tease Ira about them. The only one who ignored such rumors was Naomi. Naomi had not only believed Ira about her platonic relationship with her brother but seemed down right disgusted by the alternative. She was always one to quickly silence such rumors and would always scold her older brother when he tried to tease Ira. Unfortunately, Naomi was now living in Sterlyn kingdom with her and Damian's eldest sister and could not come to Ira's aide.

"Oh, honey dear, you know I've only got eyes for you," Damian fluttered his blue eyes rapidly.

"I reiterate… go away," Ira huffed.

"No need for jealousy honey, darling, sweet one…"

Ira scowled. "Don't make me gag."

"Come now, angel face."

"Damian, enough!" Ira snapped.

"Oh, come on, Ira," Damian said laughing. "You know I'm just playing—"

"Your majesty." A tall knight appeared around the bend in the hall.

"Everett!" Damian said, still grinning. "What do I owe the pleasure?"

"A Faithful, my lord," Everett began in an even voice that did not disguise the worry in his eyes. "Someone has been spotted using magic in a lower town just outside the city."

The hair on the back of Ira's neck stood on end, and she could not help a small shiver from slithering down her spine.

*A Faithful.*

"What?" Damian rocked back on his heals, away from the information. A brief look of shock enveloped every feature, momentarily drowned in surprise. Ira did not blame him. There had not been a Faithful sighting in Neira for years. In fact, the last known instance was back when Damian's grandfather was newly on the throne, and long before Damian was a twinkle in his father's eye. Even that had been a minor event. A squabble between two Faithful's over a few shadow market dragon bones. The fight had left one Faithful dead and the other dying, which made punishment for either offender frankly unnecessary. The bones were collected and safely given to the care of the Keepers, and the matter was settled in half a day. Then nothing. Nothing... until now.

Damian's grin had faded quickly, seeming to melt off his face like wax down a candle. Ira felt him shift closer to her, as if he might reach out for her, protectively take her elbow or arm, but he did not. In the time it takes to pull in a breath, Damian turned into Lord Lystad. His stature straightened, his eyes grew a stony blue, and his jaw was set. The kind of face that ordered armies. The type of face that kept kingdoms.

"Well, then, we better go say hello, shouldn't we?" He turned and this time he did touch her arm gently. "Make sure the girl is well. I'd like to hear more about how she is doing when you are through. Perhaps bring her around... if she is up to it, of course. I would like to thank her in person."

"Of course, your majesty." Ira nodded. Damian might be her shit stirring friend... but he was still her king.

Damian nodded and turned to walk with Everett down the hall and out of sight. Ira watched them go with a sinking feeling in her gut. A Faithful sighting... Damian had never had to handle a situation like that. He had never had reason, nor opportunity. But the laws were written, and Damian was their keeper. Being a Faithful in Neira was viewed as treasonous... devotion to another other than your king and kingdom. A devotion to dragons long gone. Over three hundred years had passed and passed by since the last dragon

37

lived. Yet the Faithful remained. Continuing with their treasonous devotions. Everyone knew the price of treason, and Damian was the collector of that debt. It was his duty. It was his responsibility. Ira knew this, and knew it well, but it did not stop her stomach from churning uneasily inside her belly.

In his few short years on the throne, Damian had never performed an execution. Ira worried what such an act might do to her ultimately soft-hearted friend, for despite his insistence on the opposite, he did have a soft heart. Ira remembered when Damian had been in his eighth year. He had cried when Ira killed a rat. Rats were vermin and could carry disease. The kitchen was no place for them, so any time one appeared, it was Ira's duty to put it down. She did not like the duty very well herself, but she performed it without hesitation. Damian, however, had walked in one day just as Ira was bringing her foot down on a particularly small rat. He had stopped, obvious horror filling his face. He had turned and left without a word, but Ira had seen the gleam of tears welling in his eyes before he disappeared behind the door. He had been a soft-hearted boy and had not changed as much as he liked to think. He had never even been to battle. Only the playful "wars" performed for tourneys that he participated in from time to time. Those would get rough and bloody, but rarely resulted in death. Damian had never actually killed anyone before. He could fight, he was a spectacular fighter, but there had been no wars, no revolutions in his lifetime. He was blessed to have been born into a peaceful age for his kingdom. The only life or death situation that Damian had been in, as far as Ira knew, had been that scuffle in the forest. Even then, he had not actually killed anyone. He had not gotten the chance. Kyana had done most of the damage there. No, Damian had not yet taken a human life, and Ira was petrified of what might happen if he was forced to do so. What might happen to her soft-hearted, playful, shit-stirring friend then?

Ira pulled herself violently from these dark thoughts. She could do nothing about them. She had no control over what would happen. Time passed by and she could only watch it go and hope for the best. However...

She turned to the door, behind which a girl had laid asleep for so long. Perhaps there **was** something she could do for the woman who saved her lordly friend's life. Ira tried to shake off that sickening feeling deep in her belly and ran a hand over the back of her neck. She reached up and wrapped her knuckles against the wooden door.

# CHAPTER 7

"Hello?" A familiar voice asked through the crack in the door, "Hello, are you awake? I've got some food." Kyana craned her neck to see who spoke and relaxed. She recognized Ira's broad grin.

"I'm awake," she answered. *Hungry as well.* The girl came through the door, a large plate in hand, piled high with bread, fruit, and a few slices of meat.

"Hi there." She smiled that broad smile as she stepped inside. She was no longer wearing boys' cloths, but a simple dress and stained apron. Her golden hair was tied in a messy bun, strands falling around her hazel eyes which looked out with hesitation. Kyana watched her caution with amusement. She was chained like a dog, and Ira was still afraid. Well, to be fair, she had held a knife to her throat. She suddenly felt rather bad about that. "Here." Ira held out the plate of food. "Augustine said you needed to eat."

"Thank you," Kyana said, taking the plate and lying it in her lap. She tore into it, realizing just how starving she was.

"Wow, slow down," Ira laughed. It was a small, quiet thing. But it was also soft, lyrical in its own way. "You'll give yourself a stomachache."

"I already have one. It's called hunger," Kyana answered with her mouth half full of bread.

"Fair enough." Ira pulled a chair from the table and sat down. "I'm—"

"Ira, yes, I remember," she said, not looking at her. "You're the one from the woods, and the one from the hall... pardon the blade, I was... confused.... just looking to get home."

"No harm done." She smiled again. She smiled a lot. Kyana was not sure if that was a good thing or a very bad one. "You seemed scared. But it's okay, you don't have to be. You're safe here. And after you are healed, you can go wherever you like." Kyana scoffed. She could not help it. She wasn't safe. Not really, not here, not with a Lystad anywhere near.

"How long will that be?" She asked.

"A few more days at most. Your wounds are healing very quickly. Augustine is excellent."

"Relative? This, Augustine," Kyana asked, brushing away a few stray crumbs from her face. She could see the deep respect and love in Ira's eyes. Such large eyes showed emotion like an open window on a clear day.

"Augustine? No, just a friend. I've known him, and his daughter Liza, since I moved to Castle Lyist." Ira smiled for the millionth time. "He's a good practitioner. He said you might be able to go for a walk after you eat... if you'd like, that is. You've been asleep for days, it would be good for you to move around."

Kyana said nothing, simply continued to clean her plate.

"Thank you, by the way."

"For?" Kyana asked, scraping up the last crumbs and swallowing them eagerly.

"In the forest. You saved us. It was... well incredible. Thank you."

Kyana wiped her mouth clean and looked into Ira's eyes.

*One.* They were hazel. Swirls of brown and green and gold that pooled and danced together around the dark pupil.

*Two.* They were sincere, no lies crept behind them. No lies... but something... something hidden. They looked deep, tired ... a little too troubled for such a young face.

*Three.* Ira was getting uncomfortable under her stare, she could tell... a light blush touched her cheeks and crept its pink fingers to her ears. But she did not look away.

*Four.* Ira felt a nervousness bubbling in her stomach and chest. Kyana's eyes had no end. They went on, and on, and she wondered, suddenly, if she would fall head first into that deep green abyss. Be lost forever in that moss. She still did not look away. Ira had never been afraid to fall.

Kyana suddenly smiled, and this seemed to surprise Ira.

"You're welcome, Ira of Castle Lyist."

"Sure," she said, taking her empty plate and slipping it onto a spare inch of the table. "Ready for that walk? And at some point, there are a few people that would like to meet you."

Kyana frowned at this. "Why?"

"They'd just also like to thank you." When she still hesitated, Ira went on. "No need to worry, Kyana. I promise."

"Do you keep your promises, Ira of Castle Lyist?" Kyana asked.

Ira smiled. "I always keep my promises."

Kyana searched her large soft eyes and knew what she said was the truth. At least it was her truth, for now.

"Well," Kyana reached down and rattled the chain. "It will be rather difficult for me to walk, with this on my ankle."

# CHAPTER 8

Kyana had to admit, the kingdom was beautiful. The cobbled streets were wide, with high amber stone walls. Giant statues of knights, kings, animals, and dragons curled the edges of the castle and marked the main entrances to the gates. Horses trotted through, their shoes clicking against the stones as groups of people bustling about in hectic grandeur. Kyana liked the sound of people. The chatter, the life, the laughter. She loved the quiet in the forest, but sometimes… a little noise was wanted. The air was crisp, clear, with only the mild passing sent of horse manure, but that did not bother her so much.

Kyana pulled the heavy cloak tight around her shoulders. It was thick, dark blue, and far too big for her thin frame, but she was not complaining. Ira had lent it to her for the walk. She borrowed it from an old room that no one used, and no one would miss. Ira had also offered her a few dresses of her own, but Kyana refused them. She could not run in a skirt, and she couldn't imagine trying to move with such long sleeves. They looked like they might touch the ground. She had insisted on her old clothes, which included trousers. Seeing as her shirt had been stained with a big blot of red blood, that dried to a dark brown that crinkled and hardened, Ira had kindly offered her a shirt she had borrowed from her father's closet. It was a shirt made for a narrow man, but still far larger than Kyana herself. The shirt was a dull gray, and dipped down towards her knees. She had to wear a belt around the waist to keep it from fitting her like a tent, but she did not care. She could run in that. She could fight in that, not some feathery death trap of a gown.

Kyana dropped the dark hood as she gazed down from the top of the wall to the bustling town below. She could see carts laden with trinkets, fruits of many colors, and a smith's shop hanging with daggers and swords. The smith himself was busy at work, pounding a glowing hot piece of metal into its desired shape, large arms gleaming with sweat. There was a resounding clank every time the hammer touched metal, but it was hardly heard over the swell of conversations.

"May we go down?" Kyana asked excitedly, not taking her eyes off the people, haggling and talking and carving their haphazard trails in the dirt.

"I don't know... do you feel up to it?" Ira asked. She had been sticking very close to Kyana, watching every step, waiting to jump in any time she looked like she may stumble or falter. "It's busy today, and people can get pushy when it's busy."

"I am perfectly fine, Ira of Castle Lyist," she said, taking a step closer to the edge and planting a foot on its top. "I have had far worse wounds then—"

"Wow, what are you doing?" Ira said, taking a step forward. "You're not jumping."

"Well... yes—"

"No! No, you're *not* You're still healing, a fall like that would one, pull out all of your stitches, and two... you know, *kill you*"

Kyana frowned at the distance and the nicely placed foot holes in the wall but decided not to argue the point. Ira may not be a practitioner... but she had a healer's eyes. Healers only see what they want their patients to see. She pulled her foot from the edge, and Ira relaxed.

"You are very strange, you know," Kyana commented, continuing down the wall.

"I'm strange?" Ira laughed and shook her head following her. "You're *crazy*."

Kyana shrugged, pulling the hood back up against the cold breeze.

"How are you feeling?"

"Fine... just as I was when you asked two seconds ago."

"Ya, well, Augustine said a short walk, and we have been out for over a half an hour."

"I've been outside my entire life. Fresh air is far more healing than any room could be."

"Speaking of which, where do you hail from?" Ira asked, eyeing her mild limp.

"The same woods you took me from. It's where I have lived, well, some of my life," she replied.

"Really? No city, no village. Is your family out there waiting for you?" Ira's face fell. "No wonder you want to get back, we could send word to your family that you're safe as soon as we get back—"

"There is no one waiting for me. There hasn't been for a long time now."

"So, you live out there all alone?" Ira asked, blinking slowly. "Sounds lonely."

"Yes." Kyana felt the fire building in her chest again, spreading to her fingertips. She clenched her hand closed, her nails digging deep gouges in her palm. "Sometimes it is."

Ira watched her, teetering on the edge of a question Kyana would rather the girl not ask. To her relief, Ira left the issue where it was.

"We better get you back to bed."

"But I thought..." Kyana gestured down to the bustling town, and the clamored calls of shoppers.

"Oh, we will." Ira nodded. "I promised. But not today." She shrugged and gave another wide grin. "I don't want to incur the wrath of Augustine."

"Alright," Kyana said begrudgingly. "Later, it is."

"And we'll be taking the stairs when we do," Ira said as they turned back to go inside.

# CHAPTER 9

It was a small village, barely outside the city limits itself. A mostly self-sufficient place with their own little fields of corn and herds of cattle flicking their tails back and forth in the breeze. Except for the yearly taxes to the kingdom and the trading done between it and Castle Lyist's inner town, the village kept to itself. Although so close, Damian could not recall a time he had ever visited.

The cattle sent their snorted moos through the cool afternoon air, and the stench of fresh manure followed with it. Damian had brought a few advisers with him to help with the ugly matter, and each began to cough as the wind changed direction, and the smell became stronger. None of the villagers, who had gathered around in a half circle, appeared to mind the smell. It was the sort of thing people grew used to over the years until they ceased to notice entirely.

The entire village, except for a few peddlers still in the larger cities, and probably those too young and fearful to watch, were gathered around with wide eyes to see what happened next. They all stood in the middle of the long dirt road. It was wide enough for two horses and two carts to ride side by side and follow the winding, twisting, and rock-strewn path to where Castle Lyist would slowly appear in the meadow. On a clear day, one might be able to stand on that road and see the castle, its four walls rising up in the distance, amber stones gleaming in the sun as the river surged by.

Damian remembered his father telling him a story of how the stones were once as dull and gray as any other, but after the last stone had been placed,

Aneira had blessed the castle with fire. Breathing against every stone, filling it with protective magic that would hold fast each wall, and ensure the castle would live on forever.

"And with every touch of her fire." His father had leaned in, eyes sparkling from the joy of the story, or perhaps the three glasses of mead he had just finished. Damian was never sure which, but chose to believe the former. "The stones glowed bright and then changed to the beautiful color they are today, and will be till the end of all days."

But the sky was not clear. A chill fog had rolled in with the breeze and the stink, obstructing the view back to his home. Even if it was, Damian had his back turned towards the path. Instead, he faced the huddled villagers. He stood flanked by a few knights donned in their armor and long chestnut cloaks that fluttered in the wind. On his other side was a few advisers from his court, including Phobos, his father's most trusted adviser. They all stood quietly, hands laced behind them, and waited. Waited with the patience belonging only to those who are afraid of what comes next.

Damian cleared his throat and raised his voice, making sure all could hear clearly over the snapping of flags, the pawing of horses in the soft dirt, and the never-ending mooing from the cattle.

"Abram Olson," he called out in a strong and booming voice, one earned after many years of practice before courts, feasts, festivals and tourneys with thousands crowded eagerly before him. Ira often called it his "King Damian tone," and gave him no end of grief for it, but she was the only one. Everyone else fell silent. It was the voice he used when he wanted to be heard. When he *needed* to be heard. It was this tone that was directed toward the slender man who stood trembling between two of his most trusted knights, Teller and Everett. "You have been found guilty of Faithful practices." It was true. It had been a long few days after Everett stopped him in the hall and told him about the disruption in the outer town. A day's ride to get there. Two days to sift through all the witnesses, statements, the evidence presented, tearful testimonies and long-winded advisement (at least in Phobos's case). Finally, it was the fourth day and all had been decided.

"You are aware," Damian said, eyes only for the man before him. "The price for such a crime, in this kingdom, is your life."

Silence fell overall. Even the wind seemed to pause for breath.

The convicted man was Damian's senior by at least twenty years. He was short and balding, the remains of his wispy brown hair had been falling out for the last four of those years. Long deep creases dipped around his soft green eyes, which nervously flicked back and forth between Damian and the ground at his feet. His hands trembled inside the shackles that bound them, and his lips and voice did the same as he finally spoke.

"I've got nothing more to say, my lord," he sputtered, like a man who has already seen the end of the road and would simply like to reach it with as much haste as possible. "I already said my piece. I already told you why I did what I did." His eyes flickered from the ground towards the crowd of villagers, but Damian knew who he was looking for.

She was a pretty girl. Young, full-lipped, with bright brown eyes and long golden hair that was braided down past her waist. The daydream of every man in that little village, Damian was sure, not just the man with flickering eyes. She stood with her arms wrapped around herself. Her fingers trembled, but her gaze was steady, and never left the man about to die.

Her gaze had been just as steady when she had given her testimony the day previous. Tears slipped slowly down her sun-kissed face, but she had remained steady all the same. She had spoken long, starting with a quiet stutter that had slowly risen so loud with earnest that Phobos barked a reminder to whom she was speaking. She had quieted once more, but the tears never stopped falling as she continued her story.

There had been an accident.

One of the more frequent peddlers from Castle Lyist had been in the village, selling and buying trinkets as was usual. There had been a recent storm which had torn the roads, and his cart had hit a particularly rough part of the road on the way into town. The cart had been jolted and rattled to the frame. As the peddler passed through a crowd of eager early morning shoppers, the cart hit a displaced cobble, and the axle snapped. The entire cart went tumbling over, spilling its cloaks, blankets, dresses, and bottles of perfumes out onto the road. Many of the shoppers were able to get out of the way, shrieking in all directions. The girl, Silvia, had not been so lucky. She had been walking close to smell a few choice perfumes and run her fingers through a soft fur-lined cloak, when the cart came down, catching her in its fall. It had crushed both her legs and cut them so deeply that blood began to pool dark and fast around her.

The girl had hesitated in her story, remembering the moment, looking like she might be sick. Everett stepped forward, ready to assist her, but the girl waived him away and carried on in a hurry.

Her life's blood was staining the dirt road, all were sure. It was too much too fast. If something was not done, she would be dead in minutes. Everyone came to her aid. Everyone dropped what they were doing, leaving their shopping things forgotten on the dirt, and their cattle to their grazing. After a short time, they were able to pull the cart off of her, but her legs were bent and mangled, and the blood was flowing even faster now. She had grown faint, and the world began to spin. All the faces seemed to lose their features, and their shouting, panicked, voices began to fade into the deep fog that blew into her mind like a cold fall morning.

She went quiet once more. Everett stood at the ready, but when she looked back up at Damian, it was neither sickness nor tears that he saw in her eyes.

"That's when he came to me," she said softly, as if telling a precious secret. A cherished dream. An elusive God.

She had known Abram since she was a child. She grew up in a town where everyone knew everyone, and Abram was no exception. She had always liked him well enough. He had always been kind to her. Respectful to her, even though he was seventeen years her senior. Not like the other boys, she recalled with a sort of loving annoyance. He was a man and treated her like a lady. He was simply one of many farmers, nothing special, no one of high power or influence in their little town. Or at least, no significant influence. For he did have something of a power, as was reviled when he knelt beside a dying girl in the street full of blood.

From inside his cloak, the farmer had pulled what looked like a smooth tan piece of stone. It hooked down, larger on one end and drawing to a point on the other. She had seen that little stone before, everyone in the village had. Good old Abram never left the house without it wrapped in a cord around his neck, or safely stashed in one pocket or another. Everyone assumed it was some sort of good luck charm or family heirloom. At first, the girl had been afraid. She did not think Abram would kill her with the pointed object, but she thought whatever he was going to do to help must be painful. She was already in so much pain. She wanted no more.

Abram had smiled at her and told her to lie still, everything would be alright. It was. And it did not hurt a bit.

Abram had placed the little stone on one of the girls shattered legs as gently as he could. He reached out, letting his hand hover over it, closed his eyes and breathed deeply.

"Then there was this... this light..." the peddler had told them. They had the peddler testify first, before Silvia. He, unlike the girl, had been short, clear, descriptive, and without a trace of admiration in the recounting of Abram and his actions.

"It was a tiny light... it flickered inside the stone... like a little fire under the man's hands. Then he placed the stone on the girl's other leg and did it all over again. Breathing. The light. Then he put the stone back in his pocket..." The peddler opened his hands and looked up at Damian with wide eyes, full of disbelief. "And the girl stopped bleeding. She stood up on legs that were moments ago a pile of meat and broken bone... and it was like she was never hurt." His voice was dark when he spoke his next words. The darkness that spills from the mouth of fear.

"He is a Faithful, my lord."

Yes. All were in agreement, and there was only one outcome. By law, and the son of Great Lawrence II, it was written.

"Step forward and kneel," Damian spoke to the man. The Faithful of a clan, no one really cared to know. Years previously he had burned off his brand, mangling the symbol that denoted his clan or dragon. It really did not matter. A clan was a clan. They all followed the way of dragons.

The man was shuffled forward. He was roughly shoved to the ground at Damian's feet, his knees popping in protest. The man was shaking hard, eyes on the ground. He gazed on it, as if it was the last thing left to see. Waiting for it to come up and swallow him forever.

With all eyes on him, Damian slowly reached for his sword. He drew it out with a soft sigh of steel against leather. The man shrank from the sound. His eyes squeezed closed, and a silent prayer fluttered against his lips.

Damian Lystad, son of Jeromy Lystad, decedent of Great Lawrence II, King of Castle Lyist, protector of Neira Kingdom, and keeper of its laws, slowly raised his blade. The crowd held their breath.

Damian let the blade fall. The entire crowd, including Abram, gave a little mousy squeak. The tip of Damian's blade went right past Abrams' neck and sunk deep into the dirt beside him. Abram looked up at his own reflection in the perfectly polished steel. He stared as if looking into the eyes of a ghost. He let his gaze slowly rise to Damian.

"Abram Olson," Damian answered the question in the man's eyes. "The punishment for being a Faithful is death in this kingdom. Therefore, I advise you to leave it immediately."

"Sire?" Abram asked as the crowd around began a light rumbling of questions and conversation.

"Leave," Damian said, simply. "Because of the extenuating circumstances of this crime," His eyes darted to the girl who would have died without Abram. She was watching him, tears flooding her eyes once more. "I will allow you to leave with your life. However," Damian continued, eyes back on the man, and they were now cold and full of warnings. "Faithful practices are not allowed in this kingdom. I give you your life. Now take it with you and go. Be out of this village before the day is through, and out of my kingdom on the quickest of paths... and if you ever return," Damian pulled the blade from the ground, wiped it against his brown cloak, and sheathed it with a practiced flip of the wrist. "Then, we will... revisit your sentence."

Abram blinked, waiting for the joke to be over. Waiting for the young king to get on with the execution. Even after the shackles were unwound from his wrists by Teller, he still hesitated. Finally, he slowly got to his feet.

"Truly, sire?" Abram asked, eyes darting to every face. Shock deepening as the knights stepped away.

"You have a horse, yes?" Damian asked, ignoring the man's stupid question. "Leave tonight. I will have someone return in three days, and if you are still here, he will be under orders to end your life on sight. Do you understand?"

"Yes, sire," Abram said, bowing low, entire body seeming to shake from fear and joy. "Of course, sire. Thank you, sire." Abram scrambled away, all shaking arms and legs, into the waiting crowd. The blond girl was the first to reach him. She flung her arms around him and fell into violent joyful sobs.

*Good gods that woman could cry.*

The rest of the village soon enveloped him like the arms of a dear friend. Because Damian noted, they were. He watched the tearful faces of the village, as they hugged and kissed and slapped the man on the back. They had known. Every single one of them. Abram was known in the village. A village that all turned up to see the sentencing. Who all came, not to see "justice" done, but to be there for a friend in his last moments of life. They had acted like Abram being a Faithful had been a discovery. That they had not known what the stone in the man's pocket was, or what it held. They had all been terrible liars. If they had not known, then they had at least suspected.

"Gather everyone," Damian said, turning to Teller. "We're leaving." He was ready to go home.

While the knights, advisers and their servants finished the last preparations to leave, Phobos stepped slowly up beside Damian. His hands were clasped tightly behind his back, and his ugly face was pinched up into a particularly displeased scowl as he watched the villagers dispersing. A small stable boy led a horse to Abram while another boy toppled along besides, fighting to keep up with the older boy's stride and finish clipping the saddle securely to the mare.

"This is a disastrous mistake, my lord," Phobos said after a moment, the remnants of his white hair floating like a cloud in the breeze about his liver-spotted scalp.

"You think so, Phobos?" Damian asked in a light tone full of humor. "I did not understand that... after the first five times you said it."

"It is these types of... decisions... that leaves the other kingdoms wondering about your readiness to take the throne, my lord."

Damian rolled his eyes. He had been listening to Phobos's griping since the moment he heard of Damian's plan to let the man live. So many, hum's, and hu's, and warning about the other three kingdoms disapproval. Kingdom Sterlyn, Kyar, and Eryl were the main kingdoms apart from Neira. All had known Damian's father well, and all had sent their most profound regret at his sudden passing. A few sent a little something extra. Rumors of the rest of the realm's trepidation at young Damian taking the throne. Granted Damian had barely reached his twentieth year when he took his father's throne, but he had been doing a damn fine job if he did say so himself.

However, it was not his age that worried the other kingdoms. Damian's grandfather had only entered his fourteenth year when he took the throne, and they had not been concerned. No one raised a finger of objection. Because Damian's grandfather had been the first born. The rightful heir. Damian was not. That was what concerned the kingdoms, not how many years he had spent in the land of the living. It was never meant to be him. It was never supposed to be his father. It was his father's elder brother who was destined to take the throne. It was supposed to be **his** son, Damian's cousin Vander, who was meant to have knelt before the priestess. It was on Vander's head the crown of Neira was meant to settle. It was on Vander's shoulders that the responsibility of Castle Lyist and Neira Kingdom was supposed to fall with the weight of a thousand mountains, that so often felt like it might snap Damian's collarbone in half. But Noah had abdicated, abandoning Neira, and Vander was now heir to a different throne altogether.

No. It was never meant to be Damian, and the kingdoms never let him forget. When his father died, they showed that clearly enough. In the case of Sterlyn Kingdom and their reigning lord Lecter Lessen, he sent along his condolences with his ever-open invitation for counsel. Damian had met Lessen before and knew what such an offer truly meant.

*Look here, boy, when you find yourself too deep, and you will, I will pull you out of whatever fire you have built for yourself. For a price, of course.*

Queen Medea Steiger had at least veiled her offer to puppet his kingdom under the pretense of her and Noah visiting to assist in whatever was needed after his father's passing. Damian had thanked, and concurrently denied, both offers in turn. This did much for his pride, but little to quell the rumors that only built as years passed on. There were even a few rumors spoken low and harsh of Sterlyn kingdom wanting to take Neira a little more securely under its wing than what simple counsel could provide.

This, Damian knew, was unlikely. After years of prosperous corporation, it would be foolish of Lessen to try such a move, unless of course, he genuinely thought Damian such a weak leader. On the other hand, Lessen was known more for his brawn than for his brains. If he ever did attempt to try to put his fingers into Neira's business, Damian would show him how hard the blue dragon could bite, proper heir or not.

"Let them wonder," Damian said simply.

"He used bones, my lord," Phobos pressed.

"To save a girl's life."

"Makes no difference." Phobos sniffed.

"Doesn't it?" Damian asked, watching Abram about to mount his steed when the blond girl grabbed him by the front of the cloak and pulled him into a tearful farewell kiss that left him more stunned then when Damian had let him live.

"The Faithful are a disease," Phobos said. "It can disguise itself as something mild, something innocent... nothing but a cold... easily cured..." He gestured to Abram who was now mounted on his horse with a few bags of gifts being shoved into his hands by the surrounding villagers. "But it spreads. It always spreads and grows. What if he comes back? And what if he doesn't come alone? What if he kills the villagers out of anger for being sent away? Because of what he is."

Damian looked at the people of the village. They were watching Abrams horse riding off now, at full gallop. Watching it slowly disappear into the distance with eyes filled with unmistakable loss. Tears rolled down faces, and the blond girl buried hers into a friend's shoulder. The friend ran a hand up and down the girls back in comforting circles.

Every one of them had known. They had known and had come to accept him anyway. Come to love him anyway. They had all lied to their own kingdom to protect him. Technically, if he followed the word of the law laid down by Great Lawrence the II, he should convict them *all* of treason for lying about Abram and the little bag around his neck. What was he supposed to do? Kill the whole village? Their lies would have worked too, Damian was sure of it. The man would have kept his secret, if one peddler with a fragile wagon had not broken down in the middle of the street, and then run straight to Castle Lyist to tell the tale.

"He won't," Damian answered.

"How can you be so sure my king?" Damian heard the slight sneer in Phobos's tone but chose to ignore it and instead answered the question.

"Because only a monster would return love with violence."

Damian had looked in Abrams' eyes. You can tell a lot about a man from his eyes, and Damian had seen it all. The man was a liar. A liar and a coward. But he was not a monster.

Damian heard Phobos give an almost inaudible snort from beside him. Damian tensed. He turned slowly eyes falling dark and cold on Phobos who froze, mouth slacking under the intensity of Damian's glare.

"Something else to say Phobos?" Damian's voice was low and warning. His tone dared the old man to snort once more.

"No, your, majesty," Phobos said, clearing his throat, and eyes darting away. "Of course not. Begging your forgiveness, sire. I did not mean to disrespect your grace."

"Granted," Damian said after a loaded silence. Phobos bowed his head once more in thanks.

"Besides," Damian went on, his hand slipping to the small lambskin pouch that had been tightened securely to his belt. He worked the knot open and pulled out the long-angled stone-like object that had been confiscated from Abram Olson after his arrest. "He's harmless now. No Faithful can perform magic... not without this." He twisted the little object in his hand, running a finger down the smooth side that tapered into a point. A point far sharper than the blade hanging on his hip could ever hope to be, because it was made from the most dangerous substance known to man. Dragon bone. A dragon tooth to be exact. Deadly in the wrong hands, but not just because it was sharp.

"In their bones, does magic still live," Damian whispered under his breath, in a low lyrical tone.

"And to willing hearts, does their magic give," Phobos spoke the next line of the children's nursery rhyme in a voice that was spectacularly tone deaf.

Damian twisted the little object to the other side, as the wind blew a bit more fog over the street. It was thick and sharp, barely longer than Damian's index finger.

"Must have been a young one." Damian mused, holding the little object up to his eyes.

"Not even two years of age, I'd say." Phobos squinted, that same pinched up scowl scrunching his features. Damian nodded in agreement. "Did you at least ask him where he got the bone my lord? Whether he has any contacts or connections to the shadow market?"

Damian laughed out loud. "Do you think me an utter halfwit Phobos? Of course, I asked him where he got the relic." They had spent many hours with Olson, using methods that Damian generally found distasteful, to make sure he was telling the truth of that matter. "It was a family heirloom."

"So he says... and you just took him at his word?" Phobos asked, his words pushing dangerously close to that impudent tone that was ever his fall back. It took a massive amount of effort for Damian to refrain from rolling his eyes, but somehow, he managed it.

"No, Phobos, I did not simply take him at his word." Along with various tasteless methods for invoking honesty from Abram himself, Damian also went about the town's folk. He asked each separately, if they knew where he might have gotten such a rare item. All the younger folk had no idea, but a few of the village's elderly swore that they had seen the little threaded pouch handed down from Olsen to Olsen, until it finally was granted to Abram himself. "Olsen had no connection to the shadow market."

"Umm," Phobos mused regretfully. "Pity."

On this, at least, Damian agreed. There were very few opportunities to catch a lead on the shadow markets operations. There had been many close calls throughout the years, but nothing definitive. With the last Faithful sighting, Damian's grandfather had believed he might retrieve a name, or a location, from one of the two Faithful that fought. Unfortunately, the Faithful's had died before the king could interrogate either, which cut off the Kingdom's avenue to find out more information about where they got the bones in the first placed. There were several locations in Neira, but they moved frequently, the shadow runners living like nomads buying and selling all that was rare, dangerous, and expensive. With the Faithfuls unable to even point Damian I in the right direction, they lost the scent, and the market continued its works in the shadows of Neira kingdom unhindered until that day. Although, by this point, business must have been dwindling.

The great majority of the dragon bones had been systematically gathered and stored beneath the castles of the Four Kingdoms after the death of dragons. Of course, a small number were distributed in secret. There were once many dragons, and they left behind many bones. It was no surprise that, despite how thorough they attempted to be, the Four Kingdoms may have overlooked a few here and there. However, these were few and the magic they contained was limited. Over the centuries, with use, the magic would dry up, leaving the stray bones worthless and powerless. The shadow market would soon be running out of relics. To be sure, dragon relics were not the only items for sale at their shops. Just the most lucrative. In the right hands, those bones could be a source of great power, and power was anything but free.

In time, however, the market relics would run dry, and when the kingdoms finally discovered how to destroy the remaining dragon bones (which was a solution that had evaded the best smiths and physicians for hundreds of years) magic itself would be wiped from the world for good.

Damian gently placed the tooth back into the little leather pouch, tightening it securely once more. He would give it to the Keepers as soon as he returned. He had no idea how much magic might still be left within the tooth after healing two shattered legs... but he would take no chances. He turned away from his adviser and the quietly mourning village. He walked over to a servant who was holding ready his horse and mounted with a graceful sweep of his long leg. The horse nickered, pawing a hoof against ground, sending a spray of soft dirt in the servant's direction. They laughed and darted out of its reach. The horse nickered again, ready to be off. Damian agreed. He wanted away from this village. Away from Phobos. Away from banishing and executions. A pit in his stomach churned and bubbled darkly as he tapped his heels into his horses' sides and clucked to him. The horse moved immediately, breaking into a soft trot. His men mounted and followed behind him with a few clicks of their own.

Dirt was churned and kicked back in soft wet sprays as they headed for the castle. Another good day's work done. Another village left saved. Saved... and weeping.

Damian remembered little of his mother; she had died when he was quite young. Both she, and what would have been Damian's little brother, perished due to a hard-twin labor. The first birth, little Naomi, was strenuous and bloody. But she was brought into the world, squalling. The boy, Simon, had passed by before he left his mother's body. This is what Augustine had called a "bygone" birth. His mother had held on for as long as she could, but that turned out to be only a few hours after losing Simon. They buried the two together, child wrapped in the protective arms of his mother. Damian's father had never been the same. He blamed himself for his wife's death, blamed the seed he had placed within her that would inevitably be her doom.

Although the king did not know it, and never would, Damian had blamed himself as well. He spent restless nights weeping silently at the ceiling over his bed, wishing that he had been a better son to his mother. If he had been a better boy, perhaps she would not have felt the need for a second son. Maybe then she would still be alive.

Because she had died so early in his years, all his memories of her were a jumble of images, sounds, smells, with a few fleeting moments that lasted in clear, perfect memory. One of these was of his mother's serious face, eyebrows pulled down close to the same eyes that would haunt his mirror for the rest of his life. He did not have a clue what he had been doing to bring about her anger. Perhaps some childish joke which had gone too far with some visiting friend or son of some nobleman. They were usually a bunch of jackasses anyway, so a young Damian would not have known what the big deal was, but his mother took unkindness very seriously, even if it was meant as a joke.

Elaine Lystad had leaned down close, blue eyes seeming to sparkle in the sunlight that spilled through his bedroom window. Damian had been sitting on his bed, head low with shame, looking back up at her. And at that moment, with that angry glint in her eyes and the sunlight pooling up behind her head, silhouetting her in some heavenly glow, Damian had been sure his mother was some sort of avenging angel. It made every word she spoke sink in like the words of the gods themselves.

"Damian... No true good comes with sad tears."

She had spoken slow and clear, and it was those words that haunted him as he clicked his horse to a gallop and hurried for home.

# CHAPTER 10

It was a few more days before Kyana was allowed another adventure into open air. She was not able to wander without supervision, on Augustine's fervent insistence, and Ira, although more than willing to be her companion, had been stuck working late hours in the kitchens. She was left instead to wander her room like a caged cat, pacing, pawing through the cabinets and closets out of boredom more than real curiosity. There was very little in there. A few clothes, bathing towels, and extra candlesticks that were as ornate as anything else in the room.

Much of the time she watched out the large window at the goings on below. Her window was wide, with double shutters that pushed out onto a north-west view of Castle Lyist and the lands of Neira Kingdom. The four walls of the castle snaking out in ever-widening amber brick. Stone dragons prowled the tops, curling up the watch towers and clambering down stone walls in various sizes and shapes. Still false leather wings spread open, casting shade on the grounds below, while frozen fire curled artfully from pulled back lips and long stone teeth. The outermost wall ended with meadows expanding miles of distance between the castle and the forests to the west, whereas the northern view was cut short by a large river that flooded and flowed south-east. Kyana often watched the ships that would hoist sail, setting off to make trade with the other major cities on the other side of the river. Sails of white fluttered high in the breeze beside flags donning the two-headed dragon of their homeland. She also watched the people in the courtyards below her window. Watched them bustling about their daily duties, moving with one another in seemingly perfect unison. It was the type of unity that came from centuries of well-worn social patterns. It was lovely in its simplicity, and elegant in its performance. However, other than the bustle of people, and the continuous glinting of sunlight reflecting off the wide river to her right, there was little else to see. A cold wind had kicked up within the kingdom. One day a fog rolled in so thick that when Kyana opened her window and stuck her hand out into the wet dappled coldness, she could not see her own fingers. Over the last evening, the fog finally rolled out, and the sun broke through the sky, lighting everything up in its golden glow and the river once again began to wink at her. Kyana was left to watch it all from her window alone.

Augustine had put her under a strict "do not disturb" policy. To Kyana's surprise, there always seemed to be people, servants usually, who Augustine had to shoo away from the door when he came to check on her.

"They're just curious is all," Augustine said, "You've been the subject of most rumors spinning around the place these days. The girl who saw demons. The girl who saved the king." Augustine had smiled at this. "Sounds like a fable now, doesn't it? Or a legend. Give um enough time they'll make you one or the other."

"What if I don't want to be either?" Kyana asked, playing into the former medic's little game.

"Oh, I don't think you'd have much say in that." Augustine laughed a little. "Legends are made without asking I'm afraid. Just like rumors. But I won't have them coming in here and pestering you right now. You need your rest if you're ever to heal."

So, for those few days, she was mostly alone. She would get visits from Augustine, and a few times from Ira, but those were always brief "hello's" and "goodbyes" with no real time in between. Other than that, she was left to her thoughts. That was not always a good thing. Her thoughts had started to run hard and fast around her mind, but they kept, inevitably coming back to one remembrance.

*A handmaid was nice enough to help change you.*

Kyana absentmindedly scratched at her forearm under her long-sleeved shirt. Augustine had tried in vain to present her with several dresses over the days. All beautiful, in pinks, blues, and dark browns, but Kyana refused each with a kind word of thanks. She was no lady to wander in garments that would do nothing but slow her down when she most needed speed. Finally, after the last few rejections, Augustine gave up on the dresses and brought in a few clean shirts that were obviously meant for a young man.

"I'm afraid I have yet to find a pair of pants to replace your old ones," Augustine said regretfully, laying out the shirts before her with a dubious expression. "But these will serve better than your old shirt I'd say. Or the one Ira gave you... which is far too large. I don't know what that girl was thinking."

Kyana reached out and felt the thick, sturdy fabric with a leather tie at the collar. She smiled.

"Thank you, practitioner."

"It is my pleasure."

Kyana pulled the shirt Ira had lent her over her head and folded it gently on the bed. She slipped on one of the tops made of light blue cotton. It was sturdy, but felt soft against her skin. It was also a little too large, but she would not need a belt which was an improvement. She neatly tucked the edge into her pants before tapping Augustine's shoulder. He had turned around to give her some privacy.

"And, your old shirt," Augustine said, gesturing towards the forgotten garment on top of the cabinet. "I might know someone who could sew up the gash nicely, but I'm afraid there is no getting the blood out of it... would you mind if I just threw it away?"

Kyana shrugged.

"Burn it for all I care." Burn it all away.

It was that blue shirt she was wearing when a soft knock came to her door, shaking her out of thoughts about some unknown maid who knew too much.

"Come," she answered, and the door creaked open. She looked around and smiled. "Hello, Ira."

"Good afternoon, Kyana." Ira's broad grin pulled wide.

"Finally got away from the kitchens, did you?" she asked.

"I did," she said, tossing her long blond braid around to her back with a flip of her wrist, as if dust from her shoulder. "Ready for me to keep my promise?" she asked.

"Oh, gods, yes," Kyana answered, already darting for the door.

The streets were a bustle. People were weaving in and out of one another, trying to reach this shop or that peddler's carts. Kyana watched several young girls holding hands in a long five-person chain to avoid being separated. They weaved through the crowd like some deformed snake, laughing at the top of their voices and tripping over their own feet as the rest of the people flooded through the streets. The crowd pulsed, moved, braking and re-merging around carts, buildings and statues. A large stone figure of Great Lawrence II stood tall and watchful in the middle of the yard, hands leaning against his stone sword. His severe, and yet unseeing, eyes gazed upon his citizens passing by below. Always watching over them. Never to fully leave them.

The laughter, conversations, heated bartering, the tromping of hundreds if not thousands of feet, and the sound of a flute playing somewhere distant in the background (where or why Kyana did not know) made a fantastic cacophony that left Kyana struck. She stood transfixed in the middle of the road, eyes wide, darting around unable to choose a spot to finally rest her gaze. There was so much to see.

Carts were laden down with fresh fruits, another with cloths of unlimited colors, a man walking between the bustle, holding out beaded necklaces and bracelets and shouting prices Kyana could not hear over the din. The smith was back at his work, sparks flying from the red-hot steel that he pounded under a large hammer. Kyana could smell oil and smoke wafting strong, but that wasn't the only smell. There was an entire cart devoted to perfumes, and it seemed someone had accidently broken a bottle, filling the air with strong vanilla scent and the sounds of the peddler's enthusiastic desire for payment. There was also the smell of apples, oranges, other perfumes, cooking meat, dirt, fire, and the overwhelming but unmistakable smell of people. Just so many people.

"You alright?" Ira asked, leaning over to get a better look at her face. "You look a little..." She did not finish the sentence, and that was probably polite.

Kyana turned to her, mouth open.

"There's so many," Kyana said, eyes finally focusing on Ira.

"So many what?"

"So many people."

Ira smiled that broad smile that belonged only to her.

"Ya. There are, aren't there?"

Kyana hesitated, then took a step forward. Then another step and then another. She moved with wondrous, uneven strides, as if a child taking its first steps into a world it did not yet understand. She was soon mixing in with the crowd. Getting lost in it. She was twirling and swirling in the bustle like a leaf in the wind surrounded by so many other leaves. She was swept up in the sound of voices until it felt like she was being pressed in on all sides. She began to wonder if it was possible to drown in a sea of people. Luckily, Ira was there to guide her through. She took Kyana's hand and lead her out into a more mellow portion of the street. There they could safely stand and watch the crowd go by without getting swept up.

"You alright?" Ira asked again.

Kyana nodded, eyes still watching everyone and everything she could.

"This is... this is..."

"A bit much, I know," Ira said, frowning out at everyone.

"Amazing," Kyana finished, looking up at Ira. "Utterly, amazing."

Ira's look of surprise melted into a smile.

"Thanks," Ira said, looking back up at the city. "We like it. It's busy, and it's loud," She looked back down at Kyana. "But it's home. Come with me." She followed Ira as she maneuvered down to a row of peddlers with fewer buyers, allowing Kyana to catch her breath a little. They walked passed small carts of more beaded jewelry matching those held by the man walking up and down the streets. They hung off the low blanket canopy like decorations that fluttered and clattered against one another in the breeze. A woman sat beside the cart, elbow resting on the table, eyes half closed with midday drowsiness, but she perked up as Kyana and Ira drew closer. She was an older woman, possibly into her seventieth year, and time had drawn many lines down her face and around her eyes. The sun had taken its toll as well, leaving her skin crinkled and discolored in several spots. She wore a thick red and green skirt with a matching shawl that had seen many years of its own. It hung over her beefy shoulders to tie in a large knot above her bosom.

"Bracelets!" the woman called in a raspy voice that seemed to stick in her own throat and an accent that suggested her origins lay a fair distance from Castle Lyist or even Kingdom of Neira. "Bracelets, necklaces, rings and more! Come, Come, see how much for! Bracelets, necklaces, rings, and more! Come, come, you'll like, I am shore!" She spoke the word "sure," like "shore" to allow for a rhyme, and this made Kyana chuckle. She turned in at the cart, and the woman looked about to burst with excitement when she did. Kyana leaned in to look at all the different beads which were woven in a rather skillful fashion. The woman began picking up different bracelets and necklaces, chattering happily about each in turn.

"This, my dear, took two days for me to complete." She raised a soft blue bracelet with four bands that interwove in lovely spirals and loops. "Twould also go nicely with that... that shirt yer wearing." The woman took a moment to realize Kyana was, in fact, a woman wearing men's clothes. She quickly shook it off as unimportant and went straight back to selling her work.

"And this one! Oh, this one took me four days!" the woman said, holding up a necklace made with three bands of mixed pink and gold beads. "I lie not! I lie not! Four days I say, and four days I mean! And I say truly also, it would go lovely with yer—" The woman broke off in mid-sentence. Her eyes met Kyana's, and her words seemed to evaporate from her tongue as if they had never intended to be there in the first place. Kyana watched her dull blue eyes widen, and her mouth go slack. A soft "oh," escaped her, as the necklace, a moment ago the most important thing in this woman's world, fell from her fingers and hit the dirty ground at her feet. Kyana stooped, picked it up, and held it out for her to take, but the woman made no such moves. She was simply staring directly into Kyana's eyes as if hypnotized by what she saw there.

"Are you alright?" Kyana asked, growing concerned now, wondering if this woman was having some sort of attack. Should she call Ira? She had wandered a short distance away, checking out a variety of colorful fabric at another cart, but not too far to call for help. And do what? Run for Augustine maybe? One of the other practitioners? Kyana was about to do just that, but the woman blinked.

"Yes..." her voice was far-off, but she reached out and took the necklace all the same. Kyana gave a little bow of thanks and started to move away from the table.

"Wait!" The woman's cry was so sudden and sounded so desperate, that Kyana flinched and swung back around. The woman hesitated, licking her lips in thought, and then she relaxed a little, a smile playing her face. "A pretty thing like you cannot leave empty-handed. No, no, not empty-handed."

"I'm afraid I have no money," Kyana said, but the woman did not seem to be listening. She turned, snagged one of the first things within reach, which was a single strand of white beads with a few larger golden beads in the middle.

"A necklace like this can bring ye luck, it can. No payment needed dear. No payment needed here."

"That is really not necessary," Kyana said, taking a step back from the woman, but the woman followed her, necklace folded in hand. She was acting very odd. Or was this normal for peddlers in the bigger cities? Kyana did not know.

"Please," the woman spoke soft and calm, but Kyana could see a trace of desperation flash across her dull blue eyes. There, and then quickly chased away by composure and a soft smile.

"Such a lovely girl like yerself... might someday be able to use such a simple thing as this." Kyana paused and then nodded, reaching out to receive the gift.

"Thank you kindly moth—" The customary thanksgiving fell short on her lips as the woman dropped the necklace in her hand. But the necklace was not all she gave. The old woman had reached out unnoticed by all the people milling around the other tables. She touched Kyana's palm with the two fingers between her pinky and the index finger of her right hand. She traced out three symbols slow and steady into her skin above the necklace now forgotten.

A straight line drawn vertically down. Taps, twice done. And a long spiral that started small and spread slowly outward.

Kyana's eyes flew up to the woman who slowly, hesitantly, finished the spiral and raised her gaze. Suddenly, Kyana saw that those blue eyes did not look dull at all. She swallowed.

"How..." Kyana could not finish the question.

"Eyes can say a lot about a woman." The jeweler woman smiled; all tension gone as if by giving her gift she was relieved of some terrible burden. "And my dear, yer's are screaming."

"Thank you, mother," she finished in a choked voice. The woman gave a slight bow of her graying head, as she let go of Kyana's hand. "Perhaps such a gift will come in handy after all."

"I truly hope not, dear lady," the woman said, blinking slowly in the bright sunlight. "Ta only people in need of luck, are those followed by misfortune."

Kyana smiled.

"Oh, mother," Kyana said pocketing the meaningless trinket, the true gift seeming to tingle against the skin of her palm. "I am no lady here."

The woman flashed a smile that melted thirty years and endless troubles from her features. Kyana saw a glint so beautiful in those eyes, she wondered how she could ever have found them dull.

"No. I suppose ye are no," she said. "Well, neither am I. Well, for goodness sake. What a pair we make, hum?"

Kyana was reaching out without the slightest idea of what she meant to do with her hands. To clasp the woman's hand or pull the woman (who only moments ago was a stranger) into her arms, she did not know. She never found out.

"Ira!" a voice called from behind them. Kyana turned to see three knights in billowing brown cloaks coming towards them. She recognized one of the bearded ones as the knight she had tripped in the courtyard. The second was a knight she had never seen. This one seemed to be having trouble growing his own reddish-blond beard, but had not yet given up the attempt. The third was the short knight from the forest.

"There you are. Cabot has been looking—" He trailed off as Kyana caught his eyes.

"Hay! It's our treetop angel!" he said happily, not looking weary at all, starkly contrasted from his fellows. The knight crossed the short distance between them, Ira and the other knights following closely behind. "I don't think we were ever properly introduced. I'm Neander." He held out his hand. Kyana resisted the urge to shrink away, eyes darting momentarily to the coat of arms sewn onto his cloak.

*No fear, no weakness, they pray on that.* So, she stood tall and took his hand.

"Kyana," she said, looking him in the eye.

*One.* His eyes were a muddy brown with thin red lines around the edges... he used to be a drinker... and still was.

*Two.* His grip was firm. If he was a drinker, it did not affect his life. His hands were completely steady.

*Three.* He did not look away or hesitate, but she saw his smile falter slightly.

*Four.* She did not blink. Those deep green eyes held his gaze captive, causing the hair rise on the back of his neck, like a dog getting a whiff of something troubling. But he still did not look away. No matter how much, as he suddenly realized, he would like to.

"Nice to meet you, Neander," she said, finally blinking. Neander took in a breath as the gaze broke. He wondered why his heart was beating so quickly.

"This here is Simon," Neander gestured to the knight Kyana had never met before, who nodded. "And this here is Cole." Neander slapped the back of the bearded knight. "But... oh, wait..." Neander grinned. "You two have met before."

"Uh, briefly." The motion felt like wrenching teeth, but Kyana made herself step forward and hold out her hand to the knight of Castle Lyist. "Forgive my rudeness the other day. I was not in my right mind."

Cole's weary expression broke into a half smile as he took her hand.

"No harm done," the knight said, in a voice a few octaves too high for his appearance. "If I thought I was seeing demons, I would have done the same."

"Speaking of which, you look better." Neander took a step back and grinned. "No more of that," He waved a hand in her general direction, "Pale fury, or passing out."

Kyana just watched him, eyebrows raised before she spoke, "Yes, your practitioner is quite skilled."

"Augustine is a good man," Neander grinned at Ira. "But another good man has been looking for you for over an hour."

"Oh shit," Ira's face fell. "Cabot…. Is he pissed?"

"Oh… that's one word for it."

Ira groaned. Kyana looked over at her. "Something wrong?"

"Ya… I gotta go," Ira said sadly. "Kitchen to clean, food to prep… I'll show you back to your room."

"Oh…" Kyana looked out at the sun-soaked town still in full swing. "Okay, then."

"Don't lock the girl away in a tower, Ira." Neander frowned, giving her a gentle shove. "Would you like to continue this walk with me, my lady?" Kyana looked up at him. He was a knight of Castle Lyist, but he was not what she would expect. He seemed… weird, but also kind. He wasn't the least bit upset about her pointing a sword at him a few days previously.

"I would like to walk a bit more…. If it is alright with Ira."

"Sure!" Ira said, then leaned in. "You're not going to try to kill him, again, are you?"

*If I needed him to be dead, he would be.*

"I promise I will not try to kill him today," Kyana answered.

"Today?" Neander laughed, and the other knights joined in halfheartedly.

"But do YOU keep your promises, Kyana of the woods?" Ira grinned at her.

"You can either trust me, or you can't." Kyana would have suggested the latter, but Ira had trusting eyes, and those eyes did not disappoint.

"Alright," Ira looked to Neander, pointing a finger in his face like a mother prematurely scolding her child. "Any teetering, or if she looks faint at all, take her straight back to her room and call for Augustine."

"Yes, Ma'am!" Neander gave Ira a salute.

"I'll be back to check on you later." Kyana nodded, and Ira turned and quickly disappeared into the bustling crowd.

"Well, my lady!" Neander said, holding out his arm. "Shall we?" Kyana hesitated.

*Oh, what could it hurt?* She stepped forward and took it. The short knight's grin widened as Kyana looked slightly up at him.

"You know, you're shorter than I remember," he said, sounding pleased. Kyana said nothing. Instead, she glanced back at the woman by her cart. She was watching Kyana go with a frightened expression, hands clasping the shawl around her shoulders. Her eyes darted from Kyana to the knights and then back again, her mouth opening and closing as if in silent, horrified, protest. Kyana smiled, gave her a reassuring wink and waved goodbye. The woman quickly disappeared through the crowds as Neander continued to lead her forward, the other knights following them like two brown flags in the breeze.

# CHAPTER 11

Unknown to that strangest of women, or the knight that lead her through the bustling city streets, the strangest of men stepped lightly through the door of a smoky bar only three cities away. This particular bar was well known to the citizens of the outer towns. The type of bar that everyone knew, but no one spoke of. It was one of those places that exist in every kingdom, although it came in different forms. This form just happened to sell alcohol. They used to sell, at an affordable hourly rate, the company of young girls and energetic boys. However, that business had drawn too much attention from the authorities after Damian Lystad I, the long-passed grandfather of the current king, had outlawed such pleasures that coin could buy. That was a disappointment for many of the customers, but the bar kept running strong. For that was not its primary source of income, not even close. It dealt in alcohol and, more importantly, it dealt in providing a safe haven for making lucrative connections. The type of connections with quick blades and no hesitation to silence whisperers who liked to talk often about things that do not concern them.

It was into this place, at the same moment that Kyana took the arm of a knight named Neander, that another strange person passed through the doors. He was tall, extraordinarily tall, with limbs that were long and willowy, and a face that was so pale he could have been leached moments before. His hair was a long, dark, and an unnatural shade of blue, but it was his eyes that caught the most attention. They were dark eyes, seeming, even in the bright lights inside the bar, not to have any irises at all. Black pupil was all that looked out from the pale face. He paused a moment, looking around the room, which was full, active, and smelled like five different levels of vomit and piss. The ground was crisscrossed with muddy footprints from the dozens of men and women who sat around tables, sprawled laughing drunkenly across counters, and in the case of one small man who looked barely older than a boy, curled up asleep in the corner. There were three bartenders behind the counter that reached from one end of the room to the other. They tried vainly to keep up with the flood of orders burped from mouths, stinking with grog and rotten teeth.

The tall man surveyed the view without expression. His deep black eyes seemed to pass over everyone and everything as if none of it was actually there. They skirted the scene, like a bug above water, passing by until he found what he had been looking for. When he saw it, every ounce of attention was poured into the gaze. The fluttering bug turned into a diving bird of prey, and he made his way farther into the room. The person who had caught his strange eye was a woman deep into her forty-sixth year. She was strong, with no chest to speak of and rippling muscles that crawled up her neck and flexed with every movement. She sat at an empty table near the back of the room, tearing pieces of chicken in handfuls from the plate before her, knife and fork completely forgotten. She ate alone, but the tall man could see there were several other tables nearby that filled with other men and women wearing the same sort of rugged well used layers of cloths as she. They pretended not to notice the tall man as he took a seat beside the hireling leader.

"Lue," the man started in a light and trickling voice. "Very nice to see you again."

"Witch," the woman responded gruffly, mouth gleaming with grease. The tall man said nothing, but a cold smile slid from one side of his face to the other.

"Any word from your little pet on the inside?"

"Not yet." The tall man sat straight in his chair, hands resting on the table, long fingers laced. "Patience."

The woman snorted a laugh, and a piece of chicken went flying to splat on the table beside her plate.

"Patience, patience, do I look like a patient woman to you, Witch?"

The man slowly drew his eyes from the discarded, half-chewed chicken, and looked back up to the woman, expression still unchanged.

"It doesn't matter what I think," the tall man said calmly. "It only matters what you do. Have you made any of those inquiries that we spoke of?"

Lue took a moment, chewing her chicken with big slopping bites, while the tall man waited patiently. She finally swallowed.

"Oh, I made some inquiries, alright."

"Any news?"

"Oh, sure. We got a little news… and lost a lot of blood as well." The women glanced over to one of the tables where a hireling with a bandaged arm sat, staring at a table in front of him as if terrified of the wood it was made from. "He was one of the few to get back from our little *inquiry.* Hasn't spoken a word since."

"I take it things became… complicated?"

"Ha," the women barked a laugh, and another piece of chicken went flying. "That's one word for it, sure is!" Her laughter died down, and she leveled her eyes to men sitting next to her. "I've been making a few inquiries about you as well."

"Is that so?" the man asked, voice coming out in an amused purr.

"Sure have," Lue said, no smile now. "I don't like doing business with people without knowing them in and out, and I gotta say, you are one odd nugget. Lots of trouble you have gotten yourself into over the years."

"Some call it trouble," the man said smile still on, "I call it successes hidden under the gauze of failure."

The woman snorted. "All of them got away. All your little plans to kill those princelings… weren't very artful. All of them survived. You failed."

The strange man shook his head, smile only spreading wider. "The little one's deaths… those were only secondary goals… a playful distraction. If successful, all the better… and if not, none the worse. They were not the primary mission."

"What was the primary mission then?"

"The exact same as it is today." His smile widened even further. "And let me assure you… that mission went beautifully."

"But those others that you hired… those that actually took those royal babies from their homes and carried them off into the night to carry out your little 'distraction,' they all ended up in various prisons or on the end of a rope."

"That was an end of their own making," the man said, smile faltering as a flash of irritation passed over his dark eyes. "If they would have followed my orders, everything would have gone as planned and those sweet little darlings would now be so much grass." The hireling scowled at this. She was a woman of loose morals herself, but she did not like the way this man spoke of killing children with the same ease as one would discuss the proper method of cooking a turkey. "They deviated from the plan. They were supposed to kill the children and scatter into the night with their prizes. Turns out a few members decided to grow a conscience at some point during the evening. Their hesitation cost them their lives, not me. Disappointing as it was… it served its purpose." That smile slid back over his lips. "When people are scrambling to retrieve their precious royal ones… they tend to forget about double checking the locked doors leading to dark caverns."

"You and your precious bones," the hireling said, shaking her head "You know," Lue pondered, grease shining on her lips like smeared gloss on a whore. "If it's just bones you're after, why not seek out the shadow market? There are several posts throughout Neira, and even more in Kyar. I have a few friends… could get you a good deal… for a cut of my own of course."

"Of course," the man said, eyes briefly flashing down to the hireling's chewing lips with disgust, and then quickly looking back up to her eyes, composure regained. "I'm afraid I'm… a little lacking in the proper coin at the moment."

"Ya," The hireling grunted and turned back to her chicken, "The price on relics has sure gone up these days. Running low on product is my thinking." The strange man paused to wonder if the woman had ever had a truly fully formed thought in her life, before moving on.

"Besides…. I am done with scavenging in the shadows, making deals with strangers, for things that never belonged to them in the first place… and revenge would be a nice aftertaste to success," the man said, eyes drifting slightly. The woman wondered if his mind had trailed off to watch grass grow.

"Well that is where our trouble starts," the hireling grumbled. "Your 'aftertaste' is our main event. You can't raid a treasury without taking the city."

"Are you concerned about my commitment?" The man's eyes drew back to her, almost regretfully. What pretty grass it must have been.

"I'm just wanting to make sure we aren't just another *distraction*," the woman replied, waiving a piece of meat in his direction.

The man shook his head. "No, my dear, not this time. You are the main event. I have been satisfied with small victories from time to time, but that time has passed and passed by." That grin again. The hireling women did not like the look of it. It slid from one side of his face to the other, like it was being oozed or sliced into place. It gave her that sickly feeling deep in her stomach that usually only came after a long night with a large bottle of wine. "It is time that I took the hall. I have the *right* to it all. And not just one or two pieces this time... as you said, you must take a city to take its treasures... you must take a city to take its relics as well. You will have your treasure... and I will have mine."

"That's all well and good," Lue pressed, still unsure about this man with the black eyes. "But I'm not so sure about your methods. You have a habit of going off half-cocked, seems to me."

"I guarantee you, that is never the case. I have a strategy, I always have. Despite outward appearances."

"Well it appears like you are an angry little boy stomping his feet after his favorite pet gets put down." The man's smile faltered, and his eyes grew deeper and darker with every moment he watched the hireling chew.

"Excuse me?" he asked, finally. His voice was as hollow as his eyes.

"Well, from what I hear," Lue went on, "it *seems* that ever since mean old kingdom Sterlyn sliced up your precious little dragon into tiny bitty pieces, you've been on a rampage with very little direction," Lue pointed a floppy piece of meat at the man's face, "And that concerns me. I don't want to put my men in the hands of a grief-stricken fool. Greif makes people sloppy. They are all filthy bastards, every single one of em... but they are *my* filthy bastards, and I'm gonna think twice about sending um on any mission of yours... no matter what the coin... Not saying I won't, just gotta think it over a bit, and maybe a little reassurance is in—"

"Never," the man's voice grew colder with every syllable uttered between his tight smile. "Never, speak of him like that again."

"Speak of who?" Lue asked, eyes narrowing, "Oh! Your precise little scaly friend? What was its name?"

The man's smile slid from his face in the opposite way that it came. It slithered away as his eyes fell deeper and deeper into darkness. His fingers twitched violently on the table like spiders in a fire. They writhed before going as still as death.

"What was it, what was it...." Lue went on, obliviously looking up towards the ceiling in thought. "S... St.... Oh wait! Wasn't it Ster—" The hireling woman looked down in time to see the knife missing from beside her plate, and the pale hand burry it deep into her chest. The woman grunted in pain and surprise which turned into a scream as the tall man pulled it from her chest and plunged it right back in. The men at the neighboring tables all scrambled, shocked, to their feet. One of the men launched himself at the tall man. The tall man reached out without looking, and caught the attacking hireling by the throat, holding him at arm's length. The hireling scrambled, utterly surprised by the thin man's unbreakable grip. The man turned away from Lue, who had fallen to the floor, blood flowing from her chest. He drew his hollow black eyes towards the man at the end of his fingertips. The hireling struggled, and the man squeezed. The hireling started choking, his face growing blue with every futile open mouth gasp. He bit the open air, but never caught any. The rest of the hirelings simply stood stunned as the desperate man tried to pull at the fingers that only dug deeper into his throat, nails disappearing into flesh. The tall man reached into his pocket and pulled out a small chain. On that chain were three long, pale objects.

Three polished bones which had once belonged to a finger far longer than any human hand could hold. The dark eyed man, never loosening his grip on the hireling, brought the bones up and gently pressed them against the choking man's face. The hirelings bulging eyes swiveled inward in desperate confusion. The man placed his hands over the three bones, pinning them to the hireling's face. He closed his dark eyes, and his lids fluttered slightly. There was a dim fluttering glow from under his fingers. It flickered like a candle, barely noticed, but the snapping sound that followed resounded in every hireling's ear that stood watching in wide-eyed amazement. Blood began to drip like tears from the hireling's lifeless eyes, nose, and ears, and his body went instantly limp. The tall man let go of his throat, and the dead man's entire weight fell to the floor in a heap at his feet.

The tall man turned back to the woman on the floor. The hireling was panting her last breaths in furious, wet gasps. Blood trickled down the side of her cheeks, painting her lips into a false, red smile. The man leaned down, upper body making a right angle to his long legs and whispered the last words Lue would ever hear.

"You don't get to speak his name. *You* don't get to speak *his* name with that filthy, faithless tongue. Now go." And with that, she went, eyes sliding closed as her greasy lips gave one last tremble. The man rose, brushed off his dark pants as if merely speaking to the hireling woman had gotten his clothes dirty, and turned to the watching men.

"Well... I suppose I will not be doing business with her any longer. Who among you will I be dealing with now?" No one spoke for a very, very, long time. And then...

"That'll be me," said a gruff voice of a hireling to his left. This man was older than Lue, with a face mangled from many years of such unspeakable services that they cannot be recounted in this tale.

"Your name?" the man with empty eyes asked, turning to him.

"Grayson," the man answered, licking a lip that was only half intact. The rest seemed to have been lost to an attacker's blade years before.

"Pleasure to meet you, Grayson," the man held out his hand, but Grayson made no move to take it. The strange man simply waited; hand outstretched.

"Friend of yours?" he asked, nodding slightly to the dead woman without taking his eyes of Grayson.

"Sister," he answered coolly.

"I'm sorry for your loss," the man said, in a voice that was the epitome of indifference.

The hireling man shrugged and took the tall man's hand reluctantly. "Was never the sharpest blade in the shop; she wasn't."

"Do we still have a deal, then?"

"You'll hold up your end of it?"

"I don't make promises I can't keep."

"No... and you don't lack for ability, then do ya." He looked back at the man whose bloody face was creating a red hallow on the floor around his head.

"You know of me," the tall man said, "You know what I am capable of."

"And you'll be doing it all with that thing then?" The hireling gestured to the string of bones still held in the man's hand.

"These?" The man lifted them gingerly in his finger, a sad, and oddly loving smile, crossing his face. "No. I'm afraid my friend here just gave the last bit that was left in him," He looked down at the dead man, "To your friend there."

"Then, how?" Grayson asked, frowning, a truly hideous sight.

"Don't fret," the man said, gently placing the bones back into the pocket of his pants. "I will have more soon." He looked back up at Grayson. "This won't be enough men," He gestured to the throng of hirelings standing about, quietly watching their conversation, and saying nothing. "You will make inquiries?"

"I have connections." Grayson nodded and licked his lip.

"Very, very, good." The man turned, "We will be speaking soon."

He left them and slipped through the still bustling crowd inside the bar. No one, other than the group of hirelings themselves, had reacted to the scene. Such shows of violence were common in this place of violent people, so little interest was given to the fight. Besides, the more you looked, the more you saw. The more you saw, the more you could say, and the more you could say, the more likely it was that you would wake one morning with a knife to your throat.

The hirelings started collecting their dead. One of the bartenders slipped out from behind the bar and began mopping up the blood, never breaking what was apparently a hilarious conversation with one of the patrons. The tall man slipped out the door, just as silently as he had come.

# CHAPTER 12

"Not much for small talk, are you?" Neander asked as he led Kyana out of the crowds and through one of the large double gates to another section of the city. It grew quieter as the bustle of shoppers faded into the background. Kyana was a little relieved. She was nervous walking with three knights of Castle Lyist, two of which were out of view behind her. Being able to hear every movement helped her nerves.

Neander chuckled when Kyana only shrugged at his question. "That's alright, it's nice actually. Some girls don't ever shut… never mind."

"Where are we going?" Kyana asked as they moved away from the nicely rowed houses and buildings, which became more infrequent, and then finally fell behind completely. Grass began to spread out in a large field before them. A soft green carpet that filled the open space between two of the massive inner walls. Kyana felt the give of the grass under her feet as they continued forward, and the smell of it made her think of home.

"To see some friends of yours."

"I have no friends here." Kyana frowned.

"Oh, don't be so sure!" he said with a grin. Their odd party moved on a little farther, and soon Kyana saw men made of straw standing here and there throughout the grass. Each had a giant target painted on the chest, and little stuffed arms which flapped in the breeze. At least two dozen knights were out between the targets, some with swords, others with bows and arrows, a few with helms and shields. Three, far off down the field, were having a sword fight while a small crowd of other knights cheered them on.

"It's okay," Neander noticed her gaze. "Their blades are dulled."

"What?" Kyana asked, looking up at him.

"Don't worry, it's all just for practice. Everyone's weapon is dull... I'm guessing you're worried... being as you're trying to twist my arm off."

"Oh," Kyana loosened her grip. "My apologies." He was mistaken. She was not worried about *them* at all. She just didn't like the proximity of Castle Lyist's knights and all their weapons... to her. Kyana nearly turned and ran when Neander called out in a booming voice.

"Hey! Everybody! There's someone here you should meet!" To Kyana's horror, the entire group of knights stopped what they were doing and looked up. They started to make their way over. Kyana tried to pull away, but Neander held tight to her arm.

"Don't be afraid, they don't bite."

*But blades do,* Kyana thought as the three knights who were battling made their way over, swords in hand.

"What is it, Neander?" asked a tall knight she had never seen before. He was a bulky fellow with a scruffy face and dark blue eyes, but Kyana noticed none of this. She only saw the sword he was holding. He rested it on his shoulder as his smile landed on Kyana. "Your latest 'true love' I assume?"

"No, it's her!" One of the three knights that had been battling pulled off his helmet. Kyana recognized him as the tall bearded knight from the forest. His face was flushed and sweaty, but she knew him quickly, just as he had recognized her.

"Nice to see you again, miss. My name's, Everett." Everett dropped his helm to his side and grinned. "You're looking well." He had a friendly grin, Kyana noticed. It was wide and open against his wide-jawed face. He also seemed to be missing a tooth near the back of his smile. Probably knocked out during one tourney or another, Kyana noted, but a nice enough smile all the same.

"Wait," asked another knight, tapping Everett on the arm and frowning. "Who's she?"

"That's the girl who saved our lives!" Everett said. There was a great rumbling of excitement, and suddenly, Kyana was surrounded. They pressed in on all sides, eager to get a look at the girl who saves kings. She was overwhelmed by the heat and the smell of dirt and sweat. She started to raise her arms automatically in self-defense, but they only tried to shake her hand and started asking questions faster than Kyana could even think to answer.

"I heard you took on five men and won. Is that true?!"

"No, no, I heard it was ten men, all at the same time!"

"I heard you knifed someone by dropping on them from the tree! Did you, did you?"

"Couldn't be! Look at her, she's so thin! And she's a girl!"

"Oh, shut up, Wayne, you're basically a girl yourself."

"What's your name?"

"Where are you from?"

"Where did you learn to fight like that?"

"Wow, everybody back up!" Neander said, stepping in front of Kyana before she got trampled. "Her name is Kyana… we are all grateful for her saving our lives and the life of our king…. So how about we don't suffocate her, alright?"

The group took a reluctant step back, and Neander smiled at her over his shoulder. "No, friends, eh?"

"Well…." said one knight after a moment of silence. "How many were there?"

"Men?" Kyana asked slowly, still in shock. "There were first eleven…. then ten, but I was only able to get five."

"Six." Neander corrected. "Remember the one you shot in the leg as he tried to get away."

"Oh, well, then, only six."

"Only, six!" A great roar of laughter came from the crowd. "Ya' hear that boys? She **only** got **six** of em… she says that like she could take on a whole army!"

Kyana opened her mouth but quickly thought better of it.

"Never mind the hirelings!" said a knight whose face was still flushed from his fight with Everett. "Tell us everything! A warrior woman of the woods? What's your favorite weapon?"

"I don't have a favored weapon." Kyana frowned at the stupid question. "Each weapon is made perfectly for a certain task." All the knights stared opened mouthed at her for a moment.

"… but," Kyana started again, realizing they would never be satisfied with that answer. "I tend to use my bow and arrow more often than—" She cut herself off, quickly turning to Neander. "My bow! Where is my bow? Is it still in the woods? I need—"

"Wow, slow down!" Neander said, laying a hand lightly on her shoulder. "We have your bow, what's left of your arrows, and your dagger. They're all back at the castle, safe and sound in our armory."

"Really?" Kyana asked, surprised.

Neander frowned at her a little.

"You think we were going to leave the weapons that saved the life of our grace out in the forest to rot?" Neander shook his head. Relief filled Kyana like fresh water being poured into a glass.

"Thank you," she said.

"A bow and arrow?" one of the knights snorted in a snippy voice that made Kyana's skin crawl. "Who uses a bow and arrow anymore?"

"And what would you use instead?" Kyana asked, locking her eyes on the boy knight who had spoken.

*One.* His eyes were small and watery, with a spattering of pimples growing below his left eyebrow.

*Two.* He had already looked away from her gaze and was watching some spot behind her left ear.

*Three.* He glanced back at her eyes and then away once more. A snarl curled Kyana's mouth. Young. Foolish. Weak.

"A crossbow, of course," the boy knight said, in that same tone that made fire course through Kyana's chest. But she did not let it show.

"A crossbow is good…" Kyana nodded. "If you have no strength nor skill. If you possess these, a bow is far better."

A loud "ooooooooohhhh!" came from the surrounding knights and a few started to chant, encouraging a contest.

"I will not be spoken to that way by a woman!" the boy knight said, his face grew bright red as the jeering became louder. The fire clawed at Kyana's neck and arms, but she only smiled.

"What would you have then…?"

"Show me this 'strength' and 'skill' of yours," the little boy knight said, puffing up his chest in defiance. "And I'll show you what a real shooter can do with a crossbow."

"Watch yourself, Li," Neander said, scowling. "She's still injured remember… you know, from saving our lives?"

"Then I will be a gentleman," the boy knight said, dripping with enough pride to drown a small city. "And withdraw my challenge."

"Put it back," Kyana was smiling, but her voice cracked like a whip against a stone. Strong, sharp, and made those closest to her wince. Even Neander cringed slightly, although he tried to hide it. "I want none of your false chivalry. Bring me a bow, and I will give you your challenge."

The knights all looked at Neander, who laughed. "What are you all waiting for? You heard the lady. Bring her a bow." A few of the knights ran off to a nearby stack of weaponry while a few others started to set up targets.

"You'll have to excuse my little brother," Neander said, leaning over to speak confidentially. "When the gods were handing out brains, they seemed to have forgotten his."

*Brother?* Kyana realized the two did look alike. The boy knight had redder hair than his older brother, but they were of a similar height and their jaw and nose seemed to have been carved by the same hand. Although the boy knight still held to his baby fat whereas his brother had long ago lost his.

"Are you sure you're, all right?" Neander asked quietly. "Augustine would kill me if I let you tear a stitch."

"I'm fine," she said, watching the boy knight as he was handed a crossbow.

"Just remember, Kina," the boy said, loading his weapon. "I offered you an out."

Kyana ignored him. She took the smooth bow and a small quiver of arrows that another knight held out to her. The bow was a little long for her, but it would do just fine. She secured the quiver over her shoulder as the targets were set up a distance down the field. Stickmen stuffed with straw and painted targets tilted slightly in the breeze. Kyana noticed their tilt and saw it well.

The boy knight was done with his chivalry. He took the first shot, and it landed dead center of the target. The knights cheered, and he shot Kyana a grin.

"Sorry, my lady!" he said, not sorry at all. "Seems like I've already won."

Kyana did not answer. She was distracted by the sound of wings fluttering against the air. She looked up to see a startled quail shoot straight out of a small patch of bushes and into the sky overhead. It dipped slightly, swerving in the breeze, travailing closer. Kyana raised the bow. She took a quick breath, pulled the arrow to her check, and let loose. With a small thudding sound, the quail began to fall from the sky. Kyana slipped another arrow into place and let loose. With another swift "thunk," her second arrow skewered the bird mid-air, and gracefully buried its metal tip deep into the bullseye of the second target. The quail swung like a hanged man over the bullseye, the breeze rustling its feathers. Everyone was absolutely silent as Kyana lowered the bow. She turned to the boy knight who was staring open-mouthed at what she had just done.

"My name is Kyana. Not Kina," she said simply. The boy turned, and a sincere grin spread his young face.

"I promise to remember that, Kyana," he said and reached out his hand. "My name is Lionel by the way. Lionel Esberg." Young, foolish, and weak he may be, but perhaps there was still some hope for him yet. Kyana shook his hand, and the knights began to whoop and laugh. A few ran down the courtyard to retrieve the bird from the target.

"There is no way..." Neander said flabbergasted. "No way could anyone make that shot! And yet... who are you?" Kyana opened her mouth to speak when suddenly the knights stopped and stood at stiff attention.

"Your majesty," they all said in unison. Neander turned and stood up straight as a voice spoke from behind Kyana.

"All at ease."

The surrounding knights softened their stance, but Kyana tensed as she slowly turned around. Standing there, with a few guards flanking him, was the black-haired man from the woods. The Lystad wore a simple blue shirt that hung loosely over brown pants. The fit was cut to perfection, obviously made special for him, and probably out of material far more expensive than the majority of the people living in Castle Lyist could imagine. Today there was no jewelry, no bracelets, no golden rings to shine gaudily from his fingers. If one did not know better, he might have been one of his own citizens milling around in those crowded shopping streets. But Kyana did know better.

"That," he said, those mixed blue eyes on the target. "Was some shot. I'm glad I didn't miss it." He looked down at her and smiled. Kyana felt the fire go to ice in her chest. This time she was the one to look away. She instinctively moved back, pulling the quiver from around her shoulder and dropping it to the ground next to the bow. She was out of arrows, and if she needed to run, she would need to be as light as possible. He watched her move with a frown spreading his face.

"Kyana," Neander said, reaching out to catch her arm, but she quickly stepped out of range. "It's okay. This is King Damian. Remember. From the woods."

"I remember," Kyana said, taking another wary step away from the King of Castle Lyist. Her voice was strained, and every word felt wrenched from her, like the knife from her side. She wanted to run. She wanted to hide. She wanted nothing more than to vanish from this place and have the Lystad king with his castle and his knights to be nothing but a distant memory or a bad dream. She should have let them die. She should have let them *all die.*

"What the *hell* is going on here?" came a voice from across the yard. Everyone looked up to see Augustine stomping his way towards them, gruff face pulled into a scowl.

"Where is Ira? Kyana shouldn't have been up this long. I said a short walk. *Short!* What have you been- oh!" He was now close enough to see the Lystad. "You're Majesty, I apologize I thought that…"

"It's alright," Lystad turned and smiled reassuringly to the practitioner, "We were just enjoying a good show. It seems that Miss Kyana here," he pointed at the target downrange, where the knights were slowly returning with her prize in hand. "is a… a rather fantastic bowman."

"Well, I should say so," the practitioner hummed as he looked back at her, eyebrows shooting up in interest. He slid his hands into the pockets of his pants, a small amazed grin broke his graying beard as he rocked back on the heels of his shoes. "My, my."

"Practitioner," she said, avoiding the Lystad's gaze.

"Weak? Faint?" Augustine's grin vanished and his thick brows scrunched together in concern. Kyana felt none of these things, only sick to her stomach with fear. Her face must have said another story because Augustine continued on without waiting for her answer: "I'm not surprised. Ira should have brought you back to rest long ago."

"It's my fault," Neander stepped forward. "She looked well, and I wanted her to meet the men. Ira wanted to take her back, but we talked her out of it."

"Ira just wanted to show the girl a good time, I'm sure Augustine," Lystad smiled. "Probably trying to ease her conscience a bit." Kyana did not know what the Lystad was talking about but was not about to ask.

"Practitioner," Kyana repeated, quietly. She felt terribly like a little girl in that moment, tugging on her fathers' sleeve. *Excuse me papa, could we get away from the scary man with the black hair and blue eyes? I don't like him much.*

"Absolutely. I'm sorry dear, let's get you back to rest," he tried to take her arm.

"N-No," she said, moving delicately out of his strong but gentle grip. "Actually, I am feeling much better and was hoping for your leave."

"My leave?" Augustine asked curiously.

"To go home," she said.

"Kyana, you're still healing from your wound... I wouldn't advise walking much more, let alone leaving the city."

"I'm not bleeding, correct? My sickness has passed?"

"Yes but—"

"And for that, you have my greatest thanks... but I really need to get home."

*And out of this city.*

Augustine looked at her, face scrunching in doubt which made his pox marks appear to be caverns against his cheeks. "My dear, your wounds are still fresh. They could easily break open. Any small fall, or blunder from horseback... You're only newly cured of sickness as well, and could be very likely retaken by it. I advise another few days of care at the very least."

"Trust me, I've had worse." Kyana nodded. She liked this man with his kind face, broad shoulders and gruff fatherly manner. She would have gladly stayed in his company... but she could not. "I will do just fine, truly."

"I strongly suggest you reconsider," Augustine nearly growled, quickly growing irritated by her apparent lack of interest in her own wellbeing. Kyana wondered how many knights, lords, and self-assured "he-men" the practitioner had to deal with on a daily basis. Those fools that insist they were fine, only to die from lack of proper care a week later. She would have liked to soothe his concerns, but had no time.

"Yes please," Neander said, leaning on the knight named Cole and tucking one foot behind his ankle. "You have impressed us with your skill at the bow... you have yet to show us your skill with the daggers and sword."

"You mean the skill I tried to use against you?" Kyana blurted before she could stop herself.

"Ya, that too!" Neander said happily. Kyana stared at him and the men smiling around him. What the hell was wrong with them? She couldn't understand.

"I attacked you... how are you all so... fine with it?"

"Well, you thought we were demons…" Everett said. "You also happened to save us first… from ten men no less."

"Pretty gods damn impressive," said another knight in the circle. The Lystad glared at him. The knight suddenly looked ashamed. "Sorry, Miss."

"Sorry?" Kyana asked blankly, not knowing what he had to be sorry for.

"I wouldn't encourage her to do any sword fighting Neander, her stitches could just as likely break from that as anything else," answered Augustine, turning his fatherly irritation towards Neander, who lifted his hands in surrender.

"Augustine's right." Everyone silenced and looked over as the king spoke. Kyana glanced up at the man, but quickly looked to Augustine instead. "I would be a fool to let the woman who saved my men out of my practitioner's care before she was safe." He looked down at her, and she glanced up. He was smiling, and his eyes were brighter than she expected. With a surprising amount of effort, she forced herself to watch them. She needed to know.

*One.* His eyes were mostly dark, but they had a shine to them. Not shining in the way that children have shining eyes. They were not glazed over with childish cheer but seemed to reflect a light that came from nowhere at all. She also noticed that the deep shining blue was broken with fissures of lighter blue. The bright blue cut from the pupil out towards the edges of the iris like lightning striking from a black sky.

*Two.* A grin pulled the corner of his mouth and crinkled the edge of his eyes. He knew exactly what she was doing.

*Three.* Those eyes did not hesitate. He did not seem to need to blink either. Long, dark, lashes held steadily open, never wavering. He knew this game and was a master of it. He watched, never faltering, and she felt herself waiver.

*Four.* He showed no signs of hesitation. No concern. No fear. Nothing. None. Kyana, on the other hand, felt a nerve-tingling up the back of her neck. She turned her eyes to the ground before she could get to five. She thought she heard him chuckle.

"So, you'll join us for the feast tonight," he said, satisfied with his victory.

"Feast?" Kyana's eyes flew open, and she looked from the king to Augustine and back again.

"If that would be alright with you, of course, Augustine," the king said looking around, to smile at the older man. "She is in your care now."

"But——" Kyana started.

"A feast should be alright," Augustine said thoughtfully, still frowning, hands sliding back in his pockets. "But not too late, of course, she needs her rest."

"Now just wait a moment..." Kyana started desperately, only to be ignored once more.

"Of course," the king said. "Whatever you say. And she is still put up in the finest guest room?"

"Yes, your majesty she is."

"Good." The king smiled at Kyana. "Until this evening then," He turned a few of his knights fell into step behind him. "Take good care of her."

"Yes, sire," Augustine called after the billowing brown cloaks.

Neander stepped forward and laid an arm over Kyana's shoulder. "Well, you sure have the king's approval, now don't you?" Kyana stared up at him bemused.

"But... but.... I don't understand." She had expected an execution, dungeon time, some sort of punishment for her actions the other day. Instead, she was being cared for against her will, given a place inside the castle itself, and would be attending a feast that evening in the king's court....

"Well, you did save his life," Neander said, scratching the back of his neck. "Not to mention his best knights and his best friend."

"Best friend?" Kyana asked.

"Ya, Ira." Neander grinned. "You know... the girl who's been watching out for you while you've been sleeping."

"She was?" Kyana asked. Ira had been kind enough to spend what time she had with Kyana over the days, but she had no idea the girl had been caring for her during her fever. This thought both surprised Kyana and made her smile. It had been a long time since she had someone to watch over her while she slept.

"And she's the king's... friend?" Kyana asked dubiously.

"Since they were kids... long before I knew either of em."

This struck Kyana as odd.

"Best friend?" Kyana repeated.

"Ya, and he doesn't do small, thank you's, our lord."

"But…." Kyana looked over the walls, to see the deep green treetops in the distance. She could smell them, hear the wind rustling through their leaves. "I need to go home…."

"And you will," Augustine reassured her, smacking Neander's arm away and motioning for her to follow him. "But first you must regain your strength. Come, follow me."

# CHAPTER 13

She was sitting on the windowsill when Ira tapped on the door. Kyana's shoes were left behind on the floor, and her small bare feet were curled up under her. Her hair was pulled back behind her ear, revealing her narrow face. She had called Ira in with a voice as far off as her gaze. She was looking out towards the flowing river, but Ira was sure she saw nothing of the sort. Those strange green eyes were fuzzy with thoughts so consuming that she barely heard Ira step in the room.

"Something wrong?" Ira asked, and Kyana started.

"What?" She blinked as if pulling herself from sleep. When she did finally refocus, her gaze fell on the tray of food in Ira's hands, and she snorted. "Really?"

Ira had brought her a mid-day snack as she had done every day since Kyana woke. Augustine was very insistent that she eat. She had lost some weight over the days she spent in fever sleep. The most they could get down her throat was some broth, and that was not nearly enough. Augustine had been pushing food on her ever since. He sent Ira to go fetch her a snack several times a day, and Ira had started to wonder if Augustine did not have an ulterior motive. He did always ask Ira to bring it to her, although there were many other servants in the kitchens that had less to do than she. She thought Augustine may have been trying to forge a friendship between the two girls. He knew Ira herself did not have many friends in the castle. That was another downside of being friends with the king. People were always nice to her, but were also, generally, afraid to be around her. At least, most everyone.

Through her friendship with Damian, Ira had also grown an attachment to his little sister Naomi. Naomi, although Ira's superior in everything but age, had come to see Ira as a second older sister of sorts. This Ira only knew because Naomi had flat out told her so. The girl was quiet in many ways, but blunt in her honesty. Ira did not mind. In fact, she was flattered. She also understood. Naomi's actual older sister was many years senior to both Naomi and Ira, and she was not the most personable woman if Ira was also blunt with her honesty. Sophia Lystad was a beautiful woman now in her twenty-eight-year and not a bad person in the least. She was, however, a distant sort of soul and one who thrived on tradition. Like her father before her, Sophia believed in high standards, and everyone knowing their place. For Naomi, that meant she should be quiet, elegant, and obedient.

"Lystad's do not cry." Ira had heard Sophia say. One day, when Naomi was at the clumsy age of eight, she had fallen and scraped her forearm while trying to catch herself on the trunk of a tree. Long red marks cut up the girl's thin skin, and tears had been welling in her large eyes, but Sophia had taken no notice of her little sister's pains. All she saw was her little sister making a scene in the courtyard with her tears. "It is not our place to cry," she had said, but she had also helped Naomi to her feet. She had wiped away her little sister's tears with the back of her sleeve, but there had been no softness in her gaze — no delicacy in her tone. No, Sophia was not a bad person... just not the type to run to with your troubles. So, when Naomi's nightmares of her bygone brother had started up again for the first time since she was six years of age, Naomi had not gone to Sophia. No. She had sought out Ira. That was perfectly alright with Ira, she liked Naomi, but Sophia had been furious. It was not Ira's place to be so close with her siblings, Damian, least of all. She had disliked their friendship from the start but grew less and less patient with their antics as they grew older. Her mild disapproval deepened into outright dislike as Naomi began to gravitate towards Ira as well. It was not their place, Sophia had warned, but this had only spurred Damian on. Sophia's warnings and disapproval only served to solidify an already strong friendship between the two unlikely fellows.

Sophia had never been rude to Ira. No, it was not her place to be rude to the help. She was polite and upright but cold in many ways. Ira knew it was probably jealousy. Jealousy that Ira had such a better relationship with her siblings than Sophia herself. Ira could sympathize, but she could not help but feel a bit of relief when Sophia had moved to Bryxston castle with her new husband, taking her chilly politeness with her. Unfortunately, she had also taken sweet little Naomi, narrowing Ira's already limited circle of friends down by fifty percent.

The knights were friendly with her to be sure, but Ira could not help that small voice in the back of her mind. The one that whispered in convincing tones, that they only did so out of respect for their lord. Besides, they too treated her differently. They were not lecherous the knights... well not all of them, but they did enjoy chasing serving girls from time to time. There were many occasions when Ira heard half stifled giggling girls recounting the antics and attentions of one knight or another. When it came to Ira, however, they made no such advances. No wink was tossed her direction. No flirtatious comment. Not even a lingering gaze. Not once. Initially, Ira assumed this was because none of them found her attractive. She was not, after all, some rare beauty of the city. In fact, Ira could admit it, she was rather plain. However, she soon came to suspect other reasons. Visiting lords and noble sons passing through the city, those that were less knowledgeable of the friendship between a serving girl and the king of Neira, had looked upon her with great interest. One or two even made some rather sloppy advances that she skillfully avoided, but this left her wondering about those within the castle itself.

Whether Damian told them to keep their hands off (in that unnecessarily brotherly manner he had a habit of adopting), or because they assumed, correctly, that she would not be interested, or they simply did not want to cross that line with her specifically, Ira did not know. One way or another, the knights saw her as off limits. But they were unusually friendly with her... out of respect to their lord. The knights were not the only ones to treat her differently.

The other servants, especially the other girls, all kept their distance. They were suspicious of her, wondering if she was listening in on their conversations, ready to repeat any criticism or misspoken word directly to the king himself. Ira would never do such a thing, but people had a hard time believing in others these days. They were always on edge around her. Conversations would stop when she walked in the room. Not to be pointed, not to be rude, not to hurt her feelings, but simply because they did not feel comfortable talking naturally around her. This always kept a distance between Ira and all the other servants of Castle Lyist. A distance that made friendships hard to forge. Kyana was a different story, and Augustine may have seen the potential friendship between the two girl and decided he could force one if necessary. Of course, Ira was more than happy to oblige. She liked this strange woman. There was something about her. That weird familiarity she could not quite place. Like when you are going about your day and come across an item, a smell, or a sound, that reminds you of a dream at the edge of memory. Something you can barely recall, but it gives you a feeling. A glimpse and then gone. Being around Kyana felt like that. Like something she was remembering and forgetting all at once. Something important.

"He knows I'm going to a feast in a few hours, yes?" Kyana asked, a small smile playing her lips.

"He just wants to make sure you're not hungry," Ira shrugged. "He worries. He's a worrier."

"Hum." Kyana's eyes went glassy once more, slowly slipping back into her thoughts. They did not look pleasant. Her eyebrows weaved together, creating a severe line between her eyes, and her little mouth turned down.

"What's the matter?" Ira asked, "You look nervous."

"I'm fine," Kyana answered automatically.

"No, you're not," Ira said, sliding the plate of bread and ham on the table, only to turn and lean against it. "You're in a strange place with strange people, and tonight you're going to be in a room full of um," Ira remembered her face amidst the crowds of shoppers. Her eyes had been wide with astonishment and excitement, but also a little fear. A childlike wonder. "You said you lived alone in the forest, right?"

"Yes."

"… If you don't mind my asking,… how long has it been since you've spent time with... well, *anyone*?"

Kyana watched Ira and thought.

"Before I met you all in the woods… Over three years."

Ira let out a little whistle between her teeth. She shook her head, sending her gold braid swinging from side to side.

"Well, that'll just about do it."

"Do what?" Kyana asked.

"Make you feel so out of touch." Ira shrugged a little. "Spending so much time alone… away from everything… away from people, away from their ways… it's not surprising you feel nervous. Why you've been acting so…

detached. On edge. Spending so much time away from things that were once so second nature… you start to wonder if you ever really belonged in the first place… or if you ever could again." Ira trailed off, mind wandering to a different time, a different place when she was practically a different person. Just a little girl listening to an old woman's stories. And what lovely stories they were. Ira shook her head, clearing her mind, and smiled.

"It's okay to feel uncomfortable… it's been a while but if you hang on a minute or two longer…" She gestured around the room, but Kyana knew it encompassed so much more. "You can find yourself falling back into the well-worn patterns you once forgot."

Kyana bit her lip slightly but nodded.

"Thank you, Ira," she said, and then looked around. "And thank you for all this."

"Thank Damian," Ira said, glancing around at the beautiful, albeit gaudy room. "He insisted you were well taken care of."

"… How kind," Kyana answered. Her nose crinkled as she spoke. It was cute, and it made Ira laugh.

"You don't like him, much do you? It's okay," Ira said when Kyana tensed and started to look even more nervous. "Honestly, sometimes, he can be an ass."

Kyana's eyebrows shot up, nearly meeting the scar that cut down from her hair.

"I heard you two were friends."

"Oh, we are." Ira nodded, "Good friends. Ever since we were kids."

"How?"

"How did we become friends?"

Kyana nodded.

Ira crossed her arms, leaning back and frowned at the ceiling. She could not help but smile when she remembered, that was how her grandmother always started her stories. She would lean back in that old creaking rocking chair of hers, knowing smile pointed at the sky. The stories would always start the same way as well. With four simple words. For some reason, four little words always seemed the precursor to the best sort of stories.

"Well, let me see…" Ira said, unable to resist. "I was about eight at the time, which would make him about seven… It was only my second night working in the kitchen. My dad knows Cabot, they worked together for a while, and so he was able to get me the job quickly after we moved to Castle Lyist. Anyway, I was just doing cleanup crew at the time. I was new at all of it and took far longer than I should. I ended up working into the late evening." Ira remembered that night pretty well. As well as any old memory can be remembered. She had been standing on a stool by the wash basin scraping, gods knew what sort of dried leftovers, off a mountain of dishes that piled to one side. She had been too short to reach them on her own. It was a time before her growth spurt, which thankfully left her taller, but also left her rather gangly.

"I was in the kitchen," Ira continued. "I was all alone... or so I thought. I was elbow deep in soapy water when I heard someone rummaging through one of the cupboards." Ira smiled. "Oh, I was scared shitless. I nearly fell off the stool and broke my wrist. I thought there was this thief there about to rob us blind and I would be blamed, and then Cabot would fire me, and blah-blah-blah... So, I screwed up what courage I had, and jumped in to confront the thief... turns out, it was Damian."

"Why was he in the cupboards?" Kyana's frown tugged her small lips into a crooked line.

"Apparently," Ira said, head tilting back just a bit more. "He had done something to upset his father. Don't know what. To this day, he won't tell me, but it upset the king, and the king had sentenced him to bed without supper for three days. He thought the kitchen would be empty and decided to snag a snack. When I caught him, he didn't act scared or even ashamed. He didn't pout or wail like I would have expected. He didn't start shouting orders or yelling or threatening. He simply stood up straight, looked me in the eye, stolen muffin in hand, and said: 'Hello Ira. Please don't tell my father.'"

Ira chuckled a little and shook her head. She remembered how Damian had looked, half buried in the cupboard, big blue eyes wide, but otherwise determinedly composed. He had even held out another muffin to Ira, not as a bribe, but as some sort of peace offering.

"I knew who he was of course, but I had never met him before. I had no idea he knew my name... but he did. And he didn't start barking orders like any other prince his age. Most young lords have spent so much time being told how precious, amazing, unique and important they are that they tend to forget niceties," Ira hesitated for a moment as if an unpleasant thought crossed her mind, but she quickly pushed on with her story. "Damian wasn't like that. He didn't order me to shut up or stay quiet. He *asked*"

Ira shrugged.

"So, I said I wouldn't tell anyone. He thanked me and left." Ira thought about how Damian had cleaned up his own mess, carefully placing every bit of food, every basket of muffins, back onto the shelf before closing the cabinet. He had grinned gratefully at Ira and left with a muffin in hand. "He came back the following night, and the one after that. On the third night, we both just sat on the kitchen floor, snacking on leftovers. We talked the night almost into the morning." Ira barely remembered what they talked about. Probably the usual chatter of little children just beginning to learn about one another. What she did remember was when Damian laughed. It was the first time Ira had heard it. The prince had flung his head back, eyes closed, and it spilled from his mouth in a loud echo. She could not remember what she had said, or what joke she had made, but Ira did remember the pride. The pride of being the one to cause that laughter. "It wasn't till a few days later that I found out the king's punishment hadn't lasted past the second evening."

"He could eat dinner?" Kyana asked. "But he kept sneaking into the kitchen? Why?"

Ira shrugged.

"I think he was lonely. I mean we were just kids and both lonely in our own way. I think he wanted to make a friend but didn't know how to ask. I think he believed us sharing a secret, like him sneaking food, would instantly bond us as friends… in hindsight, he wasn't wrong…"

"And you stayed friends."

"Weirdly enough… ya. It just… stuck."

"Are you two…" Kyana hesitated, as if unsure whether to ask, but ask she did. "Are you two mates?"

Ira laughed. It was small and muffled behind her hand, but lasted a long while.

"Are we what?" she mumbled after her laughter died down a little.

"Mates," Kyana continued, "Together. Sleeping with one another. Courting or whatever you call it."

"No," Ira said, hand dropping from her wide grin. "No, we've never 'mated.' Not us."

"Never?" Kyana asked, dubiously. She had watched the two interacting in the forest, saw the easy nature they had with one another, and the fear and anger in Damian's eyes when she had held the blade to Ira's throat.

"Not once." Ira shook her head. "Never. Many people thought so... especially after we started growing older and I started, uh, taking shape. Many whispers. Everyone loves to whisper around here, but no. It just..." Ira shrugged, grin widening. "It was just never *that way* for us. But we have always been friends."

"Hu..." Kyana mumbled, obviously bemused but trying not to show it.

"Trust me," Ira nodded. "No one was more surprised than me. I'd have thought he'd become too involved with the nobles to be interested in keeping a friendship with a kitchen girl. But Damian was never one for doing things traditionally. I think, every so often, he'll do outrageous things just to see what reaction he will get. From a friendship with me, to when you met us in the forests." Ira shook her head. "We were never supposed to be that far out from the castle. Not with so few of us. But oh no, Damian was up for an adventure and damn what anyone else had to say." Ira shrugged. "Sometimes, I think he just really likes to stir shit for no reason."

Kyana laughed. It was a high and lyrical sound. Sweet, and pure, and Ira found herself remembering. A flash of memory that never actually existed. A dream that had faded long ago. It was beautiful, confusing, frustrating, and heartbreaking all at once.

Ira said none of this. Of course not. She knew how crazy it sounded. Instead, she smiled.

"You have a nice laugh."

"Thank you again, Ira." Kyana returned her smile.

"You don't use it often, though, do you?"

"... No, not really." Kyana admitted.

"Well, I hope you'll be able to use it again tonight at the feast."

"Oh... right...." Kyana's smile melted like candle wax, drying, and withering away.

"You're not looking forward to it at all?" Ira asked. She could not help a little bit of hope from peaking around the edge of her voice.

Kyana shook her head, but she quickly perked up. "Will you be going?"

Ira laughed, "Uh, no, I'll be serving the feast, not attending."

"But you will be there?" She pressed. She was leaning forward a little from her seat at the sill, as if she may just fall into the answer she wanted. Ira felt a flutter of pride at that. The strange girl wanted her around.

"Yes," Ira nodded. "I'll be around."

"Good." Kyana nodded, and yawned, stretching her arms out over her head. That was Ira's cue.

"I'll get out of your hair and let you rest." Ira pushed off the table and went for the door. "Augustine will be up to check on you in a few hours. If you need anything, there are guards and servants around in the halls."

"I'll be fine... Ira," Kyana called her back.

"Yes?" Ira said, turning around, her hand on the door.

"Thank you. Truly." She looked so serious. Her narrow face was set, and her eyes seemed to burn with green fire as Ira watched. She swallowed, suddenly struck by a terrible and wonderful feeling that she couldn't explain. Those eyes. Those strange, strange eyes. Then Kyana blinked and inclined her head to Ira in thanks. "Ira of Castle Lyist."

"Your very welcome, Kyana of the woods," she answered, returning the little bow with one of her own. "See you soon. Rest well."

Ira gave Kyana one more smile before closing the door behind her. She leaned against it, catching a quick breath. Those eyes. Those damn green eyes. What was it about them that made Ira feel so... so... found?

She reached up and rubbed her own eyes, trying to clear the image of endless mossy tunnels from her mind. Ira pushed off the door, her mind a mess of green fire, and made her way back to the kitchens.

# CHAPTER 14

There it was. Every sound and feel of freedom. The scent of freshly grown grass traveled on the fluid air. The sharp whirl of wind that cut against her face. It all surrounded her. It held her close in its arms, like a loved one saying hello. Or saying goodbye. The night hung dark, almost impenetrable. A chasm of open space in every direction, reaching out until the end of… everything.

She was not afraid. Stars pointed her way. They glinted and winked above her, the only break in the blackness. She stretched herself into that darkness, soaking up every inch of the soft night. She opened her mouth, tasting the air, sweet and fresh. She filled her lungs with it, expanding her chest until she could hold no more. She let it howl out through her teeth, the sound building to a grumble of thunder, a growl until it sharpened to a roar.

The wind suddenly took up speed. It buffeted her shoulders, forced her off course. It tossed her flailing into the night. She spun, the stars creating white streaks in her vision. She tried to catch herself but couldn't. And so, she fell. Fell. Fell.

"Kyana." The wind whipped hard against her face, cracking like a voice in her ear. "Kyana."

Kyana's eyes opened. She looked up to see Augustine smiling down at her.

"I'm glad you found time to rest," he said.

"Hello, practitioner." Kyana yawned and propped herself up on her arms. "Is everything alright?"

"I was actually about to check if it's alright with you." He motioned to her abdomen.

Kyana nodded and lifted the bottom of her shirt, exposing the bandage beneath. Augustine changed the dressing and hummed over the red wound beneath.

"It's still very delicate," he said, putting the finishing touches on her fresh bandage, "So nothing too strenuous at the feast tonight, alright?"

"Alright," Kyana agreed. "Will you be there?" Kyana thought it unlikely, but she had to ask. The idea of being in a room full of courtiers, knights, and guards and the Lystad himself, made her uneasy. She liked this man with his stern face and kind eyes. He and Ira, they both made her feel... almost safe. Almost like they could be trusted... her eyes darted down to the little green dove tattoo on his wrist... almost. She was not nearly that much of a fool, but she did prefer them around her. With the practitioner, Kyana would only have to act like she was feeling faint, and he would quickly whisk her out of the feast at a moment's notice. He was her ultimate exit strategy. Besides. She really did enjoy the man's company.

"No, I'm afraid not," Augustine chuckled in that deep gravelly voice, as if the mere idea was absurd. "I'll be out in the lower part of town for the rest of the day, checking on patients." Kyana nodded but was disappointed all the same. She tensed at the sound of footsteps drawing closer and sat up as a small servant girl stepped through the door.

"It's alright," Augustine said, patting Kyana's arm. "This is Lilly." The girl gave a timid smile and a curtsy. "She's here to help you prepare for this evening."

"Lystad sent her?" Kyana asked, looking Lilly over. Her face was thin but healthy. Her hands were rough, worked hard. She wore simple clothes of brown, gray, and blue, but they were made from fine material, and stitched to perfection. It seemed the servants were well kept.

"King Lystad, yes..." Augustine answered. A frown creasing his face in response to Kyana's tone, but he made no comment.

"Hello, Miss." Lilly's smile was small and shy, but kind enough. She looked to be Kyana's junior by at least three years, if not more. Kyana looked the girl in the eyes.

*One.* A faint green and murky gray vied for dominance in those large irises. The gray seeming to win over in the light that flickered through the window, but green seeped back in the moments shade was cast by the curtain.

*Two.* They were soft eyes and seemed to swim with water that played heavily at the edges. Did the girl always look as if about to cry?

Before Kyana made it to three, her eyes darted to the floor. This was a girl used to being ruled by others.

Kyana gave her a smile.

"Hello, Lilly, lovely to meet you." Lilly perked up and returned her smile.

"We actually met before, miss."

"We have?" Kyana frowned, not remembering this at all.

"Well… sort of…" The girl's smile faltered. "You were caught in a fever dream at the time."

*A handmaid was nice enough to help change you*

"You're the handmaid?" The realization that hit Kyana was sudden and hard. She did her best to keep her face composed.

"Yes, miss," the girl said, giving another small curtsy, but when her watery eyes darted back to Kyana, she saw it in the gray spirals… she knew.

Kyana smiled as well as she could. No need to have Augustine become curious.

"So, should we start preparations for the feast, then?" Kyana asked, never taking her eyes off the girl, even though her eyes had once again found the floor. She seemed to have discovered something very interesting in its wooden panels.

"That's my cue to be off." Augustine rose and smiled. "I'll check on you in the morning. Have fun and get some rest."

"Thank you, Practitioner."

"Please," The gruff man smiled as he slipped his leather bag over his shoulder and headed for the door. "Call me, Augustine." The moment the door clicked closed, and she heard the practitioners slow and steady step fade down the hall, Kyana turned back to Lilly.

"Why?" Kyana demanded, stepping forward towards the girl who instantly cowered in surprise.

"W-what?" the girl stammered, seeming to shrivel and splinter under Kyana's gaze, like a twig in a campfire.

"Why did you do this?" Kyana rolled up her left sleeve, baring the smooth white bandage. "Why? Who did you tell? Who knows about this?"

"No, one!" the girl whimpered, nearly falling over her own feet as she backed away. Her watery eyes overflowed and sent streams quickly, cascading down her thin face. "I told no one miss, I swear! I swear!"

"Then, why?" Kyana's voice snapped hard against the air, making the maid flinch.

The girl hesitated, murky wet eyes darting around the room as if looking for an answer, or an escape hatch. Instead of bolting for the door behind Kyana, which was wise, she reached down and undid the laces of her right shoe. She slipped it off along with the pure white sock beneath.

Kyana's eyes widened.

There, on the soft pale skin of the girl's foot, was the thickened, healed over, skin of a brand. The name, Sterling, and the five hollow circles which underlined the name, had been long ago burned into the girl's skin. Five circles for the five dragon eggs. It was a design similar to the brand that marked Kyana's left arm.

"You're a Faithful?" Kyana's voice was low, but it sent Lilly's watery eyes darting for the large door as if waiting for knights in their brown cloaks and long swords to burst in and take her straight for the pier. When the girl was finally satisfied that no such thing was about to happen, she turned back to Kyana.

"My family was," the girl said, quickly pulling back on her sock and lacing up her shoe with hurried, trembling, fingers. "I'm a decedent of Clan Riverhast. They followed dragon Stersi and her foal Sterling, back before the end of dragons."

"I'm well aware." Kyana knew the marks of the Faithful, probably better than Lilly herself. Before all dragons were scorched from the earth by blades made of dragon egg, each clan had a mark that denoted their loyalty. They made trade between clans easy and helped to show each follower's never-ending devotion to their particular clan or dragon. After the dragons had died, the tradition continued. In the time of dragons, these brands were given when the child came of age. An age old enough to choose whether they wanted to stay in their clan or search out other paths to follow. It was an event, a celebration, an honor, an undying promise when the child chose to be marked, but those days were long gone. These days such brands were done in secret. Hidden behind closed doors with rusting tools. Sometimes those who received the mark, had no say whatsoever. Babies, barely old enough to blink their eyes let alone make such a choice, were branded by Faithful families in hiding. Devoting them to creatures, that the child would never know. Dedicating them to the memory of dragons and their fading magic. Claiming them for the dead.

Kyana did not understand why the Faithful insisted on continuing it. The marks only served to threaten their lives. Faithful practice was strictly outlawed in two of the four major kingdoms and highly restricted, and generally persecuted, in the others. Sure, there were the scattering of smaller kingdoms that did not much care if you were a Faithful or used magic, but they would never have the power, influence, or sheer ferocity of the four major kingdoms. And these Four Kingdoms spanned most of the land, making other options minimal at best. The use of Faithful magic was outlawed in all the kingdoms, but even baring the mark of faith was dangerous in some. If someone were found in either Neira or Sterlyn kingdom, for example, they would be executed on the spot. Or, in the more traditional method, brought to trial. A trial overseen by the same kingdoms that hated anything to do with dragons. It would last an hour at most and the conviction would be swift. The Faithful would be publicly executed. It served as a warning to any other Faithful, or user of the scattered remanence of magic left to this world after the dragon's deaths. The convicted Faithful did get a choice in this matter, however… to be hung, to be beheaded, or to burn. Many of the younger Faithful, brought into the fold only because of their parents and grandparents desperately clinging to a past long dead, chose the quickness of beheading. Many of the older Faithful, however, the ones that were fed more recent stories of the great dragons and their power, peace, kindness, and grandeur, would choose to burn. They believed it to be their last sign of devotion, to die in fire for their dragons. Kyana thought this was pure madness. Almost as mad as a descendant of Clan Riverhast living as a servant in Neira Kingdom.

"What are you doing here?" Kyana asked. Her voice remained low and soft as the girl wiped her eyes. She regretted her previous outburst.

"I never knew my parents," Lilly said, giving a little sniff as she pulled herself back together. "They gave me the mark. They left me with my aunt when I was a baby and never came back for me… I don't know where they went, and my aunt wouldn't say… she just told me to hide the mark, and everything would be fine. Our town started to hit hard times… we needed to get out, and my aunt had lived in Castle Lyist before. She knew people. It is a good place, it really is."

"So, you never practiced?" Kyana asked. The girl shook her head.

"Never." The girl's voice held a splash of pride. She had been in Castle Lyist for too long. She saw dragons and their Faithful as did everyone else in this kingdom of ignorance. Something to be feared. Something too powerful to be good. Something wrong... dark... evil even.

"Why?" Kyana asked again, her voice quiet.

"Huh?" The girl blinked watery eyes.

"Why did you cover my mark?" Kyana asked, tapping the cloth on her arm. "Why didn't you just tell them?" *If you think the Faithful so horrid. Why not have me killed?*

The girl looked at her, blinked twice before answering.

"Why should we be punished for the sins of our ancestors?"

Kyana wondered what sins she was referring. Living for a cause, they thought just? Living to serve a creature of magic? Giving their loyalty and having loyalty in return?

Kyana did not ask, because she did not really want to know. It did not matter... it broke her heart, but it didn't matter. Nothing changed with asking. This girl was a member of Castle Lyist. She had left behind old beliefs that had never truly belonged to her and had found a new place for her loyalty. Even if that loyalty could never be repaid in kind.

"Thank you," Kyana said because that was all she could say. She had no fear that this girl might give away her secret because she had given up her own. If Lilly told anyone about her mark, Kyana could expose the girl as well. Of course, Kyana would never do that. She would never lead another Faithful to the pier. Kyana would swing alone with a rope around her neck, feeling the air go to fire in her lungs before she gave up Lilly and her mark.

Lilly did not know this. And so, both their secrets were safe.

Lilly smiled. "You're welcome, miss."

"I think you can call me Kyana," she said, rolling back down her sleeve. Now that was settled... onto the project at hand.

"So... What sort of preparation do I need?" Kyana asked.

"Oh, well," Lilly gave her eye one last wipe, and her face lit up, glad to have those unpleasant topics behind them. "We have several options." Lilly nearly bounced over to the flip open the cabinet. Long cloths of bright blues, greens, purples, and reds hung on wooden hooks inside. "A few gowns were sent up while you were asleep. I hope you don't mind, I didn't feel the need to wake you."

"What are these for?" Kyana asked, looking at the piles and piles of fluffy fabric.

"To wear." Lilly smiled curiously. "Tonight."

"Can't I just wear…" Kyana looked down at her usual brown pants and new crisp blue shirt. She looked back up to Lilly. The answer was written all over her face. "A-alright then…" Kyana bit her lip slightly and looked back to the cabinet. "If I must."

"Which one would you like?" Lilly asked, smiling once more.

"I don't care."

"Truly?" Lilly asked bemused.

"Please… whichever you think is best."

Lilly's face light up, and her watery eyes seemed to sparkle with excitement.

"Alright, then!" She slipped her hands into the pile of clothes and pulled out a green gown.

"This would look absolutely lovely with your red hair! Besides," she gave Kyana a little smile that played between shy and mischievous. "I think long sleeves would be best. Don't you? But first," The girl laid the dress out on the bed and turned to clap her hands together. "A bath."

Kyana blinked. "A bath?"

"Yes," Lilly's eyes ran over the smudges of dirt on her neck and hands. "Definitely a bath."

Kyana watched warily as Lilly brought in a large tub and filled it with hot water. She was used to cleaning herself in cold rivers and streams, and always very alone. Even when she wasn't alone, when she had been traveling with her wandering man, he had been a gentleman and left her to her cleansing, going far off down the creek to perform his own. Then again, that was his way. He had been trained to be chivalrous after all.

"What are you smiling about, miss?" Lilly asked, looking up from a pillar of steam as she poured another bucket of water in the tub.

"Just remembering an old friend," she said, still smiling. She took a step forward to peer into the filling tub.

Lilly did not stop at hot water, no. When she had gone to get the tub, she had also retrieved a bottle of perfume that she delicately held over the water and poured in a few choice drops. The smell of flowers wafted up with the steam, and finally, it was ready.

Kyana knew the girl had already changed her while she slept, but she still felt horribly awkward as she slowly slid out of her clothes and climbed into the tub. Lilly set to work, scrubbing and washing and filling Kyana's hair with even more scented soap before washing it out once more.

"If you don't mind me asking miss," Lilly said, still busily pouring soap bubbles from Kyana's shoulders and back. "Where did you get all these scars?"

Kyana frowned, looking down at the marks that checkered her skin in so many odd angles and jagged shapes.

"Honestly, I don't remember all of them." She pointed to one on her shoulder, that cut from her collar bone over her shoulder and down her back. "That one I got when I fell out a tree. I was near the top, and I hit a few branches on the way down. This one," She tapped a spot on her back where she knew there was a dull lash mark. "That's when some man smacked me with his horse's reins."

"That's terrible!" Lilly gasped, but Kyana only shrugged.

"It's okay. I was trying to steal his stuff anyway."

"Why?" Lilly asked.

"Because I was starving, and he had an entire bag of apples just begging to be plucked." Kyana smiled over her shoulder at the surprised look on Lilly's face. "I was alone, and I wasn't always good at hunting. Sometimes I had to improvise."

"How'd you learn? To hunt so well, I mean."

"A friend taught me." When Kyana didn't explain farther, Lilly let the subject drop.

"Alright!" Lilly said, setting aside the scrub brush and pulling out a towel. "All clean! Now for the gown!"

The dress was difficult to get into. Lots of shimmying, pulling, tugging, and tying. When the gown was finally on, Lilly laced up the back with colorful golden threads. It was a mellow green and with long sleeves that fell off Kyana's shoulders and reached past her wrist to a point a few inches off her hands. The cut pulled snug around her rib cage and waist, then flowed smoothly down her hips and to the floor. Golden leaf patterns rimmed the top edge and curve of her waist. They then scattered down the skirt of the dress like stars in the sky. Lilly seemed elated in her project and hummed happily as she ran a brush through Kyana's long curls of freshly washed auburn hair. It fell in a thick mass down her back, the red-brown complementing the green fabric as Lilly knew it would.

She pulled a mirror from the cabinet so Kyana could see the end result. "What do you think?" Lilly asked excitedly. Kyana looked at the reflection. It was not at all her usual appearance, but it was not altogether unfamiliar.

"It... you did very well," Kyana said. "Thank you."

The girls face began to glow. "Thank you, kindly, my lady."

"I am no lady."

"Sorry miss." Lilly's smile faltered.

"Don't be sorry." Kyana stood there, fingers laced over her lap. "Call me, Kyana. What now?"

"Oh!" the girl jumped back to her feet and ran to the cabinet. She pulled out a few small boxes. She kept opening and closing them again, frowning, and shaking her head until she opened a little blue box with gold trim.

"Here. Here is the last piece." From the box, she pulled out a long golden braid. She brought it over but paused. "May I?" Kyana nodded. The girl went behind her, and slowly lowered the twist around her neck, looping it twice before finally fashioning the winged clip in the front.

"Finished!" The necklace was a braid of thick red thread and an elegant golden chain. The cord ran as a choker around her neck and then looped swiftly to a close just above her dress line. The clip was carved into a flying phoenix with its golden wings spread wide and its tail of flames curling above its back. Kyana smiled. Now, this she genuinely liked.

"It's beautiful," she said, stroking it with her long fingers.

"Almost as much as you Miss," the girl said, shy once more. "Eh- Kyana." She corrected herself hurriedly.

Kyana returned her smile. She liked this girl. Not because she complemented her, but because she was genuine with her compliments. Her smile was shy, but it came easily to her face. She was a sweet girl in a dark world that she did not understand, and she was getting along the best way she could.

Kyana reached out and took one of the girl's rough hands.

"Thank you." She said, lowering her head. "Truly." Lilly blinked and nodded, a light pink shade crossing her face. Kyana straightened up and was struck by a sudden idea.

"You never asked if I practiced."

"Excuse me?" Lilly asked curiously.

"You never asked if I was a practicing Faithful... if I had ever done magic, or still believed in it," Kyana said. "You just protected me... why didn't you make sure?"

Lilly shrugged.

"I didn't have to. You saved the king, after all." Lilly smiled. "You would never have done that if you were truly a Faithful."

Kyana blinked and watched quietly as the girl began to clean up after them, tiding the already immaculate room. Had it all passed so far by? Had all the children of the followers, the children of the dragons, forgotten everything? The entire point? If Kyana had let those men of Neira die, it would not have been because of the mark branded into her arm.

She left the thought in her mind, knowing that this girl would not understand. If Kyana sat down and ranted for hours, Lilly still would not have understood. She was one of those passed understanding. Kyana's heart gave another painful throb.

And so, she turned her mind to other, more pressing matters. The feast. She had her clothes, her phoenix, and a safe secret... now what?

# CHAPTER 15

The feast was in full swing when Kyana finally found herself outside the great hall. The sound of laughter and music poured from under the thick double doors. Kyana stood before their wrought iron handles, too afraid to touch them. She had never been to a feast before. Hell, she had never been in a kingdom like this before. Not her, branded with the mark of a Faithful. Such feasts were generally held in celebration of her kind's execution, not with an invitation. She did not know what to expect. She had met with nothing but the unexpected in this kingdom. She was about to walk into a room of those that hated her... although they did not know it yet. She thought of Ira's broad smile, Augustine's gruff manor and soft touch, and those knights with their playful banter.

She felt her heart sink. Kyana did not want to watch their smiles melt away. But that is all they could do. Melt from their faces like snow in summer, dripping to the floor. She would see them sink away. *Burn* away.

She felt shame bubble in her stomach like acid. She could not become attached. And despite it all, despite everything... she found herself liking the people of this unexpected kingdom. It was a nice feeling. Gods help her; it was a nice feeling. A sort of warmth in her chest, but not one of fire... softer. A softness she had not felt in years, not since her last friend took his last breath... but those smiles, given to her so freely, were smiles of ignorance. If they knew her... if they ever found out... She could not get attached. No, not to them. Not ever.

She started to turn, about to abandon the whole thing, when the door opened. The sounds of music and laughter swelled as Neander stepped out dressed in his formal wear of cheerful brown and deep blue cloth.

"Kyana!" he nearly shouted. His hair was a mess and a glass of spirits swung haphazardly in his hand. "Wow." He took a step back as the door closed slowly behind him.

"What?" Kyana asked, looking around her, tensing.

"No, nothing," Neander said, grinning and looking at her once more. "Just, wow… you look… different…"

"Yes, well, excuse me…"

"Wow, wow, where are you going?" Neander asked as she started to walk away.

"Far from here." She continued on her way.

"Hold on a moment," Neander said. He jogged forward, cup sloshing red liquid out onto the floor as he stepped in front of her. "You can't leave! You haven't even joined the party yet!"

"And I don't intend to. I was going to… but I don't think it's a good idea."

"Why not?"

"… It's just not my type of feast."

"Nonsense!" Neander said, looping his arm through hers. She could smell the strong stench of alcohol on him. "It will be wonderful fun! Besides, you wouldn't want to waste a lovely gown like that."

Kyana could have easily broken his grip and pulled away, but she did not. She let him usher her through the double doors. The hall was large, high roofed with long tables that spread from one side of the room to the other. The place was packed, people overflowed the tables, and dozens more were on the dance floor. Men in their best, and knights in their brown cloaks, girls in their bright purple and red dresses swirled the floor in dazzling elegance. Women danced with men, or other women. Kyana saw a group of three ladies all in full skirts of bright pastels, holding hands and moving back and forth in a circle, dancing in steps Kyana had never seen before. Food piled every table. Fruit, steaming meat, vegetables, and fresh bread that would keep Kyana fed for over a year in the forest. The smell was intoxicating. Kyana stared at the feast in all of its grandeur. There were players with their bows, their flutes, adding their lively tunes to match the attitude of the attendees. Smiles donned every face, and the spirit was infectious. Slowly, Kyana felt the edges of her lips begin to turn up.

"There it is!" Neander said happily, grabbing a goblet from a passing servant's tray and pushing it into her hand, "There's that smile I've heard so much about!"

"What?" Kyana asked, looking up at him.

"Ira." Neander took a swig from his glass. "She spoke wonders of your hidden smile." Neander swallowed and grinned at her. "She didn't exaggerate, I see." Kyana looked away from him, but her smile was still on her lips. Her view trailed across those sitting around the tables. Men and woman laughing and eating. She caught sight of a few other knights she recognized, chatting loudly to one another. She saw Ira, standing beside the high table, a tray in her hand. She caught sight of Kyana, and her wide grin slowly spread her face. She raised her empty hand and waived. Kyana returned her wave.

*Maybe this evening wouldn't be so bad. A little feast. What's the harm?*

Her gaze moved down the table and stopped on the man sitting in the high-back chair at the end of the hall. He was in his long brown cloak decorated with an ornate blue dragon. His tousled black hair was tamed only by a thin gold band around his head. He was speaking to a knight on his left but seemed to feel her eyes on him. He looked up to meet her gaze, and Kyana's smile melted from her mouth.

"I'll be going now," Kyana said, turning towards the door.

"Oh, not again!" Neander wrapped an arm around her waist. "Come, we have a seat waiting for you," Kyana contemplated breaking his arm and leaving anyway. He seemed to read her mind because his grip loosened, but his grin did not fade.

"Give us a chance," he said, leaning in a little to tap his goblet to hers. "Give us an hour. If you're not sold by then, I'll walk you out myself. Deal?" Kyana considered, then took a long swig from her goblet. She had no idea what it was, but it was thick, warm, and thank the gods, it was strong.

"Ha, I'll take that as a 'yes,'" Neander led her towards the high table. Kyana noticed eyes following them. People smiled as they passed. A few familiar knights, including Simon and Cole, waived. One knight, tapped another on the shoulder, gesturing to Kyana and then continue with a story involving many arm gestures, one as if drawing a bow and arrow. Kyana watched them all curiously but said nothing. Neander pulled out a chair from the high table with a small scraping sound and gestured for her to take it. It was only a few seats down from the Lystad himself, which struck her as extremely odd, but she said nothing.

"Kyana!" Everett said happily. To her surprise, everyone at the high table stood as she started to take her seat. She jumped back up.

"What?" she asked, looking around hurriedly. Had something come in?

"Oh, no angel," Neander whispered quietly in her ear. "It's alright. They're standing for you."

"Oh...," She wanted to ask why they were doing that. What a strange thing to do. Instead, she simply nodded to Neander and took her seat. The rest sat down around her. She realized that, aside from herself and the king, there were few other people not wearing a knight's crest. These few were of varying ages, wore elegant cloths in royal colors, but none of them looked like the Lystad. Kyana did not really understand royal etiquette, why should she? However, were not such spaces so close to the king reserved for members of the royal family? She doubted if any of those people, knights or not, were related to the Lystad lineage. Kyana wondered if this meant the young king simply preferred the company of these people and his knights to those of his family... or if perhaps he simply had no other family to speak of.

Neander took the chair to her right and filled her now empty cup from a passing flagon.

"So glad you could join us tonight Kyana," called Everett from down the table.

"Here, here!" called another.

"Well, she is the guest of honor," Neander said grinning. "Our little angel from the treetops." Kyana took a gulp out of her glass.

"So," Kyana started, looking around. "What exactly is this feast, well... what are we celebrating?"

"Don't you know what day it is?" Neander sloshed some more of his drink over the table in his enthusiasm to show his surprise.

"It's easy to lose track of time in the forest," Kyana explained with a shrug, but a light pink color danced momentarily across her face and ears. She did not notice, but the Lystad did.

"My dear Kyana! It's the anniversary of the Four Kingdoms!" Neander explained loudly. "It's the day that, centuries ago, the Four Kingdoms were born!... You do remember the Four Kingdoms, right? You've not been cut off from civilization for that long, have you?"

Kyana scowled, but it only made him hoot with laughter.

"I take that as a yes?" Neander grinned.

Kyana glanced up the high walls. Donned on the opposite side, almost to the rafters, hung three large decorative flags. Each represented a kingdom. The first was for Sterlyn kingdom. It was made of a soft purple cloth decorated with a silver dragon; its tail wrapped threateningly over its spiked back. It stood tall, one foot raised mid-step, wings pulled down over its back, long neck craned over its shoulder as if looking for a follower. The second was for kingdom Kyar, with a prowling black dragon. One about to pounce on its prey, eyes wide and watchful and set against a deep green field. The third was for Eryl kingdom, with a gray background and a sleeping gold dragon.

Kyana had noticed the fourth and final flag before sitting down. It hung behind the high table, large and brown with a flying two headed midnight blue dragon, meant for Kingdom Neira.

"Kingdom Sterlyn was created by the sibling Carter and the dragon Sterlyn. Kingdom Kyar by sibling Nannette and dragon Kyara. Eryl by Edwin and Beryl. And this kingdom, Kingdom Neira, by sibling Lawrence and dragon Aneira.... I do have the basics... thanks kindly." These kingdoms were born from the union of human and dragon. The dragons helped build the kingdoms, and the humans named the kingdoms after them and gave them an honored place within. From the homes they built for them beneath the castle, to the decorations on the walls, they honored each other. They graced each other with equal measure in everything. And the kingdoms grew and flourished with both. Well... at least for a time. But that time was long passed and passed by.

Kyana even knew of the annual celebration of the kingdoms, but she had always found it odd. The Four Kingdoms were created together, but they usually celebrated this creation separately. They did join in a massive celebration every twenty-four or twenty-five years in the place it all began. At those times the leaders of the Four Kingdoms would travel to the Caskcare Mountains where the siblings had found their dragons. They would hold celebration there which would last an entire month, Kyana knew this.

She did not, however, know that the anniversary was today.

"It's that time already?" Kyana wondered, watching the undeniable proof play out before her. "Time does pass and pass by…"

"As all things must," the Lystad agreed. She looked up to see the king watching the festivities with bright blue eyes and a warm smile, but Kyana thought it seemed sad somehow. "Time is not immune."

"No," Kyana nodded. "I suppose not."

"Pray, tell us Kyana," a knight she did not recognize spoke suddenly, unable to contain himself. "Tell us about that day in the forest! So many men… Where did you learn to fight like that?"

Kyana thought a moment. "A friend taught me."

"A friend?" he asked, curiously. "What kind of friend, to know so much?"

"A dear kind," Kyana said, gaze falling to the goblet in her fingers. Her green eyes seemed to grow misty in the flickering lamp lights. The other knights did not notice, but the Lystad did.

"Oh c'mon, you gotta give us more than that!" Neander pleaded shamelessly.

Kyana considered, then shrugged. "His name was Wybert. I called him Bert."

"Wait a minute… Wybert?" Everett leaned over the table to get a better view of Kyana's face. "You can't mean Zackarya Wybert."

"That was him." Kyana nodded.

"No," Everett said, shaking his head. "Nah, there's no way."

"Who?" the unknown knight asked.

"Zackarya Wybert." Kyana heard the Lystad speaking but did not look up to greet his gaze. "From Sterlyn. Wybert the Wanderer, as he is now known."

"Holy shit." Neander's mouth dropped open. "You met the Silver Knight?"

"He wasn't the Silver Knight when I knew him," Kyana said, taking another sip. It was rather delicious this drink. Thick, and strong, but also sweet, and warm on the tongue. The kind of drink that could loosen the same. Kyana put the cup back down.

"I'm still lost," the knight said, curiously.

"Gods, Teller, do you know nothing about legends!" Neander snickered.

"It's not even history yet," Everett laughed. "Give it a few more centuries for him to become a legend."

Neander shook his head. "A knight like Wybert was a legend the moment he picked up his sword."

"He was an honored knight in Sterlyn Kingdom," Lystad said helpfully to the still confused knight. "Rumored to be descended from one of the great Libras of old."

"Not just honored," Neander said, eyes wide, cup flinging so drastically in his hands that a stream spilled out and wet the table in front of him. A few waiting servants jumped forward to mop up the mess. Neander did not even notice. "Epic. A legend. A storm on the battlefield, a monster with the sword, and not bad at hand to hand from what I hear. He won tourneys with ease, fought off rebellions with minimal casualties."

"Not to mention that time when he saved that little pompous Prince Lessen," Everett added.

"That is King Lessen now," Lystad warned, but not without good humor.

"Wait, I think I did hear about that," the knight named Teller said, eyes squinting as if it would help his memory. "A bunch of traitors within the castle kidnapped him, right? Got him out of the castle to where their supporters were waiting."

"Ya," Neander grinned. "His father sent for Wybert, and Wybert went after them with an army. Killed every. Single. One of um. Brought the prince home without a hair on his head out of place. He was a walking epic."

"After that, the king himself gave him a gift."

"Since he couldn't very well knight him again." Neander interrupted, but Everett went on.

"He tried to give him a lordship, land and a castle but Wybert turned him down. So instead the King gave him a cloak."

"A cloak of a shining silver cloth, the edges were sown with actual silver thread," Neander added, nudging Teller, eyebrows wiggling.

"Hence the nickname The Silver Knight," Everett said.

"And then, one day!" Neander howled in a voice so loud a few people down the table, threw some friendly shushes in his direction. "He just gave it all up! All the fame, all the glory, his knighthood, everything. Gave his regards to his king and country, and disappeared into the dark of night, leaving his silver cloak behind."

"The only thing he took was Darkheart."

"Darkheart?" the knight named Teller asked.

"His sword," Kyana answered, taking another sip.

"No one knew why, or what he was doing, but there were scattered sightings of him across the entire realm."

"Hence the nickname Wybert the Wanderer."

"And you knew him?" Teller asked Kyana, now looking as awed as the rest of them.

"Yes," Kyana said, smiling to herself. It was a sad smile. "Rather well."

"How in the name of the gods did you two come to meet each other?" Teller asked.

Kyana shrugged. "He was wandering, and so was I. We just happened to wander into the same place at the same time."

"Incredible. What a chance," Teller said.

"Fate," Neander countered.

"Destiny," Everett nodded.

"Pick one," Kyana said. "They all apply."

"How old were you? When you met, I mean." Everett asked. "How long did you know him?"

"A while, I'd say," Neander added. "For her to learn so much about the more, uh, violent, talents." They all laughed.

This was a hard question for Kyana to answer. Time had a habit of slipping Kyana by in ways, unlike others. Spending so many years in isolation, hidden in the woods or mountains, time tended to sneak unnoticed around her. It crept like a talented thief, stealing her years, and forgetting her as quickly as she forgot time itself.

Kyana considered.

"I believe... I believe I was around fifteen... or so," At least that was the age she had seemed to Wybert. Her exact age, Kyana was not sure.

She remembered the night they met very well. She had been wandering, hungry, and alone when she came across a man. He was older in age, hair already whitened around the temples and scattered through the scruff that edged his jaw. She remembered his sleeping face most of all. He had not actually been sleeping, but she had not known it at the time. His face was well touched by the sun, tanning his skin a dark and handsome shade. Several scars cut down the temple by the right eye and split the lip of what must have once been the most handsome face in all the realms. The years had not forgotten this man, however. Deep wrinkles cut like gouges, leaving times own scars around his eyes. Another scar cut down the left side of his forehead and broke his eyebrow, leaving only half to remain like a short scratch of dark brown to match the non-gray parts of his hair.

She had crept around the sleeping figure, around the smoldering fire, towards the little satchel that lay nearby. Silent as the night itself she moved, and if he had been asleep, she would have gotten away free. Of course, he had not been. She remembered turning around, bag in hand, and nearly falling backward in surprise. The sleeping man was on his feet, a sword in his hand, watching her. He had pale blue eyes that glinted like ice by the light of the stars.

Kyana's heart had thudded in her chest like a terrified animal at the sight of him.

*Is this how I pass by?* Kyana wondered briefly as the man flicked the wrist holding the sword, loosening it, eyes never blinking.

They had fought, and Kyana had lost in mere moments. She had ended up on the ground. She recalled thinking that the sword pressed against her throat was beautiful. Long and gleaming. The man must have kept it well. The handle was wrapped in black cloth that was held down with twins of thin spun silver that circled and overlapped. Not only that, but the hilt was set with a lovely blue stone that matched the strange man's eyes. Was it really stone... or was it ice?

*If she was going to pass by,* Kyana had thought, watching the starlight filter through the blue stone, casting reflected light across the cold ground beside her. It speckled the frozen dirt with colored stars to match the sky. *If she was going to pass by, at least it was at the hand of something so lovely.*

Kyana had closed her eyes, breathed in the evening air, and let it go with the rest of it. With the rest of it all. Kyana looked up at the face, she was sure, the last she would ever see. She looked him in the eye and waited. The man paused, frowning curiously at the young girl on the ground. He grunted as if acknowledging something she said, although she had said nothing. Then he put down his blade.

"Odd little thing, aren't you?" the man had said, sheathing Darkheart and holding out his hand to help Kyana to her feet. She had taken the hand without hesitation.

Kyana pulled herself back from that moment when his hand touched hers. It was a warm hand. It was also rough. Rough from being broken open, healed and scared, a thousand times over. She pulled herself away from Wybert the Wanderer and back into the warm and lively great hall of Castle Lyist.

"We traveled together after that. About six or seven years, I'd say."

"Wow." Neander grinned, "That is amazing. I'd think you were lying if I hadn't seen how you fight."

"You became friends, you said?" Everett asked.

"Yes."

"Did he ever tell you why he did it? Why he left it, all... left everything and went wondering?"

".... Yes, he did," she said slow and soft.

"... Well?!" Neander leaned in, "Why did he do it?"

Kyana remembered that day as well. It had been overcast and cold, but not nearly as cold as Wybert's eyes as he told his tale. The ice in them seemed to splinter as he opened the wounds he had never shown to another soul. She remembered how she held the man, old enough to be her father, as he cried like a child into her shoulder. She had held him close and stroked his gray hair like a lover, although it had never been that way between them. There was love between them, but all was as innocent as that embrace and as unbreakable as the sword hanging on his hip.

"That," Kyana hesitated, "is not my story to tell."

"Well, then, tell us where he is now!" Neander asked, sloshing another splash of mead over the table. "I'd love to ask him in person."

"About six feet deep," Kyana said simply.

"He died?" they all echoed in indignant unison.

"Yes," Kyana said simply, "Men do that."

"I know he hasn't been seen in a few years," Everett said. "But I always hoped he was just off somewhere still wandering."

"Are you sure he's dead?" Neander asked, sounding almost desperate in his plea that she was wrong.

"Very." Kyana nodded.

"I mean, are you sure you're sure?" Neander spluttered. "I mean, with legends like Wybert, they can sometimes go down but—"

"He bled out in my arms, and I buried him myself." Kyana interrupted coolly. "That 'sure' enough for you?"

The table went quiet. The sounds of the festivities and music seemed to dim into nonexistence as Kyana focused on the goblet in her hands. She traced a long thin finger down one of the dragon carvings. She marveled at the time it must have taken to carve each and every scale. She also remembered.

Laying by the spluttering fire, Wybert was already long asleep. It was just by chance Kyana's doze broke in time for her to see the figures peeling from the darkness. They had not had a chance. There were five of them, armed and ready. It was not a fair fight. No fair fight at all. It was the coward's way.

"I beg your pardon, Kyana," Neander said softly.

"It's alright," she said downing the last of her drink. *To you, he was just a legend.*

"How did it happen?" Teller asked tentatively. "If you don't mind me asking."

"Just some thieves," Kyana answered, not really wanting to wade too deeply into that memory. Some memories had too much darkness. If you look too closely, stay there too long, you become lost in them. Drown in them. "Outnumbered... crept up on us while we slept."

"Thieves..." Neander mumbled under his breath. "The Silver Knight was killed by petty thieves?"

Teller shoved an elbow hard into his side, making him wince.

"Where did you lay him to rest?"

"I would rather not say," Kyana said, but not unkindly.

"Why not?" Everett asked.

"Again," Kyana answered. "A tale that isn't mine to tell."

The table went quiet once more, broken only when Neander could not hold back his curiosity any longer.

"What did he say?" The words burst from him like they had been beating against the inside of his teeth for years. "His last words? What were The Silver Knight's last words?"

"Neander!" cried Everett and the Lystad in shocked unison while Teller shook his head.

"Don't be vile, Neander."

"I'm not being- I'm just- Oh, come now you can't tell me you're not curious!" Neander said, spreading the fingers of his empty hand in self-defense.

"You can't just ask the girl such a question, you idiot." Teller thudded the back of Neander's head, causing him to splash yet more of his drink onto the table.

"Odd little thing," Kyana said over the hubbub of Neander's chastisements.

"What?" They turned to look at her.

She spun her goblet in her hand and did not look at any of them. "Wybert's last words... 'Odd little thing.'"

"... 'Odd little thing?'" Neander repeated, obvious disappointment drooping his face. "Really? That's all?"

"For the gods sake, Neander." Everett rubbed his eyes.

"I'm just saying!" Neander, eyes red with mead by this point, went on.

"Neander," Teller warned in a voice that snapped like two spark rocks by an unlit fire. "I swear, another word and I will put your head through that table, I swear by the gods."

Neander blubbered an excuse, but Kyana was not listening anymore. She was back in that dark forest, under the dappled light of the rising sun through the trees. Soft pink clouds floated high above as three of the bandit's bodies lay in heaps around them. The other two had run, hard and fast, into the forest. She had held Wybert in her arms the best she could, as his blood pooled hot and fast into her lap. She had not cried. Neither had he.

"Will you miss me?" Wybert had asked, a small smile spreading his face, so full of years. He had not looked afraid. In fact, to Kyana, he looked peaceful. He looked ready.

"Yes," she had answered, and once again she stroked that graying hair. She brushed it gently from his ice colored eyes, but they were no longer cold. They had grown a warmth. A warmth so strong and deep, it seemed like death itself could not reach it. But of course, death, as it always does, found a way. "I will not be the only one."

"Ah," Wybert reached up and cradled Kyana's face in his rough hand as gentle as any lover's kiss. "But you will be the only one that matters... my odd little thing."

"Kyana?"

Kyana snapped her head back from times passed and passed by to look up at Neander. He was watching her with a look of concern.

"Hum?" she asked, gathering her thoughts.

"You alright?"

"Oh, yes, I'm alright," she said and glanced around the room. "Is there any more of this refreshing drink to be had? I'm parched."

"Coming right up!" Neander said, turning and gesturing to one of the servants standing by. He whispered in the young boy's ear sending him scampering off in a hurry.

"Let's change the subject," Everett said, trying to smile away any awkwardness still left. "Tell us something else about yourself. We still know so little. How about your family? What are they like?"

Kyana considered.

"Complicated souls from a far simpler time."

The knights burst out in laughter, and all tension was broken.

"You like riddles, don't you?" None of them seemed disappointed, only more curious. The Lystad was silently watching her over his goblet. Kyana cleared her throat and looking around for that servant with more mead. A large steaming plate of food suddenly slid into place before her. She looked up to see Ira's broad grin.

"Ira." Kyana smiled wide in utter relief.

"Hello, Kyana," Ira said.

"Are you joining us?" she asked, hopefully. Kyana had a feeling she was about to be asked far more questions, none of which she could answer. She would prefer Ira's talk of smiles and laughter to the knights prying questions and reminders of darker days.

Ira's bright hazel eyes flitted momentarily from her smile to the Lystad and then back again.

"I'm afraid not." Her grin never faded. "I need to check that everyone's cup is full... but I'll be back soon."

"Well, while you are here!" Neander lifted both his and Kyana's goblets and wiggled them in the air. Ira rolled her eyes but filled them.

"Thank you, Ira," Kyana said. "See you soon," she said with an edge of determination.

Ira raised her eyebrows, then nodded.

"Soon. Yes. Promise." She flashed Kyana her grin once more, then headed down the table.

"Be nice," she whispered at Neander as he passed.

"Oh, please! I'm always nice." Neander waved off Ira's comment and turned back to Kyana. Kyana looked down at the plate of heavenly smelling food Ira had left. Wafts of thick steam poured from it, making Kyana's mouth water. Then she noticed something. Kyana frowned.

"Is that... a quail?" It was a beautiful thing. Lightly browned and surrounded by perfectly cooked vegetables and potatoes. The whole plate seeped delicate spirals of steam into the air. They fluttered out of sight and filled her nose with the quail's salty tang.

"Sure, is!" Neander exclaimed happily. "It's yours. From the bow challenge you won. We thought you might like it!"

"Oh, don't go on taking the credit now Neander," Everett said cheerily. "It was Ira's idea. She heard about your shot. She was sorry she missed it." Kyana smiled and reached for her fork.

"So, Kyana tell us more about your family!" And there it was. Back to the prying questions.

"What would you like to know?" she asked, slowly slicing into the quail which broke open at the slightest touch of the fork, sending even more salty steam into the air.

"Anything, everything, we still know so little." Everett leaned in from down the table. "So little... other than you have the heart of a lion, the soul of a saint, and the fighting skills that would outstrip any warrior we know."

"Well, at least we have that little riddle solved," Neander added, nodding. "But we have so many left!"

"Go on then," Teller added, gesturing with his own fork full of potato that he plopped in his mouth and chewed eagerly. Kyana considered, weighing the consequences with the sheer desire to make them all shut up. She plopped a piece of quail in her mouth, and there was an explosion of flavor against her tongue. She sighed a little as she chewed. Kyana was used to plain deer meat, and berries picked from branches. All was nothing like this salted, spiced, juicy slice of bird. She took her time, chewing slow and swallowing before continuing. She cleared her throat.

"I was born the only child to kind parents, in a small village wedged between a meadow and some rolling hills. Just inside of Kyar Kingdom in fact."

"Were you supposed to be heading back home when we met in the woods?" Neander asked, face falling slightly. "We could have sent a messenger to let them know you—"

"There isn't anyone out there to tell," Kyana reassured. "They died when I was ten." A hush fell over the long table at these words.

"I'm very sorry to hear that," said the king in an even tone.

"They passed quickly," Kyana said by way of explanation, hoping they would let the subject lie.

"Was it a sickness?" Neander pried a little further.

"Yes," Kyana's eyes landed on the king's bright blue gaze. "A powerful sickness. They were gone in minutes." They stayed quiet, waiting for her to continue. "Well, then I was adopted into another family... for whom my parents had great respect. Wybert was well versed in the art of battle, but it was my second father who showed me the grace of peace."

"I take it, you learned better the former!" Neander teased. The rest of the knights laughed, and Kyana shrugged, a little smile tugging the corner of her mouth.

"So, your second father, then?" Everett smiled. "When you had a fever, you tried to run back home to him."

"I'm eager to get home." Her eyes were back on the dragon carving. It was a lovely thing. A sleeping form with its long tail curving around the handle. "But my second father also died. Years past now. I was... thirteen, I believe."

The silence that fell on them now was deep, dark, and seemed to suck the very air from the room. It made Kyana squirm in her seat. She did not like to have so many eyes on her. Neander finally cleared his throat.

"You're... you're alone out there?"

"Yes."

"For how long."

"Long enough." Kyana looked up. All their faces were grave, and a few lined with pity which only made Kyana more uncomfortable.

"So, when Wybert found you wandering..." Teller trailed off.

"I was wandering alone."

"For two years?" Everett cleared his own throat. "And so young."

"I was starving when I found him." Kyana smiled. "I tried to steal his bag... didn't end well for me."

"So now you live out in the forest alone?" Neander asked over his goblet.

"Why would you be so eager to return to such isolation?" Everett asked his drink wholly forgotten on the table.

"It's my home." Kyana frowned. She did not understand his question. "Why would I not want to go home? It's where I belong."

"Wouldn't it be so... quite... out in those woods all alone?" Neander asked. "How do you live?"

"I live like anyone else," Kyana said. "I wake, I work, I hunt, I rest, I sleep, and then I wake once more. I find my own food and keep my own home. Well, in my case, it's a cave. Not very large mind you, but it's warm in the winter and opens out into a little break of trees... There's a small brook, only a short walk away." Kyana smiled, remembering the soft, trickling sound of the water as it danced down the rocks. "Alone or not, it's a beautiful place to spend a life. A life I live the best that I can. With all my strength. And all my heart. And the quiet..." Kyana thought. "Honestly, with all the crickets, birds, wind and water... It's never really felt that quiet... the forest has its own music." Kyana looked around at the hall, all a bustle with happy sounds, and music. It was lovely, but it was quite loud. A strain upon the ear, making her wish for the tops of the trees and the strong sappy bark under her feet. "And when it is quiet, when all the critters take a pause, that's not so bad either. It's not a cold kind of quiet, it's a good quiet. The quiet that is soft and holds so much possibility, in a way that noise never can. It's soothing. Have you ever gone out to the forest in the night, deep into the quiet? Just go there, close your eyes and let your mind wander. I promise you, it can go on forever." Kyana shrugged. "Sometimes, it can be a little too quiet. When the bird's sleep and the crickets hide, and the creek runs dry in summer. It can be a little empty... a little lonely... but I would be lost without the music of the quiet." She looked up to see them all watching her, their cups and food forgotten. The Lystad was smiling slightly. Kyana wondered why.

"That was beautifully put," Everett said. "Did your second father also teach you how to speak in such poetry?"

"My parents did," she said, taking a drink from her goblet. "My second father... well he wasn't much for words."

"I thought Wybert might have." Neander shrugged. "I heard he was as skilled in poetry as he was with the sword."

Kyana snorted.

"*That* is only legend," she said, flashing a wide grin that looked odd on her face. It was a grin that belonged to her in times passed by. It was a grin belonging to the odd little thing she once was. A ghost of a person who had died the same night as a wandering man. "Nah, Wybert could never teach me poetry. He taught me how to swear."

They all laughed and seemed to remember their meal. They turned and dug in, still chuckling. Kyana felt a buzz in the back of her mind and swiftly returned her own goblet to the table. She could not risk becoming unmindful. Being unmindful leads to the loosening of words. Words that are better left unspoken.

"You seemed to be having a hard time when we first found you," Neander said, tearing a piece of meat off with his fingers. "You're speaking beautifully now, but then..."

"Well, it had been years since I had seen anyone, let alone spoken to anyone. I nearly forgot how to put one word after another."

"That must have been frightening," the Lystad added. "A group of strangers breaking into your peaceful world ... I'm sorry we interrupted so abruptly." Kyana looked up at the young king. His face was serious, and his blue eyes seemed genuine. He seemed... truly sorry. She added it to the long list of things she had not expected.

"It's alright. It wasn't exactly your choice to be ambushed." Kyana recalled the bandit that fell in the forest. "Whatever happened to the bandit? The one I hit with the arrow?"

"Oh, him!" Neander grinned. "He spilled all he knew and the truth about who sent him. thanks to you."

"Who sent him?" she asked curiously, nibbling at the bread on her plate. Smeared with butter and salt, it tasted almost as good as the quail.

"A great enemy of the Four Kingdoms," said the Lystad.

"I'm sure you have more than one," Kyana answered.

Instead of looking offended, or surprised, the Lystad grinned.

"Yes, quite a few." Kyana waited, watching him. "His name is Rainier."

"Rainier?" Kyana looking up sharply. "The Faithful, Rainier?"

"You've heard of him?" Everett asked.

"I have heard whispers," Kyana answered, peeling off another piece of quail from her plate. Juice oozed slowly down her fork as she lifted it to her mouth. "When Wybert and I went into town or stayed at an inn along the road, we would hear stories. Many of them."

A man of severe power, Rainier was the thing of nightmares within the realm. He was the thing that hid under young children's beds at night and cackled from every dark corner of the frightened imagination by day.

In the Second War, the war that raged between the Four Kingdoms and the vengeful Faithful still furious after the death of their dragons, Rainier had been a general. He had been one of the most ruthless and relentless that the realm had ever seen and led one of the larger forces against the Kingdoms. Their efforts were bloody but ultimately futile. After hundreds of mourning clans had banded together, their forces had been significant, but the magic of the Faithful was weak. They drew their power from their dragons, and with them dead, their powers were a whisper of what they had once been. They could still draw magic in small ways through the artifacts left by their dragons, bones, scales, and relics, but there were few left to them. Most of the dragon relics had been confiscated and greedily guarded by the Four Kingdoms for just that reason. The Keepers, who had once cared for the living dragons, were reassigned to oversee the relics beneath the castles. Hidden away in the caverns where their dragons once slept.

Against the trained armies of the Four Kingdoms, the Faithful's had crumbled like paper in a fire. And those that survived scattered like ash in a breeze.

Rainier himself vanished for years but stayed in the mind of the Four Kingdoms like a bad omen. There were rumors, whispers, and sightings. Kyana heard half drunken tales of how the "bastard witch" had kept himself alive so many years by bathing in the blood of goats and young children. He would appear once every few years to cause trouble for one or another of the Four Kingdoms, nearly succeeding in an assassination attempt on the young queen of Kyar a mere eleven years ago, before he vanished once again. Rainier was notorious, hated, and few didn't know his name.

"Yes, apparently that group of bandits was actually a group of hireling scouts, sent to gather information about the goings on around Castle Lyist. They saw us outnumbered on the hunt and decided to take an opportunity. But thanks to you," the king raised his goblet, "they were unable to do either of those things."

"To Kyana!" Neander roared beside her, raising his own goblet. "Our angel from the trees! Friend to Neira!" They all drank.

Kyana watched them bemused. Where they always so festive? Did they always drink to such excess? Given a little planning, it would be a fantastic opportunity... perhaps... She looked around the table. No. Many of the knights were drinking, but dozens of other guards stood off to the side, smiles on, but they had not touched a single glass. Kyana took a long slow sip out of her goblet and mulled the idea over. A feast... in celebration of the Four Kingdoms... and her a guest of honor. How... ironic.

She watched the dancers spinning around the floor. Most were elegant and beautiful, but others… Kyana saw the young pimply knight named Lionel dancing with a short red-haired girl in a soft gray and gold gown. The girl seemed adequate in her skills, but the young knight kept stumbling over his own feet. Once he stumbled so drastically that he almost knocked the girl back into a table of food. Kyana chuckled.

"Tell us," Neander said, leaning in. "What is so funny, Kyana?"

Kyana looked up. "Just admiring the show." She nodded towards the two stumbling around the dance floor. The boy's face was bright red by this point and the girl grew more and more irritated with every misstep. Neander and Everett laughed outright, and even the king gave a chuckle.

"What?" Neander said, turning back. "You saying you can do better."

"Oh, no, no," Kyana said suddenly, leaning back in her seat. She did not like where this was headed. "No, I don't think so."

"Oh, come now, if you are half as skilled at dancing as you are at fighting, you would make a wonderful partner."

"I'm afraid you're mistaken; I would be a very poor dancing partner." Kyana's eyes were on her goblet again. "I haven't danced since… it has been a very long time."

"Well, it's time to change that," Neander said, pushing back his chair and getting to his feet. He held out his hand to her, and she eyed it warily. "Everybody needs a good dance now and then. It's good for the soul." Neander prodded.

"Not so good for healing wounds, I'm afraid," Kyana said defiantly.

"What?" Neander leaned in just enough for her to smell a strong whiff of alcohol on his breath. Her nose crinkled in distaste. "You telling me you're scared little warrior?"

Kyana narrowed her eyes at him. "No."

"Then come! Dance! Have a little fun for the god's sake!"

Kyana noticed Ira making her way down the long table filling goblets. To Kyana's relief, she was headed their way.

"You know," Kyana said, downing the rest of her glass in one gulp to the knight's glee, and got to her feet. "I think I will dance." She turned away from Neander and caught Ira by the arm as she finished filling the king's goblet.

"Dance with me?" She asked. Ira's hazel eyes widened in surprise.

"What?" she asked in an unusually high voice as all the knights, including Neander, cheered in support.

"It's been insisted that I heal my soul, so... help me? Or not?" She smiled, trying to convey playfulness. She had not done this for a while. She was not sure how it should go, being friendly, and the drink was not helping her mind be any clearer. It was, however, making her braver.

"Oh, I, uh," Ira's eyes darted to the king as she stumbled over an answer.

"Oh, why not, Ira!" The Lystad called cheerfully. "The woman saved our lives; you can't deny her a dance."

"Oh, well, alright, then," her grin widened. She set the pitcher next to Neander who happily accepted it. Kyana led the way to the dance floor, never letting go of Ira's arm.

"Now," she said, turning to face Ira. "I need to be honest with you. I haven't danced for years and am rusty."

"Don't worry," Ira answered shrugging. "I've never danced at one of these feasts before... so we are both out of our element."

"Then, we'll be fools together?" Kyana asked taking position.

"Sounds like fun," Ira laughed. To Kyana's surprise, it was. They danced around together like the closest of sisters. Ira took the lead position, seeing as she knew the dance a little better than Kyana. Only a little better, however. They stumbled here, tripped there, their laughter all but lost in the music. The onlookers seemed surprised to see the strange woman and a serving girl out on the floor together, but they were more interested than worried about it. Kyana did not mind. Not tonight. Tonight, she was having fun. For the first time in a long time, she had that warm feeling deep in her chest. It was nice.

"I hope they weren't bothering you too much," Ira said, nodding towards the head table. "They mean well, but they can act like children at times."

"No more than expected." Kyana shrugged. "Lots of questions." Kyana glanced up at the head table and frowned. "May I ask you something?"

"Sure," Ira shrugged, and quickly apologized as she nearly stepped on Kyana's foot.

"Who are they?" Kyana motioned towards the non-knights sitting in a place of honor.

"Oh, that is Morella Thyrman," Ira pointed to a young woman in a bright red dress, "Roy Pently," she motioned to the man next to her who seemed to be climbing into his sixtieth year, "Carol Carver," a woman of comparable age to

Roy Pently but taking her age with far less grace than he, judging by the make-up that clearly painted her face three shades paler than her neck. "And Andrew Phobos," the man on the far end was chatting happily with Carol Carver, liver spots visible even from such a distance.

"Relatives to the Lystad line?" Kyana asked.

"No, they're Damian's advisers."

"Is Lystad the last of his line?" Kyana asked, doing her very best not to sound hopeful.

"Does he have any other family?"

"Yes, he does. Quite a few actually." Ira's smile faltered a little. "I mean some… his parents aren't… I mean they, uh…"

Kyana looked at Ira's face and understood.

"Oh." Kyana cast her eyes briefly to the ground. It seemed that she and the Lystad had something in common.

"He's got other family though," Ira's smile was back, "he has an uncle, two aunts, two sisters and a hand full of cousins."

"But they are not here?"

"No, they live in Kyar and Sterlyn Kingdoms at the moment… although I think his little sister has been talking about moving back for some time now."

"Humm." Kyana turned back to Ira. There were more of them. If one were to fall, another would take his place. Even less reason to take drastic action. It would do no good. "Thank you."

"No problem," Ira smiled. "I'm sure it is nice to finally **ask** a question instead of having a million thrown at you."

"Yes, that did get exhausting rather quickly," Kyana said. "They had quite a few."

"Well, you are a bit of a mystery," Ira said. "The warrior from the woods. The angel from the trees."

"I am no angel," Kyana laughed.

"What are you, then?" Ira asked. "Go on, tell me."

Kyana opened her mouth, and to her severe surprise, she realized she **wanted** to tell her. This girl, with her wide grin, hazel eyes and innocent spattering of freckles down her ever so slightly hooked nose… she wanted to tell her. Why was that?

"You have wishing eyes," she answered her own question out loud.

"What?" Ira's eyebrows scrunched together in confusion, thrown by the change of subject.

"You do," Kyana insisted calmly. "You hold so much more in your heart than you let out. You are a very honest person by nature, but you hold things back... I can see them," she said, pointing a finger. "Right there... wishing to break free. Wishing to find something but not knowing where to start. They are tired eyes for such a young face." Ira's smile faded into a look of pure curiosity.

"Who are you, Kyana of the woods?" she asked.

Kyana smiled sadly. "Someone... just someone who also has wishing eyes, Ira. That's all."

Ira blinked slowly at her as if trying to read her. Like she was a very confusing recipe she was trying to decipher. A secret ingredient that Ira could not place.

Kyana turned her attention back to their feet as the music shifted. "Okay, so this step goes like this, correct?"

"Oh, Uh, well, I think so," Ira laughed.

"Let's find out, shall we?" Kyana started, but a moment later, someone tapped Ira on the shoulder.

"May I?" Kyana looked up over Ira's left shoulder to see the Lystad in his brown cloak a smile on his face. Kyana's stomach fell, and the burning fire started to kindle once more in her chest. Her cheerful demeanor was gone in an instant.

"Of course, sire," Ira said automatically but looked down as Kyana's fingers dug deep into her lower arm. Her eyes widened, in surprise, or pain, Kyana could not tell. But it was already done. Ira nodded encouragingly to her, then moved back to her duties at the tables. The Lystad took his place with Kyana on the dance floor.

"Are you enjoying yourself?" he asked.

Kyana did not answer for a moment, choosing her words carefully. This was the edge of a precipice. This was dancing on the edge of a blade, and if Kyana was not careful, she might give something away.

"I am. More than I expected," she answered. The king nodded in response. The players started a new melody, and the dance began. The Lystad moved swift and skillfully across the floor. Kyana's eyes darted straight down to her feet, fearful that the Lystad's speed would affect her balance. The last thing she needed was to step on him.

"More than you expected? Well, I suppose that's... good."

Kyana said nothing. Silence was the safest bet. She was distracted from her feet to watch her partners. Every move was so elegant, every step skilled. She never knew a man could move so... Beautifully. That was the only word for it. Her eyes were caught by a reflected gleam of lamplight, and her gaze fell upon the sword at his side. She suddenly found herself wondering how many must have perished at the edge of that blade. Her eyes narrowed, and the fire grew white hot in her chest.

"I apologize for Neander," the king said offhandedly. "He indulges in the drink a little too often sometimes, and that can make him, let's say, less than tactful."

"It's alright," Kyana answered, stepping carefully, eyes back on her own feet. "He meant no harm."

"Yes, well... Kyana..." There was a smile in his voice. "What are you doing?"

"What?" Kyana asked, eyes still cast down.

"It's very hard to talk to you when your eyes are on the floor."

"My eyes are not on the floor," Kyana corrected. "They are on my feet."

The Lystad's voice nearly trembled with the effort to hold back laughter.

"Why are you watching your feet?"

"Because I'm trying not to step on your royal toes," Kyana said coolly.

"I'm sure my feet can handle a little stepping. Besides, it will actually be easier if you look at me and not the floor."

Kyana continued to watch her feet stepping desperately around his elegant strides. She felt a light touch at the bottom of her chin, Kyana looked up to see the Lystad's smile widen. His mix of light and dark blue eyes were nearly shining with hidden laughter.

"There," he said, taking his hand down from her chin. "That's better." Kyana clenched her teeth and again, said nothing. The Lystad's smile faltered, and he looked curiously at her. "You don't like me much, do you?"

"No." The word was from her mouth before she could snag it back. She nearly bit her own tongue with anger. Stupid. *Stupid.* Lie. Lie. *Lie* if you have to. But the mead was strong, and Kyana was many things, but a good liar had never been one. To her surprise, the king did not look angry. A look of boyish shock flashed his face, to be replaced just as quickly by curiosity.

"Yes... what did you describe me as...? Someone who 'does the hurting'? Then... why didn't you let me die? In the woods, you could have let me be taken or killed, but you didn't. Why did you save us?"

Kyana thought a moment. She had not known he was a Lystad at the time, but she had known the dragon coat of arms on all their shirts. She knew who they were. At that moment, though, it did not matter. At that moment she had a reason. Reasons are sometimes as thin and fleeting as the moments it takes to create them... but they are strong while they last. And Kyana chose, as she always did, to answer honestly.

"You were outnumbered. It wasn't a fair fight," Kyana answered.

"That's it?" One of the king's eyebrows shot up and his head tilted slightly. It was a movement that reminded Kyana of a little dog cocking his ear at a strange noise. "That's why you risked your life? That's why you got stabbed? That's why you nearly bled to death on the back of my horse... Because the fight was not fair?"

Kyana shrugged. "Every battle deserves a chance. Everyone deserves a fighting chance..." *No one deserves to be caught off guard... slaughtered in their sleep or snuck up on by cowards...* "besides I was the only one around." The Lystad looked at her, mouth held open slightly as if about to say something, but he had completely forgotten what it was.

"What?" she asked, very uncomfortable under his gaze.

"You're just..." He thought a moment. "Different."

"You have no idea just how much." Kyana could not help a slight grin.

"I was right, you know," the king said after a moment.

"About what?" Kyana asked, but then she realized what he meant. They had been dancing the entire time they were talking, her head up. She had not stepped on his feet once. His graceful step made for a wonderful lead and Kyana had followed with almost as much grace as he. They had flowed, rippled, and slid like water breaking and retreating against an empty shore. They had moved with such unquestioning unison that several of the other dancers had stopped to watch the show. She glanced around to see them transfixed.

"What are they staring at?"

"It isn't every day we throw a feast and invite a stranger to Castle Lyist," the Lystad said. "I suppose they're just wondering who you are," he looked back down at her. "As are we all."

Kyana had to fight from looking away. Staring into those stormy blue eyes made her feel like he could see it in her, read it in her thoughts. The brand on her arm seemed to grow itchy, and she fought just as hard to ignore it. "I am nobody."

"Well, that is just not true."

"But it is." Kyana continued. "And come tomorrow, I'm going to leave Castle Lyist. And I will never set foot into your lands again."

The Lystad frowned. "You say that, like it's what I want to hear."

Kyana was taken aback by his answer. But of course, he did not know. "It is."

"You saved my life Kyana. And the lives of my finest knights. You even saved Ira. There are very few men that would do what you did, let alone women." The king was serious now. "Neira could use someone like yourself. Your heart. Your abilities. If you had half a mind to stay, we would find you good work." He raised one shoulder in a little shrugging motion as he went on, "You say you need to go back to where you belong, but consider the idea, that you could very easily belong *here.* Castle Lyist is a wonderful place..." The king grinned. "If you just give it a fighting chance."

Kyana watched him. She felt the fire disappearing in her chest and that soft warmth spreading like water from somewhere inside. Somewhere deep, that had been empty for so long, and her heart begged to drink it all in. But she knew, he would not offer such a thing if he truly knew her.

"Your gratitude for your life has blinded you."

"Has it now?" he asked, amused.

"It has."

"Pray, tell, to what?"

"I will go home tomorrow."

"Absolutely. If Augustine says, you are well and ready—"

"No," Kyana interrupted. "I will go home tomorrow. Well or not. I do not belong here. I am not one of your citizens, and you are **not my king.**" Kyana watched as the Lystad's face fell into disappointment, and further into frustration.

"But…" she continued, deciding it better not to anger him. "I do, thank you. For your care and kindness. I would have died without your practitioner. And the feast…" Kyana smiled warmly at the happy view and still spiraling colors. She heard a guffaw of laughter and the rattling of hands against tables. "Has been quite lovely."

The king watched her quietly for a moment. "I'm… glad to be of service. It was the least I could do." They danced a bit more, their movements taking them closer to the young Lionel and his exhausted partner. Somewhere someone dropped a large platter sending a dozen goblets clattering across the floor. Another guffaw of laughter. Kyana didn't look around, but she hoped it wasn't Ira.

"If you ever get tired of the quiet," the king spoke over the tumult. "Come for a visit. You'll always be welcome, and we never lack for noise."

Kyana could not help it. She laughed. She did not expect the king of Neira to be like this. Pleasant. Kind. She could feel that soft warmth beating against her heart, begging for entry.

*Always welcome in Castle Lyist? Ha! If only he knew. He would feel far differently.* Kyana's smile faded, and that warmth against her heart pulled back, going cold.

He would have her killed.

She looked away.

"What's the matter?" the king asked, watching her change, retreating back into herself. She did not have the chance to answer. The young knight beside them gave a fantastic stumble that sent him knocking into Kyana. He tried to catch himself on the table next to her but only succeeded in postponing his fall by a few seconds. He hit her shoulder, and the butt of his sword slammed into Kyana's side.

"Slow down you fool," the king snapped, catching Lionel by the arm before he did any more damage.

"I'm sorry, my lord!" Lionel said hastily, red face quickly finding an even deeper level of maroon.

"Apologizes to Kyana, you ran into her,"

"Of course," the young knight turned to her, face full of shame and eyes darting to the floor as he bowed. "Apologies, my lady."

Kyana was about to correct him, she was no lady, but was interrupted by a stabbing pain that ran up her side. Instead, she nodded at the boy in acceptance, and he and his partner moved off.

"Are you alright?" the Lystad asked, watching her face.

"I'm fine," she answered but avoided his eyes. She held her hand against her side as inconspicuously as possible and leaned against the table. "I think I'm done dancing."

"Of course," the king said, "Would you like to sit down?"

"Actually, I'll turn in for the night," she said, but her voice was a little too high, and another shock of pain ran through her side. She winced.

"Kyana, are you alright?" The Lystad caught her arm before she could turn away. He looked down to the hand at her side. His eyes narrowed.

"I'm fine," she said hastily, but he ignored her. He reached out and gently pulled back her fingers. A bright red was slowly seeping into the side of Kyana's green dress. The king let out a hiss between his teeth.

"That clumsy idiot."

"It's fine, he didn't mean to." Kyana shook her head.

The king caught the arm of a passing knight. "I'll return shortly," Lystad told him. "I have a few matters to attend to. Keep the feast lively." The knight nodded, smiled to Kyana, and then continued to sweep across the floor.

"What are you doing?" Kyana asked, as the Lystad took her arm, and began ushering her through the crowd.

"Ira!" The king barked as she passed by with an empty tray in hand.

"Yes, my lord?" Ira asked, stopping immediately at the call.

"Kyana's not feeling well,"

"I'm sorry to hear that," Ira said, looking worriedly to Kyana. "Would you like me to escort her back to her chambers?"

"No, I'll do that," the king said to Kyana's surprise. "Do you know where Augustine might be at this hour?"

"I'm not sure… but I can find out."

"The lower town," Kyana said.

"What?"

"He said he would be in the lower town this evening," Kyana repeated, pressing her hand into her side, wincing as she tried to slow the blood. "Checking on patients."

"I can find one of his assistance," Ira looked up to the Lystad. "They should know which house he his visiting."

"Good," Lystad said. "Send one to retrieve him. Have him meet us in Kyana's chambers at once."

"Yes, my lord." Ira nodded and gave Kyana a smile before darting out a side door.

"Lystad, what are you doing?" Kyana asked, worry cutting at her, mixing with the pain in her side.

"*Lystad...*" He scowled at the name as he led her out the door of the great hall which was pulled open by two guards. It swung slowly closed behind them and muffled the sounds of music and laughter. They moved down the hall, passing a few more guards who nodded but said nothing. The sound of the feast faded slowly behind them as they continued forward.

"That's your name, isn't it?"

"Yes, but I don't like it when you say it," he answered. Kyana opened her mouth, but all that came out was a little whimper.

"Kyana?" The king stopped.

"I'm fine," she said, pulling out of Lystad's grip and took another determined step. Another shot of pain wrenched up her side and down her leg, causing her to stumble and catch herself against the wall.

"Yes... you keep saying that." She looked back to see the king of Castle Lyist, the lord of Neira Kingdom, his majesty himself, rolling his eyes like a child.

"Did you just roll your eyes at me?" Kyana asked. She could not help it. A smile curled her mouth. "That wasn't very *kingly* of you."

"Well, you are being unreasonable. Besides, as you have pointed out," he said stepping up behind her and pulled one of her arms around his shoulder. "You are no citizen of mine, and I am no king of yours." Kyana felt his arm under her shoulder and the other at the back of her knees. By the time she realized what he was doing, she could not pull away. Instead she grabbed his shoulder for support as he lifted her into his arms.

"Put me down!" she yelped.

"Oh please, you can barely walk," the Lystad lifted her a little higher and continued down the hall with ease. "It will be much faster this way." The pain in Kyana's side throbbed, but it was no longer shooting through her. The humiliation of being carried made her woozier than any pain. The Lystad glanced down and chuckled.

"There is no need for that face, we're almost there." She fell into an irritated silence and watched him. His blue eyes were bright and clear, only slightly touched by drink. They crinkled at the corners, just like they had that day he stared her down with ease. He started up a spiral staircase without hesitation or trouble. He had lost his gold band somewhere back at the high table, allowing his black hair to fall unchecked around his forehead. He had a handsome face. Clear olive skin, free of scar or blemish, with a sharp jawline that carved elegantly down to his chin. Yes, a very handsome face. He had a very handsome soul. He felt her scrutiny and glanced back down at her.

"What?" he asked.

"You... are not what I was expecting." The drink must have hit Kyana harder than she knew.

"Oh? What were you expecting?" he asked, taking the steps slowly, gaining one floor, and then a second before continuing down the hallway.

"A self-absorbed, ignorant, evil, jackass."

The Lystad almost dropped her with how hard he began to laugh. He ended up leaning his back against the stone wall, feet planted, to balance himself. He laughed for a long while, the sound echoed off the stone walls, filling the quiet with its boisterous noise.

"That... that was unexpected," he said after catching his breath.

"I told you Wybert taught me how to swear. Besides, words don't take effort," Kyana said, rubbing her eyes. She was suddenly exhausted. "It takes far more strength to withhold them."

"True," the king said, continuing back down the hall. "So, you don't think me a self-absorbed, ignorant, evil, jackass?"

Kyana thought a moment, and a smile tugged her lips. "Well... I don't think you're evil."

The king laughed again, but he continued to walk. "You have a mouth on you, don't you?"

"You going to take my head for it?" Kyana snapped. She was getting sleepier by the minute.

The king shook his head, inky hair flowing back and forth with the movement. "No, no, I think not. Besides... it would only be treason if you were one of my citizens. As you've pointed out… you are not. So no, you can keep your head where it is."

"Well thanks, that's ever so kind," Kyana said and yawned. Drowsiness was taking its toll… at least she thought it was drowsiness. Kyana's eyelids started to droop.

"Kyana?" the king's voice spoke loudly in her ear, and he jostled her in his arms. "Kyana, stay awake now."

"Uh?" she mumbled, looking up at him from under weak lids.

"You're losing some blood." Kyana looked down to see a good section of her gown now drowned in red. It seeped in a slow but determined widening circle, like a ripple in a lake that moved in slow motion. But this was not water. "I'd prefer you stayed awake until Augustine arrives. Besides, we're here." He pushed open a door and swept into the chambers Kyana had been staying. He gently propped her on a chair and knelt by her side.

"Hey." He snapped his fingers in front of her eyes as they started to droop and her head began to loll. "Kyana, stay awake," his voice was level, even, and full of authority, but his blue eyes looked worried. He glanced down at the side of her gown and grimaced. Kyana frowned. His eyes continually darted to the door, as if the practitioner would magically appear.

"What is that?" she asked, waving a finger at his face. His mixed blue eyes followed it briefly, before waving it away and looking back down to her side. "Are you… are you worried?"

"Well, I can't have my guest of honor die from a dance, now, can I?" He grinned, but it was too tight and strained against his lips.

Kyana chuckled, but it turned into a hiss as another sharp pain went through her side. The king went straight to the cabinet and pulled out a few towels. He knelt by her side and applied pressure to her broken wound.

"Ira, where are you?" he mumbled under his breath. Kyana was drunk, woozy, and felt her consciousness slipping from her. A mere day ago, she would have been terrified to close her eyes, or even be in the same room as the man before her. Hell, just earlier that day. Now she felt quite at peace with the idea. To him, she was a simple girl who needed help. That was all. As long as he thought that, she would be completely safe. The idea made her a little sad, but she could not put her finger on why. Her eyes started to droop once more.

"Ah, no, you don't," Lystad snapped his fingers in front of her face again, and when that didn't work, he barked her name. "Kyana!"

"What?" She was getting irritated now. Couldn't he see she was exhausted?

"You need to stay awake until Augustine gets back," he repeated. "We need him to stitch you back up."

Kyana sighed and leaned back in the chair, rubbing her eyes. She gave a great yawn and looked down at the Lystad. He was grinning again.

"What now?" she asked.

"You're bleeding... all over... and you are yawning..." He shook his head in amazement. "Does nothing scare you?"

*Yes.* She thought, looking down at him and noted, not for the first time, those lovely eyes. *Something most certainly scares me.*

A knock came to the door.

"Come," the king barked. Augustine entered with Ira and Lilly close behind, arms full of medical tools and towels. "Augustine," the king sounded relieved.

"What's the trouble, my lord?" he asked, and then his eyes fell on Kyana. His eyes flew open wide. "My dear girl, what happened?"

"Sir Lionel happened." Kyana could hear the anger in Lystad's voice and suddenly felt very nervous. "The moron knocked into her."

"Oh, hell," Augustine roughly pulled back the king's fingers to examine the damage. "I'll have to take a better look at the wound to be sure.... But I think you tore every single one of your stitches." He looked up at Ira. "Could you grab some warm water from the kitchens and more towels? And tell Hilda to hurry up. I'll need her help with stitching."

"Yes, sure," Ira darted out of the room.

"I'm going to need to take a clearer look at the wound," Augustine told Lilly, who had been watching the blood spreading on Kyana's side with wide and terrified eyes. She nodded to Augustine as he spoke, stepping up beside Kyana, trembling hands already working at the laces on her dress. Augustine's eyes darted pointedly towards the king.

"I'll leave you to it, then," the Lystad said, getting to his feet. Kyana watched him go, barely noticing as Lilly tugged at the uncooperative ties at the back of her dress. Her eyes traveled down to the hands that hung by his sides. They were covered in blood. Her blood. Her stomach churned at the sight, and she quickly looked away. "Rest now."

"Is that an order?" Kyana's words were fading into a whisper, but she knew he heard her when he rolled his eyes.

"Let's not start that again," he said, slipping out the door. The door closed with a creak and a snap.

The rest of the evening passed with the practitioner's attention, Ira darting around to collect tools, Lilly helping undress and redress, and at least an hour of cleaning and re-stitching. Augustine's elusive assistant Hilda (a beefy woman in her forty-sixth year with lank brown hair) arrived after Kyana had been stripped of her dress, and hovered around her, helping with the painful work of re-stitching. Ira had to get back to her duties, but she had squeezed Kyana's hand before she left. The work went on. Kyana did not mind, her mind was elsewhere. She had left it behind. Not at the high table with its prying questions and drunken knights. Not on the dance floor with the watching eyes, or colorful spinning gowns. Not at the tables piled high with food that filled the room with a sweet and salty haze. It was not even with the stabbing pain in her side. It was left somewhere down that stone hallway, with a laughing boy king, and shining blue eyes.

# CHAPTER 16

His hands were shaking under the flow of cold water. He scrubbed at them, tugging at each finger as if trying to yank the offending digit from his hands. It would not come off. The bright red, slowly creeping to a dark murky brown as it dried into the little cracks in his palms. They branched out like some bloody roots of a dead tree. But it was not the blood of a tree, it was the blood of a girl. It was Kyana's, and he could not get it off. Not all of it anyway.

Damian was alone in his chambers, with a pitcher full of water, and a bowl that he had been working at for a good ten minutes already, to little avail. He had wanted to clean up before heading back down to the feast, but as he started working at the blood on his hands, he found the job far more daunting than he originally planned.

He had blood on his hands before. Lots of it. The blood of animals he had hunted, deer, and birds. One time, to his father's great delight, he took down a wild boar. That celebrating went on for days, with his father sloshing wine in all directions, proudly shouting that his boy was now a man.

He had the blood of his opponents during tourneys, the blood of wounded friends, all kinds of red and red splashed up his hands, and all was difficult to wash away, but this was different somehow. This made him sick.

Damian scrubbed furiously at his own fingers with a sponge, pouring on more water that did little to wash away the redness. His pulse was raised, and his breath came too short and fast for him to find any true oxygen. He watched as the image of his own hands began to blur, and he had to plant his feet to keep himself from teetering.

What the hell was wrong with him? He was never the kind to become squeamish around blood. He was not some fainting lady during battle tourneys. He was not some seven-year-old version of himself during his first hunt either. He was as grown a man as his two and twenty years would allow, and blood was no longer an issue.

Until now.

Damian finally gave up on the last mild splashes of red and sat down on the edge of his large four poster bed. He tried to slow his breathing, taking his time to let it in his nose and out his mouth. When that did not work, he gave up all his private pride and leaned forward, putting his head between his knees and cupping the back of his neck with trembling hands.

What the hell was wrong with him?

Perhaps it was the combination of the blood and the few drinks he had at the high table. Yes. Maybe that was it. But somewhere deep in his mind, it felt like his consciousness was shaking its head.

*That's not it boy. Try again.* It seemed to say.

Damian did not want to try again. He just wanted to stop feeling sick.

*So much.* He thought to himself, eyes on the floor between his feet, stomach churning. *How could one woman go through so much?* The worst part was how she had spoken of it in such a matter-of-fact way.

*Why, yes, I live alone. Family? No, they all died. Parents? Yes, them too. Oh, second father as well. Very dead, yes. My, my, isn't this a lovely quail?*

The only time she broke that composure of hers was when she spoke of Wybert the Wanderer. *I called him Bert.* When she told Neander how he had died in her arms, Damian had seen the pain there. Even that pain was veiled, though. Veiled ever so thinly behind anger she shot towards Neander, but Damian suspected that was more to shut him up. He wondered about that. Wondered if the Silver Knight could have really just been a friend, or if there was something more to it. Something more profound to bring such intense pain. Or perhaps it was just a more recent loss. A fresh wound not yet healed over into a scar.

Family, second family, and friend. And she watched it all. Gods. With that much loss, Damian wondered how the poor girl carried on so well. Then again, she was not carrying on all *that* well. Alone in the woods. Surrounding herself with as much nothing as she possibly could. The girl was offered a place in one of the most wealthy and successful kingdoms in all the realm, if

Damian did say so himself, and refused it without a second thought. In fact, she seemed scared to stay, confused by friendship and terrified by kindness. Perhaps that was it. Maybe she was just so familiar with loss that the mere idea of once more having something to lose...

To Damian's great relief, nausea began to pass, and he straightened up. He took a deep, grateful breath, and looked down at his hands. They were mostly cleaned. Just a few splotches and creases were dyed a red-brown tinge, but he scowled at it all the same. He got up, strode across the large room, and opened one of the drawers. He pulled out a pair of warm black gloves. He was glad the evening had been cold, making this little addition to his wardrobe a little less noticeable. He slid them on, covering the discolorations, to his great relief.

Damian had half a mind to simply turn and fall on the bed, going directly to sleep, but there was a feast going on downstairs. One where he would surely be missed. Seeing as it was celebrating the creation of his kingdom and all.

Damian sighed, casting one last mournful glance at his bed, before sweeping out the door, his hands securely hidden in soft leather.

# CHAPTER 17

*"Will you miss me?"*

Kyana was back in the forest. Wybert was smiling and dying in her arms. Blood, dark and thick, was filling the lap of the green dress she wore. She tried to use the endless folds of fabric to stem the equally endless flow of blood, but it was no use. She held her hand over the man's torn stomach, willing something to happen. Willing there to be a light. Willing the wound to heal, but nothing happened. She did not know how. She was never taught to use magic in that way. There was no one left to teach her. Wybert just smiled.

"Will you miss me?" he asked once more, hand touching her cheek. His voice was odd, echoing like it was from somewhere far away. "Or will you come with me?"

"Come with you?" Kyana asked distracted, still trying to stop the blood which had spilled out over her lap and begun to flood the ground around them, surrounding her like some thick and dark lake. It reflected the dream moon in eerie slow ripples. Wybert's fingers slid from her face, leaving a trail of red against her cheek. "What do you mean?"

"You know what he means," the new voice, Ira's voice, came from above Kyana. She turned, to ask her for help, but Ira was nowhere to be found. Instead, she found the Lystad. He was wearing that long brown cloak with that coat of arms. It dipped and floated, hem staining in the lake of blood. The golden band was back around his head, and for some reason, Darkheart hung from his scabbard. She knew that could not be true. Knew that Darkheart had been taken by the thieves when they ran, and yet there it was. His expression was blank, and his blue eyes looked black in the darkness. Kyana looked back down at Wybert, but he was gone. There was nothing but her, her dress, and the blood that still flooded from somewhere. It took Kyana a moment to realized that she was now the one bleeding. It poured from an open gash in her side, the spot where the hireling's blade had struck her, but not only from there. The brand on her left arm had broken open. Blood seeped down from the dragon's name like red tears. It slunk down her arm and dripped slowly off her fingers and into the ever-growing pool of blood. Kyana looked back up to the Lystad who was now reaching out to her.

"Will you come with me?" he asked, in that same far off echo that Wybert had.

Kyana began to reach for the hand but then froze in horror. His hand was covered in blood. Her blood. It splashed all the way up to his elbow. She also realized that Darkheart was not harmlessly hanging from his side but was in his hand, and it too was bloody.

"No," Kyana said, beginning to crawl back through the blood, away from the young king. "Get away from me. Stay away!"

The Lystad followed her, blank expression never wavering. His tall boots splashed through the deepening pool of blood. A few more steps, and it began to fill his boots, but it did nothing to slow him down. The coat of arms drew closer, and Darkheart started to rise in his grip. She knew he meant to finish the job he started.

Kyana screamed and crawled faster, but the pool made it difficult. She slipped and splashed down into the liquid, her heavy dress yanking her deeper. Her world went red, and she could not breathe.

*I'm going to die.* She thought, as the red turned to black and her lungs screamed in her chest. But she was able to claw herself out, gasping desperately for air, trickles of blood sliding down her face.

When she looked around, the Lystad was gone, and she was alone. She took another look, and the blood was gone as well. She sat in her usual pants and loose-fitting shirt, all clean, with no wounds, no scars, no weapons of any kind. She did not need them here. She heard a low rumbling sound. It started small, and grew into a thunder, strong enough to shake the ground. Kyana knew that sound well and nearly cried with relief.

*He's here.* She thought, staggering to her feet and beginning to run towards the sound. *Oh, thank you gods, he is here.* He was here, and everything would be okay. He would never leave her. He would always love her. He was going to save her. *He is here. He is here. Thank the gods he is—*-

Kyana woke to a knock on her chamber door. Kyana glanced around, blinking away fading visions of the forest. Her room slowly came into focus around her. A sweet morning breeze whistled lightly through her half-open window, ruffling the curtains that hung around her bed. It was such a soft, lulling motion that Kyana nearly slipped straight back to sleep. Then a second knock came to her door, followed by a timid voice.

"Miss," Lilly's voice was muffled through the heavy door. "Are you awake, miss? May I come in?"

"Yes, come," Kyana answered, sitting up and rubbing her eyes roughly with the palm of her hand. She gave a great yawn as the handmaid slipped through the door, a small tray of food in hand.

"Good morning, miss," Lilly said sweetly, closing the door behind her and turning to face Kyana as she dropped her hands to her lap. "I thought you might like some—" The girl cut off suddenly, watery eyes widening as she looked at Kyana.

"What's wrong?" Kyana asked, looking around her and seeing nothing but the small section of wooden floor that separated the bed from the stone wall.

"Oh, n-n-nothing miss," the girl said hastily, shaking off whatever was on her mind, and smiling instead. "I thought you might like some breakfast."

"Breakfast would be very nice," Kyana said, starting to slip out of bed, wincing as she did so. Her stitches were strong and thick and tugged rather sharply against newly opened skin.

"Wa — no Miss stop that!" Lilly said as Kyana got to her feet.

"Why?" Kyana asked finding the girls panicked hand gestures between Kyana and the bed, rather amusing.

"Augustine told me you shouldn't get up. We had to resew most of your stitches last night. You shouldn't be moving around, miss."

Kyana laughed.

"Not you too," she said, stepping forward. "Trust me. I'm fine. I'm a quick healer." She took the tray out of the hand Lilly was not using to point helplessly to the empty bed and rumpled sheets. It was a beautifully set plate. Perfectly sliced apples encircled a pile of strawberries, grapes, and chunks of cheese. There were also a few thick slices of bread, with freshly churned butter and a goblet full of what looked like cow's milk. Kyana frowned at the strange liquid but decided to taste it anyhow. The thing that caught her eye most was not the food at all, but a small slip of paper which had been tucked beneath the goblet. Kyana plucked It up between two long fingers and read the short message written in a sharp and slanted hand.

*Good Morning, Kyana.*

*Hope you are well.*

*My best of wishes,*

*- Ira*

Kyana smiled. That flicker of warmth budded in her chest once more. It was coming easier and easier with every passing moment.

"You two friendly miss?" Lilly asked, leaning in a little, reading the note.

"Kyana."

"Miss?" Lilly blinked curiously.

"Kyana, not miss," Kyana said, folding the note and slipping the wish in her pocket. "I am no miss, nor lady."

"Oh, yes, sorry... Kyana."

Kyana waived away the girl's apology and sat down at the wide wooden table.

"Have you eaten yet, Lilly?"

"No, not yet miss, busy morning I'm afraid." Lilly blinked again when Kyana pulled up a second chair and motioned to it. When the girl made no moves, Kyana tapped the set.

"Come join me." When the girl still did not move, Kyana tapped the seat again. "Come now, I can't eat this all on my own."

Lilly hesitated before moving forward, slowly sinking down into the seat. Kyana took one piece of bread and handed the other out to Lilly, who took it with tentative fingers.

"No one ever asked you to come eat with them before?" Kyana asked, taking a bite out of the bread, which was still warm and softened with that sweet butter. It made Kyana's taste buds sing in her mouth.

"No one I've worked for," Lilly said, nibbling at her own piece. Kyana had such a vivid image of a mouse with its little fingers wrapped around some cheese that she had to hold back a bark of laughter.

"You don't work for me." Kyana shook her head and took another bite. It only seemed to get better.

"No... but I work for the king," Lilly said, reaching out for a piece of apple, waiting for Kyana to give an insistent nod before she took any. "And his orders were clear."

"They being?"

"To get you whatever you need or want," she said, finally beginning to relax in her chair, tensions spilling from her shoulders as they started the rhythmic act of conversation. She chased a bit of apple with a chunk of cheese.

"Whatever I want?" Kyana flashed that long-lost grin of the odd little thing. "Alright, then, I'll have a knight, tall, dark-haired, and handsome."

Lilly laughed so abruptly, she nearly choked on her piece of cheese.

"Well," Lilly chuckled, wiping her mouth on the back of her sleeve. "You would have no lack of volunteers. They all seem quite taken with you."

*They are all taken with the idea of me.* Kyana thought of correcting her but decided against it.

"Oh?" was all she said, picking up the glass of milk and giving it a sniff.

"Yes. Very." Lilly shifted in her seat, breaking into a knowing little smile. "You know... the knights are not the only ones that seem taken."

"If you're talking about the practitioner, I... don't actually think that's the case." Kyana sipped at the thick white liquid. It was cold and smooth and full of a flavor utterly unfamiliar to her, but not entirely unpleasant. "He's been very kind. Gentle in his rough sort of way, but I believe that is all there is to it."

The girl smiled. "I'm not sure mi — Kyana, that you realize how much regard you create in those around you."

Kyana was well aware of this. Wybert himself had scolded her for blindly moving through the few taverns they stayed, not noticing the flirtations or invitations of the men around her. Not because he wanted her to accept any of these invitations. He would sooner kill those men than to allow them a hand on her. No, he was angry because they wanted to lay a hand on her, and she seemed blind to it.

"The only thing more dangerous to a woman than a wanting man with no honor is a drunken wanting man with no honor," he would say, frowning at her with that severe and scarred face. "Keep your head. Open your eyes. Know the dangers. Gods girl, you act like you've never known a man's attention before."

She never told Wybert the truth of this. That she never had. But over the years she had grown a better understanding of a wanting man, both honorable and dishonorable, drunken or sober. Wanting was wanting and Kyana had observed for any sign that Augustine was showing interest or desires... but she saw none. She saw nothing more in the older man's soft gray eyes as he so dutifully patched her wounds, she sitting half naked before him. She saw nothing but kindness and an overwhelming amount of curiosity. And why not? Kyana was a strange woman from a strange place, who continued to do strange things, at least, strange to all of them. But curiosity did not mean wanting, and interest did not equal desire.

"I don't believe he feels that way," Kyana said, taking another sip and leaning back in her chair. No nothing but curiosity, and he was not the only one. Ira was especially curious... but even more than that, the girl seemed drawn to Kyana in a way like no one else. In ways that far outstripped simple fascination. Kyana mulled over this while taking another cold sip of milk, and suddenly became very curious about Ira of Castle Lyist, and what secrets she may be hiding behind those wishing eyes.

"Actually," Lilly said still smiling. "I was referring to the King Damian."

"The Lystad?" Kyana eyes shot open wide. "No, no, I don't think so."

Lilly shrugged and reached for another slice of an apple. "Perhaps not... but you two did make quite the pair on the dance floor last night. Everyone was talking about..." she trailed off as Kyana shifted uncomfortably in her seat. Lilly cleared her throat, "talking about all the delicious food there was to eat."

Kyana smiled, grateful for the girls awkward segue. They ate in a comfortable silence for a time, Kyana content to watch the serving girl tucking into their shared meal. Soon Kyana's mind wandered. She wondered about that girl. She thought about the look of surprise on her face when Kyana had asked to sup with her. Such a sweet face, with such secrets to hide...

Kyana's eyes trailed down to the girl's foot, which she found curled around one of the chairs four legs. The brand was hidden under the scuffed brown slippers she wore. Kyana looked up to the girl who was now helping herself to more bread and spreading an alarming amount of butter that melted almost instantly and began to drip down the crust.

"I'm sorry about raising my voice the other day," Kyana said.

"Humm?" The girl asked, taking a bite out of the bread and not noticing when a small trickle of butter slid down her chin.

"Yesterday," Kyana continued. "Before the feast. I raised my voice at you. I believe I frightened you, and I apologize."

Lilly looked up from her bread, which was now slowly dripping into her lap, but she didn't seem to notice this either. Her eyes grew even more watery.

"No apology necessary," Lilly said, her shy smile back on her face. Apparently, she did not get many apologies either. "It was a sticky spot we were both in."

"Do you know of others in this castle, in the same sticky place?"

Lilly shook her head.

"I only know of you and me," Lilly said. "It's not like we would all start spending time together or try to get in contact if there were either."

"No, of course, not." Kyana nodded, swirling the milk, watching the thick white liquid pull to the sides of her glass. She thought about the woman by her cart, surrounded by all her beaded jewelry. The woman who had given Kyana a Faithful's blessing. A woman who had her own secrets. "That would be dangerous."

"Not to mention, stupid," the girl said, brushing off the crumbs from her apron and wiping her chin. "If there are any other... people like us... well, they are all hiding. As they should be." Kyana bit her tongue on that last comment and kept her retort to herself.

"How do you get along?" Kyana asked.

"Keeping my secret?" Lilly shifted in her seat, voice lowered, and she began to look a little uncomfortable again. "Easily enough. I just make sure I wash up on my own and check that no one is around when I change my shoes. But it's rather easy for me, having it in such a place." Lilly nodded to Kyana's arm. "How about you? How do you fare?"

Kyana shrugged. "It's easy keeping a secret when there's no one to spill it to."

"That's right," Lilly said, remembering. "You live alone." Kyana nodded. "Is it nice? Out there?" Lilly asked. "I've spent most of my life inside these walls."

"Very," Kyana said, an echo of laughter dancing at the back of her mind. "A little quiet sometimes. But very nice."

"You have to go back soon, I hear."

"Yes."

"You really have to go?"

"I really can't stay." Kyana tapped her forearm, and Lilly nodded.

"Although," Lilly said. "If you wanted to stay, I'm sure we could do something."

"Something?" Kyana asked, and a sinking feeling tugged her belly.

"To take care of that, I mean." Lilly gestured to Kyana's hidden brand. "I've not had the need... but I've heard rumors of a place. A place with closed lips," Lilly leaned in, her voice fading to a whisper. "To get rid of it. It hurts. Burns, or cuts, stuff like that. It'll leave a nasty scar, but it means you could stay. If you wanted."

Kyana resisted the hot acid that tried to flood up her throat. She understood not choosing to have the mark, refusing it for their own safety, but to remove it from their skin with a knife or hot iron... it was sickening.

Kyana forced a smiled. "Thank you for the idea, but I think I'll take it with me when I go."

Lilly nodded but looked disappointed.

"I'll be sad to see you go, Miss." Lilly smiled. "It's been nice to meet someone who... understands our particular situation."

Kyana nodded and did not bother correcting her over the "miss" this time. Lilly glanced out the window, seemed to note the path of the sun, and then jumped to her feet.

"Oh, goodness. I better help you get ready!"

"Get ready?" Kyana frowned. "For what?"

"Didn't I say?" Lilly clapped a hand over her mouth, eyes going wide. "Oh, no, I guess I didn't. The king requested a visit. He sent me ahead with breakfast and to let you know he'd be here."

Kyana groaned. The last thing she wanted to do was get dressed and washed like she had for the feast. Again, she didn't know the etiquette for receiving royalty.

"Please don't tell me I need to wear a dress," Kyana said.

"No! No!" Lilly darted to the messy bed and began to flatten and tuck in the sheets. "He expects you to be resting. I'll actually get in trouble if he finds you out of bed at all." She turned her wide eyes towards Kyana, who waived away her fear with an open hand.

"I won't breathe a word of it." Kyana pulled herself out of the chair, as Lilly finished turning down the bed and darting to the cabinet. She pulled open one of the drawers and pulled out a blue silken cloth that Kyana looked at with suspicion. "It's not a dress, I swear," Lilly said, shaking it open and holding it out for Kyana. "It's a sleeping robe."

Kyana shrugged and let Lilly slip it over her shoulder. She then followed Lilly's hasty ushering back to bed. Kyana crawled under the sheets while Lilly went back to the dresser and pulled out a brush and a small rounded glass.

"Urmmm… may I fix that for you?" Lilly asked, stepping up to the side of the bed and holding up the brush.

"Fix what for me?" Kyana asked. Lilly hesitated and handed Kyana the looking glass. Kyana held it up, blinked at her reflection, and started to laugh. Her thick auburn hair was mushed so thoroughly by sleep that the back and left side stood up in an extravagant mess. "Why didn't you say something sooner?" Kyana asked through more spouts of laughter.

Lilly raised her hands in an "I don't know" gesture.

"Yes please," Kyana said, handing back the looking glass and turning so Lilly would have easier access. "Please fix that."

# CHAPTER 18

Damian arrived just as Lilly finished clearing up the dishes from breakfast and wiped down the table. She had bowed low to him, shot Kyana a nervous glance, then darted out the door. The nervous glance did not really surprise Damian. He had known Lilly most of his life. They had not really spent any time together.... as a matter of fact, they had never had a full conversation. She worked and lived in the castle, but it was a relatively large place, and their paths did not cross often. As far as nervous looks go... well that just came with the job.

"Good morning," he said, stepping forward towards the bed that Kyana sat.

"Morning," she said, looking up at him. She looked amazingly good for having nearly bled out the night before. Her face was still pale, and her eyes looked a little tired, but otherwise she seemed perfectly healthy. She sat up against a stack of pillows, a soft blue night robe around her shoulder, and the covers tucked up tight around her waist. Her hair was hanging loose and long down her shoulders, piling in her lap like auburn water. Damian could not help but wonder if she always woke up that lovely. He shook the thought away.

"Can I help you?" Kyana asked, blinking those intense green eyes.

"I just wanted to check and see how you were doing." Damian pulled a chair from the table and sat down next to Kyana's bed, close enough to speak easily, but still far enough away for the sake of proper etiquette.

"I'm doing fine," Kyana said. "The bed arrest is hardly necessary."

Damian resisted the urge to roll his eyes with effort.

"You nearly passed out from loss of blood last night," he said, instead. "But you do look good."

"I heal quickly." She shrugged.

"Augustine has been mentioning that," he said, leaning back in his chair, and kicking up one foot to rest on his knee. "So, I'd say you'll have only a few days before you can start moving around again."

"A few more days?" Kyana's mouth fell open. "But I'm going home today."

The Lystad laughed. He noticed Kyana's expression and stopped abruptly.

"I'm afraid your little mishap yesterday has kicked your travel plans back a bit," he said an apologetic smile on his face. "I'm sorry to say, you're stuck with us for at least another nine or ten days."

Kyana's large eyes closed as she groaned.

Damian frowned, and a small twinge of disappointment cut at him from the girl's reaction.

"I know, I apologize," he said in a voice that sounded both playful and mocking. "But you'll be pleased to know Lionel has been appropriately punished for his inconveniencing you."

Kyana's head jerked up in surprise. "Punished? What do you mean punished?"

"Well, flogged, of course," the Damian said as if it was the most obvious thing in the world.

"What?!" Kyana jerked forward, eyes wide with horror.

"I thought you'd be pleased," he said, giving her an expression that was the pure picture of innocence.

"Pleased? Pleased?!" Kyana blubbered, eyes darting around for the proper words to encapsulate how she felt. "Are you *insane*?! Why, in blue hellfire, would I be *pleased*?"

Damian felt a smile slip slowly across his face, despite his best efforts to hold it back.

She was so ruffled. Eyes wide, mouth open, hands hovering in the air, seeming to anticipate the rant she was about to take, for it was going to be a long one. About how the poor kid had just bumped into her. How it was not his fault, and that such action never deserved such a severe punishment. How unfair that was. How she was fine and how dare he do such a thing, you *Lystad.*

But the rant faltered as she watched his smile slide into place.

"You're not insane." Kyana's hands slowly lowered as her eyes began to narrow into bright green slits. "You're playing with me."

Damian just smiled.

"That isn't funny," Kyana said, sinking back into her cushions, green eyes glaring.

"Come now," Damian said, dropping his foot to lean forward in his seat, elbows resting on his knees. "It was a little funny. Your face got all red. All that pent-up righteous indignation flaring in your eyes."

Kyana tried to keep up her steady glower, but to Damian's great delight, a smile broke through.

"You *are* an ass, aren't you?"

Damian paused for half a wide eyed second before bursting into laughter.

"Been talking to Ira, have you?" he asked, leaning back into his seat, eyes beaming.

"She visits from time to time," she answered.

"So, I gathered."

Kyana's eyes darted away from him, and Damian watched them go with curiosity and an odd twisting sensation in his gut that he could not quite understand yet.

She seemed to be debating something, mulling it over in her mind. Handling the thought, twisting it, contemplating it from all angles. He could almost see the question twirling around behind that auburn head of hers. When she finally looked back and opened her mouth, what came out was not what he expected.

"Do you know why Ira's eyes are so tired?"

"What?" Damian asked, trying to blink away his confusion.

"Her eyes," Kyana repeated as if it was the sanest question in the world. As if she was asking when dinner would be held that evening. "Why are they so wishing?"

Damian frowned. That was an odd question, but the women looked so serious. It was important to her somehow. An odd question for an odd woman. He tried his best to find the answer for her, recall what she might mean. *Old eyes? Wishing eyes?* He shook his head. "I'm sorry, I honestly don't know," Damian answered.

"Hum," was her only reply, but she smiled in thanks for his attempt. They fell into a comfortable silence broken only by a knock on the door.

"Come," Kyana answered.

"So how are we this mor— Oh, hello my lord," Augustine cut himself off, hesitating in the doorway. "I hope I'm not interrupting."

"No, not at all, Augustine," Damian said, getting to his feet and lightly brushing nonexistent dust from his pristine brown pants with equally pristine brown gloves. He had spent half the morning trying to wash the last stains of blood from the creases in his hands and had nearly finished the job. There was still a slight discoloration that he couldn't quite get no matter how much he worked at it. "I should actually be going."

He looked down at Kyana, still resting comfortably. "Now, I don't want you running off while I'm away. Augustine said it would be another ten days and another ten days it will be. I expect to see you again for dinner this evening if you are feeling up to it, of course." Kyana opened her mouth to answer, but Damian waived away her words before she could say them.

"Yes, yes, I know. Let me guess: Don't give me orders *Lystad*, you are no king of mine, bla, bla. Then instead," he said, reaching out a hand to her. "Do so as a friend."

Kyana blinked at the hand, waiting for it to disappear before her eyes or morph into some venomous creature ready to snack on her fingers. When it did neither, she lifted her hand tentatively and took it.

"Friends?" The word was meant as a statement but came as the softest, and most heartbreaking question. The look in her eyes as they turned back up to Damian's face was surprise, wonder and something else teetering on the precipice of belief.

"Good, then." Damian smiled, shaking her hand before letting it go and turning for the door.

"Take care of her, Augustine."

"You just keep Lionel away from her, and she'll be just fine, my lord!" Augustine called after his king's retreating back.

Kyana could hear the Lystad laugh all the way down the hall outside, echoing the cheerful sound off its stone walls.

# CHAPTER 19

The next ten days passed by faster than Kyana knew possible. Even while confined to her bed, her day was not allowed to be dull. Every morning she was woken by Lilly, who would spend the early parts of the day with her. The girl had grown quite comfortable by this point, eyes no longer afraid to meet hers, and words coming more easily to her lips. They had fallen quickly into a rhythmic routine that Kyana had grown quite fond. They would breakfast together, chatting about nothing important, until her duties called her away. She was not left alone for long, because Augustine checked on her constantly. Kyana decided this was less to do with her wound, and more to make sure she was staying in bed. Ira also took time from the kitchens for a quick visit now and then. Their conversations were not long but were always pleasant. Always full of laughter and smiles, never endless questions that dug up old pains.

The first evening, Lystad sent along Lilly with his regrets that he would be unable to join her for dinner because of various "kingly" duties. But after Augustine begrudgingly allowed her to be out of bed rest, Kyana spent every supper in front of an informal, yet extravagant, table with either a few knights, Ira, or both. Ira always brought the food, it was one of her primary duties after all, but that tended to be more of a pretense than anything. She was the king's childhood friend after all and was always invited to stay and sup with them.

There were no more feasts, no halls full of strangers dancing, but that was alright with Kyana. The group she dined with was quite boisterous enough. Usually Everett, Neander, Teller, and sometimes Cole and Simon, and on many occasions when he was not otherwise occupied, the king himself. All of which made for quite a party. The food was just as good as always, and every evening brought its own fun. Kyana's favorite night was spent with only Ira and the young Lystad. She watched them as they chatted with one another as old friends do. She was amazed by the ease of it all. Even the knights kept some sort of mild formality between themselves and the king unless of course mead had been involved. Ira was different. Alone, she spoke to her king as if he were a brother. No disrespect, just simple ease. The type of comfort gained from knowing another person so incredibly well that you know precisely what the other will say before they speak. Damian was the same. They were not a kitchen servant and king. They were friends first, before all else, and this fact struck Kyana. It was lovelier than any moonlit river or meadow of roses. It was a path of friendship carved deep by years of walking side by side. It reminded her of times passed by, and the most beautiful thing she had ever seen. As unexpected as all the rest.

As ten days drew to a close, Kyana found herself wishing that things were different. That she did not have to go. Of course, she knew that she must, so when Augustine put on the last bandage and told her it was safe to travel, she had reached out and hugged the gruff man without a second thought. He seemed startled at first but soon returned the hug with such strength that Kyana lost her breath.

"I will be sad to see you go," he spoke at her ear, in a voice even gruffer than usual. It ground like rocks in her ear.

"And I will be sad to leave," Kyana answered, pulling away.

"But leave you must?" Augustine asked, and Kyana nodded. Augustine nodded as well and began to rummage in his bag. "Well, nothing too strenuous if you can help it, and here, let me send you with a few things to help you take care of it. It's travelable, but you still must keep an eye on it." He pulled out a small leather bag, with a thin shoulder strap. He filled it with a few extra bandages and a few vials of that tingling minty paste that Kyana had grown to like.

"Thank you, Augustine," Kyana said, taking the bag and smiling.

"It has been my pleasure, dear." He hugged her once more.

She stayed only one more night in the castle. The last evening, she spent dining with Lilly and Ira in her chambers, surrounding the decoratively carved table in her room. The young king had been called off to a neighboring town for one reason or another that Kyana did not care to know. He had sent his sincere regrets that he would not be there to see her off.

"He wanted to ask if you might stay until he returned, so he could offer a proper goodbye," Ira had told her, leaning back into her chair. She pushed her now empty plate onto the table and flipped her long braid over her shoulder. "But then he changed his mind. He knew what your answer would be." Kyana smiled and nodded. She had smiled quite a lot these past days. It came easily to her face now, many times she did not even notice.

"It was a kind thought," Kyana said.

"He is a kind man," Lilly added, eyeing another piece of chicken as if it was taunting her to eat it.

"Yes," Kyana thought absently. "I'm beginning to think he is."

That changed nothing, however. She needed to go. This lovely city was no place for the likes of her. She had thought of asking Lilly to join her. The brand on her foot was just as deadly as the one on Kyana's arm, but she knew she would not. This castle was her home. Her entire world was here inside these walls and asking Lilly to leave would be like asking a flower to grow backward, a breeze to stop churning through the air, or Ira to stop grinning so broadly. It was not in their nature. So, when Kyana woke late in the afternoon of her last day in Castle Lyist, she prepared to leave alone.

The sun had already cut its path across the sky and filled her room with a bright and cheerful light, eliminating every gaudy wooden carving, which she would not miss so much. She laid in her bed a moment, enjoying the thick cushions and soft blankets. She had never been so comfortable in her life. Even the dull pain in her side seemed dim in this place of softness and sunlight. She wondered how long she could lay there in that moment. It was a good moment, she thought as she stretched. But moments fade. Her eyes fell on the dragon seal on the opposite wall. She sighed, flipped the covers aside, and got to her feet. She went to the cabinet, found her neatly folded pants and a new blue shirt, and put them on. They had been cleaned and smelled like flowers and soap as she pulled them over her head. She grabbed the little bag from Augustine and slung the strap securely over her shoulder. She checked the contents of her bag with its bandages and bottles and considered running down the kitchen to snag some bread for the journey. She would need to find some food. The small stash she had at home would have gone bad by now.

She thought about the feast and the bounty of fresh fruit and juicy quail. Her mind drifted back farther to the healthy buck they had left behind. It had simply been left to rot on that forest floor. Such a deer could have fed her for days, she thought irritably before pulling the bag over her shoulder. She was all set. Except for one thing. She checked the closet, but her bow was not there. She heard clanging noises and crossed the room to peer out the window. Down in the courtyard, she could see several knights practicing their swordsmanship. She squinted closer and smiled. It was Everett, Lionel, Teller, and Neander. One of them should know where her bow would be. She moved from the window, pulled open the heavy door, and fought the strong urge to look back as she closed it behind her. She swept down the hall, weaving in and out of scuttling servants and handmaids. She wondered if Lilly was somewhere in that stream of people scurrying off to do their duties. She would not mind another goodbye, although they had said their goodbyes the night before.

Lilly's watery eyes had grown even more watery as she waited by the door.

"Be safe out their mis- Kyana."

"Same to you, Lilly." Kyana had answered. "And be well in any and all."

"What?" Lilly blinked, confused.

"Never mind," Kyana said. "Good luck to you."

Lilly was not the only handmaid she had met over the past days. A few waved to her as she passed down the hall and towards the stairs. A few maids smiled and called her by name. It was so friendly. Warm, friendly, kind… there was a tugging inside her chest. A pain she could not wish away. With every step towards leaving the castle, it grew more painful. She pushed forward none the less. She could not allow these feelings to continue. She needed to put them aside, pack them away, she knew that. It was not the truth. It was not real. It was kindness from a lie, and Kyana knew the truth… but being here had been so… warm.

Guards opened a set of heavy doors, and she walked out into the sun. She blinked away the blinding light and moved towards the knights at their practices. They all called to her as they saw her approaching.

"Kyana!" they spoke with joy, their faces lighting up as she came closer.

"How are you, our little angel?!" Neander said, swaggering up and swinging his arm around her shoulder. His hair was in a flying mess, and his face flushed with exercise. "My dear..." He said, looking down at her clothes and bag around her shoulder. "You going somewhere?"

"I'm heading home."

"Wait, what?" Neander's face fell into a grand disappointment.

"But what about your wounds?" Everett asked.

"They'll finish healing at home as well as anywhere else."

"Did Augustine say it was alright?" Lionel asked, looking suspicious and guilty. Kyana nodded, and when Lionel's face fell into a deeper frown, she reached out and patted his arm.

"I'll be fine. You have nothing to feel guilty for." Lionel nodded but looked guilty all the same. Neander reached out and roughly rumpled his younger brother's hair. This succeeded in replacing his guilt-ridden expression with an irritated grimace. Satisfied, Neander turned back to Kyana.

"You sure you have to go now?" Neander asked, pouting like a needy puppy that was being ignored.

"Yes," Kyana said firmly. If she stayed any longer... she looked around at each of their faces... it may soon become too painful to leave. And there was no way she could stay. Not being what she was. All their sad face's, all their kindness, all their affection belonged to a girl they thought she was. If she stayed, she would be living as a lie, and the truth had a way of sneaking up on you. "Yes. I just came to ask about my bow and dagger. You took them from the woods?"

"Oh! Right! Sure thing!" Neander said, motioning back to the castle. "... did you happen to mention this to Ira... or his highness?"

Kyana nodded. "Explained to both and said goodbye to one."

"Right... right then," Neander turned to Lionel. "You know where they are right?" Lionel nodded. "Be a good boy and fetch um." Lionel scowled at the "be a good boy" comment but headed off to get them anyway. Neander turned back to her. "He'll be back in a moment. In the meantime," he wrapped his arm around her shoulder and walked her to a stack of hay that was not currently being used as targets. The others followed close behind, leaning on their dulled blades, or taking a seat on the hay bales beside them. "So, what are you going to do once you get home?"

"First," Kyana started, wondering why he was curious. "I'll need to go hunting. My food storage is low, so that needs to be fixed first. Then I'll need to check my home, make sure it's in a proper state."

"Your… food storage is small?" Neander asked, still smiling, but his voice seemed a little strained.

"Yes," Kyana said shrugging. She just said that. Why where the knights looking at her so oddly and exchanging glances with one another?

"What's your home like Kyana?" Everett asked.

"It's a small cave settled between a thicket and a thick lining of trees," she said, frowning. "It's a fair distance from here, near the forests where Kyar begins. I mentioned that before, I'm sure of it."

"Right… a cave." When Teller spoke, he sounded almost pained.

"Yes…" Kyana nodded. She had just said that as well. Why did they keep repeating things like they didn't believe her? Were they hard of hearing all of a sudden? They were watching her, almost with… that pity again. Kyana frowned.

"It's quite beautiful," she reassured them. "With the sun beaming through the trees, and the gold and greens… It's bright and warm. It's the second most beautiful place I have ever seen." Kyana looked at the castle with the sun shining off the amber bricks as the people bustling around so lively. Perhaps it was the third most beautiful place.

"I'm sure it is," Neander said grinning. "Perhaps, we could come and visit sometime."

"I don't know," Kyana tried to imagine them at her home. The Knights of Castle Lyist, knowing where she lived? "… how you would like it." Kyana shrugged.

"I'm sure we would love it!" Everett insisted.

Kyana was saved from answering by a whinnying sound. She looked up to see Lionel padding across the courtyard, her bow in his hands. Beside him walked Ira, leading the most beautiful horse Kyana had ever seen.

"Good day, Kyana!" Ira said through her ever-present grin.

"Good day, Ira," Kyana said.

"What?" she asked, stopping before her, holding the reins. "Were you going to leave without saying goodbye?"

"We said goodbye last night," Kyana said but was very glad to see her all the same.

"And one goodbye is good enough, is it then?" Ira planted a hand on her hip like a mother chastising a naughty child. Kyana could almost envision the apron and large wooden soup spoon in her hand and laughed. She was really going to miss this girl with the wishing eyes, perhaps most of all. She took her bow, dagger, and remaining arrows from Lionel and thanking him. She noted, as she slipped it into her belt, that the blade had been sharpened to perfection.

"What is this?" Kyana asked, motioning towards the horse. It was tall with a smooth black coat and a soft tan main. The tail which was also tan, flicked slowly side to side, almost brushing the ground. The horse gave a low snort and shook her elegant head, sending a small scattering of snot into the air.

"A gift from King Damian," Ira said, patting the horse on its long neck. "An apology for his not being able to say goodbye." Ira's eyebrows shot up suddenly. "You do know how to ride, yes?"

"She's beautiful. And yes, I do..." Kyana said, pulling her bow over her shoulder. "But I can't take her." Ira ignored this and continued.

"He changed his mind again."

"On what?"

"He sent word last night. He changed his mind and asks if you might again consider putting off your journey until you are completely healed." Kyana smiled but made no answer. "And he says if you still insist on going home you shouldn't have to walk."

"Well... I must go."

"Then, you also must take the gift."

Kyana shook her head but reached out to pet the horse's cheek. The horse had light brown eyes. Soft, warm, and watchful. She ran her fingers through the pale mane and over the gleaming black coat "She is unique."

"His majesty thought you two would make a nice fit."

"I can't keep her," Kyana shook her head again.

"Then, you'll just have to come back someday and return her," Neander said happily.

Kyana scratched behind the horse's ear. "What's her name?"

"Uh," Ira looked around at the knights, but they all shrugged. "I don't think she has one."

"It is bad luck to be unnamed," Kyana said, a frown tugging at her small lips.

"Looks like you're gonna have to pick one then."

Kyana thought a moment. She reached down, cupping the horse's chin in both hands, and raised her head up to look in her eyes. The horse looked back without hesitation. Animals tended to like her more than humans. They did not find her gaze quite as unsettling, and this horse was no different. She showed no fear, and she did not look away. It reminded Kyana of someone else… The horse pawed at the ground a few times, each movement an elegant pendulum swing of her long leg. Kyana looked down. She smiled to herself.

"Royal," she said, stroking her horses face. "Royal Toes."

"Royal Toes?" Neander asked, chuckling a little. "That's cute."

Kyana looked at the group around her. They were all smiles, all kindness. She knew she would truly miss them, and for a long time. She would miss them all. The warmth was leaving her, and her chest hurt with the absence, slowly growing cold.

"I wish…" Kyana trailed off slightly. "I wish things were different."

They looked confused, but for once they did not press for an answer. Kyana shook hands with the knights, but when she turned to Ira, her hazel eyes where sad. She stepped forward and wrapped the taller girl in her arms, hugging her tightly. Ira hugged her back, not dropping the horse's reins.

"Will you miss me?" Kyana asked, the words spilling from her before she knew that she wanted them said.

"Of course, I will," Ira mumbled into her shoulder. "It's been lovely having you. Kyana of the woods."

Kyana blinked. To be missed. Such a nice feeling. Nice… and painful. She pulled away and took the reins from Ira. She mounted Royal swiftly, waiving away Neander's offer of assistance. She said farewell and took one last look at the great castle. That place she had dreaded for so long. When others had nightmares of monsters and magic, she dreamed of this place and the horrors within. The people that burned, and the evil that infected every corner of its amber stone walls. But there had been no fire, and no evil. Just feasts… and ignorance. It was harder to be afraid when you are welcomed with a kind smile.

Kyana tapping her heals. Royal reacted instantly, starting at a slow trot. She continued through the arched walls of the great city. Each held its citizens, bustling, working, talking, in their almost musical rhythm. A rhythm that acted as the city's beating heart with its people pulsing swiftly around her. She passed it all, keeping her eyes on the outer gates.

Kyana soon was exiting the fourth wall of the castle, and out into the open. She looked upon the land spreading in all directions. The bright green grass seemed to shine in the light of the sun and rolled away in endless hills. It continued for miles and miles and cut only by the dirt road leading out from the castle and the raging river to her right. Beyond the smooth green hills to the left, there was the forest. Thick branches stretching up to the blue sky, and going so deep that the base of them held a cool dimness, as soft as twilight. So beautiful, so familiar. It was time. Time to go home. She breathed in the fresh air, the smell of freshly grown grass, and smiled. The forest, her haven of fluttering leaves, and songs of birds, the familiar quiet. Where she truly belonged. Where she could be herself. No more lies. No more hiding. The birds did not care about the brand on her arm. The trees did not mind. The sweet flowers and the smell of damp dirt did not give a damn who she was. That was the smell of freedom. Royal could smell it too. She snorted with excitement.

"Alright pretty one," Kyana said, leaning forward in the saddle. "Let's see how well you dance." Kyana tapped Royal's sides and whistled. Royal bolted forward eagerly.

*Home. Time to go home.*

# CHAPTER 20

"I'm gonna miss her!" Neander whined that evening, long after the king had returned from his various duties and the strange woman was long gone. After watching Kyana ride off out of sight, Neander had taken it upon himself to whimper at length about her departure. He even stomped his foot against the floor like a petulant child, threw back his head, hair flipping dramatically, to wail. He went on and on at volume, as if he the louder he whined, the more likely for her to turn around and come back. He, Everett, Teller, Ira, and Damian were relaxing in one of the many halls of the castle, sharing a few cups of cheer after supper to drown Neander's wows. Ira thought this was probably the most ludicrous remedy she had ever heard of, but brought them a flagon anyway, and did not refuse when they offered her a glass.

"We're all sad she left Neander," Everett said.

"She wasn't here long… really she wasn't, but there was just… something about her. You know what I mean?" Neander said, voice already beginning to slur. He waived a dramatic hand through the air, twisting it in circles to emphasize his drunken point. "You know?"

"I think I do," Teller said, smiling. "She was… unique… a little weird, but unique."

"I'm gonna miss that crazy lady!" Neander yowled, taking another swig from his glass.

"We know Neander."

"Ah, but you're probably relived," Neander said, leaning in and giving Ira's shoulder a little shove. "Aren't you Ira?"

"Would you please shut up?" Ira said, taking a drink of her own. Mead was not her favorite. Honestly a bit too sweet for her, but if the conversation kept running in this direction, she would happily drink anything. The knights were no stranger to the theory that Ira and Damian were an item. They used to whisper about it behind their backs, but after a short time, and realizing that no such relationship had ever been and would never be, they began to joke openly and with great gusto. Especially when alcohol was involved. Ira did not understand the humor of drunken boys. They were such children.

"We all saw it," Neander said, wiggling his eyebrows. "The sparks that were flying around those two."

"It was breaking your sweet little heart wasn't it?" Teller grinned, and Neander nodded.

"You should clean out your eyes, you're seeing things," Ira said, taking another large gulp and almost gagging. It was like drinking syrup.

She had seen the way Damian had looked at Kyana and had not been surprised. She was a lovely lady, no doubt about it. Damn near breathtaking. Any idiot could see that, and Ira had caught herself growing a little jealous of the women's sharp cheeks and long auburn hair, but not because of Damian. She was not relived to watch Kyana go, in fact, watching her go had made her feel ill. Ira spun her empty cup between her hands while remembering that day in the guest room. Kyana had looked at her with those eyes of green fire. An intensity Ira was sure she had never seen before... and yet...

Kyana had told Ira she had wishing eyes... She wondered how Kyana could have seen that. How much she could have known, or found out, by merely looking. No one else had seen it. Damian may have caught a glimpse once, but that was all. Ira thought she was pretty good at hiding it, but maybe... it was only because no one really looked. Kyana did. She looked, and she saw. In a few short days, Kyana had known more about Ira than any of these people who had spent years by her side. She would miss that very much.

*Wishing eyes.* She told Ira she had the same, and Ira hoped all her wishes came to pass.

"Hey," Neander leaned forward, snapping his fingers in front of Ira's face. "Ira!"

"What?" Ira said, jerking up slightly to wave off Neander's hand.

"You were gone there kid," Teller said grinning beneath his beard. "Where d'you go?"

"I bet I can guess..." Neander winked.

"Neander, kindly shove it up your ass," Ira answered. "Besides, aren't you tired of this stale old joke yet?" Ira knew she was.

"C'mon then," Neander continued, leaning forward eagerly. "What does our esteemed lord think of the whole... Damian?"

Ira looked around. Damian was sitting on top of the table, his shining black boots rested on the bench below. His arms rested on his knees, and a half-empty cup was dangling in his hand. He was staring off towards the back of the hall where a small side door stood open, but he did not truly seem to see anything at all. His blue eyes were unfocused, and a slight frown tugged his mouth.

"Ai! Damian!" Ira called.

Damian blinked. He looked around slowly as if pulling himself back from the deepest corner of his own mind.

"Hum?" Damian asked.

"Neander wants you to join in on teasing me," Ira said shrugging.

"They picking on you again Ira?" Damian's grin spread his face, and all traces of listlessness was gone.

"Just about her being relieved that Kyana's gone..." Everett started.

"Because of her puppy dog crush on you," Neander answered, taking an exaggerated sip from his goblet, a pinky held high in the air.

"Leave her alone Neander..." Damian warned, voice teetering dangerously on the edge of his "King Damian" tone.

"Wha?" Neander huffed. "Why can *you* tease her and not us?"

"Because," Damian said, "*I* can break your face, but *you* cannot break mine."

"Oh, that," Neander waived his hand dismissively, "We love her too you know."

"Oh, well in that case, please proceed," Damian joked.

"Okay, I'm leaving," Ira said, grabbing the empty flagon and getting to her feet.

"No!" Neander and Damian called in unison. "We're sorry! We're kidding! We'll stop! Get back here!"

"You want more or not?" Ira asked, continuing to back out of the hall while waving the empty flagon.

"Oh, well, in that case, snap to it!" Neander said, banging his cup against the table.

"For the love of the gods," Ira mumbled under her breath, but she was grinning as she left.

# CHAPTER 21

Damian took several wobbling steps down the hall, doing his best to keep his strides steady. He had not intended to drink so much. Ira had returned with not one, but two, more flagons of mead and the five of them had started a good old time.

Damian stopped halfway down the hall and leaned against the wall. He waited a few moments, pressing his forehead against the cool stones, hoping the nausea would pass. He regretted not taking Ira up on her offer. When he had poured himself his last glass... most of which sloshed onto the table... Ira, who had far less than any of the others, offered to walk Damian back to his room. Damian had loudly brushed away this offer, spewing some nonsense about a king not needing a babysitter, and how she was not his mother. Now, Damian wished he had just shut the hell up because the floor wouldn't stop spinning.

Damian leaned with both hands and groaned loudly to the empty hall.

"Shit," he said, grinding his teeth around the word.

He couldn't let anyone see him like this. It was not his place to be seen like this. It indeed was not uncommon for the king of Neira to indulge in a drink or two or six. Damian's father was well known for his enjoyment of spirits. Many a time Damian had watched his father being supported out of the great hall by two, sometimes three, guards. Everyone involved was laughing, singing, stumbling, and sometimes puking their way to the royal chambers. Damian had never liked seeing his father that way. Especially after his mother died. The drinking became more frequent. The singing and laughing faded... and then there was just stumbling and puking. It had caught up with him, eventually. Jeromy Lysted grew ill but could not seem to stop drinking. No. It stopped him instead. To everyone else, everyone who had not been paying attention, Jeromy Lystad's death had been sudden. Not for Damian. Damian had been watching his father slowly killing himself for years. With every lift of the goblet. With every uncorking of a wine bottle. With every sloshing over of his glass, Damian had watched his father's health deteriorate in helpless silence. For there was nothing he could do for him.

He had tried to stop him occasionally. One time when Damian had almost reached his twelfth year, he had actually grabbed the goblet from his father's hands and threw it on the ground. He spilled red wine like blood across the floor at his father's feet.

"She would not want this!" he had cried. "She would be ashamed!" It had been the first and only time, in Damian's entire life, that his father had laid a hand on him. Jeromy Lystad had been a good king, and a loving father, but he was not a perfect man. Then again… neither was Damian.

Damian took a deep breath and looked up slowly. The hallway which led to the staircase seemed to stretch like some sickening mirage or a nightmarish dream.

"Shit…" Damian repeated, closing his eyes and groaning once more. He gathered his courage and continued down the hall, one hand sliding against the rough stones.

How far away were his chambers again? Three flights up? The thought of it made him queasy. He let out a rather inelegant burp that echoed through the hall.

*Well, that wasn't very kingly of you.*

Damian laughed at the memory and then groaned as the floor began to spin again. He remembered the small snarky grin that had tugged up the corner of her mouth. Blood was seeping steadily through her dress, and yet, she still had the state of mind for sass.

Neander had been wailing at the top of his voice all evening about how Kyana should have stayed, and how he missed her, and how he wished she would have taught them some of those skills of hers. How he wanted to hear more about Wybert the Wanderer, and how such a girl should not be out in a forest on her own. Damian had only laughed. He had taunted Neander, and teased Ira, never telling the truth. The truth that he agreed with them.

Kyana was… odd. She was more curious than anyone he had ever met before, and more than just in her skill set, or how she had acted in a fever dream. There had been something more, something hidden deep. He had seen it in her eyes. It was stamped there against the bright sun of the training field, like a wet wax seal on a royal decree. He was able to see its presence but unable to open it and read what was inside. Unable to know the meaning woven in that deep green gaze, which seemed to have no end. Damian had seen... something. Something both fascinating and genuinely off-putting. He did not show it at the time. It was not his place to show weakness. He did not even admit it to himself except in times like these when he was alone, or out of his usual state of mind, but the truth was... those eyes had scared him. Not in a way that he feared for his safety. Not even a fear of her... just... he did not know how to explain, or even comprehend those deep, enticing eyes. They drew you in, captured you, in a way that was not... normal. It felt...

*Strange. Strange, eyes. Strange woman.*

Damian had finally made it to the spiral staircase and took it in stumbling, sloppy, strides. He had to stop three times before making it to the second floor. He rested at the second-floor landing when he heard voices on an upper floor of the staircase. Damian panicked when he realized the footfalls were headed his way. He had a sudden flash of his father, leaning against the wall with his vast stomach heaving as he vomited the remains of a feast across a guard's shoe.

Damian darted as quickly as he could down the hall, passing storerooms and a few servants' quarters. He stumbled a little farther, then noticed one of the guest rooms doors propped open. He darted inside and closed it as the footsteps reached the second floor and passed through the hall. Damian held his breath and waited for the voices to fade out and disappear. He let out a long sigh of air, praying to the gods that he would not puke as his world gave a violent jerk. The gods did not seem to be listening. Damian darted to the cabinet, yanked open the smooth wooden door and rummaged frantically through it. When he finally found the wash bowl that was kept inside, he dropped to his knees, the dish still in hand, and vomited. It was hot, sour, and stung its way up his throat. His supper and far too much mead came out in such a magnificent stream that, Damian thought bitterly, his father would have been proud. He would have slapped his son on the back, laughed, and said:

"All things must pass by my boy, and so will this."

Damian decided it more likely for his father to have pulled up a space on the floor next to him, his own bowl in hand. But neither of these things were true. His father had died and could neither say nor do anything of the sort. So instead, the king of Castle Lyist sat shivering alone on the cold wooden floor as he heaved his supper and dignity in dramatic volleys, breathing shame in sharp, desperate, gasps. When the waves had stopped, Damian rested his head against the cabinet, breathing deeply through his nose, trying to ignore the vile sour taste in his mouth. He spat into the half-full basin.

*Well, that's not very kingly of you*

He closed the cabinet door, after shoving the bowl of sick inside. He gave a staggering turn and looked around. He blinked. Damian knew this room. Well, he knew almost every room of this castle, from the servant's closest to the royal chambers. He had wandered everyone with Ira when they were both very young and very bored, inventing worlds behind every door. Dragons to fight, princesses to save, and kingdoms to rule, the usual play of young children. Although he distinctly remembered that Ira had refused to be the damsel in distress, always preferring to be a knight instead. So, they had to invent an imaginary damsel who they both saved together, side by side.

This room, however, he had been in more recently. It was the chambers he had given Kyana for her short stay.

He looked around the large room with its hanging dark blue and brown cloths, the large bed, and the two-headed dragon coat of arms on the wall. It looked… empty. Because it was empty, other than him. *Same thing.* He thought in a fit of self-loathing as he wiped his mouth on his sleeve.

*Well, that's not very kingly of you.*

"So, what?" Damian mumbled. He had been so many things before he was a king. A boy, a child, a prince, a brother, a friend, a son… a person. He was someone's person, and he had a person. Now, what did he have? His mother had bled to death. His father had drunk himself to oblivion. His beautiful sisters were leagues away, and what did he have? Damian had an empty room and a cabinet full of puke. Wonderful.

The king flopped on the bed headfirst. He buried his face into the cushions and scrunched his eyes closed, hoping the world would stop spinning if he could not see it. It did not. If he could just fall asleep, it would all be over. It would all pass by. As all things must.

# CHAPTER 22

Night fell over a kingdom at rest. The king dozed in a bed that was not his own, the people rocked their babies into dream lands, and a soft breeze lulled to sleep all the rest. There was, however, one member of that sleepy kingdom that did not dose into peaceful dreams. He was young, stealthy, and moved at a quick pace but made no sound against the dew dampened grass of the meadow as the river filled the night with its music of water tumbling by the shore. He moved at a quick pace, almost running under that open blanket of night sky. The sister moons were high overhead, casting everything in a bright blue light, and the boy felt incredibly naked under their beams. There was so much open land between him and where he needed to be. He felt exposed to any eye that may glance out from the castle walls and it felt like a hundred eyes were watching him now. His own eyes moved from side to side, like a frightened deer watching for a hunter's bow. A breeze picked up, whining in his ears and causing the long grass to curl and dance around him. It felt like the entire world was shifting beneath his feet and the boy almost whined in fear along with the wind. He drew his cloak closer around him. It was large, thick, and donned with a small midnight blue dragon on the shoulder, but this was no knight's uniform. A bright red circle surrounded the image of the dragon, trapping it, and denoting him as having a different sort of service to the castle.

He picked up his pace, his destination in sight. The meadow which separated the castle and forests to the north-west was broken by a small lake with one solitary tree standing tall and strong in the night. Its branches waved at the boy, waving him to come closer, or perhaps to turn back. The boy broke into a run and did not stop until he reached the shadow of the old tree. He breathed deeply, leaning against it. He dropped to his knees by the lake, and splashed his face with the water, trying to calm himself. His whole body was trembling. This was the first time he had done this. The first time he had left the castle since he had made it his home one year ago, and he was terrified. Terrified of being caught, terrified of not being caught… and the moons were so bright tonight. Why did they have to be so bright? It felt like they were trying to show him to the world, light up his path, reveal him to the kingdom. If they had voices, the boy was sure they would be calling out his name. But moons had no voices, and so the sisters hung above his head, watching him in silence.

The boy froze suddenly, every muscle in his body tensing to a sound that did not exist, or at least was not heard by anything other than himself. He stood up, water dripping from his trembling hands.

"Is… is that you?" his words held weakly veiled fear, as his eyes took up speed, tracing every inch of the blue stained meadow around him, analyzing every movement of grass and shifting shadows.

"Yes," a voice spoke from behind him. The boy swung around nearly falling backward in his haste but a pale hand shot out at a blinding speed, catching the boy's arm and steadying him.

"Careful, now," the voice spoke once again. "You don't want to hurt yourself."

The voice was smooth, crisp, and almost musical. The sound of a creek passing through rocks on its way from The Basin. This boy had only been to see The Basin once in his life when his family had traveled to the Caskcare Mountains to pay their respects. The three great waterfalls spilled down from the mountains and pooled in a massive lake which in turn fissured out into little streams that sent water singing happily out to the world below. Poets and songwriters and been enraptured with The Basin for centuries, never seeming to find an end to its description, beauty, and damn near worship. The sound it made when you closed your eyes… It was the most haunting sound the boy had ever heard, and the only thing he could think to compare.

The boy looked from the surprisingly firm grip on his arm and up to the man who stood before him. He was tall, strangely tall, and his limbs seemed to take up most of that height. The man wore a light blue shirt, one that was far too thin for such an evening, and no cloak to cover his shoulders. Despite this, he did not shiver, or shake, or show any signs of discomfort. He simply stood, tall and still, piles of glistening sapphire hair falling down his shoulders and back.

*He's so thin,* the boy thought, eyes trailing across the sunken cheeks and accentuated collarbones. *I never imagined him so thin... or pale.* He was indeed thin and pale, but not in the way a sick person is pale. It was a shining painless almost to match the moonlight. When the odd man moved his long-fingered hand back down to his side, it passed out of the shadows of the tree and the boy could have sworn that the man's entire arm briefly disappeared into it. Momentarily blended with the moonlight as if becoming one with it, before returning in the shadows once more.

The tall man smiled at the boy's watchful gaze, a gaze that said every thought as clearly as if he had spoken it aloud.

"I didn't..." the boy stammered taking a step backward, although he did not realize it. "I didn't think it would be... I didn't think **you** were going to come."

"Well, why not?" The man did not laugh. Then why did the boy swear he had? It seemed to reverberate in his mind in that same trickling tone as the man's words. "You are a very important child... and this is a very important task." They were silent for a moment, the man merely standing there slowly blinking his dark eyes, the smile still on his face. Gods that smile. The boy gave an involuntary shiver. He told himself it was the wind, but they both knew better. It was a wide smile. It seemed to span from one ear to the other, and the boy wondered in absent, terrible, curiosity, if the tall man ever opened his smile, or laughed out loud, if his head would not simply split in two.

"What news do you have for me?" the tall man asked, finally. "Is everything going as planned?"

"Yes," the boy gasped. He had been holding his breath. "Yes, it is."

"And the position?"

"It's mine. Six days past now," the boy answered. He hastily pulled at his cloak to reveal the image of a blue dragon encircled in red.

"Good," the man said, black eyes tracing every inch of the image before returning to the boy's face. The boy wondered if he even had irises. If it was day instead of night, would there be color around that dark circle? Perhaps a bright blue or a dark brown? He doubted it. "Did you have any trouble with… obtaining your position?"

The boy shook his head. "It went just as you said it would… sir."

The man reached out to him. The boy's first instinct was to shrink away, but he planted his feet as the tall man patted his cheek. He expected the man's touch to be cold, something to match his skin, but it was not. It was warm. No, not just warm, it was hot. It reminded the boy of the nights under the castle, when he was first accepted into the ranks of those who serviced the ancient caverns belonging to long-dead dragons. He and the other first recruit Keepers had spent hours admiring the long chasm walls, reaching out to them, but not quite touching. Feeling the strange, unnatural heat that emanated from every stone, every rock. As if a small fire burned just beneath the surface, heating the very air itself.

"Very, very good," the man said, smile widening. Then he pulled away, and the heat left with him. The cold night air seemed to hit the boy harder than before, and he shivered.

The tall man looked out from the shadow of the solitary tree and up to the sister moons that hung large and bright in the sky above, almost seeming to touch one another.

"Did you know," the tall man began in a hushed voice that sounded almost sleepy. "The four dragons were born under the sister moons?"

"I… no sir," the boy said blinking a little.

"They were," the man continued, raising a long-fingered hand to point at the moons above. "They were born when the sister moons held hands. Almost as they are doing tonight. It is a good sign my boy. A good, good sign." He looked back down and smiled. "Things are going as they should… we will be moving soon… until next time." He started for the meadow, but turned back for just a moment, "It was nice to finally meet you in person. Have a safe journey Ellis," that smile threatened to split the man's face once more, "And congratulations."

"Uh, thank you, sir," he said, bowing his head as the man turned and moved silently away. When the boy looked up a moment later, he was alone, surrounded by nothing but the flickering moonlight and shadow. Ellis leaned against the tree, feeling lightheaded. He had not expected *him* to *come.* One of his latest cronies, or a letter left under a stone was more common. That had been their routine, but for the man to meet him in person... he had not been ready for that.

Ellis leaned further down, considering whether or not to put his head between his legs for a few minutes, but found that he had no need. The general had come, and he had been pleased. Ellis had done well, and he was pleased. Ellis smiled to himself and straightened up, looking back at the open expanse where the strange man had simply disappeared.

Rainier had been pleased with him, and that was very good.

# ONE MONTH LATER

# CHAPTER 23

Kyana knelt in the branches entirely still. Her bow was up, armed, ready. The feathers of the arrow tickled her cheek as she waited. She felt the cool breeze against her face, blowing her salty scent away from her target. She watched the doe as she stepped slowly across the leaf-strewn ground. The dried brown and gold plants crunched softly beneath her cloven hoof. Her ears twitched restlessly as she nosed through the dead leaves, looking for something fresh. Kyana stayed still and waited for her moment. The doe paused in her search, lifting her elegant head and looking around to a sound behind her.

*There it is.*

Kyana held her breath and let go. There was a light whistle as the metal tip of the arrow cut through the air and a soft thud as it hit flesh. The doe stumbled, its thin legs trembling for a moment before she fell. It lay absolutely still. The shot was clean, fast, instant, and painless. Kyana jumped down from the branch and retrieved her arrow. This meat would last her a long while if she could find a way to keep it, and the pelt would make a fantastic cloak for the cold weather ahead. Or perhaps a blanket for Royal.

Kyana put her fingers to her mouth and whistled. Royal came running and pulled up short at Kyana's side. It had only taken three days for Kyana to teach her that trick. Royal was smart, fast, young, and eager to please. Like most animals, given a little attention and a little love, she would cross a sea of fire for you. It was a type of loyalty Kyana had not experienced in a long time. She liked it. She would return it with all she could. Blanket it was.

Kyana lifted the doe from the ground and hoisted it over Royal's back. She started walking, and Royal followed her without a word. They moved through the trees, the leaves crunching beneath foot and hoof alike, as they made their way back home. The mid-day sun cast light through the branches and sent patches of shade and sun scattered over the forest floor in endless blotches and patterns. Birds and squirrels darted through the thick branches as they continued forward, chattering and twittering in a language unknown to all but themselves.

So calm… so peaceful…

The image of a feast in its gold and multi-colored grandeur flew unheeded across Kyana's memory. The sound of laughter and music filled her peaceful world, so suddenly she almost believed it real. She shook the memory away, brushing it aside as soon as it appeared. No need to dwell on things passed by. The feast, dancers, and music disappeared… the laughter continued.

Kyana frowned, listening. There was laughter, and not only laughter but a soft clanging sound. That sound was not swallowed by the thick branches and thickets. Instead, it seeped towards Kyana on the breeze. There was also the sound of conversation with many voices.

Kyana raised her hand above her shoulder. Royal stopped at the signal. Kyana motioned her to stay, and Royal did, giving a small disgruntled snort as Kyana moved towards the voices. Royal was young, smart, and knew, just as Kyana did, that something was wrong.

The sounds grew louder as Kyana picked up speed, darting across the leafy ground as quickly and quietly as she could. What was in her forest? She wasn't sure she truly wanted to know… but she must. People did not wander through these woods for no reason. This was deep into the forests. Deep into "no one's land" between Neira and Kyar Kingdoms. That iffy spot where people simply did not like to go. When they did come, it was for one of three reasons, and three reasons alone. Because they were lost, because they needed to be alone, or for an intention that was less than innocent. Judging by the number of voices she heard, it was not to be alone. This left lost or ill intentions. Kyana hoped to the gods it was the former.

Soon she could hear the mumble of voices coming into clearer focus. Kyana picked up speed and darted up a tall tree, hands grabbing at rough bark, and feet scrambling in her haste to hoist herself into position. She climbed near the top and pulled down a few branches to peer at the strangers. She took a sharp breath, and her chest tightened. Her forest was being violated. Hundreds… no thousands of men were collected around makeshift campsites and deer pelt tents scattered through the trees. The men were themselves a makeshift bunch. Tall, short, skinny, strong, all covered in a fine layer of dirt and scars that came only from a history of being the type of people to cause trouble. They lumbered in and out of tents, weapons were on every person and collected in large haphazard piles.

There were no fire pits, Kyana noticed, which was wise, for smoke pillars from such a number would have definitely drawn attention from at least a few of the smaller cities outside of Castle Lyist's reach. The men were talking, drinking, taking turns in groups to fight with blades and armor that were anything but dulled. The clank of sword on shield left a ringing in the air and made Kyana cringe. They were practicing, gearing up for a fight. Fight where? One of the little Cities? No, there was too many for such a small prize. Most of the larger cities were clear over on the other side of the kingdom, at least as far as Kyana knew (although, to be fair, she did not know the populated terrain all that well these days). That left one place worthy of such an effort. They were aimed for Castle Lyist itself.

*But why?* Kyana wondered, peering around, seeing only more and more she disliked. *They are a large number, yes, but is it really large enough for the likes of Castle Lyist?* Kyana thought not. Then she noticed the one thing that would make such an effort possible. Not only possible but damn likely.

As Kyana looked back down at the hirelings, for she soon realized that hirelings they must be (no group of men such as these had ever gathered in such numbers of their own volition unless there was coin in it for them) when someone caught her eye. It was a man. He was tall, unusually so. He towered over every other man he passed by, but *towered* was not the appropriate word. He did not rigidly march around the men, but virtually glided with a silky step that pushed him slowly forward. He moved as if making his way through a waist-high creek. With his height, his long sapphire hair braided down passed his hips, and snow pale skin, the man was easy to see and easy to watch. As a matter of fact, it was hard to look away. To Kyana, the hirelings seemed to grow fuzzy in her view, her entire focus on that man in a pristine white cloak lined with gray snow cat fur. It felt like she was watching him from a tunnel, and the only light emanated from that man himself. She shuddered, shaking her head, trying to disperse that feeling, like she had the memory of the feast.

Kyana got a dark feeling about this man. He walked with long strides, his white cloak curling and shifting with every step. He stopped beside one of the hirelings, and his long thin mouth began to move. Kyana leaned forward, trying to catch even a word of what was being said, but the man spoke so low and so soft she caught none of it. The man was obviously the leader, the rest of the men submissive. They moved out of his way when he walked but did not look at him. Even the man he was speaking with, who seemed to be answering his unheard questions, kept his eyes on the sparring men.

The tall man finished his conversation with the hireling but did not move away. Instead, he turned his head slowly around. For a terrifying moment, that sent Kyana's thudding heart straight to her throat, she thought the man may be turning to stare directly at her. He did not. His head traveled passed her in that same slow watery movement and looked towards the currently out of sight Castle Lyist. He smiled. The smile was long, thin, and spread his face slowly and methodically as if it was not a smile at all, but a gash being cut from one corner of his cheek to the other. Kyana half expected to see trickles of blood as the man opened his mouth to reveal long white fangs. However, the man's mouth did not open and there was no blood. Just a long thin smile that sent another shiver down Kyana's back.

Kyana willed her gaze away from the man with the effort of pulling one's leg out of a muddy bog. She could nearly hear the slurping "thump" as she finally pulled away. She quickly dropped from the treetops, scrapping the inside of her arm with her haste. She could feel a trickle of blood blossom and seep there, but she had no time to do anything about it. Because Kyana knew who that man was. She had never met him before, only heard faint whispers, but from the moment she saw him, she knew. That was Rainier... and Kyana had no idea why or for what purpose, but he was headed for Castle Lyist.

Kyana darted back the way she came and whistled. Royal came running, her hooves crunching against the forest floor, the doe flopping limply on her back against the saddle. Kyana caught her rains and hesitated only a moment before untying and pulling the doe off. It thudded heavily against the ground as Kyana slipped her foot into the stirrup and swung herself on.

*Damn it.* She thought mournfully, as she slipped her other foot into the other stirrup. *Such a waste.* But she needed as little weight on Royal as possible. She gave Royal a sharp tap with her heals and clucked with her tongue. Royal responded instantly. She started to run.

# CHAPTER 24

Sweat rolled down the boy's long face and neck. It slipped in slow, steady streams that glistened against his skin, trying in vain, to cool him. It dripped into his collar, dampening it as if he had been walking through a summer rain. He pushed back the sticky bangs which clung desperately to his forehead and continued on.

Ellis had never been this deep into the caverns. The lower levels were strictly off limits to newcomers to the Keepers. Only sir Wilmer and sir Lake, the elders of the Keepers and the boy's superiors, were allowed in lowest caverns, the caverns where dragons once spent their nights. They were the only ones trusted to watch over the relics firsthand. The rest were tasked with higher levels, making sure no one came and went who should not come and go.

Now the boy was the intruder, and apprehension wriggled like a bucket of live worms in his stomach with every step he took. He clutched the smooth handle of his lamp between sweating fingers. He held it out and away from his body as far as possible, trying to separate him from its heat. Gods knew the tunnels were hot enough on their own.

Philip Obray had told him many stories about those caverns before his death. Stories of dragons who had lived for centuries among those red and black stones, which curved in long twists and turns. He talked about how the breath of dragons was still held like magic in every crack and crevasse. How the closer one walked to the chamber where the infamous dragons slept, the more intense the heat.

Ellis decided he must be close, because it felt like he was crawling into an oven. The boy tugged at his soaked collar as he went deeper, stepping carefully through the expansive dark space, once home to creatures he had never known. Deeper into the heat, but the heat was not the worst of it. The worst was the smell. A muggy, rotting, sweaty, sour and almost sickeningly cinnamon like mixture hung in the air so thick the boy nearly choked on it.

Phil had told him about this as well. He had crinkled his great red nose while describing how the ancient feces of the beasts had slowly built up and built up, in piles of dung. These piles slowly hardened over centuries, leaving bolder sized stones of shit that scattered the tunnels, filling it with their horrendous scent. That, along with the heat, was overwhelming and only grew stronger with every step, and with every step, Philip Obray's plump face swam before Ellis's watering eyes.

Ellis was very sorry the day Phil died. He had been a nice man. A nice man willing to spend time telling stories of the famous dragon tunnels to a strange little boy with many questions.

But he also knew why Phil had to die. He understood, he did. He saw it, plain and clear. They needed access to the caverns, and the Keepers (once called "Dragon Keepers" when dragons still lived within those boiling depths, and their job was to care for, feed, water and look after their charges, while now they only watched over their remains) had strictly numbered ranks that had not changed for centuries. Just enough to watch over the two entrances. One which entered from under Castle Lyist itself, where the royalty of days passed by would descend and visit their beloved dragons. The second opened up just inside the fourth wall on the South-West side of the city. Well, not exactly opened up. Both entrances were closed and secured by two layers of bars, and with their own specially made key which kept them secure. There had been talk in the old days, and many days since the end of dragons, about closing off the cavern and its tunnels altogether. Breaking them down until there was nothing but dirt and rock so no one could come anywhere near to the dragon chambers and their hidden treasures. This idea had been pushed aside for the sake of caution. With the tunnels in place, it gave the nobles and royals an exit strategy if they needed to leave the castle in secret, or in a hurry. Although each major kingdom had similar places that their dragons once dwelt, none were exactly the same. This left the pathways and locations unknown to all except the Keepers that kept them. Even the lords and royalty of times passed, when dragons still lived, did not know their way through. They had to rely on the guidance of the Keepers to show them to their dragons. Completely trusting the Keepers to guide them from one dark and elaborate chamber or another, because what elaborate plans they were. The dragons themselves had carved their way into the dark earth. Their Keepers had helped of course but most of the work was done by the great creatures themselves. They made their own pathways to their lairs. Years of work, different generations of dragons digging had left the caverns and tunnels sprawling and seemingly nonsensical to that day. If one was not a Keeper who knew the way or at least had a Keepers map (of which Ellis only knew of two), then you would certainly become lost within the stinking, molding, twists and turns of tunnels. More likely to find yourself bouncing from dead end to dead end only to die in the dark, never seeing a single dragon bone.

Having such close access to the relics made the position a great responsibility and few were trusted with the task. Only seven Keepers were elected at any particular time. It was tradition, and Castle Lyist sure loved its traditions. The Keepers also kept for life... another little tradition. But Ellis did not have enough time to make it into the Keeps by natural time, or natural causes. He needed to get in soon. He needed to be there a while. Not a long while, but long enough to be trusted. If he was not... the entire plan would be lost. And so, he befriended an old Keeper, one who enjoyed a good stiff drink and a good long story. One for who he could show a great interest in and a great interest for his work. One that might even recommend the boy for the post after his passing. One who no one would be surprised if he passed on a little early.

This did not mean Ellis had to like it.

He had not.

It did not mean the old man's face did not haunt him during those long nights at watch, leaning against those hot stone walls Phil had told him so much about.

Because it did.

Some things... just had to be done. Just had to be taken care of. He saw this. He knew it well, so when he was given a small packet of white powder with a note from Rainier telling him to pour it into Phil's nightly cup of wine, Ellis had done it without question. It was easier that way. The old man passed in his sleep without pain. Nice and peaceful like. When his position opened up, and having no children of his own, to whom were they to turn to but the young boy that Phil had talked so much about. The boy who had shown so much interest.

Ellis froze in his tracks, heart thumping wildly in his chest as a shot of fear and adrenaline slammed through him making him shiver despite the heat. He saw a flicker of light from another lantern down one of the tunnels to his left. Ellis cursed and blew out his light, hastily darting behind a stack of boulders. After scrunching low behind them, he quickly realized they were not boulders at all. The sticky and sour smell intensified so drastically the boy nearly puked then and there, destroying the carefully laid plans in one disgust induced instant.

He clasped a hand over his mouth and nose and searched the darkness with watering eyes. The lamplight down the tunnel grew brighter, and the sound of footsteps began to come, soft and steady, to the boy's ears. He wondered if it was Sir Wilmer or Sir Lake who so inconveniently broke their usual pattern. He had been careful, damn it. He had watched from the outskirts of the inner tunnels. Waiting to see when and where the two elders were likely to be at any particular time, or at least, as well as he could without actually going deeper into the tunnels himself. He thought no one would be down to this part of the tunnels at the moment. Obviously, he had been wrong. It did not matter. He just needed to wait out whoever it was, then he could fulfill his purpose and get the hell out of there before anyone else came around.

Ellis waited for the lamp to be swallowed entirely by the darkness before he darted out from behind the stones of fossilized dung. He took several deep breaths of semi-fresh air, before leaning down to relight his lantern. He pulled two small striker stones from his pocket, but his hands were so sweaty that it took several wipes on his trousers, and several frustrated re-strikes, before the wick took the flame.

He continued on, his eyes darting around for the slightest sign of the light from another lantern. He soon came to a fork in the tunnels, one which curved steadily to the right, and continued the twist and turns into darkness. The one on the left was more direct, and with a noticeable incline that would eventually lead to open air. Ellis may not have been down here himself, but he had scoured Phil's old map, for months and hours at a time, memorizing every twist and every turn. Memorizing exactly where he needed to go, and exactly how to get there.

He took the path on the right, picking up speed now, his large feet slapping hastily against the stone ground. His heart thumped happily in its cage, as his destination came into reach. After a few more twists and turns of red and black stones, a vast chasm opened up before him. It seemed to spread for miles in every direction, creating a tremendous circular room that expanded as high as it did wide. Ellis looked up, but the ceiling disappeared into the darkness where his lamplight could not touch. The smell was so overwhelming here, limply pressing against him, Ellis had to grit his teeth as his stomach clenched.

This was it. This was the room of the dragons. For centuries that chasm, with its jagged stalagmites and stalactites, which reached for one another with longing red and black fingers as if coated with blood and ash, had seen no one but Sir Welmer and Sir Lake. But no longer.

Ellis stepped further in the room, distracted from his mission momentarily by the sear size of it all. But the size was not the only distraction. There was no sound down in this chasm. Not just a lack of noise. It was an empty place with no sound of voices, footfalls, running water, no scampering of animals, but it was more than that. As Ellis stepped deeper and deeper, he could not hear the sound of his own feet. He lifted his lantern, giving it a little shake. Usually, when he did this, the lanterns metal arm would clatter lightly against the glass of the lamp. In this place, there was nothing. He tried shouting next. Nothing remarkable, just a few random words, but he heard none of it. He could feel the air leaving his lungs and his mouth moving around the words, but no sound reached his ears. He walked over to a stalagmite reaching up from the floor. Water was dropping slowly, making what should have been soft little plopping sounds as the water broke against the mound of calcification searched for the long out of reach the ceiling. But here, it made no sound at all. Not a one.

Ellis was amazed by this, but also very afraid.

What magic was this? It had been trapped so long in such a dark, dark, place. Trapped somewhere so empty, with no creatures of magic, for so long. Alone with dampness and darkness and... nothing, nothing, nothing. Nothing for centuries. Centuries of empty. A place where so much life turned to pain. A mass killing in one fateful night by the man, the king, they thought loved and cared for them. The place had seen so much agony, so much death. Was it possible for magic to go insane? Ellis did not think so before. But now…

He turned in the silence, eager to get what he came for and go.

Ellis started around the dark corners. Searching the edges, the small enclaves in the lower wall like shelves carved by large claws. He lifted and lowered his lamp, casting gold light across the precious treasures that nestled carefully among the rocks and dirt. Treasures. No gold. No diamonds. No precious metal, nothing so simple, and more valuable than all. They were bones. Bones of pale white and gray. Bones as small as a little finger and as large as those boulders of red and black stones they rested between. Cracks fissured across the pale surfaces in delicate twisting patterns, and Ellis tracked every turn, every line, with rapt attention. The light from his lamp shone against the bones, seeming to amplify it, gleaming until Ellis had to squint against the light.

*Beautiful.* Ellis thought, unable to stop himself from reaching out and running his fingers across their ancient surfaces. The bones were as warm to his hand as the lamp was in his other. Ellis had never seen anything so lovely in his life. After the dragons of Castle Lyist had been slaughtered, the bones of Aneira's decedents had been gathered and scattered around the large cavern to be watched over by the Keepers for the rest of eternity. For a moment, Ellis wondered what the original Keepers had done on that fateful night of The Sacrifice. Back when their job was to take care of the living dragons. Had they protested against the king? Tried to stop Great King Lawrence when he descended the tunnels with Defier and dark intentions? They had worked with these creatures for centuries, entire life times, had they cared when they were all about to die? Or were they content to go from watching living breathing things to watching over their bones? Did it make their task just that much easier?

Ellis moved in silence through the tremendous empty, eyes darting from one beautiful relic to the other. Long, short, large, small, smooth, rough, on and on they went. There were heaping piles of bones the size of large horses, but many were far larger. A ribcage stood on its back, its cage of bones pointing upward, so massive that its ends disappearing into the darkness above. Ellis passed a string of bones that reached as high as his waist and twisted off in a long chain of what once had been the tail of a massive creature. He also saw see a cluster of skulls off in the distance, one that would have taken three of men standing on each other's shoulders to reach the top. There were smaller ones as well. Piles and piles of shattered dragon eggs littered the stony floor in various extravagant colors that glinted in the passing lamp light. Young dragons the size of stallions, and babies that had been no bigger than goats lay among their shards. These would be easier to carry.

Rainier had not had any particular relic in mind.

"I leave that choice to you my friend," he had said, gracing him with another one of those skin shriveling smiles. But what to choose? Which relic would be best for such a critical mission? Which relic from this silent tomb would have the revenge they deserved upon the people that killed them?

Ellis paused in his stride, attention falling on one relic in particular. His heart thumped hard against his chest with excitement, and his mouth formed around the words that no one would ever hear.

"There you are."

Ellis reached down, gently lifting the relic in two hands. It was larger than several of the others he had passed but held very little weight. He quickly slipped it into the bag around his shoulder, adjusting the strap carefully, before making his way out the silent, dead, cavern.

He would be pleased. Ellis knew Rainier would be please.

# CHAPTER 25

Royal flew over the forest floor like an arrow from a bow. She glided over fallen trees and swept through the air. Kyana had always loved speed. She recalled her dreams of far off freedom, and could not help closing her eyes for a moment, savoring the cut of wind on her face.

It took time. Kyana pushing Royal as much as she dared. Royal, so eager to please, made good time, but they could not make it there in one day. When they rested for the night, she watered Royal at a creek, brushed her down, and let her graze and sleep for a few hours, but Kyana could not sleep. She sat up, eyes wide watching the darkness, too worried to fall into anything but a troubled doze. When the sun sent its first beams of light through the sky, they were off again. By the afternoon they burst from the trees and hit the open green hills. Royal took advantage of the lack of trees and picked up even more speed, although too soon, Kyana had to slow her again. She needed to get there as quickly as possible, but she could not make it during that day either. So, they stopped when they came to one of the smaller cities, the name of which Kyana did not know. She walked through it, allowing Royal to drink at the trough and ignored all the curious eyes that watched her as she passed. She did not blame them. With her clothes a mess and her eyes probably red and bloodshot from lack of sleep she must have looked a tad demonic. Even so, one of the many inns she passed would be more than happy to take her coin for a bed and hot supper, but she did not stay in the city. She did not like unknown places with unknown people. In fact, she had not stayed at an inn since traveling with Wybert. Kyana recalled one of his many lectures on the vileness of a "drunken wanting man," as she passed on through without a word to any of the towns people. She chose to camp a short distance outside its reach. Just that much closer to her destination. She leaned up against the base of a tree by the side of the main road and ate the stash of fruit she had picked while on her hunt. Royal slept beside her. Rain pattered light and cool around them, but the tree served as a decent cover, and Royal slept on. Kyana, again, could not. Every time she closed her eyes, her mind drifted back to that tall man, and that travailing smile.

The next morning, they were off again, and by this point, Royal was getting tired. She had been pushing herself for two days. She was young and healthy, but she was just a horse and had a breaking point, as do all animals. She kept pushing herself none the less because she could feel something was wrong. She could feel the tension pouring from her rider, the "soon to be" of it all. Most animals could. From the doe in the woods, with her desperate ears and watchful eyes, to the loyal horse or dog, which seemed able to feel their master's emotions as if they were their own. Royal felt the sharpness in Kyana's breath, her movements, the way her legs felt rigid at her sides. The horse did not know precisely what was happening, but she knew it was important. So, when the towering castle, with its gleaming amber stones, came into view across the meadow, Royal gave it all she had. Her large lungs were already burning from the time spent at a canter, but she did not hesitate, just pushed forward. Grass kicked up behind her as her hooves left deep brown gouges in the dirt still soft from the morning's rain. Sweat began to slide down her dark neck, and she smelled salt, but she did not slow down, and the hills flew by.

They were soon coming on the castle. Kyana could see the guards lounging outside the gates. The first gate was open, and they burst though, passing the guards without slowing down or heeding their yells of protest. Royal weaved effortlessly around the people, carts, and other horses which crowded the busy streets. Her hooves clicked and clattered against the cobbled streets as she went, sweat flying off her great shoulders. They darted through the second wall, then the third, all of which were open for the daily life of the people.

Kyana wondered why a castle had so many gates if they simply left them open. She soon answered her own unspoken question.

*In case of attack. Well, prepare yourself, Castle Lyist… you will soon have a use for them.*

Royal pulled up short at the inner part of the castle just past the fourth and final gate, directly in front of the giant stone steps leading to the castle itself. Knights stood in their long chestnut cloaks on the upper level. All stopped mid conversation to stare as Royal snorted and pawed the stone ground in a mixture of stress and pride. Royal had barely stopped before Kyana launched off her back and landed on the cobbled ground, her buckskin cloak billowed around her as she stood up straight.

"Who are you?" the knights called loud and with authority. Their hands rested on the hilts of their swords as she approached.

"I need to speak with the king," Kyana said, as Royal snorted a sharp gasping sound behind her.

"... uh... well our king is a bit busy little one," said a knight as he stepped forward, "So you might need to.... Wait a moment..." Neander grinned, squinting at her as if to something far away and out of natural view. "Kyana?"

"Neander," she nodded at him.

"Kyana!" Everett, who was also one of the knights on the stares, stepped eagerly forward. "You know how to make an entrance!"

"Kyana?" a knight she did not recognize asked, looking at her with sudden interest. "The girl from the woods? The one that saved the king?"

*And saw demons.* Kyana thought exasperated to herself. *Don't forget that little part.*

"How have you been?" Neander asked happily going to wrap his arms around her, but she dodged and looked him in the eye.

"I need to speak with Lystad," she said firmly. "Now."

"Something wrong?" Neander asked a frown spreading his clean face.

"Yes," Kyana answered. "Very, very, wrong."

"Well, he's in a meeting right now, but I'll let him know you are here. I'm sure he would be delighted to—"

"Now. I need to see him now," Kyana cut him off. She did not have time for this. **They** did not have time for this. "Castle Lyist is in danger. Horrible, horrible danger. I need to speak with him now Neander." She looked all three in the eyes, trying to convey the severity of her words. The knight she didn't recognize glanced towards Everett, but he and Neander were focused on Kyana. Their faces grew grave, and Neander's frown deepened.

"Find someone to take care of Kyana's horse," Neander said, turning to the unknown knight who looked confused for a moment, but soon nodded and took Royal's reins without a word.

"Follow me," Neander said to Kyana. He and Everett led her up the steps and through the castle. They made their way through a long hallway full of servants and handmaids darting around from room to room, arms laden with cleaning supplies, blankets, towels, or pitchers of water. Kyana watched them and felt a pang of pity. They all looked so content going about their daily life... but that was about to change.

They stopped outside a room Kyana had not been before. Waving off the guards by the door, Neander pushed them open to what Kyana realized was a throne room. It was a large hall, nothing the size of the great hall, but large none the less. Carved wooden chairs lined up in rows as if in a house of worship, with one long open path leading to the opposite side of the room. A long chestnut carpet with deep blue floral decorations trailed its length, only stopping at the foot of a highchair. This chair was the focus of the room, all others were either beside or facing it as if staring at its elegance with unblinking eyes. Kyana did not wonder why. It was beautiful. It was tall backed with four detail carved legs that reached to the top of a few stone steps which elevated the throne higher than the rest of the room. The legs ended in what looked like dragon claws, which curled over the top step in such a realistic manner. Kyana could almost see the claws moving, tapping impatiently against the floor. The arms of the chair were delicately shaped into dragons' wings, which curled into armrests and flowed, water like, to the floor. The back stood tall and ornate in swirls of fire, studded and flecked with red, purple, and green stones.

Kyana was so distracted by the seat that she barely heard when Neander told her to wait there. She looked around in time to see him disappear through a door on the left of the hall.

Kyana waited, eyes tracing every inch of that chair standing bright and alone at the front of the room. She hesitated, then moved forward, walking slowly to the base of the throne as if it was an animal she did not want to frighten away. She reached out with long fingers and slowly traced one of the dragon claw legs. It was a masterful thing, taken months to create, and probably made the craftsman a wealthy man. As it should have.

Kyana brushed her fingers over the false wings, admiring the smoothness, and how it shimmered in the sunlight that streamed through the rows of high windows on either side of the room. She looked around at the many simply carved seats that laid out before and around the back of the intense throne. She felt a jolt of sadness. Standing in front of the throne, she realized how vast a space there was between it and every other piece of furniture in the room. It was an extraordinary beauty, surrounded by simplicity, and very alone in both ways. So much focus. So much space.

Kyana jolted away from the throne, stepping back into the emptiness surrounding it.

What was she doing there? She wondered suddenly. Why in the name of the gods was Kyana here? Because there were hirelings in her forest? Because there may be someone who wishes to attack Castle Lyist? What then? The instant the slightest hint of danger against Castle Lyist was noticed, she ran straight back? Why?

*Because they were kind to me.* Another part of her mind insisted. *For weeks they were kind to me. They helped me. Healed me. Gave me warmth and food and care when they did not have to do so.*

*That was only because they did not know you.* The thought cut hot and sharp against her mind, and her hand curled to a fist by her side, fingernails digging painfully into her palm. She owed them nothing. She owed *him* nothing. So why was she here warning them?

There was no answer. Instead, images played behind her eyes as vivid as the feast in the forest. Ira and her broad smile as they went for a walk. Augustine's intent gaze as he bandaged her side. Neander shoving a goblet into her unwilling hand. Lionel's guilt-ridden expression. Lilly spreading copious amounts of butter on a slice of bread. A city street full of bustling shoppers. A young king's laughter echoing down an empty hallway.

That soft warmth blossomed in her chest and remained despite Kyana's attempts to push it aside. She did not understand. Did not realize what she was feeling or why... at least that was the lie she told herself. It was a paper-thin lie. A gauzy thing she still hid behind even though the shapes and outlines of truth were nearly visible through its ghostly surface. She closed her eyes to it, as well as she could... but Kyana had never been good at lying, even to herself.

She was, here, was she not? Why would she be here if she did not —

Her thoughts were interrupted by the large doors at the back of the room pushing open with the whining protest of old hinges.

# CHAPTER 26

The air began to cool the further he climbed. Ellis had turned left where the tunnel split and had ascended the long path towards an opening just inside the outer gate of the city. It had once been a gaping cavern entrance, large enough for a fully grown dragon to pass in and out with clearance to spare. Now it had been narrowed, broken down and caved in to the size of a single door that was built inside the outer wall. A gate that was heavily barred and as far as Ellis knew, had never been opened. It was a long climb to those thick iron gates, but Ellis had the keys. He had snuck them off of Phil one night after he had fallen into a wine-drenched sleep. He had taken them to the smiths and paid him quite a great deal of coin to copy them with no questions asked. He had then slipped the originals back onto Phil's belt and slid the still warm copies in his pocket for safe keeping. For this very moment.

Yes, it was a long climb, but Ellis did not mind. He had the relic and the key. All he had to do now was sneak out of the gate without being seen. He was not so worried about that. The exit of the dragon tunnels had been built behind a broken-down house pressed against the inside of the outer most wall. It had fallen into disrepair over the years, and would no longer serve as an actual house, but was perfect for hiding a small and inconspicuous gate. He would leave his Keepers cloak in the house and lock the gate behind him. He had left a horse tethered a short distance away earlier that morning before his shift. Ellis would mount the horse and simply walk out the large double gates of the final wall as if one of the many other citizens heading off to the neighboring town with a satchel full of things to sell. He would not head for another town, however. He would head for the forests. Soon it would be all over. Soon he would have his, Rainiers, approval. What was a little time? No, he did not mind at all. Until he heard someone calling his name.

"Ellis?"

Ellis froze, turning slowly to see a boy, barely older than he, staring with wide brown eyes. Although a little older than Ellis, the boy's rounded face gave him a youth that would follow him long past when youth had left him. He was teased around the dinner table by the other Keepers, Ellis included. It was all in good fun, and Patryk never complained. He always laughed it off.

"You'll all be singing a different tune when you're all haggard and old, and I look barely past my twentieth year!" He would always grin, deep dimples devoting his soft, beardless cheeks.

But Patryk was not laughing now. His eyes were wide, and his mouth hung open slightly in surprise. It made him look more even more innocent and childish.

"P-Patryk?" Ellis stuttered in a tremulous voice. "What are you doing here?"

Patryk had been part of the Keepers since his thirteenth year, long before Ellis had even come to Castle Lyist. The position was passed down to him when his father died of the gray cough, and he had served it gracefully ever since. He served in the outer tunnels towards the castle where all younger members of the Keeps served, Ellis included. So why, in the hell, was he here?

"I was bringing a spare lantern to Sir Lake." Patryk raised the lantern in his left hand, while the one in his right flickered its orange and red glow across the stone walls where they danced with the shadows. "He mentioned his was…. what are you doing here?" Patryk's eyes moved slowly from Ellis's face to the bag that hung heavy around his shoulder. Ellis swallowed as Patryk's eyes widened further.

"Patryk…" Ellis said as the boy's eyes traveled the direction that Ellis had just come, then back to the bag around his shoulder.

"You're not supposed to be here, Ellis," Patryk said slowly as if piecing together the answer to a particularly challenging riddle. He would get there eventually, Ellis knew. Patryk may look young, but he was not stupid.

"Neither are you." Ellis pointed out, trying to laugh it off, but the sound that came out of his throat sounded more like a choked whimper than a laugh.

"I already told you why I'm here." Patryk looked back into Ellis's face, and Ellis swallowed once more. "What are you doing here, Ellis?"

"I... I... I'm here to... just..." Ellis's mind spun in frantic circles, like a squirrel in a hunters trap. Desperate. Panic blurring out all coherent thought. Scrambling uselessly against the inside of his mind, doing nothing but scratching futilely and bloodying its claws.

"What's in the bag, Ellis?" Patryk asked, taking a step forward. Ellis nearly jumped back, as if Patryk's movement were hot coals under bare toes.

"Nothing!" Ellis was even squeaking like a squirrel now. And round and round his excuses went.

"Give it to me, Ellis." Patryk's face had grown hard, as hard as a young face could. He set down the unlit lamp without taking his eyes off of Ellis and held out his empty hand. "Give me the bag." Ellis took another step away, scrunching the bag to his chest.

"Y-You, don't understand," Ellis said, taking another step back as Patryk stepped forward. "I can'-t— I can't do that."

"Yes," Patryk insisted, smiling a little now. "Just hand me the bag, Ellis. No one has to know. It's tempting I know... all the stories... stories of power, or the price it would fetch... the shadow market value on relics are so, so high, it would keep my family for the rest of our lives and perhaps our children as well... I'd be lying if I didn't say I wasn't tempted from time to time... so, just hand over the bag. It'll be our secret, okay? Wilmer, Lake, nobody needs to know, as long as we put it back safe..."

"Patryk, I can't." Ellis whimpered again. "I can't, don't you see, I can't."

"No, I don't see Ellis."

"He'll *kill* me if I do." It was the first time he had spoken these words out loud, but as soon as he heard it, he knew the truth of them. That man with the dark eyes and that long smile. He needed what he needed. He had made that clear when he had gotten in contact with Ellis and began making his plans. Never in person. Always through someone else or through letters, but somehow, they always found him. Before moving into the city, Ellis had flitted from little town too little town, outside the reaches of Castle Lyist. He ran desperately, not from Rainier, but from a past that haunted Ellis and filled his dreams with panicked nightmares. He kept moving, looking, and failing to find a place he felt safe. A place to call home. No matter where he went, no matter how long he stayed, the dreams always followed him and Rainier always found him. Ellis always got the same message. That all his wishes could come true.

*I know what you want dear boy,* He had written. *I know your darkest secrets. Your darkest wants. No. Your darkest **needs**. I can make it come true. I can make **all of it** come true. You need not be alone.*

It was a few years passed, that Ellis had finally begun to listen. Night terrors and desperation drove him to follow the man he knew only through legend. He had no idea why the Faithful Rainier would be interested in one piteous waist of a Faithful like him, branded at the age of four by a mother who had died on his ninth birthday. He destroyed the mark, sliced it a hundred times with that little pocket knife that his father had given to him. The scars crisscrossed in an ugly mas on his left leg just above his knee.

"It must be done boy," His father had said as he pressed the blade into Ellis's trembling hand. "You must do it. It must be taken care of and you must take care of it."

Ellis had felt ashamed of the ugliness. Even as he carved his own flesh into unrecognizable ridges, he felt ashamed. Not so much because of the mark itself, but because it was the last thing he had of his mother. He had not known much about being a Faithful after his mother passed by, but Rainier had reminded him and he simply no longer questioned him. Pretty promises made Ellis follow him, but not follow blindly. He must listen to him… and never fail him. And if Ellis failed him, he would not get a second chance. Rainier's approval would turn to anger, and Ellis knew the man's anger was something he never wanted to see.

"Who'll kill you?" Patryk frowned. Ellis did not answer. Instead, he continued backing down the tunnel.

"Ellis, I can't let you leave with that." Patryk's eyes were wide again.

"Please, just…" Ellis kept stepping desperately back, feet scrambling for purchase on the rocky ground. "Just let me go—"

"I'll get Wilmer." Patryk threatened suddenly, like a boy promising to tell on his older brother for acting out of place. "Wilmer and Lake. I swear, I will."

Ellis froze, in his step. He would, wouldn't he? Patryk and Ellis had gotten along well since he joined the Keeps. Being the youngest in a position mostly held by men in their fiftieth years, they naturally gravitated towards each other. They had spent a lot of time together in their off hours, and Ellis had liked to think of Patryk as a friend… but he was right. Patryk would go to

Wilmer and Lake, who would then send people after Ellis. Ellis was fast but not fast enough to outrun the knights of Castle Lyist on horseback. Even if he did shake them, there was still the threat that they would track him to wherever the general was hiding in the woods. Rainier would not like that, no, not one bit.

"Patryk, you can't." Ellis stepped closer to his boy faced friend, pleading now.

"Sir Wilmer!" Patryk raised his voice nearly to a shout, eyes still on Ellis as if proving that yes, in fact, he could.

"Patryk!" Ellis hissed, stepping closer. "Patryk, stop!"

"Sir Lake!" Patryk's voice rose, bouncing off the stone walls, echoing long and hard against Ellis's ear, making him shrink in horror.

*No!* Ellis thought, squirrel mind running circles, clawing bloody tracks in his brain. *Not so loud. So loud! He'll hear you!*

"Sir Wilmer!" Patryk continued, stepping away from Ellis now, but wide eyes never leaving him. "Sir Lake!"

"Stop, barking!" the words burst out from Ellis in a half sob, adding to the echoing chorus.

"Drop the bag," Patryk said, voice quiet once more.

"Okay." Ellis slipped the bag from around his shoulder with one hand. "Okay, Patryk, okay." He gently rested it against the stone floor and took a small step away.

Patryk's shoulders relaxed a little, and a small relieved smile curled his plump lips. He stepped forward and leaned down to pick up the bag. The moment his fingers touched the rough woolen cloth, Ellis made his move.

He swung around the lantern in his hand and crashed it against Patryk's down turned head. Patryk shrieked as the base broke and spilled hot oil across his face and into his eyes. He wailed, throwing his head back, stumbling and trying to rub the oil from his eyes as it burned his face and hands.

"Be quiet!" Ellis hist desperately, sidestepping the woolen bag and moving towards Patryk. "Please be quiet!" But Patryk wasn't quiet. He was wailing at the top of his lungs as blood began to dribble from his check, and the smell of burned skin filled the sticky air. Ellis darted forward, weaving to Patryk's back, and swiftly wrapping his arms around the boy, one across his mouth, and the other around his neck, cutting off his wails of pain.

Ellis felt the boy's hands tugging against his arm as Patryk fought back. He shoved backward, slamming Ellis into the hard-stone wall. Pain shot up his back and hip, making him want to shriek, but he bit it back hard. Patryk tried to shove him again, but this time Ellis was ready. He lifted his legs as Patryk moved, and caught the wall, pushing back and away from it with the force of his legs, toppling Patryk to the floor. A sickening snapping sound and a muffled wail of pain told Ellis that Patryk had fallen on his leg in just the wrong way.

"I'm so sorry," he whispered as Patryk's fingers scrambled desperately, uselessly, against Ellis's arm. "I'm sorry. I'm sorry. I'm so sorry. I don't want to, I have to, you see? You see, don't you? He'll kill me. He'll kill me, he will. You see, right?"

Patryk was not seeing much of anything by this point. Large dark spots had popped up all over his vision, slowly consuming the light. At first, they chewed away his sight in little nibbles, but they grew more ravenous every moment until his whole world turned black. His lungs flailed, shriveling in his chest, completely empty.

"I'm so sorry." Tears slid down Ellis's face, mixing with his sweat, salt with salt. "I'm so sorry."

The frantic scrabbling of fingers slowed to a pathetic patting. Ellis thought about the puppy he once had, the one with the soft paws. The one that patted at his arms and licked his face in the morning when it was time to get up. That sweet little puppy face. That sweet, innocent face.

Ellis's father had not liked that sweet face, no, no indeed. He liked it even less than the brand on his son's leg. He barked a lot, don't you see? He barked and barked and barked and drove him crazy, and Ellis's dad got scary when he got angry.

"I'm sorry, I'm sorry." Ellis was weeping now, tears flowing freely down his face as the hand gave one last desperate tug. He felt fingernails digging slowly into his arm, and hot blood seeping across his wrist. "I had to don't you see?" Ellis simpered. Rainier was scary when he was happy. Ellis did not want to see him angry. He could not see him mad. Not like his dad had been.

Ellis tried to make him stop. He had tried to train the puppy with a sweet face and soft paws. But the puppy was a puppy, and he knew no better. He was loyal to his very nature, and so he barked. So, Daddy said, take care of it boy, take care of it, or I'll take very good care of you. And so, Ellis did.

The puppy had splashed a while in the bucket of water and scratched up Ellis's arms good and bloody but in the end…

The fingers fell limply away from Ellis's arm, and Patryk stopped struggling altogether.

"Good boy, good boy." Ellis sputtered, body shaking, sobbing so intensely that it took his breath away. It took all his energy to chase it back. "I couldn't let you bark good boy, it's fine now, its fine now. I'm sorry. I'm sorry. I'm so sorry. You see, don't you?" he asked, cradling the body of a boy he had once called a friend. "I had to. I had to don't you see?"

The dead boy's eyes stared wide and surprised at the ceiling, frozen in this last emotion, and saw nothing at all.

Ellis waited until his sobs died down. He wiped away his sweat and tears with the back of his sleeve and hiccupped miserably. Then he gathered up his pieces and got to his feet. He reached down, grabbed the boy under the arms, and dragged him into a side tunnel. He drugged and shoved him securely into a dark corner. Once he got him there, half out of breath, he began to pile dragon dung stones on top of him. He worked as quickly as possible, dragging larger stones, while nearly throwing smaller ones. He did not smell the stench this time. As a matter of fact, he blessed it. Patryk was a favorite of the Keepers, and would soon be missed. If Ellis was unable to come back and retrieve his body, the smell of the stones would overwhelm and cover up any scent of Patryk when he began ripening. By the time that stopped working… well, Ellis hoped to be long gone by then.

Ellis finished stacking the rocks. The last stone clicked on top with a finality that was damn near deafening in those quiet caverns. He stumbled over to the bag which lay safely to the side. He reached down and replaced it over his shoulder, tightening the strap with a tug on the rough fabric. He discarded the shattered remains of his lantern, tossed the one that was supposed to be Sir Lake's, and picked up Patryk's, which still flickered with light. As he did, his shadow rose monstrous and dark up the stone wall behind him. It hulked there, hovering over him, watching him with eyes unseen but that saw everything… and never forgot. Ellis continued up the long path to the lip of the forest, without a single glance back at the pile of stones he left behind. His shadow followed him step for step, as it had always done. As it always would.

# CHAPTER 27

A door opened behind her, and Kyana turned hastily away from the glorious throne like a child caught doing something she shouldn't. Neander had returned with Everett and Teller, all in their shining knight's uniforms. All trailed behind the king himself.

"Kyana." The Lystad swept into the room his chestnut cloak fluttering behind him. He smiled as he entered, his blue eyes lighting up when they found her. This surprised Kyana, but she had no time to think about it. "How have you been?"

"There's a battalion building in the forest," Kyana said flatly, brushing right by civilities and stepping forward. The king's smile faded quickly, and his bright eyes grew dark.

"A battalion? How many? Whose arms do they wear? Was it a silver dragon?" Kyana shook her head and briefly wondered why the King of Neira would be worried about armies of Sterlyn, before moving on.

"No coat of arms. Hirelings. I didn't take the time to count. They were scattered throughout the forest. I'd say around a thousand or so."

The king seemed to relax. His smile nearly spread his face once more.

"A thousand? Is that all?" He frowned, more irritated than anything. "They're probably planning ongoing after one of the lower cities." He started to turn and speak to Everett when Kyana called back his attention.

"No," she said firmly. "He's coming after Castle Lyist."

"He?" The king asked, turning back.

"The hirelings are being led by a man," Kyana went on. "A tall man with long sapphire hair."

"Did you catch a name?" he asked, eyes narrowing.

"No…" Kyana hesitated distracted by two sides of her mind screaming at one another.

*Why are you telling them anything?* One half of her mind was shrieking in a voice not quite human. *Why did you tell them any of this?*

*Because he's dangerous.* The other side shot back furiously. *Because Rainier obviously has something up his sleeve. If I don't tell them, he might find a way to kill them all.*

*Good!* The other shrieked, loud enough to make Kyana wince. *Let him burn it down. Let him burn it all away. They killed the dragons, they killed your people, they killed them all, let him do the same if that is what he wants! Why are you here talking to them? You should be there **helping him**!*

Then Ira's broad grin flashed briefly across her mind. The streets full of people. The woman with her beaded jewelry. An echo of laughter down a long hall filled her mind and Kyana shrank from the harsh and violent raging of her heart. Soon enough, all the voices went silent.

"It was Rainier," she finished hastily, as if getting the truth out before the argument in her head could begin again.

Neander and Everett exchanged worried looks, but the Lystad only watched Kyana, face sinking deeper into darkness. "Are you su—"

"Very."

He took a deep breath, closing his eyes for a moment.

"Wonderful," he said in such a sarcastic tone, Kyana's mind darted back to the eye roll in the hall after the feast "Why? And where?"

"To the west of the castle," Kyana answered. "Deep in the forests where Neira meets Kyar. Two nights as the horse runs. And as for why… well, I have no idea. I don't know what he hopes to accomplish, but he's headed this way. I'm sure of it."

"Everett," the king spoke over his shoulder.

"I'll gather a few scouts and see what's going on," Everett said, already headed for the door.

"Be careful. A thousand men does not an army make," Kyana said. Everett looked confused.

"What do you mean?"

"From what I hear Rainier is a shrewd fighter, a warrior, he was a general that was successful in many a battle… he would not attack one of the most powerful castles in all the realm with just a thousand straggling hirelings and nothing else in mind," Kyana said, eyes on Everett. "He's got something else planned... something massive."

"Everett," the king turned to his knights. "Take your scouts. Neander go with him. And Teller check on the gates, won't you? Make sure they are secure... no mishaps with the structure, care, or management. Let them know they may be in need soon."

"Yes sir," All the knights bowed to their king, nodded to Kyana, and disappeared out the door. The king and Kyana were left alone in the throne room. Kyana yawned and rubbed one eye. She had made it, and now her adrenaline was used up and her sleepless nights were catching up with her at last.

"Kyana, are you alright?" the king asked, stepping forward.

"Yes," Kyana said, noticing for the first time that her arms and legs were trembling. She was sore, tired, wore out. "Royal, and I just raced here as fast as possible."

"Royal?" the king asked curious.

"Royal Toes," Kyana said, without thinking. "The horse you lent me."

"The horse I *gave* you," Lystad corrected, then realization caught in his eyes. A smile slowly spread his lips, and his eyes regained their brightness. "Royal Toes?" he asked. Kyana watched his expression change, a bubble of embarrassment churning her stomach. His eyes were glittering, and he looked like he might start to laugh.

"She didn't have a name," was the only answer she gave. They fell silent for a few moments.

Lystad cleared his throat. "How are your wounds?" he asked.

"They're fully healed now," Kyana said, pulling at the collar of her heavy cloak. It was quite hot in there.

"Are you alright?" he asked again and then answered his own question. "No, of course, you're not. You ran here from the forest, your exhausted. Please, come with me." He held out a hand, and Kyana's green eyes fell on it, narrowing a little. Lystad noticed and rolled his eyes.

"Oh, come on, Kyana. Enough of the doubts. Have you learned nothing from your time here?"

No, she had learned a great deal. More than she ever meant to. More than she had ever *wanted* to. Enough to send her running back at the first sign of trouble. Everything she had expected, from the moment he had lifted her off the ground and taken her to this dreaded castle, had been brushed away like so much dust. The evil knights where kind. The starving peasants were treated with kindness and fairness. The tyrant king, who fed off the poverty of his nation and the death of so many rivals, was a loyal leader. He was a king who had earned the love and respect of his knights and countrymen. He was a man who could put aside his pride to thank a stranger. He was a boy who rolled his eyes.

Kyana felt no fire in her chest, just that soft, persistent warmth. The anger was gone, and the gauzy lie fell from her eyes, leaving nothing but clarity. No, they did not know who she was. They did not understand, and that was all. They did not understand... not really. But she did not really care. She had not had kindness, pleasantness, friendship, for so long. Not for years. She had forgotten what it felt like to have that soft warmth in her heart, the one that told her she cared. The one that told her she still had *the capacity* to care. She cared for these people. In the short moments she had spent behind these walls, and despite everything she knew to be true, she cared. Although they would sentence her to death if they ever saw that name branded to her arm, she cared. She cared for them, with all that remained of her beaten and broken heart. It was not much... but it was theirs.

She could never belong in such a place, but it was a good kingdom he had built. This son was not his father, nor his grandfather, nor his grandfather's grandfather. He was a man from a different time who walked a similar, and yet varied, road. It was paved with a lie, but it was a lie Kyana dared say, had been told to him from birth. A lie perhaps weaved into every bedtime story. Dragons are evil. The Faithful are poisoned, manipulated, insane, and out to ruin the world. He knew no other way. But the damage was already done, and the kingdom he was creating was a great one of peace, wealth, and loyalty. It was not perfect. Not by any means. It was not a safe haven for the Faithful, but they too seemed to have found a place here in one way or another. Kyana thought of Lilly, and how the girl would never live anywhere else. Her smile, her dress, her health said she was happy, as did everyone Kyana had met. So, what if she had to hide her brand? The girl never believed in the mark anyhow. Why would she? Dragons where long dead and the most well-known of the Faithful was Rainier. Rainier, who stirred up nothing but trouble and pain. Who was Kyana to judge the girl for making a home for herself in this place? This place that had been blinded by old fears of an old war. It may be blind... but it was not bad. Kyana knew, she would never belong here. Her time, and the time for those like her had passed and passed far behind. She belonged to a time long gone and perhaps, that was also alright. This was no kingdom of hers, but that did not mean it did not deserve a fighting chance. That was why she came back to Castle Lyist... and that was why she reached out and took the hand of its king. He led her out of the throne room and down a very familiar path.

"You look tired." The king said as he led her back to the room she had occupied a month ago. "Get some rest, wash up, I'll send up a few maids to take care of you."

"Wait," Kyana said, stopping outside the door. She should probably go now. Just because she cared... did not mean it was a good idea to stay. She had told them of the threat, and she could do little more than that. "I should really—"

"You look like you haven't slept in days, and you ran straight here from the forest,"

"Yes," Kyana frowned. "But I should probably just—"

"If you think I'm letting you go back in that forest now, you're crazy," he interrupted her again, voice cold and flat, one eyebrow cocked high above his eye. "You said yourself it's crawling with hirelings. The safest place for you is inside these walls."

Kyana tried not to laugh. "I live nowhere near where they are camped out. And... You do realize these walls are exactly where the army is headed correct?"

"I do," The king nodded. "And they will never pass them. This kingdom has stood tall for many years and will stand tall for many more. Thanks to your information we can get a head start on preparations. I just don't know how we could have missed their advances for this long..." He shook his head, drawing his attention back to her. "No, you'll stay here until the forest is safe." Kyana opened her mouth to protest, but once more she was silenced with an exasperated bark. "And if you fight me on this, I swear I will throw you in the dungeons."

"On what grounds?" Kyana snapped, snatching her hand back. "I am no—"

"No citizen of mine." The king did not roll his eyes, but she could tell he was fighting the urge. "Perhaps not, but I could decide you're an ally of Rainier. Keep you in custody until we are sure."

"An ally who just gave away the location of his men?" Kyana asked, now fighting the urge to roll her own eyes.

"We have yet to hear back any confirmation from my scouts that your information is legitimate," he spoke in a voice reserved for throne rooms and royal announcements. Kyana suddenly had a flashing image of him saying those exact words while sitting on that elegant throne, one ankle rested crossed on his knee.

"You are doubting me?" Kyana's eyebrows shot up.

"You are. Not. Leaving. This. Castle," he said, breaking each word down, driving each like a hammer against a nail, trying to make the point stick firm. "Not until this is all resolved. Do you understand?" Kyana narrowed her eyes at him but said nothing. She just nodded. "Good," the Lystad said, opening the door for her and motioning to a nearby guard, who quickly took a post outside her door.

"I don't need a guard," Kyana protested.

"I know," he said, brushing back his black hair. "But you're getting one anyway."

"I don't **want** a guard," Kyana scowled.

The Lystad rolled his eyes. "Well, that's just too gods damn bad."

Kyana tried not to laugh at the guard's stunned reaction. He must never have heard his king speaking in such a manner, especially to a woman. Kyana reluctantly nodded once more, and the king returned the nod before turning to leave.

"Kyana," he said, looking back. "Thank you for letting me know. About Rainier."

"Oh," she said, taken aback. "You're... welcome," she answered, and Damian Lystad left her. Kyana watched him go in silence, but a small smile flickered across her face. She turned to nod at the guard before entering the room. She closed the heavy door and looked around. It was exactly the same. The closet in the corner, the flag on the wall, and the bed full of soft cushions and smooth sheets all sat in their perfect state, seemingly untouched since her last visit. She walked straight for the bed, dropping her bow and quiver of arrows on the rug before crawling between the sheets, pulling them snuggly over her head. She was so exhausted.

# CHAPTER 28

They found him in the dark. He was standing beneath the shadows of the trees, sunlight glinting through the branches with a cheeriness the boy himself did not feel. His hands trembled and clutched the thick, woolen bag. He held it to his chest as if every beat of his heart depended on its contents... because he knew it did.

The hirelings appeared first. They slunk silently out of the trees like shadows themselves, faces half visible beneath twines of unkempt hair, but Ellis knew they were watching him. They all seemed so big. All arms rippling with muscles, all clad in dirty wool, weapons hanging sharp and glinting on their hips. A few even held their daggers in their hands, always ready for a fight. Ellis shrank from them like a scared little puppy with soft paws.

"What do you have there, boy?" one of the taller men asked, a bow slung over his back. His voice was deep, crackling from years of familiarity with the pipe, and full of something akin to good humor. If, Ellis thought, such a man with such a scarred face had any good humor left. Such a scarred face it was. Year old burns carved up the left side of the man's neck and mangled his ear. His skin twisted, rough, red, tanned, and looked more like ruined leather than anything else. The right side of his face was no better. A dagger scar ran deep into the man's lips, curling it into an uncontrollable scowl which showed a few rotting bottom teeth through the cavern of missing skin.

Ellis swallowed, clutching the bag even closer.

"A-A-I have a gift for the general," he spoke in a trembling voice to match his hands.

A great chorus of laughter peeled out from the surrounding men, making Ellis shiver.

"There is no general here, boy," the hireling said grinning the best he could with what was left of his lips. The result almost made Ellis piss himself.

"Rainier." Ellis pressed desperately, like those fingers against his arm, so desperate for air. "I'm looking for the general Rainier."

"The witch?" the man barked a laugh that made Ellis flinch.

*Please Don't Bark.* Ellis thought desperately. *No barking, don't you see?*

"Oh, he's here boy." The man leaned in with a leer, and Ellis took a stumbling step back which almost sent him directly on his ass. "But he's no general. Not anymore."

"No, Grayson?" A cool voice swept in on the breeze, making all their hair stand on end. Ellis could feel the goose flesh rising on his arms, neck, and back. Despite this, hot relief filled his chest and spread out like fire to his finger and toes. He had been good. And he would be pleased.

He turned to see the man standing a few yards away. Ellis did not know when he had stepped into the circle of hirelings but judging by the baffled expressions that they cast to one another, neither did they. He moved with silent, silken grace, his pure white cloak sifting around him, every move like water. His blue hair was tied up on his head, pulled elegantly away from his pale face and dark eyes. Dark eyes that watched the hireling named Grayson, with nothing less than amusement.

"No general, am I?" he asked, coming to stand next to Ellis. He could feel that strange, unnatural heat. It wafted from him, calming the boy's shudders. "Then pray tell me, boy... what am I?"

Grayson, who was not at all accustomed to being called "boy" by anyone, let alone a man who looked less than half his age, scowled deeply and licked his shattered lip.

"A man, and a *Faithful*," he said, attempting to capture his old, long gone air of importance, and spitting the last word as if it was a curse.

"Yes. Both of those are true..." Rainier nodded slowly, eyes never leaving the mercenary.

"but please go on..."

"You are also a man that has promised a great deal... a great deal to all of us." He gestured to the surrounding crowd. The crowd grunted brutishly, nodding their heads. A few tapped their weapons to the ground or against their thighs, creating a volley of snapping and slaps.

"Big promises... that you have yet to deliver." A few around the circle hooted in agreement, but Rainier ignored them. The Faithful watched Grayson with those cavernous black eyes. They seemed to grow darker and darker, the longer they watched, the longer he didn't blink. Ellis saw the man's jaw tighten, and small crinkles edge his eyes as he narrowed them. When he spoke, the entire forest seemed to go silent.

"Are you calling me... a liar, Grayson?" Ellis watched as Grayson's once tall and proud demeanor slowly ebbed away under those cold eyes.

"No," he swallowed slightly, taking his time and picking his words very carefully. "But... I believe a little proof is wanting."

There was another flurry of incoherent grumbles around the circle, but the tall man's eyes were only for Grayson. He never blinked, thin mouth set, and Grayson seemed unable to look away. Everyone around the circle watched in silence, leaning in as if ready to fight, or ready to run.

Ellis watched Grayson's shoulders slowly slump, and his eyes widen. Ellis knew he was being swallowed by those eyes, sucked into the darkness's uncontrollable pull. Feeling the iciness spreading, that cold, that hollow, that... empty. As empty as that cavern beneath the city. The type of empty where magic goes insane and young boys are strangled before their twentieth year. The kind of empty with a history of pain and a future of silence.

Ellis smiled. He smiled because those eyes were not on him. He smiled because those eyes were *with* him, beside him. He smiled because he did what he had to do, you see? Those eyes would be pleased with him. Those eyes would protect him. As long as they did not look at him like that... he was going to be alright. Ellis would follow him like the shadow that followed his every move, just as long as those eyes were looking like that at someone else.

The silence broke.

"You're right, of course," Rainier said finally, blinking and letting Grayson breath. "Proof is what you all want... proof is what you all will get." He turned to Ellis, eyes casting down to the bag. "You have it, then?" he asked, in a soft voice.

"Yes, sir," he answered, hastily holding it out to him. "It wasn't easy... but I have it." Rainier reached out with long fingers and took the woolen bag from his grip. He slowly and carefully untied the knotted string at the top and pulled it open. A wide smile began to break his face. It slipped from one side to the other, cheek to cheek, as his dark eyes began to gleam. They shone silver as the sister moonlight despite the burning midday sun.

He reached into the bag and pulled out the skull. It seemed larger in his gentle hands Ellis realized, then it had in that stinking, massive cavern. And far more beautiful. It was larger than a human head, and missing the bottom jaw, but the baby dragon skull seemed to shine, glorious in the sunlight. The teeth, still embedded in the skull, hung down low and sharp from the extended snout. The ridges on the top and back of the head spoke of a time when the dragon who owned it was just beginning to grow her spikes. The empty sockets were broad, deep, and dark, and reminded Ellis suddenly of his eyes, his general's eyes, which were looking upon the skull like a loved one who finally came home.

"Isn't she beautiful?" Rainier whispered.

"Yes," Ellis answered in an equally hushed tone.

Rainier looked up at him, and Ellis was shocked to see tears had begun to well up in the corners of his eyes. They did not fall, but rested there, glittering, making his black eyes look like a night sky filled with stars. An eternal night sky. Ellis could still feel that odd empty… but this time he was not afraid.

"You did very well," Rainier said, reaching out to pat his cheek in his warm palm, "You did so very well, my important friend."

"What is that, then?" Grayson grunted, stepping up to have a look at the skull.

"This, dear boy," Rainier raised it slightly, looking at it from another angle as if reading a trail of invisible words down the snout. "This is the answer to all our prayers."

"Alright then, you've got your bone." Grayson frowned. "So, now, what are you going to do with it?" Rainier did not answer, his eyes continued to praise the skull. He ran an exploratory finger down one of the fangs. He pressed against the tip, and a drop of blood instantly blossomed against his skin. He drew it back and placed his finger in his mouth.

"Did you go deaf, man? I asked what you're going to do with that," Grayson snapped, watching him with what might have been disgust growing on his face, but Ellis thought it was hard to tell. He could be smiling happily for all he knew. His face was far too gone to know anymore.

"Oh, Ellis my boy you did so very well," the man mumbled to himself, ignoring his question once more. "Very well indeed... we can now get started." He glanced back at Grayson. "Send word to the rest of the men. Bring them here at once. All of them."

"Why?" Grayson crossed his arms over his broad chest. He was definitely scowling now.

"Because it will be very difficult for me to keep my promise when most of the men are too far away to accept it," he answered. He looked up at the sky. The sun was almost to the center by this point. A few more minutes, and it would be directly overhead. "And as you are sending word... I'll get started."

"Started on what?" Grayson sounded exasperated and tapped his large, callous thickened fingers against his arms.

The man wasn't listening. He had started brushing away loose leaves and branches with his feet, clearing an open circle of dirt. He knelt down in the sunlight, and placed the skull in the circle, flicking away any remaining twigs with the wave of his hand. He reached out with long fingers and began to draw in the damp dirt. Symbols, symbols Ellis did not recognize. They were spirals and scratches, marks like words but that belonged to no language Ellis had ever known. He surrounded the skull in them until no part of the open dirt was untouched.

He stood and turned towards Grayson. He motioned the hireling to come nearer. He took a tentative step forward. Rainier motioned him to come nearer still. The hireling leaned towards him. Rainier reached out, grabbed a hand full of his hair between his long fingers and ripped it out in one harsh movement.

"What the hell?" Grayson pulled away, hand flying to his scalp that stung and now bore a small section of bare reddening skin. "Crazy bastard," Grayson snapped.

"Would you rather I cut out your tongue?" the man asked absently, turning back to the skull on the ground. "I just need any piece of you, really. I'm not fussy about which piece."

"What for?" Grayson asked ruefully, dropping his hand from his head.

"You want proof," Rainier said, kneeling before the skull. "I'm going to give it to you." The general reached out and discarded the little clump of hair under the skull, gently lowering the snout over the top of it. This done, he leaned back and closed his eyes. Ellis could see his lips moving but heard no word, not a sound. He thought about how he must have looked, screaming silently in the empty cavern, and shivered. No, he heard nothing... but he smelled something. The smell of burning hair wafted from the skull, and Ellis saw the faintest flicker of light within the dragon's eye. Like the tiniest flash of fire. There and then gone. For a few minutes, there was no sound but the rustling of leaves and the random cough from the waiting crowd. Soon enough, his lips stopped moving, and his eyes opened.

"There," he said, pushing off from the dirt and rising slowly to his feet. "It's done."

"What's done?" Grayson asked bemused. "Nothing happened."

"Ellis," he said, turning to him and smiling. "May I borrow your blade for a moment?" Ellis blinked confused, but tugged his dagger from his belt, all the same, flipping it around and offering the handle to his general.

"Thank you," Rainier said kindly.

"What are you prattling on about Faithful," Grayson started up, chest puffing like some cock about to fight for his territory. "Nothing happened. I don't know what game you are playing, but we have a dea—" Grayson did not have time to finish his complaint as Rainier took a swift step forward and buried the dagger deep into the man's neck.

"You asked to be invincible..." he said, twisting the blade, drawing a pathetic howl from the man. "So here... have a taste of what it is to be unstoppable." Grayson sputtered, stumbling back. He pawed at the blade, no longer like a cock, but a puppy in water. The crowd around gave a gasp and then a roar of fury, leaning forward, but one warning look from Rainier, and they all stepped back.

"Have patience," he said, and they did. Grayson stumbled, spluttered, spit flying from his mouth as he finally got a hold of the blades handle and pulled. It slid from his neck with a sickening squelch that made Ellis want to vomit, but there was no blood. No spurt of red, no gush of life onto the dampened dirt. Nothing but a thin, jagged line where the blade had entered, and as Grayson looked back at the Faithful, wide-eyed, even that slowly shrank and slipped away. Grayson ran a hand across his neck, panting, eyes still on the tall man.

"Well?" Rainier asked, blinking those dark eyes. He raised his hand, motioning for the dagger. "Do we have a deal?"

Grayson looked at his hand, then down at the skull eyes widening once more. A small trail of smoke was wafting luxuriously out of the dragon's nose, and his hair was gone. As if it had never been. He looked slowly back up at Rainier, and with a slow and weary movement, placed the clean dagger back into his hand.

"That we do general, sir," he said, a wide grin breaking across his face. "That we most certainly do."

"You get the gold. All of it," Rainier said. "I get the bones. All of them."

"Sounds fair to me." Grayson grinned, and the rest of the waiting crowd hooted their approval. Another volley of slaps and cheers filled the air. Rainier smiled as the sun beat down hot and bright overhead.

# CHAPTER 29

Kyana slept the day into the night and did not wake until dusk had settled on the second evening. She stirred and twisted a few times, but only to fall back into an exhausted sleep. When Kyana finally opened her deep green eyes, she wished she had not. The days she had spent riding had taken their toll. Every muscle in her body seemed sore. And she was thirsty. Very thirsty.

Kyana pushed herself groggily to a sitting position and looked around. The sun was setting, casting long and dark shadows over the floor, but there was still enough light for Kyana to see a tray of food and a pitcher of water waiting for her on the table. She slid out of bed, groaning as she did, and made her way over. She picked the pitcher up, ignoring the glass sitting next to it, and drank greedily. The water filled her mouth and splashed down her face wetting the front of her shirt. When she finished, she put down the pitcher and got to eating. That bread and sweet butter were there, along with a few apples, cheese, and other choice snacks. Kyana dug in gratefully. She winced a little as she sat down, deciding to check on Royal when she was done. She was, after all, the one that did most of the work. If Kyana was tired, Royal must be dead on her feet.

She finished her dinner, got to her feet and stretched, looking around for the things she dropped when she came in. Her bow, her cloak, and her dagger had been picked off the floor and laid neatly on top of the dresser off to the side. She went to them, frowned down for a moment, and then decided to slide the dagger between her belt, slipped the cloak around her shoulders, and left the bow where it was.

Kyana pocketed a bright red apple before she went to the door and pushed it open easily. The hall outside was empty. Empty except for the tall man in guard's armor standing to the left of her door. Kyana jumped when she saw him there and leaned up against the door frame to catch her breath.

"You scared the blue hell out of me," Kyana said, looking up at the man, who made no reply, but gave apologetic incline of his head. The man looked to be around his thirty-seventh year, with a neatly trimmed brown beard and close-set brown eyes. The man was not only tall, Kyana noticed, but broad. He towered silent and still beside the door like so many stone statues in the courtyards.

"Have you been standing here this whole time?" Kyana asked curiously. The man just shrugged. Kyana looked around at the empty halls, usually bustling with servants and handmaids. "Everyone going off to bed then?" Kyana asked, and the man nodded. A smile crept Kyana's mouth.

"Not much for talking, I see." The man shrugged.

"Alright, then." She looked around, hesitating, "Do you happen to know," she asked, looked back up at him. "Where they might have taken my horse?" The man thought, shrugged, then nodded. He went over and plucked one of the lamps off the wall and started down the hall. Kyana following close behind. They went through the hall, down a staircase, and out a side door to the courtyards which were as empty as the rest. The sun had set entirely by this point, leaving no light except the one in the guard's hand, but Kyana thought this man could find his way around the castle with his eyes closed. He led her to a building off to the side, and as they approached, Kyana began to hear nickering and the thudding of hooves against dirt. The guard opened the door and held out the lamp for Kyana.

Kyana took it gratefully and went inside. The stables where long and spacious and Kyana passed many fine, young, beautiful horses along her way down its rows of stalls. Most were dozing, snorting a little as the light cast briefly over their faces and moved on. She was over halfway through when she found her. Royal was in a stall next to a tall black mare, who nickered at Kyana as she drew close, but Kyana did not notice. Royal was laying down.

"Shit," Kyana cursed under her breath. She tried the locks on the little double doors to the stall, but they were firmly latched. Instead, she carefully dropped the lamp over the doors and vaulted over to the other side. "Royal," She went to the large animal that lay there and felt a bit of relief when she saw the mare was still breathing. "Royal..." She rested a hand against the mare's neck, and suddenly her large head shot up sending her tan mane flapping. Kyana had to jump out of the way as Royal scrambled to her feet. The horse swung her neck around to see who or what had just appeared in her stall. They both stood, looking at each, before Kyana burst out laughing. Royal nickered, realizing who the intruder was, and tapped the ground playfully with her right hoof.

"Well, I guess you're fine," Kyana said. She rummaged in her pocket, pulled out the apple, and held it out for Royal. Royal snagged it and bit it clean in half, sending the other half falling and rolling to the corner of the stall. "Good girl," Kyana said, reaching out and patting Royal's nose. Royal leaned into the touch, still happily chomping the apple. "Good girl." Kyana spent some time petting and checking on Royal's legs. They seemed fine, no cuts or scrapes except for a small one at the top of her left back hoof, but it had already been cleaned and bandaged. In fact, Royal had never looked so clean. She had been brushed, and washed down, with a pile of hay in one corner of her stall and a bucket of water in the other.

"They take good care of you here," Kyana said, almost regretfully. When all this was over, when the issue with Rainier had been resolved, and she went home, Kyana wondered whether or not she should leave Royal at Castle Lyist. She did not want to, but she could never give Royal the type of pampered life she would have here. Even as the thought crossed her mind, she knew she could not leave her. Would not leave her. She leaned in and planting a kiss between the horse's eyes. It was selfish, but Kyana wanted to keep her. She was tired of losing. Maybe this once it would be okay if she kept something. Just this once.

Kyana gave Royal another pat before sliding the lamp back over the door and pulling herself over as well. As she straightened up, she noticed her saddle was propped up on a long wooden bar beside a few other saddles. The bag Augustine had given her was still tied to the back. She went to it and pulled it open. All the bandages and vials of mint paste had been used up over the month, and the bag was now a jumble of random belongings, including an extra dagger, a few strips of cloth, extra arrowheads, and a white and gold beaded necklace.

Her lucky little charm.

Kyana reached in, grabbed the necklace, and pocketed it. She returned the bag, picked up the lamp, gave Royal one last whispered goodnight, and slipped out the door where the guard was waiting patiently in the dark.

# CHAPTER 30

*Well,* Everett thought as he ran, beard and long ponytail flying out behind him as he pushed through the searing pain in his legs and chest, forcing himself to go faster, just a little faster. *Kyana had been right.* They were all there, exactly where she said they would be. All the hirelings with their arms and their tents propped up haphazardly throughout the forest. A thousand or so, of no concern really, except for the fact that they were not alone. He had been with them. The faithful with such a vast reputation, and Rainier did not disappoint.

Part of the hireling's numbers had separated from the main group and had moved off to the outer reaches, closer to Castle Lyist on the far side. Everett and his group had followed to see what they were doing. They thought they had been quiet, unnoticed, but they had been wrong. He had noticed. He had noticed them very well.

Everett nearly bit at the air around him, willing his lungs to keep functioning despite the searing pain and sweat that poured down his face. He did not know how long he had been running, but by the desperate throbbing of his heart, he knew it must have been quite a while. Cole was running at his side, also gasping, also sweating, also desperately tired but from more than exhaustion. Tears slid down the man's face to mingle with the sweat. Everett might have also cried if he had not been using every ounce of his energy to keep putting one trembling leg in front of the other.

There had been five of them. Five of them moved slow and swift after the small cluster of hirelings who had separated from the main group, but only two were able to get away. Arel, Darrius... Simon... they were left behind and passed by. Arel and Darrius had died quickly. As they had all been observing the small group of hirelings, trying to decipher their purpose out here away from the rest of their numbers, they had been found. They had been leaning out around the trees to get a better look at the hirelings, when the smooth voice had spoken directly behind them.

"Hello Gentleman... may I be of service?" Six more hirelings stood beside a tall, thin, pale man with a smile that made Everett's stomach shrivel up into a raisin. Arel and Darrius had been run through the instant they turned around... but... Simon.

Cole broke his stride, stumbling to his knees, gasping, whether for lack of air, or from sobs, Everett did not know. He turned back, grabbing the man by the lower arm and yanking him back to his feet.

"We don't have time for that now," Everett barked into the older man's face, which was red with exertion, eyes bloodshot by sorrow.

"He's gone, Everett," Cole gasped desperately, a fresh stream of tears spilling down his cheeks as his chest shuttered. "Oh, gods Everett, he killed Simon. Simon is gone." Everett knew this. He had watched it happen in wide-eyed horror. In the scuffle that occurred after they were found, Everett and Cole were able to break away. They thought Simon was right at their heels, but when they turned around, he was gone. They backtracked to discover him surrounded by hirelings... and the tall stranger.

Cole had tried to jump right in, ready to fight and die for the man who was forced to his knees before the stranger, but Everett held him back. He wrapped one arm around his waist, and the other pressed hard against Cole's mouth to prevent him from drawing attention. There was no use in trying to save Simon, Everett could see that. They would only succeed in getting themselves killed as well. Cole struggled viciously against his hold, but Everett was stronger, so all he could do was watch in horror as the tall man walked in slow liquid strides to where Simon was held in a kneeling position.

"Hello there," the man said, voice just as slow and slick as his strides. "What is your name?" Simon said nothing, teeth-gritting into a scowl as one of the hirelings gave him a swift kick in the hip. Cole gave another violent thrash, but Everett still did not let go.

"Oh, that is not necessary," the tall man said, lifting a long-fingered hand towards the kicker. He jerked back as if the tall man had slapped him. The tall man stepped closer and knelt down, coming face to face with Simon. "Now... shall we try this again knight of Castle Lyist? You are a knight of Castle Lyist, yes?" Cole still said nothing. "Come, come, my good man, don't be shy," the tall man said pleasantly. Simon hocked loudly and spat into the man's face. Cole froze in Everett's arms, and Everett could feel his heart beating wildly, picking up speed as panic rose almost palpable in the air.

The tall man did not react at first, just knelt there, the spit sliding down his face in a slow, sickeningly green sludge. Then, he smiled. It was a horrible thing that smile. It traced from one side of his face to the other, breaking wide to reveal bright white teeth. He reached up and wiped his face with his sleeve.

"Okay," he said, standing slowly to tower over Simon, casting him in his long willowy shadow. "Okay, boy." He moved away from Simon and moved to a little bundle of cloth beneath a nearby tree. He picked it up with a gentle hand and brought it back to kneel before Simon once more.

"Have you ever seen dragon bones?" the man asked, slowly unlacing the silken tie that held the lip of the bag closed. Simon made no answer, so the man pushed on. "Funny really. How you all seem so reluctant to even acknowledge their existence. You created them. You killed the flesh and left the bones. Then you hide them away. Forget about them... or at least you try." The man looked up briefly, that smile spread a little wider. "Is it shame that makes you do so? A little regret? If that is the case... then perhaps your souls aren't quite so damned. The first step on the road to redemption is to acknowledge the wrongs you have done. But it is a pity." The man reached into the bag. "They are such beautiful things. They deserve better than to rot in the dark... don't you think?" The man pulled out the skull of a creature that had not existed for centuries, and Cole began to struggle once more. "Pretty isn't she?" the man asked, drawing a long finger down the dragon's snout. "So young... she would probably still be alive today if... it is a pity, it truly is... can't you see that? Surely you must see that... ah well..." The man rested the skull on top of the cloth bag and put his hand gently on the creature's forehead. He looked back at Simon, reached out, and touched his shoulder. There was an ominous, loud, snapping sound. Simon began to scream. Cole nearly launched himself out of Everett's arms, but Everett was able to hold on. Simon's arm hung from his shattered collarbone and shoulder like a rag doll's limb. It flopped uselessly at his side, as Simon continued to shriek in pain. The tall man's expression did not change. It remained absolutely neutral as the sound of Simon's screams reverberated throughout the forests, and birds took wild, frightened flight into the midday sky. The man raised his hand once more, black eyes oblivious to the pain he was causing.

"No!" Simon shrieked. "No, please, for the love of the gods, don't. Please."

"Shhhhhhh." The man patted Simon's cheek, and Simon shrank from the touch, his ruined arm flopping awkwardly. "Shhhhh, boy. Do not be afraid. I'm going to *help* you. I'll make that nasty pain go away. I'll make it *all* go away. What is it you and your kind liked to say? Oh yes," That smile broke his face once more, and his black eyes suddenly lit up with a sickening pleasure. "I'm going to **liberate** you. I am sure you will appreciate it, as much as I did." The man reached over and placed his free hand against Simon's forehead, the other still resting on the skull. There was another sickening snapping sound, and Simon's eyes ran with blood.

Everett had to drag Cole's shuddering body away, and it was then that they began to run.

"I know," Everett said hollowly, giving the man another rough yank on his arm. "I know, but we don't have time to mourn him now. We need to get back to the horses. We need to get back to Castle Lyist. That is the only important thing right now." Cole gasped, still sobbing, but he nodded. They turned and continued forward.

They needed to tell King Lystad. Kyana had been right.

Rainer was here.

And they were fucked.

# CHAPTER 31

Ira grunted in frustration as she balanced a platter of goblets and a flask of fresh water in one arm while trying to open the council room door with the other. The guard that stood by the door watched her struggle, an amused grin playing his face.

Ira gave one last effort, almost tumbling the platter to the floor. She sighed and glared up at the guard, who was now choking on his held back laughter.

"Do you mind, Gerald?" Ira snapped.

Gerald was a dipshit who only got the position in the castle because he was the youngest son of a lower nobleman with ties to Castle Lyist, and no other talents, or brains, to speak of. He spent most of his days fidgeting with his armor, leering at passing handmaids, and saying the only three words he seemed to know: "yes sir," and "huh?"

Taking his time, Gerald reached over with a gloved hand and pushed the door open, still holding back his laughter.

"Thanks," Ira spat the word. *You ignorant, pig-headed, self-absorbed piece of shit in armor.* "Ever so kind of you." The guard finally burst into laughter as Ira walked through the door. Ira kicked it closed behind her. It snapped into place with a loud thud that made the men in brown cloaks, who had been huddled around the small square table, look up.

"Sorry," Ira mumbled, making her way over and sliding the platter onto the table between them all, avoiding the maps that were spread wide. No one responded, merely picked up where they had left off.

"They were exactly where she said they would be," Neander said, tapping his finger against one of the maps crinkled surface.

"How many?" Damian spoke in his 'King Damian tone' of voice, and Ira couldn't help a worried glance. Ira had not been told what was going on. She had only been told to bring drinks to the council chamber for an impromptu meeting, and impromptu meetings never meant good things. The fact that Damian had on his extra authoritative voice, and that long crease between his brows, told Ira that something was very, very wrong.

"We counted nine hundred and eighty-seven men in the forests. But part of the group broke off. Everett went with a few scouts to check their numbers. He should be back soon, as well."

"Any sight of Rainier?" Damian said, taking a goblet and carefully filing it with the pitcher.

"Rainier?" the name fell fast and hard from her mouth as Ira glanced back and forth from one knight to the other. Was Rainier near? Was he making an attack on the castle? For the god's sake, why? What the hell was going on?

Neander shook his head. "But he's not usually one to be seen, now is he?"

"No," Damian agreed, calmly sipping from his goblet as if simply discussing an irritating fly in the room and not one of the most powerful and oldest of Faithful ever to have existed in the lands.

"What's going on?" Ira was standing, arms loose by her sides, mouth nearly hanging open.

"We aren't quite sure yet," Damian answered simply. Neander jerked a glance in her direction as if suddenly realizing she had entered the room.

"Is there an army coming for Castle Lyist?" Ira asked, taking a step closer to the maps spread open wide as if they would tell her everything he wanted to know, show the advancing armies like images from a sorcerer's crystal ball.

"We believe so," Damian continued, that same calm, cool, commanding tone as before. He slowly rested his cup to the table and squinted down at the maps himself. "We heard news of a threat from Kyana and are checking into it now."

"Kyana?" Ira's head jerked up. "Kyana's here?"

"A few nights passed," Damian said. "I sent her to get rest while we assessed the situation—" He was interrupted by a tremendous banging noise, as the counsel room door was flung open and Everett marched in, Cole by his side. They looked exhausted and sweaty as if they had been riding hard. They also looked alert and tense as they stepped up to the table and bowed to the king.

"Your majesty."

"What happened?" Damian asked.

"We followed a group of the hirelings that broke off my lord. They moved to forests nearer the meadow and just seemed to be waiting there."

"Waiting for what?" Ira knew she sounded flustered and was speaking completely out of turn, but she was a little too panicked to give a damn. Besides, it did not matter, no one was listening to her, anyway.

"How many?" Damian's voice was as smooth and cool as ice on a creek.

"A few hundred," Everett said.

"Just a few hundred?" Damian frowned. "What were they doing?"

"I don't know your majesty," Everett answered gravely. "… but the Faithful… he was with them. And your majesty… he saw us. We lost Simon… we lost them all… they know their surprise is blown."

A hush ran through the small gathering. Ira looked from one grim face to the other and finally stopping on the King of Castle Lyist himself. Ira wondered what must be going on beneath that inky black hair. He looked calm, thoughtful, but Ira knew he could not be. How could he be?

The Faithful. Rainier. The mere idea of him filled the room like an evil laugh, distracting, and disquieting.

"Gather the men," Damian said finally, lifting his goblet, taking a long slow sip, before speaking again. "Prepare for an attack. Close the gates and tell the people to go to their homes… try to do so as calmly as possible. We have little time, and we don't want to start a panic. Think of an excuse. Any excuse. Meet back here once preparations have been made. But first, get ready."

"Yes, my lord." The knights bowed to their king, before quickly turning and heading to make preparations.

"Damian," Ira said, looking at the man now rolling up the scattered maps and sliding them into their smooth brown bags. "What the hell is going on?" Damian looked up at her, blue eyes as cool as his voice, and a cold shiver ran down Ira's spine.

"Their plans to attack are out in the open… they will either retreat… or continue on in force, and as far as legends go, Rainier never turns tail," Damian said, taking another sip from his cup. "So, either this is a futile waste of time by a Faithful whose legend has far outstripped his nature… or something very bad is headed our way. So, nothing good Ira… nothing good."

# CHAPTER 32

Days passed with little change. Kyana spent most of that time in the stall with Royal, brushing her down, feeding her apples and giving her, some well-earned, attention. None of the stable boys that tended to the rest of the horses seemed to mind. The only time they became uncomfortable was when she tried to muck out Royal's stall.

"We can do that, miss," one of them, barely past his twelfth year, said kindly, holding out his hand for the shovel. Kyana brushed off the offer with a smile.

"She's my horse, I can handle a little dung. And I'm no miss, nor lady."

When Kyana was not in the stall with Royal, she was in her room resting and growing increasingly bored. She had no idea what to do and did not know if she could or should go wandering alone. She did have the guard, but he only followed behind her like a silent phantom which Kyana found unnerving, to say the least. Even if she wanted to find an old friend, Kyana did not know where Ira might be. She mentioned she worked in the kitchens, but as far as Kyana knew there were at least two kitchens if not more, and she had no idea where any of them were. She could go wandering and hopefully run into a knight or servant she recognized, but she wondered if that was a good idea either. As much as she would like to spend time with Neander, Ira, Everett or Lilly, she did not see the point. It was hard enough leaving the first time and seeing them would only make it that much harder to repeat. So, she went between Royal, her room, and sleep. Food was brought in to her, but only by strangers. She did not see anyone she recognized until one morning when she was woken by a soft and familiar voice.

"Miss…. Kyana, miss, wake up."

"Lilly?" Kyana asked groggily as the girl's face came into focus.

"Hello, miss," Lilly said, smiling down at her. Behind Lilly, a second girl was laying clean clothes out on the wide wooden table. "Nice to see you again."

Kyana smiled.

"Lilly," Kyana reached up, and wrapped her arms around the girl, nearly yanking her into a hug. "How have you been?" she asked, pulling away to look over the girl's face, which was now a little pink.

"Very well, thank you, Miss." Lilly's watery eyes sparkled for a moment, but the sparkle quickly faded. "Although it's been a little tense around the castle for the past few days… I think something's wrong, but no one will tell me what."

"There's an army gathering outside the reach of Castle Lyist," Kyana said bluntly.

Lilly's mouth dropped open, and the girl who had been flipping out, what looked to Kyana like a chestnut blanket, stopped and looked around.

"Oh," Lilly said.

"Why wouldn't anyone tell you that?" Kyana frowned.

"I don't know," Lilly shrugged as the girl in the back, slowly turned back to her work. "Worried about… well, worrying us, I guess."

"That's stupid," Kyana said. There was an attack planned on Castle Lyist led by a Faithful of extreme capability and a history of near successes. There was definitely something to be worried over.

Lilly just laughed and shrugged, her watery eyes shining once more. Kyana was amazed at how easily the girl had shaken off this information. Was she so sure of the castle's safety? Or did she just find comfort in the idea that it was none of her business?

"We're here to get you cleaned and dressed," Lilly said. Kyana's eyes darted towards the other servant girl, hand going automatically for her forearm. Lilly eased her silent concern. "I told Brea about your shyness at being bathed and changed… I'll be helping you with that. On my own." She gave Kyana a shy wink.

The girl was not exactly subtle, but Kyana was grateful all the same.

"Thank you," Kyana said, and playfully returned the girls wink.

Kyana got to her feet. It was awkward being bathed and dressed, but she took a deep breath and allowed Lilly to do her work. The other girl, Brea, waited outside while Lilly helped wash and clean Kyana's hair. She was not allowed back in until a smooth white cloth was wrapped like a bandage on the inside of Kyana's left arm, and a thin white undergarment had been slipped over her head.

When Kyana was fully bathed and dried, she stepped slowly up to the table. Beside the laid-out clothes was a small tray of food and a glass of milk. Kyana noticed a small role of paper tucked under the little dish of sweet butter and unraveled it. She smiled at the familiar slanted handwriting.

*Hello Kyana,*

*Welcome back. You've been missed.—Ira*

Kyana carefully folded the little piece of paper before turning to look down at the clothes that waited for her. She frowned at the fabric, as Lilly let Brea back in, and picked up a brush from the table.

"Are these…" Kyana reached out and fingered the bottoms of the dark brown cloth. "pants?"

"Oh, yes!" Lilly said, running a brush through Kyana's hair as she spoke. The thick auburn curls sprung back into place as the brush reached the ends. They bounced like brown and red rain off the street. It had dried so quickly, Lilly noted, as if Kyana had been sitting with her back to a fire for hours, and not just stepped out of the tub. "The king had it made specially. He was told you were uncomfortable in skirts. That you're used to trousers."

"He had them made?" Kyana looked around, running a hand absently down the white slip she wore. "When?"

"A month or so ago. Before you left, I believe," Brea said, fluffing the waiting fabric. "He thought you would be staying longer."

"And he… kept them?" Kyana wondered.

"In case you stopped by for a visit. He wanted you to be comfortable, I suppose." Brea smiled at the material as if seeing the young king himself. Reverently. "He is a kind man, our king."

"Brea's got a thing for him," Lilly whispered in Kyana's ear.

"I do not!" Brea protested, her cheeks turning a bright shade of red. Kyana could almost see the steam begin to pour out of the girl's ears.

"He is… handsome, I suppose." Kyana squinted at the fabric as if thinking hard. It was an act, of course. It was not hard to remember his face. His smooth olive skin. How his inky black hair seemed to liquify in the sunlight. How his laughter echoed… how his eyes light up when he saw her.

Kyana shook her head, nearly flinging the brush from Lilly's hand. This was a dangerous train of thought. Very dangerous. He was not her king. He was nothing to her, and never would be. Nothing but a strangely happy memory left behind in a stone-walled hallway.

"Well," Kyana said, turning to the girls, one of which was still gleaming red. "Let's get on with it."

The new clothes seemed a compromise between Kyana's useful, comfortable forest wear and the traditional, elegant, Castle Lyist style of a long skirt. It had long sleeves, but they did not hang cumbersome around her fingers. They snug tight around her wrists, keeping them out of the way. It also had slim pants with a half skirt tapering down the back. The skirt was a deep, chestnut brown and held on the hips by silver dragon head clips whose long silver teeth dug into the fabric. The girls then pinned the top of Kyana's hair, allowing the bottom to fall around her shoulders in a natural auburn mass. She let them finish lacing up the back of the dress with smooth brown ribbon before she slipped the dagger into her pocket. Kyana looked at her quiver and bow, and debated only a moment, before slipping them over her shoulder. If things had grown tense around the castle... well, better to be prepared for everything. It was about time she found out what was going on.

The last thing she did before leaving was to slip that little beaded necklace off of its place on the bedside table and gently fasten it around her neck. Pretty and simple, it rested against her chest. Kyana found comfort in the weight of it.

*A little luck,* she thought, *never hurt anyone.*

Kyana thanked the girls, giving Lilly a knowing wink before all three left the room behind. Kyana had walked only a short distance when she remembered her phantom. He was trailing behind her as she stepped swiftly down the stone hall, his footsteps falling almost silently behind her. Kyana tried to ignore him, padding towards the staircase that leads to the other levels of the castle, but soon found it impossible. Instead, she slowed her step until the guard was walking by her side. He hesitated, seeming to decide whether or not to slow his step farther. He glanced down at her, his gruff, bearded, face questioning.

"I prefer walking with someone, than in front of them," Kyana answered the silent question with honesty. The guard said nothing but smiled as they continued on their way.

"Do you know what's been happening?" The guard shook his head. "Have you heard anything about the hirelings? Or Rainier?" The guard frowned at her. Another question.

"I take that as a 'no.'" Who was in charge of spreading the news in this city? They were doing a piss-poor job of it. Kyana sighed.

"Well, let's go find out then."

Kyana picking up speed and this time the guard matched her stride. They moved swiftly through the castle and up the stairs. They met very few people along the way, and that worried her. The castle was usually bustling during this time of day, but now the halls were quiet. Tense. Foreboding.

Kyana and her armored shadow made it to the top of the staircase and the door that waited there. She gripped the cool metal handle and pushed it open. Bright, fresh air greeted her as she stepped out on top of the castle walls. A bird swept so close overhead the guard cursed and ducked, but Kyana ignored it. She walked to the edge of the wall and looked down to the goings on below. A hiss of air slipped between her teeth and came back out as a sharp woeful whistle.

The streets below the walls were hectic, a rush of people moving here and there. They flowed like water in a river during a flood. Desperate and fast, they streamed around carts, statues, and each other, sometimes knocking into one or several of them. Some seemed to be scurrying for their homes, quickly shutting their windows and barring their doors the moment they did so. Several mothers wrangled unruly children like a farmer herding chickens, arms raised and voices calling names Kyana could not hear over the endless stream of voices, trampling of feet and the clicking of horse's hooves as they joined the flow, doing their best to avoid stepping on any of the aforementioned chicken children.

Others were preparing. Knights in their brown capes and guards in their gleaming armor lead horses with carts filled with weapons through the crowd. They bellowed at the rest to get out of the way. A few heard, and a few did not. One boy, no older than his ninth year, had to jump out of the way as a cart full of spears came careening passed, led by a large black stallion, which whinnied and snorted before passing by. Gates began to close. Kyana watched as far as her eyes could see, the four large gates of Castle Lyist, slowly sliding shut with the grinding sound of infrequently used hinges that made the crowds grown and wince in unison, before continuing on their way.

Kyana looked past the hubbub, passed the hurrying masses, past the whining gates, and saw what was coming into view over the hills outside of the castle's reach. A small dark army was descending upon Castle Lyist. Kyana squinted to them, trying to make them out, make anything out. At this distance they looked more like a little swarm of black ants, descending on an unfortunate picnic laid out for an unobservant couple. The black mass slowed to a stop.

Kyana frowned at this. It did not make sense. Why would they just stop? Right there, out in the open under the midday sun? They were giving Castle Lyist time to prepare, whether accidentally or otherwise. Was there something wrong with their original plan? Did they just realize that their rumpled group of only a little over a thousand men would be no match for the famous armies of Castle Lyist? Where they merely altering their plan? Whatever reason, the sight worried Kyana.

"Well, this…" Kyana looked out over the descending darkness and scowled. "This is not good."

"No, not a very pretty sight, is it?" Kyana turned to see Ira standing beside her, arms weighed down with bags of shining, newly sharpened, daggers. Her face was severe and wan but switched to a half smile as Kyana looked at her.

"Ira!" she said. Kyana might have reached out to the girl if her arms were not otherwise occupied. She was struck by the happy intensity. She knew she had missed Ira's grinning face, but she did not realize just how much until she was standing before her. Kyana had missed so much about this castle. The people in this city. That warmth blossomed in her chest, and this time, she did not try to hold it back. It bloomed there, petals spreading wide, triumphant in its victory.

"I heard you were back in the city," Ira said. "I was hoping to see you… before it all started…" Her eyes darted back to the army which still held still. Too still. "How've you been?"

"I was doing well until this commotion," Kyana waived a hand towards the mess of activity. She turned back to Ira. "Would you like some help with that?"

"Well, uh, sure just be careful," Ira said as Kyana reached for two of the bags. "They're quite heavy and..." She trailed off as Kyana easily slung one over her shoulder and wrapped the other securely around her wrist. "Uh, never mind, then." She flashed her another grin.

"Where are we taking these?" Kyana asked. "Also, why are *you* taking these? Don't you work in the kitchens?"

"Down to the knights," Ira said as they took the same stairs that Kyana and the guard had come up moments ago. "Everyone is mostly ready, but the king thought it best to have the extra blades on standby in case they were needed. And I volunteered," Ira shrugged, "Nobody is in the mood for food right now, anyway."

"Why would you ever not have all blades ready?" Kyana asked curiously. The idea of having so many weapons at your disposal, only to have them rust and dull in the darkness of a closet damn near insulted her. In the forest, Kyana had to make her own weapons. Arrows, spears, even her bow she had made by hand. It had taken her days, nearly costing her a finger at one point. During that time, she would have killed to have a single one of the blades that Ira now carried in a haphazard bundle under her arm like they were nothing more than a basket of stale bread.

Ira laughed and shrugged. "I dunno. It's usually not needed."

"Today on the other hand..."

"Yes, today is quite different," Ira's grin slipped slowly from her face like rain down a window pane. Kyana could almost see her usual cheerful nature dripping off her chin and to the ground below, slowly left behind with every step. "They say you saw him," Ira said. "Rainier."

"Yes," Kyana answered, taking every step with care.

"... What is he like?" Ira asked, voice low, and Kyana thought she heard a tinge of fear folded within the question. She thought about the man's slow gash of a smile. Thought about how his black eyes had passed by her, and how cold they had felt. How *hollow* they had felt. What had those eyes seen to cause so much darkness? To suck out all the light?

"Nothing good," Kyana said, hoisting the bag a little higher on her shoulder. To her surprise, her answer made Ira laugh. It was a short, nervous thing, but a laugh all the same.

"What?" Kyana asked, but Ira only shook her head as they made it to the bottom floor and started down the hallway.

"It's nothing. Never mind."

Kyana cast a glance toward the guard, to see if he knew what Ira was laughing at, but he was missing from her side. She turned to see that he had once again started trailing behind her. She scowled and watched him with unblinking green eyes, never faltering in her step. The guard's eyebrows shot up at her glare.

"Why?" the question cracked, sarcastic, and sharp. The guard's eyes darted from side to side, confused, until realization struck him. He quickened his pace until he was walking in line with Ira and Kyana.

"There," she said, satisfied. Kyana looked back to Ira, who was watching her curiously. "I don't like people walking behind me," she answered. "It's creepy."

"In this city, it's usually a sign of respect," Ira said, shrugging. "Guards usually follow behind their nobleman or their charges."

"Well," Kyana crinkled her nose absently as if smelling something old and rotten. "Not where I'm from. When you walk, you walk side by side, or you shouldn't be walking together at all." Kyana saw that grin tugging at Ira's lips once more.

After they stepped out into the busy courtyard, they caught a ride with one of the horse carts laden down with weaponry. They road it all the way to the fourth and outer most wall. The wall that would be attacked first. They were dropped off at one of the stations where knights were gearing up for battle. Long tables of endless weapons were lined in an orderly fashion. Ira told her they had stations like these set out beside every gate in the castle. The inner gate was the least likely to be used, seeing as if it was needed, that would mean the other three barriers had fallen, and the castle was nearly done for. They thought it wise to prepare all the stations anyhow.

Kyana watched the flurry of brown and blue movement around the stations and listened to the yelled of orders. Armor was being locked in place on knights by their frantic servants. The armor was fresh, clean, and shown almost blinding in the bright reflection of the sun. Kyana thought how all those gleaming metal plates would be a little less shiny in a few hours. A little less shiny... and a lot bloodier.

Kyana helped Ira neatly line up the remaining daggers on the last empty spaces. Every point turned upward, sharp, and ready.

"Kyana!" Kyana turned to see the boy knight Lionel coming up to her. He was already donning his armor, and to his credit, he wore it well. There was no hesitation in his gait, and no fear in his young eyes as his red tinged hair tumbled in the breeze.

*Ah,* Kyana thought, a tightness in her chest began to twist painfully. *The immortal gait of someone who has not yet been to battle... that will also change.* Many things would by the end of this day. She could feel it. She felt it when that pale man's gaze passed through her like a ghost through flesh, freezing her and setting her on fire all at once. She felt it then. The change that would begin with that pale man, and end... Kyana didn't know... She supposed she would find out in time, once time had passed far enough behind.

*All things must eventually... time is not immune.*

Kyana pulled her mind back to the boy knight who had come to stand tall and confident before her.

"What are you doing here?" Lionel asked in sincere wonder. "Are you planning to fight with us?"

Kyana was taken aback.

"I..." She had not thought about it. She had come to the castle without hesitation and stayed because there was no other option available to her. She was already helping with the preparations... but to battle with them? She had not thought about it. Fight against that man? Rainier may be a violent and well-feared... but he was a Faithful. One of Kyana's own kind. Would she really take up arms against her own... for the sake of Castle Lyist? For the sake of any of the Four Kingdoms, who had persecuted the dragons for which they had once cared so deeply. Kyana did not know. In not knowing she suddenly felt cold, and the little blossom of warmth seemed to wilt, delicate petals falling slow.

*How far will you go?* She asked herself in a voice as cold, dark, and sharp as the edge of a dragon shell blade. *How far will you turn from yourself, from your kind, from what you know you are... for the sake of these people? Are you truly so lost, little girl? Are you truly so needy? Are you truly so desperate for affection,* **any** *affection, that you would fight what you are?* Kyana tried to shake away the voice. Tried to reassure herself that she was doing nothing wrong. This was a fine kingdom with good people. People that were just lost in an old hate.

*Old?!* The voice nearly screamed, battering around in her skull, fighting against its captivity. Desperate to escape, to be heard, to be free. *The hate is not old, you fool! It's as young and fresh as the first four dragons when they came into this world and will last far longer than they ever could. It will live past us, it will live past us all, and when every Faithful is dead by fire and scattered like so much ash, the hate will live on. They have no love for you, you stupid girl. They cannot love what they hate.*

"She's just helping me get set up here, sir," Ira said helpfully, casting a worried glance at Kyana, who seemed unable to speak.

"Well, I'm glad to hear that," Neander said, appearing by Lionel's side. His armor was only half tied down. He leaned an arm against his brother's shoulder, a few leather straps hung awkwardly out of place. "We wouldn't want that."

"Why do you say that?" Kyana asked. She felt a pang of disappointment. Something almost like hurt.

Neander seemed to notice her reaction and chose to clarify.

"Oh, don't get me wrong, angel. I'd feel a lot safer with you by my side going into battle. You could probably whip twelve of those hirelings at once… but there are a lot more than twelve…. And none of us want you getting hurt."

"I can handle myself."

"Oh, I know you can," Neander laughed and nodded vigorously. "Doesn't mean we want you in harm's way."

"Neander…" Ira broke out, not able to hold it any longer. She had been watching the leather straps swinging all out of place with building annoyance. "Who's doing up your armor…. Because it's all wrong. Just, *all* wrong."

"This guy, uh, William… Wilbert…. Something with a "Will" I think. He's new."

"Come here." Ira stepped forward, taking his arm and properly strapping his armor. "We need to fix this, or it will fall off two seconds into a fight. Where's the rest of it?"

"Back at my station," Neander said, gesturing vaguely, and Ira started tugging on his sleeve. "Alright, woman, alright, hold on then." He reached out and gave Lionel a quick rumple of his hair, which his little brother unsuccessfully tried to dodge. "And you. You come find me before this all starts right?"

"What for?" Lionel asked.

"Keep you from getting yourself killed obviously," Neander laughed. "Grams would have a fit if I sent you home dead."

"Okay, let's go." Ira, losing all patience, gave his arm a hard jerk.

"Easy, Ira," Neander said as Ira tugged on his armor with surprising strength for such a thin frame, almost making Neander stumble. "I'm coming. See you soon, Kyana! Stay out of trouble!" he called as Ira ushered him away. Ira looked back and waived, her skirts flipping lightly behind her. Kyana waived and watched them disappear through the crowd.

"I better get going as well," Lionel said, checking the sun in the sky. "Need to finish getting ready." He looked back at her and smiled. "Take care, Kyana."

Kyana's stomach gave a violent tug as she watched the young boy turn away.

"Wait," she said, and he turned back. She reached out with the two fingers between the pinky and index of her right hand and drew a straight line down his forehead between his eyes, which watched her confused.

"Let there be cunning," she spoke the words slowly, quietly, as if each was the most delicate word in the world. As if spoken without the deepest of care would cause each to break and shatter on her lips, lost forever. With the same fingers, she tapped twice under his lightly stubbled chin. A baby's beard. What was this boy doing with a sword by his side? Didn't they see he was too young to be a man? A battle could only do three things to a boy… make a coward, make a man, or make him dead. Which would he be, when the time had passed him by?

"Let there be courage." She moved to his smooth chest plate and traced a spiral against its shimmering surface, one of the few layers protecting that still beating heart.

"Let there be fire," she finished in a whisper and drew back to see Lionel staring at her, a mixture of confusion and wonder circling his face.

"For luck," she said simply. She half expected him to say he did not need luck. That he was a knight of Castle Lyist, and that he was untouchable and that he would give Great King Lawrence II himself a run for his coin, but he did not. He simply smiled a young boy's smile.

"Thank you," he said, and he meant it. The people of Castle Lyist did not believe in magic, but they did believe in good old-fashioned luck. They bid their goodbyes, and soon Kyana was alone with her watchful guard. She stood there, unsure of what to do next. She watched the people flowing by her in swirls of browns and blues and glinting armor. Servants tripping after knights, and horses prancing past, snorting. They felt the tension, and so could Kyana. There was a heat sparking in her lower chest, and the pressure was making her edgy. The pressure... and something else.

Kyana looked around and noticed an old servant watching her. He had been raking horse excrement and tossing it into the back of a hand wheeled cart, but he had stopped mid-work to stare directly at her. His face was traced with years, and his eyes whited by cataracts, but he had seen. He had seen her giving Lionel the Wish for the Traveler. Lionel was too young to know about the Faithful's charm for luck and guidance. It was once a common practice for Faithful's going on a long journey or coping with a great loss. It was once performed in a small ceremony by the Main of a dragon, someone who had direct access to a dragon's magic, making the charm have actual powers. However, as the years passed, the Mains and their ceremonies began to dwindle with the dragons, and it was a practice taken up by many Faithful mothers who gave it to their sons before sending them to fight against the Four Kingdoms during the Second War. More of comfort to the mothers then actual protection for the children by that point, but Kyana knew the power that resided in comfort. Comfort and hope have lead thousands across deserts in search of fresh water, into war with pride, and towards death with grace.

Lionel was too young to know such things. This man apparently was not. He watched her with a narrowed, white gaze, and Kyana felt a shiver run down her spine. In those eyes, she saw it. That distrust.

*That's hate my dear.* That cold voice corrected. *That is pure, unabashed, hate.*

Kyana moved away from the old man and his cream-colored eyes, swiftly moving through the hordes, putting as much space between them as possible. Her guard followed her like a billowing brown shadow, silent but swift, oblivious to the old man and his glare. He had been too busy helping a servant carry a particularly large stack of shields to the nearest station to notice what Kyana had done.

"What's your name?" Kyana asked the guard as they moved together, he only a step behind, by the simple fact that he did not know where she was going. Neither did she, but no need to talk about that. "I feel like I should know by now."

"Killian," he answered.

"Have you always lived in Castle Lyist Killian?" He nodded. "Have you always wanted to protect this kingdom?"

"To be a guard, you mean?"

"... Sure." Kyana said after a pause.

"Of course," he answered, as swift and steady as his gate. "My father and my father's father have all been guardians of the castle."

"So, you took up the post because of tradition?" Kyana sidestepped a servant carting a wagon full of horse's armor. She thought of Royal and wondered how she was doing with all this commotion. She was a smart animal and must know something was wrong.

"Partly," Killian said. His voice had a questioning tone, as if wondering what she really wanted to ask. He was a perceptive one, this Killian. Quiet, but quick. She liked that very well.

"And the other part?" Kyana paused in her steps, turning to look at him over her shoulder.

"Well... it's what I have always known I suppose..." Killian shrugged. "But it's also what I wanted. To stand for something.... More."

"More?"

"More than just me," he finished. He frowned at her. "Why are you asking?"

"Can't I be curious who you are?" Kyana flashed a grin and continued forward.

"Sure..." he said slowly. "Doesn't mean people usually are."

Kyana pondered, stepping carefully around the passerby's, but being careful not to leave Killian behind.

*Something more. Humm...*

# CHAPTER 33

The midday sun burned bright overhead, Castle Lyist itself in view, when the Faithful man ordered them to halt. He stood before them, a tall and thin figure between their small rag tag masses and the four high walls of the Castle Lyist. His white cloak dragged against the grass as he stepped closer, face upturned, black eyes on the sun.

Grayson watched him warily. He did not like the man. Not one bit. From his snake-like strides to his horrible smile, he hated Rainier. Hated his airs, the way he acted like a noble of a kingdom and not the skulking, grief-driven, revenge-driven, outcast, that he indeed was. Not even his own kind liked him. If they did, he would have gathered an army of Faithful's to his side, not men of coin. Or in this case, men for so, so much more.

Grayson's hand ran over the spot on his neck where the Faithful had stabbed him. There was not a single mark left behind. *Invincibility.* The word hung in his mind like a dream, and he was waking slowly to realize it was now his reality. The Faithful may be a monster in the skin of a man, but he knew what he was doing. He had kept himself alive for gods knows how many years by this point, and he did not look older than his thirtieth year.

"Now," Rainier said, eyes coming down from the sun and landing on Grayson. "Now is the time." He held out his hand to his sniveling boy, Ellis, Grayson though his name was, came up to him like a mouse approaching a cat. He held out the bag with both hands, eyes cast to the ground. The Faithful took it gently as if taking a child and then reached out to pat the boy's hair. To Grayson's great disgust, he saw the boy's eyes damn near sparkle before stepping away, still watching the ground. The man untied the bag with pale white fingers that looked like they had never seen the sun a day in their lives and pulled from it the skull. They had spent hours earlier that morning, every member of their army lining up to take their turn with the thing. They stepped up, pulled, cut, or yanking parts of their hair or beard. Those that had no hair or beard to speak of, resorted to other methods. Teeth were pulled from mouths; skin was sliced from arms and legs. In one case, a very determined hireling cut the small finger off his left hand. As Rainier had said, he simply needed a piece of each of them. Any piece would do. After their parts were given, Rainier gathered the bloody haired mess into a small bag. Grayson had grown a little suspicious when the Faithful had asked him to do the same.

"You already did me," Grayson said, scowling at the man's outstretched hand. "Why do I need to do it again?"

"Because," the Faithful spoke in that low and sweet voice that made Grayson's skin crawl. "The spell I am doing today will be a blanket spell over everyone near. It needs to touch every person in our little regiment, or it may not work at all." When Grayson still hesitated, the man held his hand higher. "You want your gold, don't you?"

Grayson frowned, mind drifting to Castle Lyist and the endless treasures it must hold. How Grayson wanted to step foot in those halls, taking what he pleased, all he pleased. That was their deal after all. Grayson and the other men would have invincibility in battle and all they wished from the riches of Castle Lyist. The Faithful got revenge on one of the cities that helped to slaughter his precious dragons, and the caverns under the Castle and town would be his and only his. Grayson wondered how sweet the revenge would end up being for the man. After all, the dragons were killed off over three centuries ago, and the men that lived inside those walls where only the decedents of their killers. What would it be like killing a grandson for something their great-great-grandfather did? How much pleasure could be squeezed from that? One drop? Two? He did not mention this to the witch, however. He was offering far more than Grayson ever dreamed, and he was not about to let such an opportunity pass and pass by. Besides, revenge was an "after taste" at best. It was all about those bones. Grayson had asked the Faithful one night around the fire, if he wanted to kill the Lystad king himself.

"Why?" he had asked, dark eyes blinking slowly at him. "Why would it matter? I don't care who kills him... as a matter of fact, I don't even care if he dies. I just want the Kingdom left in ash. Let the Lystad live the rest of his life wandering with no home… that would be enough." He had looked down at the bag of bones that he had slept with since his sniveling little boy had presented it to him. "I just want to lay **them** to rest. All of them to rest. They deserve more than a dark cave. They deserved to be buried with honor."

"And that magic inside um…" Grayson goaded. "Hundreds of thousands of bones held enough power to keep a Faithful like yourself alive forever… what a Faithful like yourself could do with all that power… that has nothin to do with it then?"

Rainier had glared up at him, and for a flashing, terrifying moment, Grayson thought he would leap at him. Fling himself across the fire, untouched, like a hellish cat, but he did not. Instead the Faithful shrugged and turned back to stroking his little bag with long fingers.

"They would not begrudge me a few bones, so that I may go and release their brothers and sisters. There are other caverns beneath other castles… full of other dragons. They all deserve to pass and pass by with grace."

Grayson had pulled himself from this memory. Who cared what the Faithful's reasons were? Revenge, retrieval, bones, power, loyalty, what did Grayson care? As long as he had his prize… Grayson did not give a damn what the Faithful's motives were, and it was a pretty-pretty prize waiting for Grayson behind those walls as well. He wanted it. Oh, he had never wanted anything so much in his life. An entire kingdom's treasury laid open and waiting like a bride on her wedding night. Eager for the taking. All his. All that was left, was the means by which to take it, and that was just a moment away from his reach as well. What was one more clump of hair?

Grayson reached up to tug hard at another section of his head. It came out with a ripping sound and a flash of pain, but Grayson did not mind.

Now, Castle Lyist just within reach, the man placed the pale skull on the open meadow and pulled out his dagger. He could not simply draw in the dirt like he had done before, so he began to cut into the grass, carving out the symbols and spirals surrounding the skull completely. He then stood, brushed off his cloak, and handed the dagger to his boy. He placed the little sack full of the pieces of hair and skin gently under the skull. He then closed those hollow black eyes, and his lips began to move. They moved quick and steady, fluttering open and closed with gaining speed, arms held to his chest. Grayson looked down at the bones. A wide grin crossed his face as pillars of smoke began to flurry out the nose, eyes and ear holes of the dragon's skull. The smell of burnt hair filled the air, making all of their eyes water. The Faithful man opened his eyes. He dropped his hands and turned to Grayson. That smile traveled slowly from one cheek to the other. He blinked.

"Well, then... shall we begin?"

# CHAPTER 34

A bell rang loud overhead, signaling something Kyana did not understand, but the people around her seemed to know. They started yelling and running in hasty, jarring, movements. A few scrambled in circles, needing to be somewhere fast, but not knowing where that was.

"What is it?" Kyana turned to Killian.

"The enemy has started to advance once more." Killian's voice grew low, and he placed a hand on the hilt of his sword. Kyana looked around disoriented.

"Should… Should we go see?" she asked. Killian shook his head.

"We should get you back inside the castle."

"No," she said. The word was pulled from her like the gut reaction to a question. Her first response and it was just as unexpected as everything else in this kingdom of strange and unexpected things. Killian stared at her bemused.

"It will be much safer back at the castle, Miss."

"Do what you will, guard of Castle Lyist," Kyana said. She turned and darted through the rushing crowd. She assumed the direction the brown caps where going, and the last straggling peasants were fleeing, would be the right way. Killian tried to follow, but he and his protests were lost in the crowd behind her. She swept in and out, moving back toward the station beside the large iron gate which rose like an uninterested sentinel above the chaos below. It had been opened, allowing the knights and guards to pour out and meet the oncoming army outside of the gates. A short distance away, Kyana could hear the clang of metal and shouts of men. The battle had begun. Kyana caught sight of the men with bows and arrows lined above the castle wall, waiting for the enemy to come within distance. Kyana ran for one of the wooden doors, nearly flying up the spiral stairs and bursting out on top of the wall. She moved down the lines of knights, arrows drawn, and armor gleaming, ready for their orders. She found Everett walking up and down the line of men, barking orders and surveying the newly born battle below. He caught sight of her.

"Kyana!" he called, "What are you doing up here?"

"Watching the show," she said, without humor. Kyana looked down at the black and brown mass clashing together with dark ferocity. Armor gleamed, weapons flashed, men fell, and blood had already begun to run. Kyana saw a man in a knight's uniform lying motionless as his fellows stepped on and around his body. She could not see his face, and she hoped it was not anyone she knew. "How is it going?"

"Not sure yet," Everett said, stepping up beside her, dousing her in shadow from his outrageous height. "Should you be in the castle?"

"Should I?" She frowned at the battle below. She could see more than most, and what she saw worried her. The hirelings were sloppy, sending haphazard attacks in almost listless movements. On the other hand, the knights of Castle Lyist, who rode on armored steeds or ran on foot, all fought with precise accuracy. Their blows landed steady and true... and yet....

"Something's wrong," Kyana said, a sour taste building at the back of her tongue like blood bubbling up in a fresh wound.

"What is it?" Everett squinted down.

"Oh, something's very wrong." Kyana nearly had to spit the taste away it was growing so strong.

"What do you mean?" Everett asked with a little frustration. "The battle has barely—- wow hey, don't do that!"

Kyana pushed aside one of the waiting knights without apology and stepped up on the edge of the wall beside a tall statue of a crouching dragon. She steadied herself against the creature's stone shoulder as the wind threatening to tilt her forward and into the open air that lay between her and the ground far, far, below. She ignored Everett and the other knight's curious glances. She tugged her bow from around her shoulder, slid an arrow from her quiver, and pulled it to her cheek. She felt the wind, focused on one of the dark hirelings far below, waited, breathed... and let go. The arrow found her mark, cutting through the neck of the hirelings, causing him to jerk back from the knight he was about to skewer on a spear. He fell to the ground in a heap.

"Holy shit," Everett said. "That…. was amazing actually."

Kyana ignored him, squinting at the man she should have just killed. He remained motionless for a moment, then stirred, got to his feet, and slowly pulled the arrow from his own neck.

"What the hell?" A knight she had pushed aside spoke in a hollow voice. His eyes widened at the hireling who tossed the arrow aside like an old corn rind, gave a crude hand gesture towards them up on the wall, before returning to the fight. Kyana's suspicions were answered.

"They need to be called back," Kyana said, turning to Everett. "The hirelings, they're enchanted. Some sort of undead curse."

"Curse?" One of the knights whispered in awe. "More like a miracle."

Kyana knew it was no miracle. A spell like that… she knew of them. They came up in Faithful history, not often, but enough times to find their way in children's tales of misused magic. Those tales, like the true stories they were based, never ended well for anyone, especially not those who were under a spell. Magic was a gift given by dragons to humanity. It was to be used with discretion. A powerful, self-interested spell like this was tantamount to spitting in the face of the giver. Now was not the time to explain this, however.

"No weapon will kill them," Kyana said firm and loud enough for the rows of men to hear. "Castle Lyist needs to pull back." Everett stood there for a moment, looking shocked.

"I can't just call back the attack. They aren't—"

"If you don't," Kyana said, looking the knight in his shocked eyes. "They will all die. Castle Lyist will fall. You will lose it all. They need to be *called back.*"

Everett turned and barked the orders to several knights who dropped their bows which clattered to the floor, grabbed their swords, and darted down the steps.

"That will take too long," Kyana said, shaking her head.

"It's the only way," Everett answered, but his face turned back to the battle, fear growing plainly in his eyes.

"Or not." Kyana looked down the side of the castle wall and then glanced back around to an unfamiliar weapon that hung on Everett's hip. It reminded her of some sort of heavy structured hay hook. "May I borrow that?" she asked.

He gave it to her curiously and gave a yell of horror as she turned and pushed lightly against the dragon statue, forcing herself off the wall. She was falling, faster and faster, the wind ripping at her hair and clothes as she picked up speed. About halfway down the wall, she swung the hook as hard as she could into the cracked stone. It caught on a jagged edge, and her speed slowed as the hook dug through the mortar, rock, and stone. The force of it jerked her arm, dislocating her shoulder in one swift movement and Kyana bit back a scream. The hook screeched and sparked beneath her hand as she made her way down. She still hit the ground at a fast pace and rolled, but it was no longer a fatal fall. When she finally stopped rolling, she laid there a moment, looking up at the sky. The men looking back down from the top of the wall, mouths open, shouting in voices Kyana could not quite hear. She waited for her lungs to remember their job, then pulled in a deep, ragged breath. She tried to get up and screamed as pain sang through her wrist and shoulder. She gritted her teeth, trembling. If her wrist was broken, there was nothing she could do for it now, but her shoulder... She gently laid back down. She lifted her arm above her head and curled her hand down as if going to scratch the back of her neck. Instead, she drew a deep breath, and then quickly reached as if going to touch her other shoulder. There was a sickening pop, and Kyana breathed out a sigh of relief. She slowly got to her feet, using her other arm for support. Judging by the sharp pain every time she breathed, Kyana had broken a few ribs as well, but she could not think about that right now. She began running for the battle, slowly and unsteady at first, but quickly picking up speed as she regained her balance. She waded into the battle of blue and black. She darted around one dark form or another, ducking swords, knives, lances and the hard thud of horse's hooves. She was looking for their leader, their king. He must know by this point, that the enemy could not die, but he was not acting on it fast enough for her liking. A hireling on the back of a stolen knight's steed came at her, spear raised. She sidestepped the spear, grabbed the horse's reins, and jumped. She landed hard behind the hireling, making the horse stumble and snort in anger.

The wafting scent of sweat and blood filled her nose as the back of his dark and tattered clothes flapped in her face. She slipped a dagger from around the man's waist belt and jammed it into the side of his neck, driving it to the handle. He went limp with shock, but she knew it would not last. She pulled the dagger from his neck and shoved him off the horse. He flopped like a sack of wheat and was instantly trampled by thousands of feet as she pulled the horse around. She looked about in frustration for that stupid Lystad. She let go of the horse's reins and carefully placed her feet at the front and back of the saddle, standing to see over the battle. Midnight blue and glinting armor were everywhere. Capes flapped here and there on several knights, but none of them was the Lystad.

Kyana cursed, wondering why any of them wore those stupid things to begin with. Would they not simply get in the way? She turned directly around, nearly falling off entirely when she found him. He was fighting alongside his knights at the front of the battlefield.

*A silly place for a king to be.* She thought, slipping back into the saddle and kicking the horse into a run. *He may get his precious, kingly head cut off.*

She jumped from the horse as she came close and it ran from the battle, in search of the calmer meadow. Kyana thought about following its lead… but she was already here. Might as well finish what she started.

The Lystad was battling a wiry hireling with an ax strapped to his back, and a sword in his hand. The king fought like he danced, Kyana noted. His movements were smooth, swift, elegant in battle. His opponent, on the other hand, was heavy-handed and clumsy. He was no match, or at least he should not have been. The Lystad landed what should have been a fatal blow between the man's shoulder and head, slicing into his skin, severing the color bone, but there was no blood. The Lystad pulled back his blade, as the hireling straightened up, arm hanging awkward at his side, as his shoulder hung open, revealing bone, tendons, but no blood.

"Wha?" The hireling slurred, grinning with yellow, rotten teeth. "That all you got, boy?" The king did not have time to answer, because a moment later, an arrow went through the hireling's left eye. He keeled backwards, severed arm flailing, and fell onto another hireling standing close behind, causing them both to tumble to the ground. The Lystad looked around to see Kyana pulling another arrow from the quiver on her back.

"What the hell are you doing here?" he shouted over the sound of battle.

Kyana frowned. Why did they all insist on asking her the same question? Stop asking. She barely knew herself.

"Behind you," she called instead. The king turned to cut down another hireling, who fell, momentarily, to the ground.

"They aren't dying," the king called back to her.

"I know," she said, releasing another arrow into the crowd of darkness that was slowly making its way towards the open castle gates. "They're cursed. You need to pull your men back. Now."

"We can't give them the city." The king swung around to cut down another hireling who had been sneaking up to his left.

"I'm not saying that," Kyana spat, doing her very best not to roll her eyes in the middle of the bloodshed and chaos. "I'm saying pull back until we know what will kill them. There is always a way. Every enchantment has a weakness. But we can't," she darted forward shouldering a hireling with all her weight as he tried to creep up behind the king, "do that," she turned, grabbed a hirelings blade from his hands only to run it though his chest, "if we are dead."

The Lystad looked around, seeing the numbers of brown uniforms that already carpeted the meadow floor. They would not be getting back to their feet anytime soon.

"Alright, then," his voice rose to a yell. "Back to the walls!" The surrounding knights echoed his call, and they slowly began to seep back into the castle, fighting as they went. Kyana stood atop a few stray wagons by the gates, shooting arrows, trying to give the knights as much opportunity as possible. The knights on the top of the wall began firing down as the darkness came closer. A flood of arrows cascaded through the air, whizzing past, dropping man after man, giving a little breathing room for the rest of the knights to get inside. The black metal gates closed behind them with a creak and shuttering clank. Kyana had slipped in just in time, leaning and panting against the inside of the castle wall. She felt the hirelings clamber and hammer uselessly against the gates next to her. It sent reverberations up her back, and she sent another string of pain flutter in her shoulder.

"What the hell was that?" one of the knights yelled.

"Monsters!" another called breathlessly.

"Faithful!" a third yelled, who was nursing a bloody arm.

"Nothing killed them! What the hell do we do?" cried a fourth.

"That," the king said, wiping his blade on his shirt, before sheathing it. "Is exactly what we need to figure out. Call the practitioners and the nurses. All of you get patched up. Lionel," Kyana was relieved to see the boy step up beside his king. His eyes seemed blurry, and blood smeared his young face. That charge of pride was gone. Kyana wondered if it was laying in one of those puddles of brown cloth back outside that iron gate. But he was alive. Perhaps he would make it to a man after all.

"Round up Teller, Everett and the others. We'll meet in the hall." He frowned at the red smear that dripped slowly down Lionel's face. "And go find one of The Seven... make sure you get that fixed up."

"Yes, sir," the boy said and moved off down the wall. They all dispersed, momentarily safe behind those gates. They went to tend to wounds, each other, and their weapons. Murmurs of fear spread like a shiver down a spine. Magic and Faithful. The things they feared most stood in mass behind those gates. The horror was palpable in the air, thick as paste and as suffocating as smoke.

Kyana watched them all. There was no more desperate energy, they were too tired for that. Fighting an enemy that was invincible.... That will take out all the fun. Kyana shook the thought from her mind. She heard her name and looked up to see the king of Castle Lyist watching her.

"Are you coming?" he asked. Kyana blinked, then nodded and pushed off the wall. She followed him and a few stray knights towards the inner castle. "How do you know about curses like these?" Kyana scrambled for an excuse that was close enough to the truth but did not leave her tied to a pier.

"Stories, mostly, told to me by my second father," she answered. "Dark fairy tales... you know the kind?"

"Yes," he agreed, "But mine generally didn't go into detail about curses." Kyana did not doubt it and waited for him to turn on her with suspicion, but he simply continued to stride for the castle.

"How much do you know about these types of enchantments?" the king asked, as they stepped through a door to the second wall. It was held open by a guard and quickly closed by the same.

"A few things. For an undead curse like this one, they need exactly four," Kyana answered. "They must be done by a powerful Faithful... I mean incredibly powerful, and very practiced," Rainier. "They are usually attached to some sort of celestial event or motion, an eclipse, or track of stars. They also require the piece of those being cursed."

"Blood sacrifices?" Neander asked, appearing beside them. Blood was smeared on the side of his cheek, neck and temple. There was no sign of a wound, so it must have belonged to someone else.

"No," Kyana shook her head. "Wrong type of magic. Blood magic is usually more specific, destructive, and generally aimed at one person. Three at the most. They also require death to be performed. Hence, sacrifice. This is more of a prick of the finger, section of skin, lock of hair, type of curse. Not a slit of the throat." Neander nodded but still looked confused. Kyana would have happily sat down and explained how they differ, but time was short, so they moved on.

"You said four things were needed," Neander said, "What's the fourth?"

"Just like any magic, blood sacrifice or not," Kyana said, "It needs the power of a dragon relic to be fueled."

"Dragon relic?" Teller asked, falling into step beside them as they made it to the small door in the next wall which another guard unlocked and let them pass. Their footsteps echoed through the empty stone halls as they went. It was a haunting sound. Ominous, eerie and oh so hollow.

"The shell of an egg. Bone of a dragon. Scales. Teeth," Lystad explained as they pushed through another door and out into the yard between the second and first gate. Green grass crunch softly underfoot as they picked up the pace. "Pretty much any part of a dragon, old or new." He shot a grin over his shoulder at Kyana. "See, I know things."

"So, these dragon relics," Teller pushed on, "They hold the most powerful of magic."

"Actually," Kyana corrected, "They hold the **only** magic. You can amplify it by using incantations at certain times, during certain seasons, but magic itself was born to this world in dragons and through them, or a part of them, is the only way it can be harnessed."

"So, this Rainier bastard," Neander said, pushing open yet another large wooden door that lead out into the courtyard. Kyana had barely noticed how fast they were moving. Tensions were too high to walk slower than a trot. "He's got some sort of relic in his possession?"

"Yes. To enchant so many men, he must have at least one." Kyana nodded. They had reached the castle by this point and had just pushed open the large double doors, sweeping in a sweating mass into the entryway.

"How?" Neander asked, eyes wide. "How the hell did he get one? I thought all dragon relics were in possession of the Four Kingdoms for that exact reason! Under lock and key, guarded too."

"Yes," Kyana nodded, although she knew that was not entirely true. Dragon relics were a very rare but profitable item on the shadow markets. Kyana herself had never dealt with the shadow market, but she and Bert stayed in many a below board inn that conducted many a below board deal. She had seen dragon relics pass from one hand to another on many an occasion. The first time she had witnessed such a deal being conducted, Burt had to grab her arm and hold her in place. He did not know why it had made her so furious, or why tears had begun to slide down her cheeks, and he never asked. He only whispered in her ear that life was a filthy place, full of battles, but that you had to choose them with care. If you threw yourself into every opportunity, you would find an end to your road much faster than you might like. Kyana had listened and watched in silent seething hate as the two bone dealers exchanged prizes and moved on to conduct more deals. However, Neander was right about one thing. Most of the relics had been collected by the Four Kingdoms after the death of dragons. Each kingdom had turned the homes of their dragons into protected treasuries for their bones.

"But, heavily guarded or not," Kyana said, "Nowhere is impenetrable."

"Do you know any way to stop the enchantment?" the king asked Kyana.

"Depends on what type of enchantment and what type of relic it's drawing power from."

"What do you mean what type of relic?" Neander asked, frowning. "Does it matter?"

"Absolutely," Kyana nodded. "The older the relic, the more intense the magic. It also matters if it has been used before. Dragons were a living breathing source of magic, but without life their relics are limited. If it has been used previously, the magic would not last as long or be as strong."

"How in the hell do you know all this?" Neander asked. He was shaking his head, and Kyana could not tell if it was in amazement or frustration.

"Do you really want to hear my life story up to this point?" Kyana snapped, harsher than she meant to, "Or would you like to stay focused on the problem at hand?"

"Okay, okay, then how do we figure all that stuff out?" Neander asked as they pushed into the great hall. All the long tables stood empty. There was no feast, no celebration, just long, empty tables. The rest of the knights, what Kyana guessed where those with the highest rank, were waiting for them. They looked tired, blood smeared and on edge. She saw Cole among them but did not see his usual companion Simon by his side. Kyana tried not to think of why. They all stood together in a circle, eyes flying to the king and a few towards Kyana.

"There are a few different options," Kyana said. "Most require the same thing."

"What do we need?" the king asked, turning full attention on Kyana as they came to a halt in the large quiet room. The only voices were their own and they echoed off the high ceiling in a ghostly manner that made Kyana's hair stand on end.

"Someone under the curse," Kyana said.

"We have to capture one of those monsters?" Everett asked. He had entered the hall almost a moment after them. He stood, dumbfounded at the mere idea of capturing one of those dead, undead, things scrabbling outside the outer gates.

"There are a few ways to find out exactly what curse they are under and how to break it… but yes, we need one of them… alive…" Kyana shrugged. "Obviously."

"Should I even ask how dangerous that would be?" Lystad asked, relaxed and calm. Blood was smeared on his neck, and Kyana felt the need to take a closer look, make sure it was not his. She resisted. Instead, she met his steady blue gaze. Blue and blue. Light and dark storm. A night sky broken by bright lightning.

She yanked her mind back in place like tugging the reins of some surprisingly strong beast. What on earth was wrong with her?

"Almost certainly deadly," Kyana answered. The room went quiet. "But… there is another option."

"What is it?" the king asked.

Kyana knew one way. A way that would destroy any magical creature with just the slightest touch… only one touch and… gone. But she could not tell them about this possibility. This she could not suggest. And so, she answered with the only other way she knew.

"We wait it out," Kyana said, looking around the room. "The one useful thing about an enchantment as massive and powerful as this is the fact that it can't last. We could simply barricade ourselves inside. Wait until the magic within the relic dries up, or the spells amplification changes. But since we don't know the relic, or what cosmic factor is amplifying its effects, there is no telling how long it will take for the spell to wear off. It could take hours, days, weeks, years. It all depends on the enchantment, but it can't last forever. Stars move, storms end, full moons fade, time passes by, suns…. suns set…"

Kyana drifted, mind going back to the image of the small dark army halted in the vast meadow, for no apparent reason. Suspended beneath the midday sun.

"The sun," she said, looking around to the Lystad, who was still watching her with that unblinking storm of blue. "He attached the spell to the sun."

"How can you be sure?" he asked, leaning in. She could hear the eagerness in his voice, the pure desire for her to be right.

"I can't," Kyana said, honestly. "But I'm pretty sure. It's a powerful conduit. Dangerous even, when attached to the wrong spell. Not commonly used because it only lasts a day at most... but a day is all Rainier would need."

"Is 'pretty sure,' really good enough?" Cole called.

"It might be all we have," Kyana answered, looking over at his face, which bore a nasty cut above his left eye. "We could wait for sundown and see if the spell has worn off. If the spell does break with the sun, you will have to attack before the next morning, or else Rainier may do the spell all over again." If the relic still had magic left. Kyana doubted it. Spells of this magnitude took too much magic and energy to maintain, and relics held only so much. However, it was better to err on the side of caution when it came to such as Rainier. "And if it's not connected to the sun, then the worst thing it will do is kill some time."

"And perhaps the knights that go out to test your little theory," Cole spat back.

Kyana scowled, a crackle of fire erupting deep in her chest, but she held it back with effort. This man had just been in battle against an unbeatable enemy. He had just watched many of his comrades passing by. He was hurting and angry, and that sometimes made good men act stupid.

"Actually," Kyana said, nearly chewing on her tongue to keep it civil, "I was thinking of having a few knights shoot some arrows from the safety of the castle walls, and just wait to see if the sons of bitches stay dead."

A murmur and a few nods ran through the circle. All eyes turned towards the king.

"Do it," he said firmly, hand resting on his sword. "We will hold out until sunset and then see where we go from there."

"Yes, your majesty." They all bowed and turned with a great twirling of capes, emptying out of the room in a chestnut stream until the king and Kyana were left alone. Kyana had watched them go, wondering if she should follow, unsure about what she would do if she did. She had no idea how to prepare for a siege, and so she stayed where she was. The room was silent for a few minutes.

"What the hell were you thinking?" Lysted said from behind her. She turned around.

"What do you mean?" she asked, surveying the king of Castle Lyist with a frown.

"I saw you," he said, his voice was stern, but there was a smile trying not to break through. His soft black hair was a sweaty mess around his face, but she could not see any signs of wounds, except for the small amount of blood on his neck. "You jumped off the wall... why on earth did you think that was a good idea?"

"I needed to get down fast," Kyana said as if the Lystad was being purposefully obtuse. The king shook his head.

"You are... you are the weirdest... no... the *craziest* woman I have ever met," he said.

"Quite possible, yes," Kyana shrugged. She shifted her stance and a shock of pain made her wince.

"Are you alright?" he asked, leaning forward as if he might go to her.

"I'm fine," Kyana said, waving away his concern. "Just a few broken ribs... maybe a broken wrist," she said, looking down at the hand which had begun to swell into an ugly purple and brown mess, making a break seem ever more likely. Now that things were quieting down, she could truly appreciate the throbbing pain that emanated from it and winced again. "I hit the ground a little faster than I meant to."

"You hit the ground.... A little faster than you meant..." the king repeated, raising an eyebrow so high it was almost lost in his hair. He watched her with unblinking, exasperated, curiosity.

"Yes... that's what I said," Kyana frowned at him. "Are **you** alright?"

The king laughed loud, almost manic, and ran an absentminded hand through his dark hair, pulling it away from his sweaty forehead, leaving a small streak of dirt as he did.

"Yes... I suppose. My kingdom is held hostage, with magical monsters surrounding my castle.... I have lost men, good men.... My people are terrified... but yes... I suppose I'm alright." He looked up. "That is thanks to you. Again."

"I'm sure you'd have done the same." The sarcastic bitterness came automatically to her lips. The Lystad blinked.

"Of course, I would," he said, blinking again, "Why do you think otherwise?"

"Does not matter," she said, holding her wrist as if it would stop the pain from reverberating up her elbow. Mead and pain, she was finding had something in common. It made her far more honest than she should be.

The king watched her confused, head cocking slightly to one side. Kyana had another flash of a little puppy dog looking curiously for a treat. He opened his mouth to say something but was interrupted as Everett burst back into the hall.

"Your majesty!" he said skidding to a halt before them. "Rainier is with the rest of the hirelings... he's bringing down the gate."

"He's what?" the king spoke softly as if Everett must only be having a good joke on his lord's behalf.

"The gate, he's using magic or something... the outer two gates have already fallen... he's about to break down the third gate."

"Already?" Kyana felt her mouth go dry. "How.... So quickly?" How could everything have gone so wrong so quickly?

"Magic," was Everett's only answer. It was spat like a curse as his eyes flared with hate. A hate Kyana recognized all too well. The rest of his words came out in desperate out of breath gasps. "The gate. It's about to go. They are near to the castle already. They're waiting to flood in. What are your orders, your majesty?"

Kyana looked at the king who stood, silent and grave. When he spoke, it was in a voice of calm resignation.

"Split the men into three," he said quickly. "Have one group lead the civilians out through the old dragon caverns. One tunnel will lead them to the outer wall of the city. The Keepers can show you the way. The hirelings are few and are all distracted at the inner wall. They won't have time to back track to the outer wall and stop them, if you move quickly. The other end leads to a section of the outer wall near the... apparently now broken outer gate. From there they can run from the city." The Lystad thought a moment. "The caverns themselves are large, but the exit of the dragon caverns is small. Not many can go that way at one time. Have the second group go towards the old northern gates. Break them open and take everyone to the river front. Take the ships to the cities across the waters. Neira cities or even Sterlyn if they have to. Go till they are safe. Get out as many as you can and fast. Have the rest of the men meet me at the inner gate… we need to give everyone as much time as possible to get out." Kyana stared at him. Everett nodded grimly and left to carry out his orders. The Lystad turned his back and leaned his hands against the table.

"That plan," Kyana said slowly, watching the king's back rise and fall with slow, steady breaths. "Is most certainly suicide for anyone at the gate… have you already forgotten? Your enemy won't die."

"We need to get as many people out as possible," the king said. "I won't leave my people here to be slaughtered by the likes of Rainier."

"So, you will be the slaughtered instead?" Kyana asked, turning away from the king and looking at the giant dragon seal that hung in the back of the hall. It hung high and proud above where she and the knights, and the king himself, had shared a feast for the Four Kingdoms.

"How very…. *Gallant* of you." She drew out the word as if it was an insult.

"And what would you suggest, Kyana?" He was trying to be fierce, but all that came out was a bitter laugh. "Leave my people and run?"

"No. That would be cowardice. You are many things Lystad," Kyana said, still eyeing the crest. "But cowardly is not one of them. I just… I never saw you as the type to be defeated either."

"You know what?" the king chuckled humorlessly, turning, a small smile on his face. "Neither did I."

"You can't leave your people without a leader," she said flatly.

"And I won't send men to die while I run," he answered.

"Stop it!" Kyana spat. Glaring at the two-headed dragon now, wishing it would melt straight off the wall. She would watch it drip dark blue and chestnut, spark into a flame and burn, burn all away. Burn away the memories. Burn away that soft warmth in her chest. Burn away the smiles, the laughter, the kindness, the confusion, the unexpected, burn, burn it all away.

"Stop acting like this," she ordered.

"Like what?" The Lystad asked curiously, straightening up and tightening his sword belt.

"Like some good-hearted, noble, loyal…. King," she spat.

"Oh, well forgive me," he said, tugging the chestnut cape from his shoulders and laying it gently, on the table. "Didn't know I was playing a part."

"Well, you are," Kyana mumbled. "You must be."

"Why is that?" His voiced sounded like his only dream in the world was to take a long, long, nap.

"Because you… you are not supposed to be like this," she said dully, her anger and frustration fizzling away as quickly as it had come. It was replaced by a something cold… mournful… empty. An empty space with no fire, no warmth, nothing at all.

Memories flooded her. Memories spent happily in this castle about to crumble. Every laugh, every smile, every arm wrapped around her shoulder. It all passed, and passed, and that empty space grew deeper, and deeper as it all passed her by.

*As all things must.*

She heard a chuckle from behind her.

"You should go with the civilians," the king said a click of shoes made Kyana aware he was preparing to leave. "Out the tunnels, or across the river. Follow the knights, they'll lead the way. I'd say grab Royal on your way out, but that may take too much time, and I'd like you out as soon as possible." Kyana felt that empty space tighten at his words, twist, like a knife, but hurt so much more. It bled, not blood, but something far more valuable.

She could not just leave; she knew that now. She did not want to. She had found… something here. Something she had told herself she would never need again… but now she knew. She did need it. Yes. She was a needy little thing. She did not want to go back to the forest, not alone. She did not want to be alone. She had been abandoned for so long, so damn long. And she had lost, so, so much. Watched everyone and everything she loved go up in smoke or down in blood and she was tired of watching it all pass by while she, always, stayed. She could not do it anymore. She did not want to leave these people, and that little bit of warmth they made her *feel.* Yes, if they knew her, they would hate her. But she cared about them. She did not want to leave them to die. Leave them to die as she lived on. No. Not again. She could not. She would not. And so, what did that mean for her?

*All things must eventually pass and pass by… time is no exception… and my time is done. So, let it be done.*

Kyana sighed.

*What the hell.*

"You know me and unfair fights," she said straightening up and allowing a small almost bitter smile, "A battle between a doomed army and enchanted invincible soldiers? I can't pass that up. I'll see you at the gate." She turned to go.

"No," the Lystad said, flatly from behind her.

"What? Why?" Kyana scowled. That empty space gave another twist, a jarring motion that almost took her breath.

*Don't trust me?* Kyana wondered. She still would not look at him. If she had, he would have seen the disappointment on her face. "Think I'd get in the way of your little suicide mission?"

"No, actually," he said simply, "I think you would be invaluable. Absolutely invaluable."

Kyana blinked, confused. "Then why—" She turned to ask, but did not get the chance to finish her question. In one swift movement, Damian Lystad had her face in his rough hands. He pulled her to him. Kyana's first instinct was to jerk away, but surprise made her hesitate, and Damian did not. He pressed his lips against hers, capturing her upper lip. The kiss was forceful and insistent. It was the kiss of a man with nothing left to lose, and only one last thing he wanted. His fingers curled in her auburn hair, and she tasted him on her tongue. She tried to compare it in her mind, to describe it to herself, but it lost all meaning. There was no food, no drink, no spirit, nothing like this warm feeling against her lips, as his lips moved against hers. She stood, thunderstruck, as he finally, slowly, pulled back. His blue eyes opened and looked down on her from mere inches away.

"Just… listen to me *for once* and leave with the rest… won't you?"

Kyana said nothing, only watched as the King of Castle Lyist pulled away, warm, rough hands sliding past her cheeks. He turned without another word and left the hall, leaving Kyana alone with her tangled mind.

# CHAPTER 35

Gods, it was a mess. All of it. Everything. Ira watched her home, her livelihood, her people, and her life of so many years, slipping from existence. No. Not slipping. Running terrified.

They were all running. All the civilians, mothers, fathers, daughters, sons, tottering babes they all ran. They were herded like cattle into endless streams for the waiting ships in the river to the north, or the dragon caverns beneath the castle. Ira had never been down there before. It was always off limits, home only to the relics of a bygone time and the Keepers who protected them.

Ira had always wanted to see what they were like. Those tunnels and caves belonging to the great decedents of Aneira herself. Stories said the caves spread for miles; a maze so intricate and dark that you would surely be lost forever. It was also whispered, to all who had never been down there to see, it was the type of dark that only dragon fire could pierce. Of course, that was not true. Ira had spoken with several of the Keepers on multiple occasions, and they had a far less romantic view of the place.

"It's a dark, hot, shit hole, child," the gruff eldest Keeper Philip (or Phil by his friends) had said. "It's dark, and damp, hot, and stinks of fossilized fesses of the dead, dead, beasts that dropped loads larger than you, girl!" Ira heard that Phil had died only a few months before and had been replaced by a young boy of only seventeen. Ira had not spoken to Phil in years. The last time was when Phil had caught Ira and the young price trying to sneak through the first gate of the cavern below the Keepers tower connected to the castle. Not having a key made this completely impossible, but he had given both of them a hefty whack on the back of their heads as a reward at any rate.

Even at the very mouth of the tunnels they noticed one mysterious thing. Ira had asked about it while rubbing the slow building bump behind her head.

"Aren't caves usually cold?" Ira had asked.

"Yes," Phil had answered, a calloused and hairy knuckled hand running over his full beard which reached towards his belly in brown and gray tangles. "I suppose they are."

"Then why is it hot in there?" Damian had asked in that young voice that still clung its last traces of a lisp.

"Well…" Phil's gruff voice had trailed off, eyes traveling to watch something that evaded both Ira and Damian's view. "Well, child… because… *dragons.*" That was the only explanation they were allowed, but it was enough. They made several other attempts to sneak down to those tunnels, but when Damian's father was finally informed, he quickly put a stop to that. It had taken an entire month for Damian to be allowed to see Ira again, and a month for two ten-year-old friends as close as they, it was a long, long time. They decided their desire to see one another outweighed their interest in a "dark, hot, shit hole."

But Ira had always wondered.

Today, however, it looked like everyone would get a chance to see what the caverns were like. People stumbled over one another, not really trying to push the others aside, or trip one another into the dirt, but it seemed to keep happening all the same. When panic takes over the mind, little else gets through. Your thoughts become a pinprick of fear, with one way out, and that is all you can think about. Those tunnels, although dark and smelled like shit, was one of the few ways out now.

The three outer gates belonging to the walls of Castle Lyist had been either broken down or broken open. Ira had actually seen the third one fall. She had watched, open-mouthed, frozen in place, as the large metal gates, which had stood tall, firm, and unbreakable for centuries, had shattered. Simply shattered as if it was made of glass and not steel. They had trembled like a leaf in the wind, their dark shade going glossy in the light of the sun which beamed off of it in beautiful rainbows. For a moment it looked like the gates to heaven had been brought down to earth. Its shining beauty finally revealed to the world of mortals as was told in prophecies of old. Ira half expected the God of Time himself to open them and bid this world to come to the next.

But of course, he did not.

Instead, the gates gave a violent shake and then splintered into pieces. Shards of gleaming metal rained down on the knights below, skewering two, killing them instantly. The rest ran from the falling shards, holding up their arms, hiding under their shields, trying to protect themselves. Once the metal had stopped raining, however, the real threat stepped in. And he was no god. No. He was a Faithful.

Ira had never pictured Rainier, never tried to place an image of him in her mind. She heard many stories, those of terror, and Faithful magic, and power beyond human comprehension, but she had never tried to "see" him in her thoughts. She never tried to build a picture in her mind, because she always assumed, if the stories were true, it would never do the Faithful justice.

The moment that tall figure in that pale cloak stepped through those shattered gates, Ira knew she had been right. The man moved with a grace that was anything but human. He glided every step over those jagged chunks of metal and wood. His pale skin seemed to glow as he came to a stop just inside the third wall. Ira did not see his face at first, because it was covered by a mask.

*No...* Ira realized as she leaned closer from her perch on the innermost wall. She had been delivering new arrows to the knights stationed at the top with some other servant girls when someone had begun to shout that the Faithful was approaching. *That's not a mask...*

What Ira had first taken to be a large, white, war mask, was actually the skull of a young dragon. Its bones were pale, almost as pale as the man's skin, with large empty sockets, where eyes had been, and long teeth that reached down towards the man's long neck. He stopped a short distance past the ruined gate, hands hanging loosely at his sides.

The knights, after straightening up to see what was happening, began to swarm towards him, shouting for Castle Lyist. Shouting for their kingdom and their king. The tall man calmly reached up with one hand as they ran for him, swords raised. He gently pushed back the dragon skull on his head, revealing his face.

Ira could not breathe. He was... beautiful. He was the most gloriously beautiful person, man or women, that Ira had ever seen. An unnatural beauty, but this did not surprise her. Magic was not natural. It was magic after all. It was home in the breasts of dragons. Anything else was an insufficient vessel, but magic was crafty. Magic could adapt. It had a way of changing those that used it. Altering them, adjusting them, refining them from the inside, making the user a more hospitable host. After years of use, those alterations sometimes presented themselves in a physical manner... like shining sapphire hair, for example.

His features were sharp, his cheeks sunken, and his eyes... they were as deep and dark as those caverns beneath the castle. They seemed to go on and on for years, and Ira was reminded of how it felt looking in Kyana's eyes for the first time... but this was different... this time Ira was afraid.

Rainier waited until the knights were mere feet from him, and then, he smiled. Two of the closest knights faltered, stumbled, clutched at their chests, and simply dropped to the ground. Ira did not know how it happened, but she knew they were dead.

"How...?" One of the knights beside her had asked, bow and arrows all but forgotten in his hands as his wide eyes moved from Ira to Rainier, and back again. Ira did not answer him, but Phil's gruff voice flitted across her memory, bright like the day, only to be swallowed by the other thoughts that twisted her now frantic mind.

*Well, child... because... dragons...*

And from there, it had simply gone to further shit. Rainier's charmed hirelings flooded through the gate after him, catching the temporarily startled knights by surprise, and they began to fight. They had only been fighting a few short minutes, five at the most. To Ira, it felt like years.

The civilians were being hurried by shouting knights waving their arms, ushering them into two streams. One was led to the old and narrow secondary gates leading to the back of the city to the north. The second stream was led down into the tunnels which, Damian had said, lead to an exit just inside the outermost wall. From there they would make their escape to... where? The ships would probably take them across the river, delivering them safely to the other side where many of the other cities of Neira were living on, happily ignorant of the misfortunes befalling Castle Lyist. Those that came from the caverns could exit the city and either back track to meet up with the ships, or scatter to the forests. Perhaps even head for Kyar. Or simply scatter to anywhere at all. Ira supposed, anywhere was better than here.

Ira had been in the process of helping a woman gather her scattered belongings, which had been accidentally tossed aside by a man who darted carelessly for a spot in the line of exodus, when she heard her name being called. She turned to see Damian making his way swiftly from the castle. Even in their time of panic, his subjects parted out of his way as he came. At this moment, like no other, Ira saw the king in him. The man that did not flinch. The man that stood tall and ready and regal even when his castle, his kingdom, literally came crashing to the ground around him. He did not look afraid. He did not look abashed. He looked calm and ready for everything which came next.

It was all a big fucking lie, of course, Ira knew he was scared. Damian was as human as any of them, but he would not let it show. Ira did not know why. It usually ticked her off, how Damian would whine and complain to her how no one treated him like they used to, or acted around him like they used to, and then turn around and did the same. It usually pissed her right off. But now, as everything fell apart, every little piece just fell out of place, she saw Damian walking towards her as if it was just another day. And Ira loved him for it.

"Ira," he said, as calm and relaxed as his stride. "Is this the last of them?"

"No, my lord," Ira said, handing the woman back her bag and watching her quickly be swept away towards the castle and down into the private stairway belonging to the Keepers. "There are a few more groups left, but we're nearly there."

"Good," the king said, smiling as if Ira had just told him that it had stopped raining and he could go on another hunt before the day was through. "And the inner gate?"

"Still holding," Ira said, glancing around to make sure this was true. The last gate stood tall and strong against the sky, but she could hear the clamor of crowds on the opposite side. "Rainier, he seems to need a moment to rest between each gate. It's been a while though... so I don't know how much longer it's going to last."

"Have they started pillaging throughout the outer parts of the city?" Damian asked.

"No, my lord," Ira shook her head. "They're all still waiting by the gates... it looks like they're waiting to break every single one down before they start... anything else."

"Well... how *efficient* of them," the king said coolly, but the calm never left him. His blue eyes, which had been watching the gate, drew back to Ira. "Leave with this group."

"What?" Ira asked.

"Leave with this group," Damian repeated and jerked his head to the crowd. "The knights have things under control. You need to get out, and they obviously need someone to help keep people calm, so go with them, help with... why are you shaking your head at me?"

"Because I'm not going anywhere," Ira said simply. Damian gave a great sigh, but Ira could see the smile trying to break his face.

"Why does everyone feel the need to ignore my orders today?"

"You're staying, aren't you?" Ira said, shrugging. "You're staying. I'm staying."

"What about your family?"

"They went out with the first group," Ira said. Her mother had wailed and clutched at her sleeve, terrified eyes spilling over with tears as she begged Ira to come with them. Ira had told her she needed to help everyone else get out first. As Ira's father dragged her mother through the tower door, she had wailed and begged Ira to promise. Promise that she would follow them soon. Ira had called after them, saying that she loved them both, but she made no such promise. She always kept her promises. She would not lie to her mother's face. "They'll be alright."

"Get out of here Ira." In an instant, king Damian was replaced, not by a prince, not by a common man, but by the boy Ira had met in that kitchen cupboard all those years ago. Gods... how long ago had it been? Yesterday? A century? "Go see those damn caverns."

"Nah," Ira said, shaking her head and grinning. "I heard it smells like shit down there, and I've got a delicate stomach."

"Ira," Damian pulled himself up to his greatest height, which was, Ira had to admit, no small matter. "As your *king*, I order you to leave this castle with the civilians."

"And as your *faithful servant*," Ira said, drawing out the last word as long as her breath would allow. "kindly *go screw yourself*." She grinned. "I'm with you. I'm not going anywhere." Damian tried to look angry. He tried to look furious. He tried to muster up another order, to yell at his friend to run and save her own damn life, but she could see the shock of poorly disguised gratitude across his face.

"You're... being...." Damian started.

"I'm not leaving you here Damian," Ira said flatly, without fear, without hesitation. "I'm just not."

Damian opened his mouth to protest, "Ira..." but Ira simply shook her head, that wide grin of hers covering her face and Damian knew it was no good. Ira had made up her mind. It was as good as a promise made and Damian knew Ira never broke a promise, no matter what the cost. Damian sighed, his gaze softening. He reached out and briefly pulled her into a hug. "You are insane woman..." he spoke in her ear. Ira gave a little chokeed laugh in his shoulder and held him tighter. "Thank you," Damian whispered. For a brief and breathless moment Ira was back in a lonely kitchen with a little boy steeling muffins. Oh, to be back at the beginning. Now that they were so close to the end, she would love to play the story again... just one more time. Would she do things differently? Would she have said more, done more? Taken more chances? She would never know. Time never turned backward, it only passed by.

"So." Ira said as they pulled apart to watch the civilians trampling on, as a nearby guard yelled at them to go faster. "What now?"

"Now..." Damian said, turning towards the last remaining barrier between Castle Lyist and her destruction. "We hold on. As long as we can... and then I guess..." He looked over at Ira and Ira to him, "We see what comes... when all things have passed by."

"Well," Ira said, shrugging. "All things eventually must... right?"

Damian smiled. It was a bitter thing, but true.

"Yes, I guess they do."

"Doesn't mean we're gonna be ready for it though."

"No. I suppose not."

"You know..." Ira glanced over at Damian. "I'm glad you pissed your dad off that day when we were kids. I'm pretty damn glad I met you."

Damian threw back his head and laughed. He reached out and took Ira's hand as his laugh continued. Ira was glad. If things were about to pass and pass by... she did not mind her friend's laughter being one of the last sounds she heard. She squeezed his hand in hers.

"Ah, ya, so am I, Ira," Damian said squeezing her hand tighter. "So am I."

"Owch, Damian," Ira winced as his grip became painful.

"Killian!" Damian called, ignoring Ira.

"Damian, let go of me," Ira said, pulling against his fingers, but he refused to budge an inch. Kyana's metal plated shadow appeared by their side.

"Sir," Killian said in his gruff voice.

"Get her out of here," Damian ordered.

"What?!" Ira yelped as Killian took her wrist from his king.

"Drag her away if need be," Damian said, still ignoring her. "I want her gone."

"No!" Ira barked, now trying to pry off Killian's grip, but it proved even stronger than Damian's.

"Did you really think I was going to let you stay?" Damian finally turned his attention towards her, and her heart sank as she saw the broken smile on his face and the unmistakable sheen in his eyes.

"Damian, no," Ira hissed as adrenaline started to course through her chest. He was saying goodbye. The son of a bitch was saying goodbye.

"Tell Naomi and Soph," Damian's voice was trembling slightly, and it broke Ira's heart. It stomped on it, shattering it, cutting her from the insides with its jagged edges and she bled. She bled memories. She bled love. Love for this infuriating man who had become her brother. No, she was not ready to say goodbye. Not like this. This was not fair. "Tell my sisters I love them." Damian leaned down and kissed her forehead. "Goodbye Ira." He looked back up at Killian. "Go."

"No!" Ira yelped in fury and despair as Killian began to pull her away towards the last retreating crowd. Angry tears began to stream down her face. "No, this is not… no, Killian stop it. Damian! This is not how it's supposed to go! Damian! Damn it! Damian! Don't do this! You don't have to be alone! Damian!" She tried to pull away, tried to wriggle out of Killian's grip, but he only held on tighter, and when she did finally start to break away, he hoisted her thin frame into the air and over one shoulder.

Damian laughed. It was a manic sound he could not help. It tumbled from his lips in short bursts as he watched his friend of over fifteen years being hoisted like a sack of grain over Killian's shoulder and taken away. She yelled, and she cursed, and she planted a few hard hits on Killian's back, but she slowly disappeared into the crowed flooding for the back gates of Castle Lyist, towards the lake where the boats were waiting to take her somewhere safe. Damian almost protested.

*Take her through the caverns,* he thought weakly. *We always wanted to see the caverns,* but he supposed whichever way she went, she would be saved. Besides, she would probably be too busy cursing his name to enjoy the tour.

Damian Lystad turned and started for the inner gate. No, he was not ready to see what came after everything passed by. He was not ready one bit. He had not yet done his father's name proud. He had not seen his sisters in almost two years. He always meant to visit, or send for them, but he had simply not taken the time. Been too busy. He had not done many things, but at least they would be safe. Ira would sail for Sterlyn Kingdom, find Naomi and Soph, and tell them everything. They would take her in. All three of them would be alright, and he supposed, that was enough. It would be enough.

*All things must pass and pass by... I am no exception.* Damian made his peace with the God of Time, cast one last wish for strength up to his mother, and moved with a steady stride towards his fate.

# CHAPTER 36

Rainier paused, breathing heavily under his hood of dragon skull. The skull was powerful. From a young dragon, but from long ago, and full of magic… but not an infinite amount. Rainier wielded it to the best of his ability, trying to spread out its gift as long as it might go. However, the invincibility spell had taken a great deal out of the little dear, and with every gate that came down its power grew less and less. It was slowly but surely emptying itself. With every act, with every falling piece of metal, with every inch he moved closer to the inner part of the city, Rainier gave thanks to the dragon's gift. A great gift it was… so great in fact, Rainier was growing weary with the effort.

His chest rose and fell quick and steady. He tipped the dragon skull back on his head to look up at the massive metal gate before him. They had made it to the last. The last gate left of Castle Lyist's great defenses. Once those were down, the hirelings could charge for the treasury, emptying Castle Lyist's vaults like magic from the skull, until it was empty… and finally, truthfully, dead. A kingdom's gold was like the blood in its veins. It kept everything running, pumping through the world, keeping it functioning. Without it… well, veins shriveled, and hearts stopped beating.

Rainier looked around, watching the terrified civilians unlucky enough to be beyond the innermost wall. They scattered like ants from their homes, away from the hirelings, from the shattered gates, from the lives they had known. The safety they had taken for granted was being ripped from them, everything important stolen away… Rainier knew what that was like, and as he watched Castle Lyist falling into chaos around him, he waited for that feeling. The feeling of victory, the satisfaction of revenge... but it did not come. He felt nothing. No gleam of glory, not a dash of satiation, not even an aftertaste. These people... these scrambling, weeping, wailing mongrels were not the ones that owed him revenge. None of them... not a single one had seen a dragon in their lifetimes, not in their father's lifetime, or even their father's father's lifetime, let alone had a hand in their deaths. He wanted revenge... but not against these **children**. Time had taken those that deserved his wrath. Time had swept them into the past, steeling his chance. His aftertaste of revenge... It was just one more thing he had lost.

Rainier sighed and forced his breath under control, slowing it to a steady rhythm in his nose and out his mouth. No matter. No matter. As soon as all the ants left their hill... he would have what he came for. There was enough magic left in the skull for that, at least. *Thank you, little Docent.*

"What's the holdup?"

Rainier turned to see Grayson, ugly face twisted into a horrid grin, eyes glinting with malice and greed. Rainier had seen that look on many a man... and every single one had been a fool, ready to push forward when a pause was wanting. Ready to eat when it was time to fast. Ready to trust... where trust was foolish.

"Patience," Rainier said, eyes sliding back to the wall. "You will have your gold."

"Not till that gate comes down I won't" Grayson said, but he spoke in an almost jovial, friendly tone of voice. "Come, man, we are so close! So close now!"

"Has not anyone told you the old adage... anticipation is half the joy?"

Grayson barked a laugh as his men caused destruction around them. They had begun raiding nearby houses, businesses, and shop carts in their impatience. They scattered the contents across the cobbled streets, taking what pleased them and kicking aside or destroying the rest, to the great grief of the shop owners. Several hirelings had taken up a lively game of "chase the peasants." Girls ran screaming from laughing hirelings who tore at their clothes jeering with browning teeth. Anyone who came to the girl's aide was allowed a few choice shots, a sword in the shoulder, a knife in the neck. Then the hirelings would pull the weapons from their chests with a laugh and kill the would-be hero with their own blade.

"Witch, I was never one for foreplay." Grayson grinned seemingly oblivious to the chaos, and still in that congenial manner. Rainier wondered if the hireling had actually grown a liking to him… the thought made the Faithful's stomach churn in disgust.

Rainier looked back up to the gate. "Get your men under control, Grayson… we will be moving momentarily."

"Ai, shit heads!" Grayson barked over his shoulder, "We're pushing on. Let's go!" They came. One begrudgingly letting go of a half-naked peasant girl. He blew her a kiss before she scrambled, screaming out of sight, clinging her torn garments against her bare chest.

"Last one," Grayson barked another laugh, looking up at the tall barrier. "Good gods, witch… you sure are something, let me tell you."

"I will take down the gate." Rainier said, ignoring Grayson's compliment as if it had been the sound of a bug's wings buzzing against the air. "You and your hirelings clear out the rest of the people. I will be back when they are gone."

"What?" Grayson looked back around to him, frowning. "Your leaving? You're not going to stay for the whole thing?"

"No."

"Why not?"

"You do not need my help for the rest."

"Well, no…" Grayson said, watching Rainier with an odd, curious expression that morphed his ruined face into an even more unpleasant mass of flesh and bad choices. "But don't ya want to enjoy the show?"

"No, I am quite finished, thank you," Rainier answered. Time had already taken his revenge… and left him nothing but bitter bile at the back of his throat and the ever-present hunger for the remnants of what was forever lost to him. All he wanted now were the bones. "It will be easier to do my work when the castle has been emptied." Get all those little ants out of the way, and then he could take his time ordering all the bones… testing their strengths… begin their burials. He did not want to start those sacred rights with screams still infecting the air… or any Lystad life still on the premises, tainting the land. No, it had to be done right.

"Fair warning Grayson," Rainier continued, "If I find out a single one of my bones has been taken… if any of your men happened to ponder the price that would be fetched on the shadow market for the relics below… if any of what belongs to me is taken by anyone of you… I will kill *all* of you."

"And how would you plan on doing that?" Grayson barked another laugh that shriveled into a small whimper in his throat as the Faithful's eyes fell on him, dark, empty, hollow… so very hollow. "That won't be a problem," Grayson said, clearing his throat, forcing down the lump that had risen there. "An entire castle's treasury… what more could we possibly need?"

"A man's greed knows no bounds," Rainier whispered softly in that trickling voice like water down a creek. Grayson's skin began to crawl.

"I'll make sure it doesn't happen," Grayson said, firmly. "A deal is a deal. Those bones belong to you… sir," he added as those dark eyes watched him without blinking.

"Good… very good." Rainier turned back to the gate, lightly tipping the skull back down over his eyes. "Shall we?"

Grayson nodded. The rest of the hirelings gathered around them in mass, and as Rainier placed his hand on the last gate, they began to cheer and chant in one harmonious voice, united by greed, united by desire, united by everything but their better angels. No… their better angels sat weeping tears of blood on their shoulders… but no one was listening. They could hear nothing over their upraised chorus.

"Bring it down!" they screamed in savage joy, in vicious lust for destruction. Grayson even took up the chant, all discomfort forgotten in the rising emotion and a shared need for power. "Bring it down! Down! Bring it down!"

*How so very human they all are,* Rainier pondered as they continued,

"Bring it down! Bring it down! Bring it down! Down! Down! Down! Down!"

Down it came… and Rainier felt nothing.

# CHAPTER 37

Kyana crouched in the middle of the empty room, in the abandoned castle. A castle that had been so alive, so loud, just a few weeks previously was then so hollow. So barren. So quiet. But not a kind quiet. A dark quiet. An evil stillness. An insane silence. The forest was supposed to be quiet, but this city was not. Kyana could hear the distant sound of voices. They were panicked... desperate... running.

Kyana ran her hands through her auburn hair, eyes closed tight.

She was falling, falling through the empty sky of her mind with nothing to grab onto, no solid answers to catch herself. What should she do? The castle would fall. The Neira coat of arms could crumble to dust on this very day. These people would die. So many people. The people in the caverns might make it to the forests, and those in the boats may sail to safety, but those at the gate... The knights. Neander. Everett. Teller. Lionel with his babies' beard.... The Lystad.... All of them would die. She could do something. She could, but if she did it... if she did the one thing that could save them all... She would be....

Kyana snarled into empty air, an inhuman sound ripped from the deepest part of her soul. It attacked the air like a rabid snow cat, claws out, teeth slick with saliva, desperate to hurt, harm, and pass on some of that pain which was eating her slowly from the inside.

This was not supposed to happen. She was not supposed to care. She should have let them die in the woods. Then she would not care. She would not… she should not… they were the Four Kingdoms, haters of dragons, haters of Faithful… haters of her kind and she… she… she was…

Kyana reached up and ran the tips of her fingers over her lips. She could still taste it. That kiss. It still held on her lips and tongue like a snowflake that had fallen on a leaf. It hung there, clinging lightly, soon to melt.

She should not do it…. It would all end if she did. It would be the end of things. The warmth that had been building in her chest since she came to this kingdom of unexpected things. That soft warmth that she had missed so dearly. The kind smiles. The friendship. The talks of laughter. All of it. All the soft eyes. The sweet, stupid, need that she had for it. If she did what she knew she could do… it would end it… end it all. Their smiles would melt away… *burn* away.

But it was already ending… they would all die, and she would lose them, anyway. They would pass and pass by, and she would still be there. As always. Alone and left behind.

*So, let it all burn.*

Kyana stood. She opened her eyes, and her mouth was set. She walked up to the head of the high table. Stood before the chair she had sat in all those weeks ago. She glanced around the room, remembering the smell of fresh food, the tripping dancers, and the chaotic sound of life in a happy Castle Lyist. The joy of it. It was a beautiful moment. But moments end. Moments pass and pass by.

Kyana looked over to the high chair. She ran her fingers lightly over her bottom lip and thought of the way the gold band settled lightly on that soft black hair. She thought of how rough his hands had been on her cheek. What king had rough hands? Were they not supposed to be smooth and soft from years of pampered pleasures? That is what she had expected. Then again, nothing in this kingdom had ever done what she had expected. What was one more surprise… what was one more change? Just one more time?

Kyana dropped her hand to her bow, removing it from around her shoulder and placing it on the table before the seat. She put them gently beside the brown cloak that the Lystad had left behind only a short time ago. She set the quiver of arrows beside her bow and pulled her dagger from her belt as well. She left behind all her weapons on that high table, as if an offering to the empty hall of evil quiet, and turned to leave.

Kyana stepped outside into the bright and beautiful day. The sun shone; the clouds churned by in slow rhythmic puffs of white against a powder blue sky. Beautiful, serenity, as if the world was mocking the horror that lay obliviously below it.

People were running in all directions. A few knights were trying to rally the remaining women and children into a tower entrance against the castle wall, which Kyana assumed lead down to the dragon tunnels the king had mentioned. She ducked around thunderstruck families and under the reins of a particularly startled horse, who nearly kicked her in the face as it reared up and whinnied in panic. She ignored this and made her way towards the last remaining wall at a slow and steady walk.

It would all end. Everything. The angel of the treetops. Kyana of the woods. The kind faces and gentle words. The friendships, the caring, the acceptance… the rolling eyes, the echoing laughter… she would lose it all. No, worse than lose it. The death of a cherished thing was sad, but that cherished thing changing, turning away from you… that would be so much worse.

Kyana did not stop. She ducked and dodged and continued to walk through the hectic crowd, leaving them behind for the distant, last remaining gate. The noise died away as she walked. The people became fewer and fewer, until she was alone, and listening only to her own muffled footsteps against the cobbled streets. Everyone had been evacuated from this section of the city, and the quiet was interrupted only by the bustling sounds fading in the background. Kyana continued forward, watching the large gates slowly come into better view. She saw people scrambling around at its base, but she was not close enough to see who, or how many.

*Should I be sad?* Kyana wondered suddenly. *Should I cry?*

She did not feel like crying, but her heart ached as if she should. It was the same ache she felt as she tossed shovels full of red dirt over Wybert's last resting place. An ache that told her she was losing something important, but really, what was she losing here?

A lie.

It was a lie she told them. A lie she told herself. The truth was a drink better tasted fresh, for when aged with deceit, it grew sour… and when spiced with affection… poisonous.

Kyana could do nothing about that, however. It was far too late, and all things eventually end. She just wished it could end better than this.

She found them all, all the knights of suicide standing beneath the creaking, straining gates of the inner wall. Magic was slowly breaking the bonds, metal panels, and thick wooden posts of the gate. She could hear them straining and snapping in turn. The entire thing shuddered. Soon the enchanted unkillable men of coin would flood those cobbled streets. They would fill them with a noise that did not belong. The sound of death, dying, and destruction to replace the bustle of joy. Kyana did not want that.

Family and Faithful forgive her, she did not want it.

Several knights noticed her approach, and despite the fear that filled their faces, they peered curiously as she stopped a few yards back from the gate. One knight nudged another as she started unclipping the skirt that hung around her hips, leaving the snug pants to stand alone. The Lystad was there, right out in front of his men. He was rallying them, calling out orders and telling them to remain steady as the giant gates shuddered and groaned like a magnificent animal before them.

Kyana smiled, a sad little thing it was. *He looks so serious*, she thought as she unclipped the delicate white and gold necklace from around her neck and laid it gently on top of the discarded skirt. Her luck had run out it seemed.

His black hair danced across his ferocious face in elegant inky waves. This would be the last. A last look at the young king who was kind to her. She drank in the view as a drowned woman might gasp for air. He must have felt her gaze. He looked around, and his eyes landed on her.

"What the hell are you doing here?" he yelled, clearly frustrated.

"Why do you all keep asking me that?" Kyana wondered aloud, taking another step forward, eyes now moving towards the gate which had taken on a strange gleam that looked more like water than wood.

They kept asking her that question. All she knew was what she did not want. She did not want to watch these people she had grown to care about die, and that gave her the strength to take another step forward. The fire began to crackle deep within her chest.

A long crack appeared across the face of the gate with a sharp snapping sound. The knights jumped and looked around. Kyana jumped too, and fear shot through her heart. Because she did not want to die. She had spent years, countless years, avoiding that very thing. Running and hiding from whatever may come when time passed her by.

*What does it matter?* Kyana wondered. *We all die eventually.* What did it matter? And the reasons? What did they mean when it all passed? Whether they were selfish, or foolish, or wrong, or right, or in between. Time would not remember.

Doing. Moving. Choosing to do one thing or another. That mattered for a moment, but nothing more… and the reasons… they were wisps of light before the night swallowed them whole. There one moment and gone the next. Momentary. Ever so fleeting. And this choice she was making, at that moment, whether right or wrong, would haunt her for only a short time. Because she did not expect to live very long after it was done.

A moment there. A moment gone. Time would pass on.

Kyana watched the gate cracking and let the spark of fire flit into a quick flame within her. She closed her eyes. It had been so long since she had felt that fire. The heat resonated from her chest to her neck, feet, and fingertips. It had been so long, so many years. The spark of fire within burst to a steady flame which filled her with heat. Not a soft warmth, but a roaring, singing, burning heat. She resonated with it. She WAS it. She could feel the air begin to heat. If she had been standing in water, it would have begun to boil. Kyana opened her eyes to the sky above. The beautiful bright day mocked no longer. It seemed to sink away from her, dimming from her view as if the sun was frightened away by the light it saw within her.

*Yes.* She thought, smiling, and smiling wide. The fire licked at every inch within her chest, burning her, but not hurting her. It could never hurt her. Would never hurt her. Would never leave her… because he promised he never would. She felt that light inside, that light that could burn the world to ash. Burn it all away.

*You are right to be afraid.* She told the sun. *Run, run, run away little one. Run before a true fire comes.*

Kyana let out a breath of air, and it appeared in the form of steam. Another breath, and it was smoke. She let out a small gasp of pain as she felt her bones creak, strain, and then began to snap. Kyana fell to her knees as the high gate splintered with a shuddering cacophony. No one noticed Kyana screaming as the shards of wood began to fall, and twisted metal hit the ground with a thunderous, shuddering, crash. No one saw that Kyana shattered the same way. Her skin began to tear and break and peel away in bloody strips. But it was not bone and meat beneath… it was her real skin that began to show.

Dark scales began to grow under her false skin, and her body began to open, making way for her true form. The uproar of the swarming hireling men which had started to stream through the chasm left by the broken gate was overpowered by the guttural roar that emitted from Kyana's broken lips. Lips that shed like snakeskin, peeling backwards and away and dropping to the ground as long white teeth began to slide into place. As the last piece slipped from her mouth, Kyana could not help but think that the snowflake had melted for good. It was gone. Passed away. *Burned* away.

And that was okay. It was the last shovel of dirt on a lonely grave.

Despite themselves, the knights glanced around, only to turn and stare. The hirelings, who had been pouring through the entryway, began to slow their stream as they saw what was happening. Kyana began to rise from the dirty ground. The knights and hirelings alike shrinking before her.

The fire was a roaring inferno, and it filled her with power. It began to spill from her nose and mouth in steaming flutters of flame. Kyana's human skin sloughed off her scaly body as she stood on her newly formed claws and paws.

The courtyard of knights, hirelings, and kings stood together in silence as Kyana took form. Temporarily united in their sense of wonder. None of them had seen a dragon in their lives. They had been dead and gone for centuries. They had never felt the heat that emanated from the mere proximity to such a creature. This dark, black-scaled, monster felt to them like a hundred burning piers as it stretched wide its enormous, leathery, wings. Kyana's green eyes, large, with horizontal slits, looked down upon the humans that gaped at her. She breathed deeply, enjoying the feeling. It had been so long. Too long. This was it, her lie, her secret. And it was beautiful.

At her feet, the humans began to scatter. They had regained their minds and had begun to panic. Kyana made her move. Carefully she stepped over the knights in brown capes, leaned down and let a burst of fire roar from behind her teeth and into the dark mass of hirelings. They screamed and ran. They scattered, tumbled, running around, over, or crawling under each other, desperately grasping for the gateway they had just entered. Kyana followed them, ducking her magnificent scaly head as she barely slipped under the remains of its arch. The dark masses scattered like ants beneath her, and they burned like dried twigs under her breath. Their enchantment was strong...

but her magic was pure. Straight from the tap, and it brushed away that relic magic like dirt from a dress.

Her tail whipped behind her, causing a gust of wind that sent a stray knight flying into a far wall. He slammed into the thing and fell flat on his stomach, not moving. Kyana did not have time to turn back and check that he was alright. The hirelings were trying to escape, and she could not have that. No, she could not have that at all. She moved forward, following them in their retreat. She stepped heavily, every footfall sending a small quake across the entire city. One of her steps came down hard against the tall solemn statue of King Lawrence II. It split under her claws like a hot knife going though butter. The statue fell into pieces where it had once stood so tall and watchful, but Kyana was too wrapped up in her pursuit of the hirelings to notice.

She let out another burst of fire that curled through the panicked crowds and followed their retreat out the second, third, and towards the fourth and final gate. Kyana's massive claws left foot deep scars in the burning, scorching earth. By the time she ducked under the last gate, the hireling's numbers where over half destroyed. The rest of the masses scattered outward, running desperately through the meadow for the edge of the forest, while still others ran for the safety of the glittering river. But they had a long way to run and no time to get there. Kyana stopped a short distance from the gate, breathing heavily, smoke escaping her in sharp puffs.

It had been a long time since she had taken this form, and the intensity of her actions had already taken a toll. She could feel exhaustion creeping up on her, waiting to cover her face like a cloth of dream weed, but she could not stop now. Not yet. It was almost done. They were almost safe.

She steadied her stance, leaned her great neck down to the ground, and pulled in a long breath. She sent a streaming inferno like a whip across the open field between her and the running men. It whipped out and threw a crescent wall of flame sizzling over the grassy ground. The fire ate the grass ravenously, ferociously consuming everything it had. It left nothing behind but blackened, ashy, earth. The hirelings panic made them fast, but not nearly fast enough. Kyana heard the shrieks that were quickly silenced as her fire caught up to them. The dragon fire bounded over the rolling hills, roaring and crackling towards the edge of the forest. It pillared and writhed in greens, golds, blues and reds. She watched it dance smiling with wide scaled lips and long pure white fangs.

It had been so long.

Kyana slipped slightly as a wave of exhaustion washed over her. Her fire petered a few miles from the forest as Kyana shook her great head, trying to clear her vision. She blinked a few times and noticed something far out in the dimming light of her fire. A man. A man who was tall, with dark blue hair, thin face, and eyes of the deepest black. Kyana had no idea how he had gotten so far away from the castle so quickly... and then she cursed herself as a fool. The man was a Faithful after all.

Rainier watched Kyana in the light of her dragon fire. He was so close to it, but he was not running, not afraid. On the contrary, the man stepped closer, completely fearless of its ravenous power. Instead of fear, he stood watching Kyana, the skull relic in his hands, eyes wide with an expression of pure... ecstasy. There was no other word for it. It gleamed in his eyes, mingling with the reflection of the fire, writhing there amongst the empty dark. Kyana did not like that look. Not one bit.

She would burn it away.

Kyana tried to gain another breath, to end that bastardization of a Faithful right then and there, but she could not pull it in. She gasped for it, wished for it, but it did not come. It had been too long since her last change, and it always took time to adjust. She had never spent so much energy directly after a change. She had never risked it, and now she was feeling the price of her impatience.

Kyana's fire died out at the edge of the forest, and her eyes grew blurry, extinguishing her view of the Faithful man. Kyana stumbled and fell, the earth shuddering under her weight, a wing crumpled beneath her. Kyana's feet scrambled for a few moments, kicking ash and dirt into clouds in the air, trying to regain her footing. Perhaps if she could make it into the trees... if she could make it that far... but it was futile... it was over... it was all over. Kyana could already feel her true form shrinking, her scales receding, her wings folding and dissolving into her back.

*All over.* Kyana thought to herself as her pink human skin began to reform over her scales, and her snout returned into her skull and was covered by a human face. *It's all over now. Was it worth it?*

Kyana's human fingers dug into the scorched earth as her naked human form, half enveloped by smoke, finished coming into shape with a last creaking of bones.

*Was it?* Kyana blinked black ash from her eyes and looked at the sky. The bright blue was back to taunting through a haze of smoke and dust. The sun beat heavy and hot against her skin, seeming to tease her with its fake fire. Kyana smiled, out of joy or bitterness she could not say.

It was all over. She would be dead in a moment… maybe two. She could already hear the sound of horse's hooves approaching from the castle behind her, but she was far too tired to do anything about it. Too tired to even be afraid. Kyana's eyelids began to slip closed as the sound came nearer. A few muffled calls from familiar voices washed over her fading consciousness.

*Was it worth it? Was it really, Kyana of the woods?* Her own voice spoke harsh and hateful within her blurring mind, which was slowly spiraling into a darkness she was sure she would never wake from. *Tell me… how long will it take them to kill you for what you are? Tell me little girl, stupid child. Tell me, truly. Were they worth it? Were the hateful human's worth this?*

Kyana did not have time to answer. Her eyes fluttered closed as the voice went, thankfully, silent.

# CHAPTER 38

"We had a deal..." The words dripped from his mouth like the blood from his lips. They slid slow and thick, down his ruined cheeks, dropping in drip after drip of steady red tears that broke against the forest floor. They splattered in small red explosions, only to be swallowed by the soft and hungry earth. Swallowed into nothing, and leaving nothing but a browning stain, which would pass with the next rain.

Grayson was on his knees before Rainier. He reached out to the Faithful with one bloody hand, the other clutching a fatal wound in his belly, desperately holding in his own intestines with the will of trembling fingers.

"You swore to us... in... invincibility..."

The general watched him with eyes as indifferent to the hireling's pain as the sun looking down on the churning earth.

"No," he said as if speaking to a particularly dull child. "I promised you a *taste* of invincibility. A *taste* lasts for a moment. And your moment is over. You should be more careful when making deals... although I suppose you won't have to worry about that anymore." He looked up to the sun, watching its steady descent to the horizon. Reds, purples, and oranges streaked the sky, dying the pillowing clouds the softest of pinks. He had needed to pick a celestial anchor to enhance the magic from the dragon bones, and he once more congratulated himself on his choice. They had to admit... it was poetic. If things had gone as planned... if Castle Lyist had fallen... the sun would be setting on the day, on a kingdom, and on the hireling's dreams, although they would not know it until their purpose had been fulfilled. But honestly, did they really think he would give them lasting invincibility? Them? So, they could pillage and kill and rape at leisure? More than they already do? Unworthy, stupid things humans could be.

However, things had not gone as planned. No... not one little bit as planned.

"You... lying bastard!" Grayson spat with as much ferocity as a dead man could possess. Rainier's eyes dropped from the sun and looked into the hireling's dimming gaze so full of hate. His eyes grew terribly deep as fury fluttered inside his chest, while that terrible traveling smile spread wide, white teeth flashing in the sunlight. He leaned down a little, better for the hireling to hear his words, and hear them true.

"I am many *unpleasant* things Grayson. But a liar is not one of them. Of course, I deceived you" He nearly hissed into the dying man's face, "You stupid, useless piece of walking meat. Of course, I led you astray, because you made it so *easy*. I did not lie; I did not **need** to lie. I did not lie, although I owe you no truths. I owe you no honesty. I owe you absolutely *nothing*. I told you the truth, and you heard it in the way you wanted to hear it. You humans... you always like to take what you hear, but you do not keep it as it comes. You take it as if it was clay. You bend it, you mold it, to fit your own desires, your own purposes... you morph it to fit your own story, a tale of your own creation, and then you act *so surprised* when you are shown to be wrong. Because," Rainier reached out and took the hirelings trembling outstretched hand. The contrast of tanned, broken, bloody, thick fingers against Rainiers elegant, moon pale, thin grip was almost comical in a sickening sort of way. "Because little boy... you were never handed clay. You were handed stone," the Faithful leaned down closer and whispered in the dying man's ear, so low no one, but they could hear. "No, you deserve nothing. Nothing but liberation. So, go then, and pass us by. Let there be any and all waiting there when you arrive."

The man glared; bloody teeth bared at Rainier as if he might take a bite out of the Faithful's face. Perhaps lean forward and tear off that thin ear which hung dangerously close to his reach. Just clamp down and spill it out among the blood droplets, adding it to the rest. He did not, however.

Grayson's furious grimace froze on his broken face, and he keeled forward, face burying into the soft dirt. Rainier let the hand drop from his grip reaching down and wiping a smear of blood on the dead man's shirt. He stood, pale cloak shifting around him, caressing every elegant movement.

"Any other complaints?" he called to the crowd of remaining hirelings who had gathered after realizing their spell had broken. There were few left, perhaps forty or fifty at the most. The rest had been consumed in fire. They had been watching in terrified silence. No one spoke, merely stared with blank eyes, cradling their own wounds and burns.

"No?" Rainier said, smiling and turning away. "Very good then."

"Was that really a dragon?" asked a man in his thirties. The timid highness of his voice made him sound like a child no older than his tenth year. He was supporting his friend, who seemed only half conscious with his head lolling against his shoulder. Fresh burns had eaten up his right arm and right side of his face... Rainier knew he would not last the hour. The man watched the Faithful, gaze wide and desperate as if praying his eyes had been lying. "Was that... was that real?"

The Faithful general turned his full attention on the hireling, all traces of anger and irritation gone. In its place was a gleam that lit up his dark eyes.

"Yes, my boy," he said. "Yes, it was. Gods be good, it was."

There was no rumble of conversation, no flickering of expressions, just pure silence. Soon the crowd began to disperse. They slithered into the shadows of the night in sluggish singles or pairs, leaving their own trails of blood behind. Soon it was just the tall man, Ellis and the still form of Grayson in the clearing. The sun was over half passed the horizon by this point, and darkness had taken up most of the sky. Stars began to dapple the dark, sending pinpricks of light into the blackness and soon moonlight would flood the world.

Rainier could feel the boy's eyes on him. They had not left since Rainier found him in the forest, and they watched him now with a burning curiosity. The Faithful knew all the questions the boy would ask, and he did not mind them one bit. However, he was too wrapped in his own thoughts to speak first. His mind obsessed over the image of that beautiful dark creature rising from behind the walls. He watched and re-watched in his memory as it spread its massive wings, mouth opening wide. The roar it had made shook the ground, vibrating the earth all the way out to where Rainier had been standing in the meadow beyond the walls. It had shaken him, shuddering through him, filling him, consuming him, and when the fire had started to spread... oh how he wanted to be touched by its light. To step inside of it, to have it all around him, to be claimed by the heat. He remembered those green eyes, those eyes that floated forefront in his mind, holding him captive, but he did not mind those chains. The emptiness Rainier had been feeling, that lack of feeling altogether, it had been burnt away by that fire, and swallowed up in those eyes.

They remained in silence a short time more. The boy waited, watching the Faithful's forever eyes flitting from star to star at a tireless speed. Soon enough, however, his curiosity got the better of the silence. Ellis shifted his feet and moved the dragon skull in his grip.

"What… what now sir?" he asked in a small voice.

The tall man took a deep breath, eyes closing, a smile spreading wide across his face.

What now? Oh, so many things. So many, many, beautiful, beautiful things.

"First my dear boy," he said, eyes still closed. "We bury our dead."

"Oh, right of course," Ellis said hastily. "Should we bury Grayson here? Or would you like me to—"

"Grayson?" Rainier's eyes opened. He frowned down at the body, scrunched at his feet. "Why would I mean this piece of filth? Leave the meat for the animals boy, I meant the bones. We must bury the bones."

"Oh, uh, of course," Ellis said again, hugging the skull close to his chest. "But… won't we still need it?" The man shook his head, stepping over Grayson like a puddle of mud he would rather not step in.

"I'm afraid our dear friend has given everything she could. The bones hold no more magic. They gave it all in the battle." He looked down at the skull in the boy's hands, reached out and stroked the long nose. "It is time to lay her to rest. Once and for all." He looked up. "But not here. Not among the blood of non-Faithful. Not this tainted ground."

"Where then?" Ellis asked.

The traveling smile slipped slowly from one side of his face to the other, splitting him.

"I have just the place. Follow me. We have much to do." He turned, and Ellis followed without hesitation.

"After we bury the bones," the boy said, scampering behind the tall man like a puppy with soft paws and stumbling stride. "What then general sir?"

"Then my boy," the man spoke soft, but his heart was thudding hard, pulsing blood and adrenaline, and that feeling he thought he would never have again. That feeling of hope. That little creature that twittered from the recesses of its cage within his chest. The one that he thought had died long ago. The one that had been beaten, burned, strangled until its song was forced from its body. It had lain there still and silent until, without warning, it perked up its little head, opened its little beak and began to sing a song that Rainier had forgotten, but now, beautifully, he remembered.

He could feel that joy rising, that anticipation, the knowledge that everything... everything was different. Something beautiful had happened, and there was... oh *so much* to do.

"We start something new."

# CHAPTER 39

Ira's shoes crunched against the shattered stones, and the hem of her gray dress was drenched in black ash. She made her way towards the twisted and torn remnants of the inner gate. It was burnt. All of it. Carts, barrels, even a few houses slumped smoldering in black and gray ruin to the sides of the street, still wafting smoke and pulsing with heat from the fire which had extinguished hours before. The road itself, once filled with elegantly laid cobbles, had a large black scar down the main street. The stones had darkened, fissured, or wholly shattered into ragged pebbles that ground together as Ira and others bustled trancelike through their city. Their city, suddenly so foreign. Their city suddenly so changed with embers and ash slashed out across its street like a wound across flesh.

Ira watched them all, the hordes of families staggering in a trembling, stumbling herd, drunk on shock and fear. She watched them lumber back to their homes, back to the lives they once had, not yet realizing such lives had died the moment a small woman stood before an army, shedding her skin for all to see. Shed it like a lizard. Shed it like a dragon.

*A dragon…*

Ira stopped a short distance from the gaping wound in the inner wall, no one else came near. This was the place. This very place where hours before history had been rewritten. Reborn in fire. Ira had seen it. She had watched from the deck of a ship that had not yet set sail as the massive creature had risen into the sky. She had watched the ancient legend pierce reality with its mere existence. She had seen the green eyes, bright even from such a distance, and she had known what it meant. So many things suddenly made sense.

This place had been given a wide berth by all. Only Ira stepped across that invisible circle and knelt down between the scattered shards of metal and wood still crackling with heat that sent ripples of warmth into the air.

It was a terrible thing that she stooped to see. The flesh that had fallen from Kyana's body like wrapping from a prize. It lay in a forgotten puddle of skin, hair, teeth, bone, and blood now as dark and black as the ash and stone it had dried upon. The smell was the worst of it. There was nothing like it. Soppy and rancid, it churned through the hot rippling air and made Ira want to gag like so many passerby's who plugged their nose and squinted watering eyes, quickly hurrying away.

Ira did not cover her nose. She did not run away. Instead she reached out, lungs full of putrid air, and reached into the huddled mass with a trembling hand. A few people watched as Ira gently pulled something out of the mangled mess, something that had caught her eye. They said nothing, merely going back to their wandering with a sniff or a retching sound. One man finally succumbed to vomiting as Ira pulled the string of beads into the air, and a chunk of flesh clung to it like thin, sticky fingers.

They were lovely, even covered in blood. That simple string of white and gold beads. Ira had pretended not to notice when the woman in the market gave them to Kyana. Pretended not to see the Wish for the Traveler that the woman had tapped into her palm. Ira knew Faithful were living in Castle Lyist. You would be stupid not to know. People were people, and they tend to live where they can live best. By gods Castle Lyist was such a place. Citys held businesses, people, prosperity and opportunity, and Castle Lyist was one of the most prosperous in the lands. Besides... where else did people have to go? To Kyar? Where they had just started to quarter off sections of cities that allowed Faithfuls to live openly? It was a transitional period and was sure to be a life seeped in a constant state of danger and persecution. However, it was not like any of the other major cities were much more tolerant. Except of course, for Wayriver in Kingdom Eryl. The "quite kingdom," as it had been somewhat affectionally named by the other three kingdoms, had never quite outlawed being a Faithful per se. The king, old and withering Edwin Amnon XII, allowed the Faithful to live within the kingdom, with punishment only for the trading of bones and practice of magic. Eryl Kingdom, however, rested on an island far out in the icy Ocean of the Four Winds, a considerable distance from either Neira Kingdom or even Kingdom Kyar. Few wealthy families had the opportunity to travel such distance safely, let alone any Faithful's, whose main job was to keep quiet and keep their secret.

Ira wiped the necklace on the bottom of her shirt and saw that the clasp and short chain at the back had been snapped. She pocketed it, careful to not let any beads escape the line, and slowly got to her feet, hands still trembling. There was something in her, something strange. Something that had been building and building since the gates rained down around their heads. Ever since that pink skin turned to black scales and those green eyes showed their true history. It was a building, and flowing and churning sensation in Ira's chest, hot and growing hotter with every passing moment. With every breath of that putrid air she breathed and every flash of memory, she felt a flicker of prophecy. Yes. The city had changed. The world had changed. Their old lives had passed and passed by, and all that was left was what was ahead. She could almost see it, feel it, and she knew what it was.

*Fire.*

For the first time in a long time, Ira remembered.

# CHAPTER 40

The knock came hours after the sun had set low beyond the horizon. Night had taken the streets, shooing home all stragglers from the afternoon's pilgrimage back into the city, leaving them empty. Or so the jeweler had thought.

She looked up at her husband, who had stopped on his way towards their room. He turned, white nightshirt shifting in the orange light cast from the candle in his hand. Their eyes found each other, then turned back to the door that now stood silent. The woman grabbed her thread worn shawl and pulled it tight about her shoulders as her husband stepped forward. She waited, fingers digging into her arms as her husband reached out and unlatched the door, pushing it slightly open.

Behind the door stood a girl. A girl with fine, blond hair, a thin but sturdy frame, and a face that she recognized instantly. The jeweler was an older woman, pushing reluctantly towards her seventy-fourth year but her memory was as sharp as it had ever been, better even. This was the girl from the market, the one with the woman who had such unnatural eyes.

Ira stood in the doorway but made no move to come inside. Her head was tilted down towards her hands, which twisted slowly around a string of beads, one the woman also recognized well. It had taken much time to make, and mere seconds to give away. Like a pretty song, or those three words that people found so difficult to say these cold, impersonal days. However, the woman supposed, it was not the words that were the problem, but the act of giving them over to someone else. Such a selfish world it had become. The jeweler had not hesitated, however. She was a giver at heart, always had been. It was how her mother raised her, and her mother before her. Her husband liked to tease, saying that perhaps that was why they were always so poor. She would always answer with a smile, and a reminder, that there was more than one way to be rich.

She had given that necklace to the woman without hesitation, both the necklace and the wish, and she never regretted either, not for a single moment. Now, she pushed forward, jostling her husband violently out of the way in her haste to stand before the girl with the beads.

"Twas her, twasn't it?" the woman asked, in a voice that defied the quiet night without shame, without fear. The girl looked up through her golden curtain of hair. In her eyes the red and orange candlelight burst into a glittering flame. In that fire the jeweler knew, such a girl would not be a mere child for much longer.

"It was..." she said, holding out the string of beads, and jeweler instantly reached out to accept them. "And... she is."

The woman did not bother asking if the girl was sure, or if it could have all been a mistake, or some cruel trick. She could tell by her eyes she was not lying, and she could tell by her own thudding heart that she already believed.

"Wake ta boys," she said, turning to her husband. "Stew and Waylen. Wake em both. Ta sooner ta better."

"What about Kyden?" the man asked, already moving towards the back of the house, headed to their youngest sons' room. The woman shook her head.

"He's clear on ta other side of ta city. Besides, Stew and Waylen are young, healthy an fast. We'll call on Kyden come morn. Better send Stew and Way off now. They've gotta lot of distance to cover in a very short time." She turned to the girl who stood, almost dazedly in the doorway. A cool breeze fluttered the cloak that hung off her slumped shoulders, but she made no notice.

"How much time?" the jeweler asked her.

"Don't know," Ira said, blinking slowly. "They haven't... hurt her yet.... So, they'll probably wait till she's awake. There are rumors of a trial..." The jeweler cackled. A harsh sound, more akin to fingernails braking against stone than any sort of mirth.

"Yes, yes, I know of their 'fair' trails." She frowned, and mumbled more to herself than to him, "Better start up a few letters too. They'll be slower ten da boys, but at least it'll be something."

"I've got someone I can send word to," Ira mumbled, in an almost embarrassed, childish tone. The woman glanced up.

"Do so, child. Do so fast. As fast as ya can. We have little time." She watched the young girl's face with concern. "You alright child?" she asked, stepping forward and placing a soft hand on Ira's cheek which was flushed with the chill. Ira started as if waking from a dose.

"Yes, I'm... I'm... I..." She took a deep breath and the firelight from the lamp on a nearby table swam once more in her hazel eyes. It danced there, brighter than the flame itself.

"I remember," the girl said, a warm, wondrous smile breaking her face. The smile of someone who had stumbled in the dark for a long age and had finally found their way home.

The woman smiled and patted her cheek.

"So, do I child. So, will they all."

# CHAPTER 41

Kyana stirred, a soft groan escaping dry and cracked lips. She regretted the movement. Her entire body felt sore. Every muscle seemed to pulse and throb from the change. She was always sore coming back, but it was never this bad until the third day. With the way she was feeling, it had been at least that long since she fell in the meadow outside the city. The sun was gone, and so was the soft grass which had turned to ashy earth. Kyana felt cold stones pressed against her side. The air was thick with humidity. The sickly, stench of mold, stale water, and dirt grew until Kyana nearly had to swallow it down. Wherever she was, sanitation was not a priority.

Kyana groaned, sat up and opened her eyes. Yes, the sun was gone, replaced by a dark stone room. There were no windows, no natural light, only a few torches hung against the far wall. The orange and red glow flickered through the bars, stretching their shadows in long dark figures across the dirty stone floor that made up her cell, for it was a cell after all. It was a dungeon.

Kyana raised a hand to her throbbing head and pushed back a strand of hair. She felt her forehead. No fever. She reached down and pulled at the edge of her clothes if they could be called that. They were barely cloth, tattered, old, stained brown, and fraying from numerous uses. It was basically a sack with a hole cut in the top and sides for arms, with a cord of rope wrapping the waist. The same material was sown into baggy sleeves on the sides that fell down past her fingertips. She supposed it was better than nothing. They could have left her naked.

She pulled up the old cloth to inspect her wrist and side. The wounds were gone, as she knew they would be, replaced by fresh and beautify untouched pink skin. All her old scars would be gone. Every injury she had collected in the forest over the many years she had spent alone, vanished. Even the one on her side that Augustine had tended too with such diligence would be gone. Kyana had left them all in the inner wall of Castle Lyist. She imagined them molding there on the cobbled street next to her reputation and her lies. She wondered which was stinking worse by this point.

Kyana jerked her shirt down, and a clanking sound drew her attention to the shackles wrapping her wrist. They were thick, heavy chains, connected to a metal band which wrapped around both wrists. She frowned down at them. It was made of an odd metal. It was heavy, heavier than it should be. Something that small, almost an exact fit for her tiny wrists, should have been light, but she could feel them trying to drag her arms to the floor. That was not the only odd thing she noticed. The color was off, so dark, it was almost black. It looked charred as if burnt and brittle around the edges. That should have made the metal weak, but this was anything but weak. They wrapped both wrists and dipped to the floor where they spun through a loop sutured to the stone ground and then back up to another heavy band that curled snug around her throat. Kyana flicked the thick chains testing their strength. They clanked heavily against the stone ground, letting out a sound more like a growl than a clatter. No, not normal metal at all. In fact, she knew precisely what these shackles were made of.

*Well,* Kyana thought, *they aren't stupid enough to put me in typical irons. I'll give them that little at least.*

She was curious at her predicament. She had never expected to wake after her eyes slid closed on that field of ash. She had expected to be slaughtered the instant the knights slid off their horses. The mark of the Faithful alone was considered treason in Neira, and she was... well a dragon after all. The real deal. The main event.

Kyana stretched her sore legs and tried to stand, but the chains only allowed her the most minimal of movement. She could sit up, but no more. The cell was cold, as she expected all cells must be, for the constant discomfort for those unlucky enough to be inside one. The only form of comfort came in the scattered flakes of hay that littered the floor. It looked as if it had seen many a resident. Black mold grew in oily colors along its edges. Kyana's nose wrinkled as that heavy smelling air came to her once more.

Her stomach gave a throb almost to match the one inside her head. This made sense, of course, she had been asleep for days. She usually planned her hibernations with care, feasting beforehand and finding a far more comfortable place to rest than the likes of this. A deep cavern where predators would not find her or perhaps nestle in that hollowed out sections of those giant trees at the very heart of Kyar Kingdom. Those old things, older than dragons themselves, stood tall, quiet, and peaceful. The perfect place to rest and recoup from a change.

Kyana's mother had told her stories of how spirits had once lived in those trees. Ghosts of the ancients, those that had come first and would come again when the God of Time descended to claim the world. The spirits had made those trees their homes. Her mother insisted that their essence had left a mark, leaving a place of peace, kindness, where no evil would dare to stray.

Kyana was grown now and had shaken the fantasies of her childhood. She knew better now. Evil did not care what came before. It would go wherever it pleased, despite the pretty, pretty, stories. But at times like these, when she needed to heal from a change, or simply needed rest, Kyana would curl up in those hollowed out spaces. She would hover above the world, enjoying the secluded comfort and imagining a time of gossamer spirits, sparkling lights, where evil was outlawed, and all was right. A few times she swore she heard her mother's voice, telling and retelling those tales in her sleeping ear. She swore only to herself, of course, because there was no one else to tell. No one left to swear to. Because evil did not care about sweet stories.

Kyana heard the scraping sound of a heavy door being forced open somewhere out of sight. By the complete silence, not even the sound of breathing, the dungeons had been empty except for her. Now, however, a figure in a guard's uniform and long chestnut cloak stepped into sight. He had an unfamiliar face that stared at her in wide-eyed surprise, as his gate jutted to a stop. She sat as dignified as a chained animal could be, and allowed a wide venomous smile to flash across her lips.

"Well, hello, handsome," she said, deep green eyes boring into his. His eyes grew as large as supper dishes and fear poured into them like water from a spigot. Kyana wondered if he had already pissed himself, or if he would have the dignity to be out of sight before he did so. "How's it going?"

The guard did not say a word, merely stood frozen, eyes locked on hers. Kyana smelled the sour scent of urine and knew the poor man had not made it. She blinked, allowing him to breathe. He took the opportunity, turned around, and stumbled out of the room. He tripped over his own cape in his haste and Kyana barked a humorless laugh. She heard the heavy door being damn near slammed closed behind him. Once again she was alone in the dimly lit cell. Kyana did not see anyone else for a long while, but she knew they would come for her soon enough. She sat silent, waiting, thinking, wondering why on earth she was still breathing. She could think of no good reason, and all the viable ones left her feeling ill. What did they want her for? What would they do with her? Dissect her? Make an example of her? She was the last dragon to be seen in centuries. Any plans for her would not be good ones, and every possible purpose ran in bloody circles through her mind.

Kyana waited. Time seemed to slide sluggishly by as she waited for her fate to come in the form of a brown-cloaked executioner. A brown cloaked knight did eventually appear, four of them in fact. She waited as one of them stepped forward to unlock the heavy gate as the other three waited behind, swords already drawn. They flashed ominously in the torchlight, by they did not worry Kyana half as much as the shackles that wrapped her wrists and neck.

She waited patiently as the guard detached the shackles from the floor and onto another long chain made of the same chard looking metal. These he held in his hands. The guard motioned for Kyana to follow with a sharp tug on the chain. Kyana followed without hesitation or question, knowing neither would do any good.

She knew she would die, and she had come to accept the fact. Well, as well as anyone could come to except such a fact. Kyana did wonder if they would take care of Royal after they had executed her, or if they would take the poor beast's life for the pure shame of having been owned by her. She hoped not. She hoped for nothing but a long and happy life for that creature.

The steps out of the dungeon were spiraled and long, a continuous twist that curved up and up into the darkness, only dispersed by the torches which sent the same warm light against the cold walls. They ascended, two guards flanking her, and the other two walked ahead. One held the chain and the other a torch to guide the rest as sentinel. The two at her back never lowered their swords, and every so often she felt a sharp edge graze her lower back. A small reminder not to make a move in the wrong direction, not to stray a single hair. She heard it loud and clear. They soon reached the top where a gatekeeper with a somber face opened a heavy wooden door for them. It opened with an angry creak as if frustrated to be losing its only captive. The guard tugged on her chain, and Kyana followed through.

Crisp night air brushed across Kyana's face, and she gulped in eagerly, glad to be rid of the rancid rotting smell down below. She had expected to be taken directly into a throng of eager watchers, cheering before the stone block and waiting headsman. She had seen two executions in her life, both very different. One she cared to see, the other killed her to witness. One was the death of a man, the other the end of a boy. One happened on a summer day with the backdrop of a beating sun, the other on a fall night filled with rain. One by ax, the other by fire. Very different, but both shared two things and two things only. The executioner and the crowd.

The executioners were not the same man, but close enough. All dressed in black, with a bored expression on his face. A face that had taken too many lives to see them as worth anything more than the swipe of an ax or the throw of a torch.

The crowd was also the same. All voices cheering, eager for the "monster" blood to be spilled. The strange, savage desire to see harm come to someone they found undeserving of life. Whether or not worthy themselves… Kyana did not know. But they thought they knew. They all thought they knew what was right and what was wrong. They sentenced accordingly and took great joy in it. A sickening pleasure, that crowd always had.

Kyana had expected a headsman and crowd waiting for her in the dimming light of evening. Or would they burn her for witchcraft? That would be a silly mistake on their part. Surely, they were not be that stupid. To her surprise, she found no stone nor pier in those streets. There were no angry throngs, in fact, there was no one at all. The entire courtyard was empty. This was odd being as Kyana could hear voices talking, yelling, calling, bickering, at some distance, but no one in sight.

The guards led her through the empty courtyard and into an inner wall. This was also cleared, except for the few guards standing frozen around the edges. Again… odd. Kyana found only more surprises when she realized what direction they were leading her. Towards the castle? Why would she be brought there? She did not have to wait long to find out. She was soon being ushered through a side door to the castle. Walking down the empty hallway, Kyana heard the sound of many voices arguing. This sound grew nearer and nearer as she continued forward. Two guards watched outside the double doors of the throne room. They pushed them inward as Kyana and her entourage approached. The yell of voices reached a deafening peak and then died to silence as Kyana stepped inside.

She looked around. People dressed in either knight's uniforms or official public garb surrounded her. Fabrics of bright reds, greens, and blues sparkled on every side. The servants stood in stark contrast, lining the back walls in simple, understated colors, half out of sight. Faces, old, young and in-between, stared as she was ushered further into the room. A fireplace at the side of the hall crackled, sputtered and heated the room, but did nothing to thaw the cold glares of the onlookers.

Every chair was filled, not a single seat open. Not even the high throne at the head of the room. It was truly gorgeous, Kyana noted not for the first time. It waited beyond the long hallway of chairs, its back stood tall and ornately carved into swirls of flame. The stones inlaid within the throne sparkled in the firelight.

However ornate the chair, it was nothing compared to the man who sat upon it. He wore his court armor, polished to a shine. His chestnut cloak tumbled from his broad shoulders and spilled across the stone steps at his feet. The modest golden band from the banquet was replaced with a jewel-encrusted crown to match his throne. From beneath the crown, the Lystad's blue eyes were a war of day and night. They watched her, as cold and hard as the stones beneath his boots. All traces of boyish joy and echoing laughter had vanished from the hallways of Kyana's mind. She was not looking up at the boy with royal toes, she was coming eye to eye with the king. The King of Neira, King of Castle Lyist. A king of blue storm, born from the lineage of needless fear. And in those eyes, she saw it. That look she had been dreading since that blossom of warmth opened defiantly in her chest.

*There it is, little girl.* The voice whispered, soft and slow in her ear. *There it is. That hate you know so well. Well? Was it worth it? Was it worth this?*

At that moment, Kyana regretted everything. Regretted saving him. Regretted saving them all. She should have turned her fire inward. She should have scorched the ground where they now stood and turned to ash this kingdom and its obsession with old wars. This kingdom of hate. Burned it all.

Burned it away until even the ashes passed by. However, there was no going back. There was no undoing the done, and so she stepped forward, her shackles clanking at her wrists. When she reached the head of the room, she stopped and faced the tall chair.

The room was silent as the king stared down at Kyana. After a moment, the Lystad finally spoke.

"Kyana," his tone was loud, authoritative, glorious, everything a king should be. "Stranger from the forest, you have been brought before us today, on charges of witchcraft. How do you plead?"

Kyana could not help but smile. She smiled, and soon, a light chuckle bubbled from her chest and left her in raucous laughter. It echoed sharp and boisterous off the ceiling, seeming to bounce around the hall. She saw a few people flinch as if it was a thing to be avoided, not to be touched.

A trial? She was being put on trial? A civil society should have a trial, Kyana supposed, but did it still count as a fair trial when everyone already knew how it would end? After a few moments, she stopped laughing. She let the sound die in an instant. Let it fall to the ground hard, swallowed by the silence.

"Not guilty," Kyana said, calm and clear. A murmur ran across the room. It bounced from hushed whisper to hushed whisper, dulling back into silence as the king raised his hand. His eyes never left Kyana and Kyana never blinked.

"Not guilty?" he asked, sounding astonished.

"Correct," Kyana answered.

"So, you did not change yourself into an ancient magical beast three nights past? You did not scorch the earth with unholy fire?" called an old man in lavish colored robes. His wrinkled head still clung possessively to a few patches of white hair, but it was fighting a losing battle. His veins stood out blue and vivid against his skull and neck, but Kyana was not concerned with that, she was concerned with his eyes. Light eyes, but not like Augustine. Augustine's eyes were soft and looked for light, this man was not. This man only saw hate. Hate and something else... fear. Hate and fear consumed him, blinded him. Give him a year or two, and he would have nothing left to see.

"If you recall," a familiar voice spoke, and made Kyana look over. Down a few rows to the kings right stood Neander. He did not look at Kyana but glared at the man who just spoke. "It was that "unholy" fire that lets you stand here today, Phobos. It's the only reason we all weren't killed by an army of magical monsters."

"*She* is a magical monster!" the man screamed, waving his thin arms in her direction, fingers twisted into claws.

*There it is.* Kyana thought. *Monster, monster, kill the beast! Spill its blood and let it die. Kill it, burn it, burn it all away. Monster, monster! Burn it all away!* Did they ever tire of their hoarse tune? Kyana knew she did.

"Careful boy," Kyana said, green eyes flashing so ferociously towards the man that he shrank under their intensity like a sheep from a wolf. "You might hurt a girl's feelings."

A rumble of voices leaped up once more.

"Not guilty?" the king repeated, and the voices petered. "Explain."

"The charges are of witchcraft," Kyana answered. "I am no sorcerer or witch. I am no trickster, or mimic, or anything of the like. I'm no relic using Faithful. They use magic that doesn't truly belong to them. They steal it from those that can no longer give it." Not all Faithful's were meant to channel magic. When the dragons were alive, they would pick the humans they deemed worthy to receive their power. It was a gift to be given, not a power to be taken. Now that the dragons were dead, Faithful's like Rainier scavenged for bones, the last remnants of a once beautiful promise. Kyana understood their desires... those bones were the last whisper of a time when they belonged in a community that loved them. It was a far-flung daydream from the world that they all now lived. To hold those bones was to read a letter from a lost friend, a lost world, and to wield their power was to connect to the life you miss with all of your heart. Kyana understood... that did not mean she agreed with them. "They rob graves, but instead of gold they take magic. It does not make them any less of a thief. I am no thief. That is not what I am."

"What are you then?" the king asked, slow, and even.

"Couldn't you tell?" Kyana flashed him a grin with no real mirth. "Well, your *self-righteousness...* if you need it spelled out for you... I'm a dragon." There was an uproar from the crowd that lasted until one knight banged his fist against the end of a table.

"That is impossible!" the old man, Phobos, proclaimed. "All dragons were eliminated years ago."

"Besides," called a voice Kyana could not see. "You're human."

"Yes... sometimes I am."

"Faithful!" called another disembodied voice.

"Monster!" called another.

"Burn her!" cried a third. Kyana rolled her eyes.

"Yes, please, burn me, for all the good it will do you." Humans burn. Dragons do not.

"How could you be both?" the king asked once the voices dimmed down. "Human and Dragon?"

"It's a long and tedious story," Kyana said coolly as the fire gave a loud crackle. "One you will not like, and I do not enjoy telling. Why don't we just skip to the part where you murder me?"

"There will be no murdering here," sniffed a tall knight, also to the king's right. "This is a trial. If you are to die, it will be by the will and discretion of the king. An execution, no murder."

*Either way, I will be dead, yes?* Kyana thought, but she felt the fire building in her chest at the knight's words.

"And what about my family?" Kyana asked, voice rising as the fire flared in her belly, the clawing of her other half, fighting to come out. "Do you call their deaths a trialed execution as well?"

"Your family?" the Lystad asked, and for the briefest moment, Kyana saw a flicker of boyish surprise. The face of someone who was best friends with a simple kitchen girl. Then it was gone. "Explain."

She thought about refusing him. Thought about telling him to shove it straight up his ass, and have done with it, but she did not. Her family deserved their story. Their voices deserved to be heard, even in this stony hall full of ears that would not listen, and refused to understand. She owed them that, and so much more. She also owed it to herself. For Neander, who would not look at her. For Everett who stood beside him with fearful distrust. For the Lystad with his stony expression. For Ira who she did not see anywhere, and for Lilly who was standing off in a far corner watching her with nothing less than utter terror. When she noticed Kyana was looking at her, the girl's eyes fell to the floor, hands trembling so hard she looked like she was holding an angry mouse between her fingers.

Augustine was also there. He was off in one of the side chairs facing the throne. His gray eyes were wide, too bemused to be afraid or hateful. Give him time and Kyana was sure he would get there.

Kyana owed it to herself to tell these people. These people that had made her care. Forced her to care. Against her will, she craved their friendship, and now that the truth was free, she owed it to herself to tell them the whole story. If these people were going to kill her, they were going to know precisely who it was they were killing. She hoped it haunted them till their dying day.

"I was born in a fall that rained yellow and red leaves. I was born into a family," Kyana began. The room was quiet once more, seeming to lean in from all sides, eager to hear what tales this creature may tell. Curiosity winning out over fear. "Into a good family. People of love and loyalty. I grew up on the hillsides and meadows of Pastenfair between Neira and Kyar Kingdoms. At least, it was called Pastenfair at the time. But that was long ago, it might have changed, and I haven't been back since...." Kyana cleared her throat and went on. She must tell it all. From the very beginning. "I was born into the Faithful, and I lived a faithful life." The room remained silent at this. Confusion seemed to pass over every face. Every face but one.

"Continue," the king ordered. Kyana obliged, but not for his sake.

"This was just before the Time of Turmoil, about six years before the First War. As I grew up, there were few scatterings of battles and skirmishes between the newly forming Iver Faithful and the Four Kingdoms. But none of this was near Pastenfair or my people. We thought if we kept our heads down the trouble would pass with only a momentary mark on history... we were very... very wrong." The room remained silent, so Kyana continued, "I was the only daughter to a mother... full of stories and songs of spirits and... hope..." Kyana trailed off, choking around the lump in her throat. She cleared it, trying to find her voice. When she did, it was steady once more.

"And a father full of kindness and poetry. We were the Faithful to the dragons Kyaper, Sterya, and their young foal Kyaru. My great grandfather had been Kyaper's Main... his personal human. His "first" and most honored and trusted out of all his Faithful, the kind granted the gift of magic, for all of you who have forgotten your history. My grandfather was his Main when Kyaper and Sterya left Aadya Castle and kingdom Kyar, seeking the solitude of Pastenfair. My grandfather followed his dragon, and for generations, my family was the faithful keepers of this magnificent clan. This great family. My mother and father lived in loyalty and love and brought me up in the same way."

Kyana remembered those times with difficulty. Vague images of twirling grass under a pale-yellow sky. There were other children toddling about around her. Her mother's smile. Her father's rasping laugh. The magnificent roar of Kyaper in the distance and the sweet little whooping of a baby Kyaru trying a roar of his own, but not yet old enough. All images briefly swooped across her mind. There one minute, gone the next. What remained was something far more powerful. It was a feeling. That feeling of a soft warmth filling her chest. That soft warmth that heated her very soul. The feeling of love. That feeling of being safe. That feeling of being *home*.

"There were others in our clan, but my parents were the two most favored among the Faithful. I spent most of my young years in the presence of the great dragons and played alongside the young Kyaru. The foal was barely older than I was at the time, and we were... he was my best friend." Kyana had to stop again. She was having trouble finding breath. Anger and pain fought for dominance inside her and both were doing an excellent job of wreaking havoc, tearing, breaking, burning the broken thing in her chest in place of a heart. She continued,

"I dare say, I would have had the honor of being Kyaru's Main when we both came of age... but Kyaru wouldn't see his second decade.

In the year I turned ten, The First War had ended. The Iver faithful had been beaten down. That was good. They were violent and angry and stood against everything we at Pastenfair believed. What we had separated from the Four Kingdoms to get away from. The politics, the old pains, the old fury, resentments, and constant squabbles for power. We didn't want power. We didn't *need* power. We had each other, and our meadows and that was all we needed. That was everything.

"With the Iver Faithful defeated, we thought the war was over. Everything went back to peace, quiet and calm. We thought the fighting was done... but one day... we were startled by a great sound. It shattered the peace of our homeland. Can you guess what it was?" Kyana glanced around the silent room, daring them to speak. They did not. They all knew... they must know.

"It was an army. Two armies. One made of black and green, with the crest of Kyar Kingdom shining so bright and proud on their shields. The other was an army in brown. An army of brown and blue. An army with the coat of arms of a midnight dragon. Thousands of knights came. Came with dragon egg swords to cut through dragon scales." Her eyes raked around the knights standing or sitting, their chestnut and blue cloaks hanging so bright and so proud of their shoulders. She wanted to rip them off. Throw them on the ground, stomp on them and set them on fire. She wanted to hold them under their noses, show them just how much blood it took to make those browns so bright. She wanted to show them that day. Show them the blood and the pain and the destruction. The smoke, the glint of swords before they broke through flesh, soon enveloped by red, red, and more red.

"They claimed to be liberating us… freeing us from an evil tyranny. They came to end a reign of dragons and their evil, controlling, tempting, seductive, manipulative magic… they came only for the dragons… but they were **ours**." Kyana thudded a fist against her chest, and her chains rattled violently. "They were **our** dragons, and we were **their** Faithful. We tried to tell them. We yelled it. We screamed it. We tried to convince them we were under no spell, no tyranny. We tried to convince them that our dragons were peaceful. We tried, but they would not listen. They said we were under a curse to follow them, controlled by them. But we were not. Those dragons were our home, our family. My *family*," Kyana's voice rose as tears burned in her eyes, but she did not let them fall. She would not let them fall. They did not deserve to see her cry. She would not give them such a pleasure. She would not grant them such a gift. "And they were trying to kill them. So, we fought for them." Kyana swallowed. The painful memory cutting open wounds that had never truly closed, and began to bleed her dry. When she spoke again, her voice was low. "Both Kyaru and his mother Sterya were killed that day. Kyaru was dragged away between two horses, back to some far-off castle to hang on some cold stone wall in Kyar Kingdom itself. He was a decedent of Kyara after all and therefore belonged to the kingdom of green and black. Sterya was too large… so they cut her to pieces while we watched. With that hideous dragon egg blade, they cut her and took her that way… piece by bloody piece."

She remembered the screams. The wailing of Faithful was deafening in her little ears. She had fallen to her knees, hands clasping her face as she screamed into the muddy ground red with blood. She could still feel it squelch beneath her legs and fill her shoes with dirt and red water. People ran in all directions around her, but she saw them only as vague flashes of brown, white and black. All she could see where the two figures lying side by side in that muddy earth. She heard the long wail that ripped from her own chest like a sword from a sheath.

Kyana continued.

"They weren't the only ones. Two-thirds of the Faithful of Pastenfair lost their lives... My mother and father among them..." Kyana's voice trailed off for a third time. The two figures in the mud stared up at the bright blue sky. No more smiles. No more laughter. No more stories or poetry. Pale faces and wide eyes which, no matter how long Kyana watched, held nothing but empty.

Kyana's voice shook with fury as she began to shout at the cold, collected, sons of bitches. Those sons of killers. Wearing their shields of death with such pride. "We were peaceful! We were peaceful you unholy bastards! We had no weapons, no armies! You massacred us! You killed us so easily. As easy as slapping away a fly, and do you know *why*? How you killed us with such ease? Didn't you find that the least bit **strange**? How you won despite the *three* dragons you claimed were so evil? With their dragon fire and their powers and their strength and yet sons of men came and killed these creatures of magic?" She bared her teeth, and a small trail of smoke seeped through them. Most did not notice. Those that did screeched and threw themselves back into their chairs, hands covering mouths.

"It was because our dragons *wouldn't* fight you! They didn't want to kill you, you blind bastards! Three dragons drape themselves in light blue, become ambitious, call themselves Iver Faithful. Only three become killers, and you think they are **all** the same? You were wrong. Dragons were kind. Peace was their true nature. Dragons did not drive humans to evil actions. If dragons became something else, something angry, something dangerous, something **evil**, it is only because humans **drove them to it.**

"Our dragons didn't even want *us* to fight. They didn't want to hurt anyone... and their hesitation cost them their lives. We were dying, all of us, side by side. Side by side, just as we lived... side by side." Kyana's eyes flashed with green fire, and all the onlookers shrank away. The king himself leaned back, as if from a flame that had grown too hot. "Sterya, Kyaru, the countless Faithful, my... my parents. Tell me, where was their "trial"? Where was their "fair execution"? What had they done to you and yours? What crime did they commit? Living? Loving in a way you do not understand?" Kyana expected someone to interrupt, someone to call out in protest, a counter-argument, but there was nothing. No sound. They were waiting for her to continue, and so she did, "At ten years, I was without a mother or father, but not parentless. Kyaper had lived through that day. We both did. We had both lost our families.

We were both left lost and wandering. Wandering and angry. From that day forward, Kyaper took me even more securely under his wing. With the straggling remains of our Faithful we pressed on, from the hillside and meadows of our homeland and deep into the forests where we hoped we would be safe. There we stayed. Hiding, sneaking, for three years, as the end of The First War passed into the time of a new war... no, that is not right... a time of *massacre.* Time of genocide. The endless... meaningless... the murder of dragons began. That is what it was. You can try to hide behind the veil of some "greater cause," the "freeing of the Faithful," and "Eradicating seductive monsters from the world, those corrupting dragons," or some other bull shit notions you like to feed yourselves so you can sleep at night. But you'd be wrong. You weren't saving anyone. Murder was all you did. No trials. No courts. Just swords and knights and death and blood.

"They hunted dragons. Killing whether they were connected with the Iver Faithful or not. Whether or not they or their Faithful had ever used magic to hurt a single soul. Whether their Faithful had ever used magic *at all.* Many didn't you know. Practice. Many dragon clans believed humans where not yet ready for the responsibility, for the power involved. Many didn't even have a Main! They just lived with the dragons, and practiced nothing but love, affection, loyalty. They weren't there for the power... oh, but you didn't care. You weren't freeing anyone. You were scared and angry and killing, killing, killing. Like a frightened child with a stick, at a dog that bit him, you beat and beat and beat until it was bloody. Until it was dead. A dog that wouldn't... Wouldn't. Fight. Back." Kyana breathed heavily, calming her voice so she could continue. The room was stone still. She was beginning to wonder if anyone was even blinking. She hoped not. She hoped all their eyes dried up and fell from their skulls like so many raisins.

"For three years, we hid like animals in a hunt. For over three years we stayed safe, sending scouts out every morning to be sure we weren't found. Then on the eve of my fourteenth year, our scouts didn't return. We waited for days, and still nothing. On the third night of waiting, a great smoke filled our forest. They had found us. We were being burned out. Our Faithful scattered. Kyaper and I were separated in the upheaval. I got lost in the trees and smoke, losing all the other Faithful in the process."

Gods, she could see it now. Smell the smoke that had filled her lungs, choking her, making her eyes water, spilling down her face like tears. She had fallen three times, each time ripping open her knees, hands, face. She had been bleeding, but she had not cared. She needed to find Kyaper. She needed to find her family.

"It was hours before the smoke cleared enough for me to find my way back to them," Kyana remembered the ground charred and blackened trees standing, smoldering and dead. "The ground was black and hot..." They had burned it... burned it all away. She had to jump out of the way as a tremendous creaking snap sent a smoldering tree down to thunder against the ground. It made the earth shutter so hard Kyana had fallen once more into the hot dirt, burning up her arms. The fallen tree sent black ash puffing into the warm air to mingle with the remaining smoke. The stink of burnt flesh filled the sky in a heavy musk that choked her as badly as the smoke and ash.

"Faithful laid dead everywhere... everywhere... and Kyaper? I found him." His towering form laid among a scattering of burning knights. "He hadn't been harmed by the fire... but had been disillusioned in the smoke and he was not as young as he once was... and he had enough pain. This time, he had fought back." Kyana remembered the smell of burning human flesh. The smoldering silver armor burnt to black. There had been too many of them to count. She could not see whose colors they wore, or which dragon adorned their crest. All their bright cloths had been burnt away, and their shields scorched beyond recognition. It did not matter. They were all the same. All four of the kingdoms were the same. All four were killers.

"It took the murder of his mate, his foal, being cast from his home, and the destruction of his remaining Faithful. It took the loss of absolutely everything for him to finally fight back. You broke him. You finally broke him with all your destruction. You did it. Are you proud?!"

She had run to him. Run to her second father, the last thing left to her in this world. She fell to her knees like she had years before, but she did not scream. She spoke softly to the dragon who breathed in sharp, ragged gasps around the blade thrust in his great black scaled chest. It was an odd blade. Made of a dark, chard, metal like substance. Chard dragon egg.

*Something*, Kyana thought absently, looking down at her hands, *which looked a lot like these shackles around my wrists.*

"Kyaper was nearly dead. He had put up a noble fight but, in the end..." Kyana had begged him to fight, just a little more... "But he was old, tired... and had little to live for. He couldn't stay... he didn't *want* to," Kyana's voice fell almost to a whisper. "But he still loved me. He loved me and would never leave me. Dragons... they can't speak the way humans do. They do not speak in words, or voices of the average sort. No, they had something far purer. They had their minds and their magic. They speak... they spoke... through feeling. They could send it from themselves to another, and with that beautiful language, he told me how much he loved me. How much he wanted to protect me. How he would never leave me, even as he passed by." Kyana remembered the softness of his thoughts in her mind. The gentleness that had followed him all his long life. How he had held her consciousness in his like a father's arms around a child as she held his massive head in her small hands.

"It was there among the hot, dark, ash, and death, that he showed me how. He gave me a gift... a gift never given to another human. No Main, no man, no mortal creature was ever given such a gift... but for me... my Kyaper gave it."

Kyana had knelt down before her dragon, as he accepted her into his family like no human had before. Dragons had gifted Faithful's access to their magic. Taught them how to use it, how to channel it, but this was different. Kyaper had opened his mouth, revealing a light so blinding that Kyana almost shielded her gaze, but she did not. She leaned into it. That light came to her, filling her, killing her, and giving her life all at once.

"With his last breath Kyaper, my second father, a decedent of the great Kyara himself, gave me the greatest gift he could give. The greatest honor. He breathed into me his life. He breathed into me his fire, his magic. And in his fire, I was reborn. With his last life's utterance, he pronounced my new name to match my new truth. That day, knee deep in the blood of killer knights, I was no longer little brown eyed Ana, daughter of Cara and Royce of the Pastenfair Faithful." Kyana glared around the room with eyes that burned green fire.

"No. I am no witch, nor trickster. I am no user of others magic. I am no scavenger of bones. Because I don't need to. I am pure magic. I am *true* magic. I am Kyana. The sole survivor of the Pastenfair Faithful. Human, reborn in dragons breath. Reborn as the daughter of Kyaper, and sole remaining heir of the Kyara bloodline. I. Am. A. Dragon."

There was an uproar. The sound rang deafeningly off the stone walls for what felt like hours. Finally, a voice broke coherent above the rest.

"Impossible!"

"How so?" Kyana asked, turning to look at Phobos.

"How could he turn you into a dragon? You say he gave you his fire? That has never been heard of before."

"Dragons themselves had never been heard of until the four siblings pulled them out of the mountains," Kyana countered.

"That can't happen!" called another voice from somewhere Kyana couldn't see.

"Are you blind or just stupid?" Kyana called back.

"Well, how do you explain it?" Phobos snapped.

"Well…" Kyana grinned at the hateful old man made of wrinkles and liver spots, "it's magic."

"The end of dragons was hundreds of years ago," called a woman in a dark blue dress. "You can't be alive!"

Kyana nodded.

"I spent much of my life in my dragon form. First within the caves of the Kyar forests and later in the mountains of Caskcare after Clan Winterhast and their Faithful had been cast out. Their caves and homes were deep, dark and stood completely empty. I am not proud to say, I took advantage. I found the safest places I could. I hibernated much of the time hoping for brighter mornings… not sure what much else I could do." Kyana shrugged. "Dragons age slower than humans. Besides, even some Faithful can slow their aging using dragon relics. Rainier is over a couple hundred years old himself… but he looked fairly youthful the other day."

"Liar!" called a voice.

"Proof!" called a third. Kyana rolled her eyes. Becoming a dragon before their eyes was not enough proof? Kyana reached past her shackles and rolled up the tattered sleeve on her left arm. Someone must have seen it by now. Her clothes were torn off when she changed, but she supposed they must present it in court for it to count. Respectful civilization and all. Branded into the skin of her forearm was proof of her allegiance to the Pastenfair Faithful. It was a name with five circles hovering beneath it. *Kyaru.* It stood dark and proud against her skin. Kyana had asked her mother to give it to her on her ninth year. It was a young age for the choice, but she was determined, and her mother and father did not object. She still remembered the pride in Kyaper's eyes and the full roar that Kyaru had given in celebration. Even the pain and nasty sharp smell of burnt skin could not dull the joy she had felt on that day.

The king motioned for a few of the men standing in the back to check its authenticity. Kyana grinned as they slunk forward, but made no moves towards them. They poked at the mark, running their thumb over it as if half expecting it to rub off. Kyana had to fight the urge to snap her teeth at them as they inspected the brand. Give them a reason to look so scared. When they seemed satisfied, they retreated to their places by the wall and gave the king a curt nod.

As they did so, Kyana finally noticed the tall girl in the back of the room, behind the throne itself. How Kyana had missed her bright hazel eyes before, she would never know. Unlike the other familiar knights, courtiers, and servants, Ira met her gaze intently. She watched and waited for the girl to look away in shame or fear, but she did neither. Her gaze never wavered.

"You realize," the king spoke slow and soft. "That saying you're a Dragon... is no better than saying you are a Faithful. In fact... it's far worse."

Kyana looked back to the throne.

"Only to you and yours," Kyana laughed. The sound cut through the hushed voices leaving them quiet and trembling. "Ironic isn't it? Dragons. You say it with such hate... and yet you decorate your tables, your walls, and your throne room with dragons... hell boys, the name of your damn kingdom is in honor of a dragon." She looked up at the king and smiled. "There are two sides to that pretty, pretty, story of the end of dragons and freeing of the Faithful. So, hear it well, and understand if you can. We were never enslaved. We *adored* our dragons. I am what I am. If I am going die for 'being,' then I will die under the proper title. It is a title I find nothing but pride in... I feel no shame for my lineage... can you say the same?" Another rumble ran across the room. The king made no reply, but Kyana watched as his cool blue eyes flickered away from her gaze. An involuntary, childish movement... so childish...

Just like that, her anger, the rage bubbling like thick lava in her chest, fissured and dissipated. It petered out until there was nothing but a mild throb in her chest. Because yelling at these people, all these wide eyed and open-mouthed fools, was like yelling at a child. Screaming in a baby's face. They were all so new to the world. None of these men and women, none of them had a hand in the past. They were just the product of their history, not the cause. She could scream in their faces all she liked, but it was not to them that her anger was truly meant. It was for their grandfather's great grandfathers.

It was for those of their linage, and it was not enough. All her yelling and screaming and righteous indignation, it slumped and lay sullen and slacken at her feet like a drowned lizard, limbs splayed helpless, broken and twitching.

*Babies.* She thought, looking around at them all with new eyes. *Babies all.* She was the only one here that had a hand in any of it, any part in those times passed by. All of a sudden she felt very tired. Old, and tired.

*Enough then.* She thought, eyes sliding closed, letting the entire world slip by in a dark moment. And for that dark moment she felt how alone she was in the world of unknowing children. World of babies. Babies with so many one-sided bedtime stories. History was told by those who survived it, and they told those stories to these children. She was the monster under their beds, and nothing she did or said would change that. Nothing she did or said would change anything. It would not bring back her life or those she loved so dearly. It would do nothing. *She* could do nothing. *Enough then. Let it end here. Let me end, and let the babies sleep soundly in their beds tonight, if that pleases them. I am the last… so let it end with me. Send me away, to any and all that awaits me.* She wondered if Kyaper would be there, wings stretched wide and ready to receive her. She envisioned herself finding them all, all those from Pastenfair, Kyaper, Sterya, her loving parents, maybe even dear gruff Wybert. All with smiles on their faces, all blood gone from their mouths, and all blankness from their eyes. They would be full of laughter and poetry. She would hold them in her arms, only to turn away when she heard *his* soft rumbling purr. She would turn and there he would be. Her dragon. Her Kyaru. She would run to him, and he would greet her as his sister. Together they would spend the eternity that stretches on, after time has passed and passed by.

Kyana smiled softly to herself and opened her eyes.

*Enough then. Send me home.*

As if hearing her thoughts, the Lystad started.

"Very well, then," he said, straightening in his chair. "Kyana. Member of Pastenfair Faithful an-" He was about to continue when a small mousy boy darted into the room and tapped the nearest knight on the arm. The knight gave the boy an odd look and then nodded. The boy scampered off, and the knight crossed the room to lean in and whisper into the king's ear. The Lystad looked equally puzzled. That boyish look of curiosity passed his face, quickly followed by kingly concern.

"We will continue this tomorrow," he called to the room at large as he stood. "There is an urgent matter I must attend to. Guards, please lead the prisoner back to her cell. Knights, with me." With that, the king swept from the room, his cloak and knights billowing behind him. The room filled with a confused rumble of conversation. Kyana was taken aback but had little time to dwell on it. They quickly led her out the same way she had come. She looked back before the heavy wooden doors closed on the bickering crowd. She looked for bright hazel eyes, but they were nowhere to be seen.

# CHAPTER 42

The trial did not continue the following day. Nor the day after. Three days Kyana waited in the darkness, chained to the floor, straining for any news. None came. Only the silent guard who slid half molding scraps of bread between her bars to keep her from starving to death before her execution. What fun would that be?

She had no knowledge of what was happening outside those cold stone walls. What great happenings they were. The word of a dragon in Castle Lyist had spread like fire on the wind, picking up in ferocity with every passing moment. The people of Castle Lyist were stirring, churning with fear, excitement, anticipation, but they were not the only ones. Others, far from the stretches of the kingdom, were beginning to receive word. They were the ones who felt it the most.

It rippled through the segregated cities of Kyar. The persecuted and isolated. The lost and the ones still fighting and dreaming of times passed and passed long by. It surged through the valleys, forests, small kingdoms and even smaller townships.

Word of a dragon sparked a light in those shadows. Heads began to rise from dreams to look towards Neira Kingdom. It was on those outskirts, in those dark places of the mind, that word of Kyana lit a force. A force, unstoppable which began to crackle and spread like fire. It was only fitting.

# CHAPTER 43

"Shit..." They were spread out across the ground, spilling around the outer wall like water around a rock. They were people of all ages, young, old, healthy, thin, scarred, and fresh. So many. So different. Their voices filled the air in a low steady rumble like continuous thunder, making it impossible to catch a clear word.

Ira leaned over the edge of the wall, not far from the giant gaping hole where a gate once stood. Carpenters had been out there for the past few days, trying to erect a temporary barrier between Castle Lyist and the outside world, but it was far from complete. None of the strangers tried to enter, but many were still pouring out of the forests, over the hills, towards the castle at a slow but steady pace.

So many. Ira thought in awe. She had no idea there were *so many*. She knew there were still plenty of Faithful, and even a few organized communities of various sizes at the outskirts of the realms, away from the four kingdom's grasp. She also knew of at least one community, small and timid as it may be, that lived in the lands between Caskcare and Kyar kingdom. She even knew that some must live hidden within their own walls, but never in her wildest dreams did she imagine there were so many so near.

Ira could see the old jeweler woman with her shawl wrapped tightly around her. She was wandering up and down the little tents and shacks that had been erected, not selling her beaded bracelets, but offering food and water. She, along with her sons and husband were out there now. They had been one of the first to step from their doors after their two youngest had returned from spreading the news.

Ira had watched them leave that night, hastening off into the darkness to retrieve their horses from stable. Ira had not stopped them but had mournfully wondered what good it would do. Even if news of Kyana had spread, would it be fast enough? Would there be enough ears that wanted to hear the news, that it would matter? When they returned a few days later, however, it was not alone. Hundreds came, by horse and by foot. More came after that and continued to come as those within the walls began to make their own moves, starting with the woman and her sons. They stepped out, bags in hand and side by side marched past the knights who watched them go, too confused to understand what was happening. They were the first to choose the Faithful over the kingdom, but most certainly not the last.

People of the city, a few hundred the last Ira had heard, had come out of hiding. They had left their homes, walking straight past the other open-mouthed citizens as they went to stand with the gathering crowd who had pitched camps outside the fourth gate. They knew revealing themselves to be Faithful's could mean death, and at very least rejection from the lives built in Castle Lyist, but they went anyway, and they went smiling.

Ira was too busy watching the swarms of people below to notice that Neander had joined her.

"Holy blue hell," Neander whispered, making Ira jump and clutch the wall so tight, her knuckles went white. "You alright there, buddy?" Neander grinned and patted Ira gently on the shoulder.

"I'll make it," Ira said, loosening her grip and returning Neander's smile. They turned back to the goings on below.

"I never knew…" Neander said after a moment. Ira glanced up at him. He was wearing his uniform, sword slung on his hip as he leaned against the wall. His brown eyes darted from person to person, a look of amazement on his scruffy face.

"Me neither," Ira answered quietly.

"So many…" Neander glanced over at Ira. "There haven't been dragons for centuries… why are there so many?"

Ira smiled. "They're Faithful, Neander… faith doesn't need… well… anything." She shrugged.

"Well," Neander sighed and ran a hand through his thick brown hair, brushing it back and away from his face. "They sure got something now."

"Ya," Ira agreed. "I guess they do."

"A dragon…" Neander shook his head. Both he and Ira exchanged a look. "This is going to end badly, isn't it?"

"Oh, you never know Neander," Ira looked. "Maybe not."

"What?" Neander barked a laugh. "This looks like the makings of a smooth conversation to you?"

"Oh, no, this is going to go very badly," Ira nodded, turning back to watch a few of the Faithful talking indistinctly in their own small huddled group. "I'm just thinking… it's probably not an 'end' at all."

Neander nodded beside her and barked another laugh.

"Shit. A *dragon.*"

"Ya." Ira looked up, a grin uncontrollably spreading her face. "Ya, I know."

"I can't believe it." Neander shook his head.

"Better to start, my friend," Ira said simply, hands going back to the wall.

The end of dragons… The Second Peace… it all teetered on the edge of this very moment. Things were about to fall. About to change. This world, this way of life, had grown familiar to the realms. Everyone had known their place, whether they liked it or not. They had become comfortable with it. Accepting of it. But that had passed the moment one girl shattered in a castle yard.

It was passed and passed long by.

Ira watched it go with a smile on her face, and a spark in her eyes.

# CHAPTER 44

The great hall was sparse. Damian thought it was better to keep it simple. Phobos wanted this meeting held in the throne room with all of its authoritative elegance, to throw the Faithful off his sure footing. Damian had decided against it. Nice and small. A few of his most trusted advisers, closest knights, and a table would do.

He did wear his crown, however.

They were all gathered about the table, his knights Neander, Everett, Teller, and his advisers, Andrew Phobos, Carol Carver, Roy Pently and Morella Thyrman. The king himself was at the head of the table, waiting as they all were. Quiet and calm. Or at least, most of them. Damian could feel Phobos's eyes darting to him with quick and agitated glances. He had been against the meeting altogether and had made his opinion on the matter very clear and very loud. Damian had grown tired of his indiscriminate yapping over the past years, but Phobos was one of the elders of the court and was once the most trusted adviser to his father. To send him away from his place would not only be an insult to his father's memory but a shame that would surely send the aging adviser to an early grave. The old man's wife had died ten years past, and his children had never made it past their second years of life. He was alone, and his only purpose left in this world was to be adviser to the king. Even though this king found him to be one of the most unpleasant, ill-mannered, and frustratingly ignorant old coots he had ever had the misfortune to meet, he would no sooner send him away than to cut off the fingers of his right hand. So, there he sat, stiff and sullen at the table. Waiting.

Damian watched the double doors to the hall and waited. He did not wait long. The doors opened shortly after they had all taken their places. It was pushed wide by the guards with a halted squeak that made Damian flinch and make a mental note to have the hinges oiled.

The old man walked through on quiet feet that made no more sound against the wooden floor than a dove's feather on the breeze. He wore pale green robes which swept softly around his ankles and brown cloth shoes. His skin was thin and tanned, pulled tightly over sharp features. Blue veins rippled out from under his collar, around his eyes, and over his hands. They spread like little rivers, unfurling under the thin skin. Damian could almost see the blood beating in time with his heart beneath. It gave the man a strange, pulsing image, even when he finally came to a standstill before the high table. His hair was almost completely gone, leaving only a small halo of wispy gray clouds around his head, covering his temples. He looked thin and tired, with large blue circles dipping below his eyes, but his eyes themselves were steady and bright brown.

*Those eyes,* Damian thought to himself as their gaze landed hard and steady on his own. *Have seen more than I could begin to imagine.*

Their clear, knowing intensity was marred only by an ancient scar that cut down the lower half of his left eye. It burrowed deep into his cheek, leaving mountains and ridges in the thin skin, forcing his left eye into a permanent wince. The king noticed something else. Almost lost in dark, golden tanned skin, were scales. Dragon scales. They were dim, silver, and scattered lightly up from under his collar and around the pulsing veins. The king knew of his kind. The Faithful that had seared the scales of dragons into their own skin to show their loyalty, to prove their worth, and to gain their powers. His father had told him stories of these people when he was a child, and Kyana had reminded him during her speech at court the days before. The Faithful called them a "Main" and had been held in as much respect by their clan as knights to their kingdom. With the transfer of the scales, there was also a transfer of power. An open access to magic. At least, when his dragon was alive, that is. Now those scales were but a whisper of the power they once were. They were relics and could still hold some magic, but the main driving force behind it was dead and gone, making them now little more than decoration. A show of devotion to a time passed and passed by.

The old man stepped up slowly to the table but did not take a seat. The guards closed the double doors with another painful creak and a light thud that echoed slightly in the silent room.

A young page of no older than fifteen, judging by the pimples dotting his beardless chin, stepped out from a corner of the room to perform his one and only duty of the evening.

"Your royal highness," he spoke loud and clear to the almost empty room, bouncing ominously off the walls and high ceiling and back to the king's ears. "I present to you Temper Worsing. Member of the Everhast Faithful, and the chosen voice for those calling themselves The Rekindled Faithful." Temper stood tall before them. A few people exchanged looks around the table. By this point, it was traditional for the one being presented to the king to kneel, or bow, in a show of respect and reverence. Temper made no moves to do so. He stood still, barely blinking before the king, and did not even look at the empty seat waiting for him.

"Welcome," Damian said, finally breaking the silence. "I'm glad you could join us." Temper said nothing, merely nodded his head once in response.

"What is wrong with him?" Phobos whispered under his breath to Morella Thyrman at his side, but Damian overheard. "Absolutely no respect. Doesn't he know he's speaking to a king?"

"Phobos, do not whisper," Damian said, loud enough for all to hear. "If it's not something for everyone to hear, then it's not something that should be said. Besides," he continued, looking away from Phobos's abashed expression to Temper's steady gaze. "As far as he's concerned… I'm no king of his."

Temper watched Damian closely for a moment. He could almost feel those eyes looking straight through him, seeing everything that there was to see. Reading his very thoughts. A smile broke across Tempers withered lips.

"Thank you for having me… *your* majesty," Temper said, tilting his head with respect.

Damian smiled at Temper's emphasis on "your." For a moment, he thought he saw a flash of green in those brown eyes.

"Please," Damian motioned towards the empty chair at the other end of the table. "Let's talk."

# CHAPTER 45

Days passed in the dark and damp cell. They churned by in a slow succession of waking, sleeping, and waking once more. There was very little else to do. Kyana occupied herself by staring at the wall, lost in thoughts of things passed by and all the possible paths before her. Thoughts on the past occupied her longer. Thoughts on the future tended to pinhole into one outcome and it was not pretty. So, she languished in memories and tried to ignore the future. She spent hours like this, without moving or even blinking. The guards that watched her began to wonder if she had not merely died, and it was nothing more than an empty shell sitting stalk still on the dungeon floor. Just when their suspicions teetered on the edge of certainty, she would blink, turn her head towards them, and wink or snap her teeth.

On the morning of the fifth day, someone finally came. Kyana thought it would be the guard with her scraps, but there was something odd about the timing. They usually waited till mid-day to feed her, but dawn had barely broken. Despite this, she could hear the distinct sound of feet slow and careful, patting down the stairs. The steps were also odd. They were light steps, not the usual clanking, sloppy, trod of the dungeon guards with which she had grown familiar.

Kyana looked up and, to her surprise, found Ira standing outside the thick and rusting bars. She was holding a plate in one hand, which was covered by a silken green cloth. Kyana yanked her eyes away from the plate as her stomach grumbled eagerly. She looked up to Ira's face. Ira's hazel eyes were watching her with something as unfamiliar as her footsteps. They seemed full of surprise, fear, but not of her. And something that looked like pain. But also, something else. Something…

Ira turned to the guard and asked him to open the door.

"Be careful in there," the guard said solemnly, eyeing Kyana. Kyana grinned at him slowly, allowing the motion to spread her face like something thick and slimy sliding across a table. She snapped her teeth like the animal he expected her to be, making the guard flinched. Kyana laugh, letting the harsh sound echo off the stone walls and making even the hair on the back of her own arms stand on end.

Ira looked back at Kyana, eyes running over the dragon iron chains. She recognized *that* look instantly. Disgust.

"I think it'll be fine," Ira snapped. The guard shrugged and opened the bars between them. Ira stepped inside, and the guard closed the gate behind her, standing back with his arms crossed.

"Privacy would be nice," Ira said coolly. The guard shrugged again.

"Call if you need help," the guard said, slowly plodding down the hall and out of earshot. Ira's scowl melted into a wide smile as she turned back to Kyana.

"Hello, Kyana."

"Hello, Ira," she answered her own smile crossing her face. Somehow, she could not help it. Even in this dark, damp, disgusting hellish hole, Ira's smile was infectious. She began to wonder if the girl had magic of her own.

"What on earth are you doing here?" she asked.

"Thought you might be hungry." Ira pulled away the green cloth to reveal two thick slices of bread, several slices of steaming meat, three hunks of cheese of various types, and two shining apples.

Kyana's mouth watered, and her stomach gave an empty throb.

"Why?" she asked unnerved by the kindness.

"Because I want to."

"Why?" Kyana asked again, frowning at her. "Won't you get in trouble, coming down here… spending time with me?"

"No, I have permission," she said, sliding the plate across the stone floor and into Kyana's reach. "From the king himself. He knows we, well, we get along and all. He thought it would be best if I explained things… quite right if you ask me. The guards are less than…" She glanced back over his shoulder. "… pleasant."

Kyana frowned. It could not be from mere kindness that the Lystad allowed her here.

"And?"

Ira shrugged a little, still smiling. "And... everyone else is a little, uh, leery to do so themselves."

"And you," Kyana widened her leer like a dog showing fangs. "you are not afraid to be near me?"

"Should I be?" Ira asked. Kyana paused, lips sliding back down over teeth.

"So, you're here as a messenger of the Lystad then?" Kyana made no move to take the food, although the smell wafting from the plate was enough to make her cry with hunger.

"Partly," Ira admitted, sliding the plate a little closer. "But... only partly."

"What's the other reason then?"

"Two."

"What?"

"There are two other reasons," Ira said, scooting the plate almost directly under Kyana's hand, but she still refused to take anything.

"Spit them out," Kyana's voice was crisp and sharp. It made Ira blink as if she had snapped her fingers in front of the girl's face.

"You saved us," Ira continued slowly. "You keep saving us, and they keep forgetting that. You are our friend... and they keep forgetting that. I haven't. And I never will." The honesty in those gleaming eyes was visible even in the dim light of the dungeon torches.

"That's one reason. And the other?" Kyana asked, her voice softer this time. To her great surprise, Ira took a breath, looked back to make sure the guard was still out of view, and began to roll up her sleeve. There, on the pale skin of her right forearm, hidden for years, was a name underlined with five circles. *Steryln.*

"That..." Kyana leaned in, momentarily forgetting her chains which tugged painfully against the movement. "That is..."

"A mark of the Winterhast Faithful," Ira whispered, glancing back over her shoulder, to make sure the guard was still out of earshot. "Yes."

"You're a Faithful?" Kyana looked back up at the girl and suddenly saw so much more. She could see the caution, the fear that must have breed wild and strong, being such a person, with such a mark, in such a place. And the Lystad! Ira's best friend. To be so close with a man, who would have turned against her if he had known her devotions. Such a burden. Kyana suddenly understood the reason for the wishing in Ira's eyes.

A sad smile crossed her lips.

"You're a long way from home, mountain girl."

"What?" Ira asked eyebrows scrunching in confusion.

"Nothing," Kyana shook her head. "An old joke. But... how...?"

"My grandmother," Ira explained, rolling down her sleeve. "Her own grandmother passed down stories of when she had lived with the Winterhast Faithful before they were cast out of the Caskcare mountains and scattered across the realm. She taught my grandmother, and my grandmother taught me."

"You practice?" Kyana asked, amazed, but Ira shook her head.

"No. Not really. Just the forms, the words, the bare bones of it, but I've never used magic because, well..."

"You never had any bare bones," Kyana added. Ira smiled and shrugged.

"Yes, that. It would have also been a bit dangerous these days. You know." Kyana chuckled, and Ira continued, "My grandmother, well, she never lost her belief in dragons, even if her daughter, my mother, did. My mother married a traveling merchant from Castle Lyist and had me shortly after. For a time, we lived near my grandmother in a small village past the forest to the south. My mother wasn't one for... well mothering, so I spent most of my young life with my grandmother. Helping her, being with her, listening to her stories." Ira's eyes drifted as if looking for someone or something else in the cell besides Kyana. "Stories about the times before this, The First Peace, the war against dragons, and so much more. Through these stories and my grandmother's teaching, I became a believer. A believer in dragons and what they stood for."

"But... what are you doing here in Castle Lyist?" Kyana insisted. "Why the hell are you here?"

"My parents moved to Castle Lyist when I was seven. They noticed how much time my grandmother spent with me, teaching me, and they thought it was dangerous. My father reconnected with his friends and family back in Castle Lyist, and we moved here. They told me it was for business reasons. Work was scarce in my hometown, but really it was to get me away from my grandmother. Her and her "poisonous stories," Ira snorted at this. When she rolled her hazel eyes, for a moment, Kyana was back in a stone hallway. She shook her head as Ira continued.

"My mother had completely rejected Faithful ideals by this point. She thought it was useless to keep devotion for creatures that no longer existed. The Faithful revolved around dragons, and with them gone, she said it was a useless, futile, and dangerous. To be a Faithful is banned in two of the four major kingdoms and highly restricted in the others. Not to mention the scattering of small cities along the outskirts that also hold Faithful's in contempt."

*Well… she's got a point there.* Kyana thought but kept it to herself. Ira was on a roll, words falling quickly from her lips and Kyana did not want to interrupt. Her eyes kept darting down to where the brand hid beneath her shirt, barely believing it was there at all.

"My grandmother," Ira said, tapping her forearm. "gave this to me the night before we left for Castle Lyist. The metal piece had been handed down from generation to generation. She heated it in the fire place the night before I left. 'Never forget,' she said. 'It is only truly gone when we choose to forget.' And I'm sorry to say, I did forget." Ira's eyes sparkled and her face beamed with the joy only hope can create. "I chose to. I almost choose to forget it all. Put it all away. All her stories, all her time, all my faith in something greater than what is easily seen, heard, touched. Put away the hope that one day, something might change. That it all didn't truly die with the last dragons. Almost packed it away. Packed it in with the trash, ready to burn it away." Kyana looked up with a jerk, but said nothing. Ira's eyes were shining on her. There was so much joy there. So much emotion and Kyana shrank from it. She knew what that look was. She did not deserve that look. She hoped Ira would stop, almost told her to. She did not stop, she continued.

"Then you stood there… before an army… and you changed. You brought back to life all the dreams of a little girl sitting at her great grandmothers' feet. You have made me remember, and I am forever in your debt… Now…" Ira tilted the plate under her hand. "Will you please just eat the damn food already? I can hear your stomach from here."

Kyana watched her a moment longer, taking in every inch of that smiling face, and those still gleaming hazel eyes. She plucked a chunk of cheese from the plate and began to eat. She did not bother eating with any delicate airs. She was not a delicate lady, and she was famished.

Ira leaning back on her hands, satisfied as Kyana tucked in. "Kyana…"

"Yes?"

"You're a dragon."

"Clearly."

"So… can you… I mean, you're still down here, so I assume for some reason you can't but…" Ira's voice trickled off.

"Spit it out, Ira," Kyana said, crumbs spraying a little in her irritation.

"I mean," Ira looked back up from beneath her lashes, looking oddly cowed, "could you break out of here?"

"Not really, Ira," Kyana chuckled, and raised her shackled wrists.

"No, I don't mean changing into… I mean… can't you use magic to break out?"

Kyana paused, cleared her throat, and a shock of pink briefly flushed her cheeks.

"Actually…" She wiped her mouth on her sleeve, "no."

"But you—"

"Yes, I know, I'm a dragon and made of magic… but…" she looked up to Ira, and Ira noticed an odd look reflected in the strange woman's eyes. Shame. "I was only a child when the dragons died. I had not become Kyaru's Main or even granted the gift of magic. That gift was only given to those that were ready. Those that were worthy. You must be at a certain age, a certain temperament, possess a certain spirit. I was but a child. I was not ready to be judged for such a gift, let alone able to receive it. What Kyaper did for me… was unprecedented. It changed who I was, to my very soul. Changing into my other self, my true form… is as natural as breathing. But in my human form… I do not know how to use the magic inside me. Not without changing," her eyes cast down to the dirty ground, and her fingers picked listlessly at the fraying edge of her sleeve. "I was never taught how," Kyana remembered holding her hands over Wybert's wounds as he lay dying on the cold and filthy ground. Willing a light to appear between her fingers, willing him to heal, but in vain.

"Oh," Ira breathed. Kyana had lost so much. So many things that should have been second nature to one such as her, a Faithful from the time of dragons. A different time, a time that had passed and passed by before Kyana had learned all that it had to teach. However, was that not the way of time? It always disappeared before we are ready to watch it go. Before we even realize it is leaving. We try to catch it between desperate fingers, but it twists and slips away all the same, like fog. Or like smoke.

"So, this…" Kyana gave the shackles a light shake, and they jingled beneath her hands. "This is it for me, I suppose."

"…. Not necessarily…"

"What do you mean?"

"May I ask one more question first?"

Kyana frowned. Ira was stalling.

"I suppose," Kyana said slowly, "I've got nowhere else to be."

"I've been wondering," Ira said, "your brand…"

"What about it?" Kyana asked voice muffled as she began to cram as much food into her mouth that would fit. She knew her cheeks were bulging like a squirrel gathering for winter, but she did not care. She was only hungry.

"It's still there," Ira said, watching her without a hint of disgust as crumbs fell like rain from the Kyana's mouth and she replaced them with more food. "Your skin… your scars, your wounds, every blemish is gone. Even that small scar on your hairline," she pointed to her own face, where on Kyana, there had once been a jagged mark. "They are all gone."

"I left them behind." Kyana shrugged simply, thinking once more about that lovely pile of flesh and blood in the courtyard. She did not envy the servant who was sent to clean up that mess. She had a sudden nasty hope that the chore would fall to the old man with hateful cataract glazed eyes. She hoped he slipped and fell in face first. The thought made her grin before she tore another piece of bread between her teeth.

"Yes, but your brand… shouldn't it have been left behind as well?" Ira asked, doing that slow and curious blink, lids closing and opening like thick black curtains, and for a moment, Kyana marveled at their dense, and long lashes. Those lashes must be the envy of every woman in Castle Lyist, and for one silly girlish moment that was quite unlike her, she felt a tinge of jealousy of her own. Kyana wiped it easily away like the crumbs on her chin.

She shook her head at Ira's question and swallowed before speaking.

"Scars are scars. They are only skin deep. So, when I shed my skin, they go with it, but this," she tapped the cloth on her forearm, "This is no scar. It is not a mark forced on me by someone else. It wasn't a mark of an angry hand, an ignorant metal, or a stupid stumble from a tree. This," she tapped again, "This is a promise. A promise I made out of love and solidified in dragon fire. This will last for as long as I love my family, both dragon and human. It will last until the day I die." Even if Kyana had wanted to take Lilly up on her long ago offer, her offer to mar the mark, it would not have worked. If burned, it would heal. If sliced off, it will grow back. Such methods may work for those who never chose to be a Faithful, or never truly believed in dragons, but for her, it would never disappear. Her mark would never leave her. Because she simply never wanted it to go. So, it would remain.

"Incredible…" Ira spoke the word so softly that she almost missed it. Kyana turned back to her food and began shoveling once more. She had many questions for Ira as well. How was her life after moving to Castle Lyist? What was it like being a kitchen hand in a castle such as this? How was she never discovered? Had she been back to see her grandmother since her parents took her away? Did she know there was another servant in Castle Lyist with the exact same secret as she?

Unfortunately, there were more immediate matters.

"Any news?" she asked around a mouth full of bread and cheese.

"Yes, there is." Ira had a curious expression, one that Kyana could not decipher. Joy? Worry? Anger? It seemed to all mingle and swirl across her face like clouds in a strong wind. She frowned.

"The new date of my execution?" Kyana asked as calmly as if she had been asking her to pass the salt at a dinner table.

"No!" Ira burst out, so loudly the guard came shuffling over to check on her. Ira quickly waived him away, and he shuffled back down the hall, leaving them alone once more. Ira lowered her voice. "Sorry… no, no, nothing like that. Actually, it's good news… sort of."

"Sort of?"

"Yes…"

"Yes, meaning…?"

"Yes, sort of. As a matter of fact. The execution has been postponed… indefinitely."

"Oh?" Kyana looked up. Relief and utter confusion flooded her. "Why is that?"

"Well, that's where the 'sort of' comes in," Ira said.

Kyana continued to chew, waiting for her to continue.

"Well, eh, let me start from the beginning… quite a lot has happened in the past few days. Henry, the kid who interrupted the trial the other day, he was bringing news."

"News?"

"Ya," Ira grinned wide. "News."

Kyana resisted the urge to roll her eyes with impatience.

"Ira… news of what exactly?"

"A gathering." Ira said, and before Kyana could ask, "A gathering of Faithful. Right outside the city walls."

"They heard of a dragon in Castle Lyist?" Kyana asked, and Ira nodded.

"And the trial for your execution… they all came running."

Kyana frowned. "What good is a few Faithful stomping their feet outside the city?"

"Oh… there were more than a few." Ira grinned.

"How many?"

"Last I checked, over three thousand… and still growing."

"Three thousand?" Kyana's mouth fell open, a few crumbs taking advantage of her surprise to escape across the cell floor. Three thousand. She could not believe it.

"How?" She asked. "From where?"

"All over. All types of clans," Ira answered. "Everhast, Winterhast, Rivershade, Bellway, I also suspect even a few Iver Faithful decedents are mixed in there. Not to mention at least a few hundred from inside this very city. And even some from Kyar."

"How did word spread so quickly?" she asked, pulling apart another slice of bread.

"Kyana, these people have been waiting for this moment. They've been waiting for any word, any excuse, to be justified for their faith in dragons… and you… well, you just sent the message." Ira shrugged. "They're just answering it." Ira had not quite answered her question… but she let it pass by. Kyana supposed she did not know herself. Why would she?

Ira continued.

"Anyway, they all came in mass, and they all come armed. They sent Henry with word to the Damian, that if he killed the last decedent of Kyara that they would attack the castle."

"… So they came to fight… for me?" She tried to imagine it. The undoubtedly ragtag swarm of Faithful, coming together with their sticks, twigs, pitchforks, and shovels at three thousand strong. How… ridiculous.

"Well, that is foolish," Kyana frowned. "Even with such numbers, they are no match for Castle Lyist's army."

"They know that." Ira shook her head. "They aren't expecting to live Kyana."

"So, they would just…"

"Fight to the last man."

"That… is *stupid.*"

"That… is *loyalty,*" Ira corrected.

"Has anyone told them I'm half human?" Kyana said, licking her fingers and glaring at the empty plate, willing more food to appear.

"Think they'll be disappointed?" Ira asked.

"I think…" Kyana considered, "I think they're expecting something extraordinary. Something to match their dreams." Kyana glanced up. "You said it yourself, they came for something that proved their faith… and answers their loyalty. A dragon." Kyana motioned to her state. "Not a girl chained to the floor."

"They know," Ira said.

"And they don't care?"

"You're a dragon, Kyana."

"Yes, yes I am…" Kyana hesitated. "But that's all."

"What do you mean "That's all"?" Ira let out a bark of laughter. "That's everything!"

Kyana opened her mouth, only to close it again in silence.

*Fight to the last man…*

Kyana thought back to the king and his men, and their futile fight against the magic army, pummeling against the walls of their kingdom. They did not see a way out either.

"Why does everyone keep trying to 'fight to the death'?" Kyana scowled. "There's always another way."

"And you weren't planning to die when you turned into a dragon in front of an entire kingdom with a history of slaughtering dragons?" Ira asked, eyebrows raised.

"Okay… I see your point." Kyana shrugged. "So, they threatened to fight."

"Yes. They knew they would lose, but Castle Lyist would take a hard hit. The gates are still broken down and they would have easy access to the city until the knights finally beat down their forces." Kyana watched Ira as she continued. She noticed how Ira kept using "they," and "them" in reference to

Castle Lyist and its people. She decided not to mention it. A question for another time.

"So, in light of this, Damian decided to pursue other options for your… uh… punishment."

"The king was cowed?" Kyana asked, surprised.

Ira shrugged. "Well, the king took into mind that you didn't actually harm any of his citizens in dragon form…. While…. Well… saving the kingdom." Kyana watched Ira's face closely. There was something different there. There was an edge in her voice when speaking of the Lystad. An edge that had not been there before. It was small, but sharp, like the prick of a splinter after running your hand across an unfinished carving. This worried her a little. The Lystad was Ira's friend of many years, and she had always spoken of him with kindness, familial tenderness even. Right now, however, since her change…

Kyana suddenly remembered.

"A knight," Kyana said, leaning against her chains. "When I changed, there was a knight. I think I hit him."

"Ya," Ira nodded. "He's fine. A few bruises, but he'll be alright. All of them are, and the king agreed to stay the execution for the use of witchcraft." Kyana rolled her eyes, leaning back. "I'm an actual magical being, not a witch using relics. How does no one understand this?"

Ira smiled and shrugged. "You are still a Faithful though… which is technically treason." Kyana snorted. *Treason to no kingdom of mine.*

"Alright. So, what happened next?"

"The Faithful's sent a representative, Temper. He's one of the elders of the old Everhast Faithful. He seems very respected within the Faithful communities."

"There are still communities of Faithful?" Kyana frowned.

"Um… well yes," Ira said, scratching her cheek. "Didn't you know? I thought for sure you'd know."

"I've spent most of my life hibernating in dragon form, and the rest of it hiding out in the forests… why on earth would I have any idea what the Faithful are up to?" Kyana asked.

Ira blinked. "Well, I guess I get your point."

"So, communities of Faithful?" Kyana waved her hand, motioning for her to continue. Her chains rattled lightly.

"Ya, well, Temper agreed to a sit down with the king, and they came to terms."

"What terms?" Kyana frowned.

"Although you've been 'granted a pardon from the death penalty for heroic actions,' I believe it was, you're still a dragon... which is a powerful, magical, creature."

"A powerful, magical creature, they are afraid of."

"Yes... And... well... the only living breathing source of magic to be known in this world for centuries."

Kyana did roll her eyes this time. Ira was stalling. She knew that Kyana knew all of this. The news would be bad, but she wished the girl would get to the point already.

"You will live... but you will have to stay in Castle Lyist, in the custody of the kingdom."

Kyana froze, eyes fixed on the last remaining crumbs of cheese in her hand, mouth going dry, and appetite completely gone. Remain in Castle Lyist?

"Why on earth would they want that?" Kyana asked evenly. "I would think they want me gone as far from here as possible."

"Exile was suggested, but some of the king's closest advisers didn't think it safe to have a powerful creature... as yourself... to be... uh, out of their immediate control and supervision."

Kyana chuckled darkly. "I'm sure it doesn't hurt the king's perception among the other kingdoms, either." A kingdom that held captive a dragon, the likes of which haven't been seen since the end of dragons, would be the most feared and respected kingdom in all the lands. This was not mercy. This was politics.

"For how long?" Kyana asked. In her heart, she already knew the answer.

"... For the remainder of your life," Ira said dully.

Kyana's heart sank, dropped, and seemed to roll away across the stone floor in the dirt and filth. Forever? Here? Doubtlessly chained to this same stone floor until her dying breath. No air. No sky, no wind at her face and breeze in her wings to bring her, guide her, quickly up to the clouds... to freedom.

"I would rather die," Kyana spoke softly. She hated to hear the break in her voice, but she could not prevent it. She would not live like that. Like some dog. Like some beaten down bitch. She needed her freedom... she needed her sky and her forest. The idea of never stretching her wings again... She had missed it so much. The change in the courtyard had reminded her of how it felt. To be herself, her pure form. Opening her great wings. Feeling the light of day glinting off her scales. The warmth of fire raging wild within her chest. It was her. It was all she had left of the family she loved. She would not live without it. Not any longer.

"I would rather die," Kyana repeated firmly.

"Wait," Ira said, hurriedly, as if worried Kyana would simply drop dead with the intensity of her will. "That's not all. Not down here. There were more terms. Although you have to stay in Castle Ly—"

"To protect the world from – oh me – evil me," she spat bitterly.

"You'll have to stay," Ira went on. "But you won't live here. Not like a prisoner in a dungeon. Temper was very clear, and the king agreed. Your charges will be completely dropped when you become a ward to the Kingdom." Ira raised her hand, quitting Kyana before she could protest. "You'll live in the castle, in the style and comfort as any ward of the king. You'll have your own quarters, a seat at the table, warmth, space, comfortable living with a handmaid of your own. A Faithful as a matter of fact, Temper also insisted on that. Freedom to roam the castle as you wish. Courtyards to…. But you can't leave the outer wall. The moment you do, the terms fail and you… uh…"

"Can be executed on sight." Kyana finished for her.

"Yes."

"And how exactly do they plan on doing that?" Kyana grinned, more a show of teeth than a smile. She watched Ira's eyes dart downward as if she was expecting to see sharp fangs replacing the usual smooth white teeth, but there was no fear in the glance. It was curiosity. Excitement even. "I am a dragon, after all."

"Kyana, you're a dragon, but you're also human. You nearly died when you were stabbed, remember?"

"Vaguely," Kyana joked.

"Well, I assume they plan on doing the same thing… except make sure it sticks this time."

"So, I'd have to stay in human form."

"Yes."

"And why on earth," Kyana asked slowly, allowing her words to sink into the air, wanting them to weigh as heavy as possible. "With such freedoms, why would they trust me not to run… or burn down the entire damn kingdom? Why wouldn't I just change?"

Ira took another deep breath. "Because you won't be able to." Kyana raised a brow.

"Oh?" she asked. "Why not?"

"Ya… it's another term. Temper nearly crapped a brick and burst a blood vessel when he heard it. I swear that man's skin, bone, veins, and nothing else—"

"Ira!" Kyana barked. She was a master of stalling, but Kyana had never been terribly patient.

"Okay… so you see these?" Ira pointed at the shackles around her wrists, ankles, and neck.

"Yes…" Kyana rolled her eyes. "Rather clearly in fact."

"Do you know what they are made of?"

"Dragon Iron," she answered without hesitation.

"Oh, so you know about it?"

Kyana looked up to the dark ceiling of her cell and wished to whatever soaring spirit of Kyaper remained, to give her patience.

"Eggs," she said evenly. "It's not Iron at all. It's made of dragon eggshells. The Four Kingdoms made blades out of them in The First War. It's the only reason they won."

Kyana knew all of this. Because the eggs were part of the dragons themselves, it was the only thing that could break through dragon scales. Magic used against magic. She also knew that during the end of dragons, there was a total of twelve swords made from dragon eggs. Four of which were kept by the kings and queens of the kingdoms, and the other eight were given to the most skilled and trusted knights of the realms. These knights speared into action, led the armies onward, and brought the dragon lineage slowly, methodically, and violently, to its end.

These knights, known as Liberators or Liberas, were revered as heroes of the realms, and as respected as the dragons they slew. Never mind asking who was being "liberated" or if they even wanted to be 'saved.' But their visages were immortalized in every kingdom. Kyana had seen a few standing solemn and stony around Castle Lyist, both decorating the Castle itself and the courtyards. Watching over the people who they thought they saved. Never stopping to wonder if they were really saving anyone at all.

Kyana dragged her wandering mind back to Ira, who was still talking.

"Some say," Ira continued, trying to hide the real topic behind matters of fact and days passed by. "Because of the magical properties in the shells, they were able to break dragon scales," Ira added. "And for some reason, manmade fire—"

"Yes, yes, a manmade fire could bend it," Kyana hurried, eager to move on. "It was used in times of old to slay the dragons. Yes, Ira, I know…. Remember…. *I was there.*"

"Ya…" Ira said, a light pink color rising to her cheeks and nose. "So, uh, you know how if you tried to "change" right now… you would uh…"

"Be decapitated and have my hands and feet come off?" Kyana said matter-of-factly. Not only would the Dragon Iron break through her newly grown scales if she trying to change, but it would *slice* through, leaving her bleeding out on this moldy floor.

Ira nodded, but said nothing, waiting for the realization to hit. She did not wait long.

"Oh….," Kyana said, eyebrows rising. "Oh…."

"Ya." Ira nodded.

"So, I may not be chained to the floor…" Kyana began to laugh. It was a rumbling sound, low and rough in her chest. It scratched and scrambled up her belly like a cat drowning in a well. It clawed its way up her throat and past her teeth, leaving a bitter taste on the back of her tongue, and a raking pain left in her chest. "But I'll still be in shackles."

"Just one," Ira insisted. "One around… uh, well, your neck."

"… like dog collar." Kyana muttered, rubbing her tired eyes.

"They thought… if you tried to 'change' with just the one, you'd be decapitated. Having any others would be…"

"Overdoing it?" Kyana nodded, almost amused. Now if that bitter taste would just leave her mouth. "A death noose," Kyana said, looking at Ira's worried eyes. "Anything else?"

"Just a few other terms. The Faithful promised to disband their forces once arrangements had been made. They promised to go quietly, with the exception of your new handmaid, who Temper insisted, should be a Faithful from their group. To make sure you are properly cared for."

"And how can they be sure that the Lystad wouldn't just kill both I and this handmaid as soon as they've dispersed?" Kyana asked.

"Damian wouldn't do that." Ira shook her head. "If he signs the agreement, he will uphold it. He is a man of his word. All that's needed now…" Ira looked up sheepishly. "… Is your consent to carry out the terms."

"Do I really have a choice?" Kyana grumbled.

"Death," Ira answered glumly. "I really hope you don't choose that option. There are a lot of people," Ira motioned to the unseen throng of distant travelers that waited outside the broken walls of the kingdom. "Who see you as... their last remnants of true, visible... well... proof. All their dreaming, all their remembering, all this time... they believe you're the answer to it all. They believe your appearance, your change, it affirmed their long-suffering beliefs. You are the last known remnants of an entire area, an entire... way of life. The last gasp of their long-held loyalty. You brought them hope for the future."

Kyana was shaking her head.

"I'm not... Ira, I'm not what they think I am."

"What do you mean?"

"They think I'm some sort of... some... Ira, I'm not what they're looking for. I'm not what they *need*."

"What do you think they need?" Ira asked, blinking slowly.

"A god." Kyana answered, "A savior. A leader."

Ira smiled.

"The Faithful never needed a God, Kyana. They only ever needed a Dragon. And as for a savior... you've already saved them."

"I've not done anything!" Kyana said and tried to throw her hands up in exasperation, only to have them painfully yanked back down by the chains.

"You exist," Ira said simply. "That's enough for them."

"No," Kyana shook her head. She looked up at Ira, desperate green eyes landing on her. She tried to show the girl, tried to convey the emptiness, that hopeless, hollowness, the knowledge that she - which *they*, didn't seem to understand. "No, it's not. They may not know it yet... but it's *not* enough." Ira watched her face carefully. Kyana could almost see the girl's thoughts swirling behind those hazel eyes, but she did not speak them. Not yet.

"I am not going to be enough, Ira," Kyana said simply.

Ira thought a few more moments.

"Do you think you're not enough for the Faithful to carry on?... or not enough for yourself?"

"What are you talking about?" Kyana frowned at Ira. She was acting more confusing than usual.

"Never mind," Ira said, eyes darting away.

They fell silent for a few moments. They could hear the stamping of the guard's feet as he moved up and down the cells out of sight.

"What if I choose death?" Kyana eventually asked. Ira watched her, jaw tightening and loosening slightly, biting back words she wanted to say, eyes swirling wildly with thoughts unspoken.

"Kyana... you were... you ARE a Faithful," Ira began, slow and calm. "You were a Faithful long before you were a dragon. You know this is everything to them. YOU are **everything** to them. Everything has been taken from these people. Everything. Their freedoms, their livelihoods, and many times, their lives. All they have left is their belief, their trust and loyalty to dragons... their loyalty to *you*." She sighed eyes blinking slow. "If they lose you... after everything they've been through, after all this time, finally having you... if they **lose you...**"

Ira trailed off into silence, but she did not need words. Kyana knew. Kyana had watched her dragons die. She knew what that felt like. She knew what it felt like to have nothing left. To lose and lose *everything*. She knew.

Kyana watched as Ira stood, brushing off her dress and apron and made her way for the gate. "But it's your choice, of course," she said, "I'll be back tomorrow with your breakfast. Think about it."

"And you Ira," Kyana asked the girl after she called for the guard. "What do you believe?"

Ira turned, and her eyes gleamed with a light that did not belong in that dark place. It was a look that sent a shiver down the dragon's spine because behind that gleam was something strong. A power that outstripped any magic. Outstripped any god.

"I believe... you're a woman who couldn't possibly begin to comprehend her future importance in this world. One which will change... everything." Ira then shrugged, the gleam in her eyes was gone, replaced by its usual sweet sparkle, and her broad grin spread her lips. "Besides, I'm selfish. You're a good friend... I have very few of those. I'd hate to lose you." She paused. "Things will change... things will get better. Things always get worse, just before they get better... if you give it time, patience... and have a little faith." She gave Kyana a wink, leaving her alone in the room of stones, with much to think over.

# CHAPTER 46

"Think about it?" Damian repeated with disbelief. He and Ira were alone in Damian's chambers. He had sent for Ira under the pretense of a late meal, but they both knew better. Damian did not need a meal. They had matters to discuss.

Damian paced with an agitated, jerking step. He moved back and forth in front of the fireplace which crackled happily, blissfully unaware of the situation developing in the castle where it burned. A situation with deep green eyes and a secret that was a secret no longer.

"She has to think about *what?*" the king asked again, anger crackling along with the fire and seeming to flow from every agitated movement. "What is there to think over?"

"This isn't exactly an easy thing to accept Damian," Ira insisted, pouring mead into a goblet and holding it out to him. Damian waived it away. Ira shrugged and took a gulp of her own. It was hot and warmed her throat and chest as it went down. Ira scowled at the cup and clucked her tongue against the sickening sweetness.

"This isn't exactly easy…?" Damian repeated, sounding more than exasperated. "It's live or die. How is that not easy?"

"Well," Ira said, leaning against the table laden with forgotten food, and taking another gulp of mead. "It's not quite that simple."

Damian turned to her; blue eyes wide with exasperation. He had not touched a drop of spirits since Rainier's attack on the city, and yet he looked as disheveled at that moment as he had on the evenings when he went back to his chambers stumbling from drink. Granted, it was not often, but Ira knew the look. Disheveled, wide-eyed, clothes wrinkled and as out of place as if he had just rolled from the bed, although Ira knew the king had not. Sleep had not come easily to any of them since this whole thing began, and to Damian least of all. His face was paler than usual, and a blue stain played around the corners of his eyes and dipping into premature wrinkles.

Ira felt concern bolt through her stomach, making her set down the goblet. Her friend had a rough few days, she knew, and it was taking its toll on both his health and temper.

"Life." Damian lifted one hand in the air. "Death." He raised his other hand, holding it about a foot away from the first. "I know this is a little complex, but even you should see it."

Ira took a deep breath, reeling in her irritation with some effort. Damian was baiting her, but Ira would not bite. Not today.

"Life," Ira pointed to the kings open hand, "A life of imprisonment. A life of captivity. A life with no true freedom."

"And so, death is better?" Damian scoffed, dropping both hands to his sides, where they curled into fists.

"To her," Ira picked back up the goblet, turning it in her hands. The thick liquid swirled, catching light and shadow in equal turns as they chased each other inside the rim. Around and around, it went. "Maybe."

"Then she's a fool," Damian bristled, turning to face the hearth. His features instantly lit up in its orange and gold glow.

"You know that's not true," Ira mumbled miserably.

They fell quiet for a time, listening to the fire crackle, and the cold wind slowly picking up speed outside the shuttered windows. Damian sighed and covered his closed eyes with his "life" hand.

"And should she?"

"Should she what?" Ira asked, watching Damian's broad shoulders slumping at his own words. They hung low and heavy under all that weight they had to bear. When Damian made no answer, Ira asked again. "Should she what?" The King of Neira dragged his hand slowly down his face, back straightening as he turned to face Ira.

"Should... gods Ira, *should* she live?"

Ira's heart sank, and she felt something dark and empty come up to greet it. Her hand trailed absently over the hidden mark on her arm. The brand she had never shown anyone, not even her best friend of fifteen years, *especially* her best friend, until this morning. She remembered how Kyana's green eyes had widened when Ira pulled back her sleeve. How Kyana looked at her then, realization spreading like ripples in the water. A pebble of truth breaking its cool surface, widening until understanding filled every feature.

Ira had wanted to ask her then. That very moment. Ask her the question that had been burning in her heart since the moment she stooped down to pull a string of beads from a pile of blood and gore, but it had not been the time. Kyana's eyes had soon gone dark, and in them, Ira had seen the resolve. The resolve of a knight going to war, with no hope of return. The determination of a dead man.

Again, she had wanted to ask Kyana. Show her she was not alone. To prove it with a question. It was still not the time, and Ira would not use this request to manipulate her. She would encourage. Tell Kyana exactly how it was. She did not want to lie. Not to her. Never to her. She would not ask her question, the most important of requests, out of desperation. She was the bloodline of Kyara, and it was her decision.

Unless of course, Damian chose to take it from her.

"What do you think?" Ira asked slowly.

"I think she's a dangerous... magical... thing." Damian said, voice as low as the crackling fire. "One that holds the only source of replenishing magic in the realm. The bones were supposed to be the last of it. The bones were supposed to eventually run dry, but now she... she..." Damian's eyes widened as he swung round. "Oh gods, Ira! She's not just a dragon. She's a Faithful. A Faithful with an inexhaustible source of magic. Herself! Access to her *own* magic. She could use it. Break out of her chains, break out of her cell. Gods, I'm such a fool, I must go and—"

"Whoa, whoa, Damian, Damian, stop," Ira went to him, catching him as he made for the door. "Slow down, breathe..." She took his shoulders in both her hands and turned him back to face her. "It's okay, she can't get out of her chains."

"Ira, dragon iron only works on dragons, for Faithful it's just another stone, it doesn't prevent the use of magic, it just prevents her from turning into... into that..."

"Damian breathe," Ira said, squeezing his shoulders tight, trying to steady him. "I promise you, she can't magic her locks open."

"How do you know that?" Damian asked, breathing starting to slow, blue eyes desperately searching Ira's for the truth of her words.

"She told me," Ira explained. "She was never taught how. She can change. But no magic."

"Truly?"

"Truly," Ira insisted. "Besides. If she could... she would have done so already. Alright? Trust me." Damian nodded a little, and Ira dropped her hands. She moved back to her place at the table. Damian's tired eyes looked dejectedly up.

"My people are afraid."

"Not all," Ira countered, but she kept her tone conversational. Now that Damian was back down, she wanted to keep him there. "There are many asking for her life. She saved the kingdom, your majesty."

"And could just as easily destroy it if she likes," Damian said, face stony.

*Not with a metal noose around her neck.* Ira thought, but she chose to keep it to herself. The king already knew all of this. So that left only two more questions.

"Why are you asking me this?"

Damian glanced over at her as if surprised.

"Why?"

"Yes," Ira said, taking and holding out the goblet once more. This time, the king took it. After a moment of glaring down into the liquid, as if it had said something extremely offensive, Damian downed it in one gulp.

"Because," Damian wiped his mouth on his sleeve. "I'm in untraveled territory, Ira. And I..." The king trailed off. For a moment Ira thought she saw a flash of fear in the king's blue eyes, but it was gone so quickly, she decided she must have imagined it. Damian took a seat at the table, elbows resting on his knees, and looked into the fire once more. "I have many advisers, and they do love to whisper their never-ending buzz of opinions in my ear, but, I'm frankly tired of it. And although I like to tease and joke with you... I respect your opinion. And it is you, above all others, that knows her best." Ira opened her mouth to protest, but Damian pushed on, "No, I know you could never have foreseen this. I don't mean you know all her secrets... although if that woman is hiding any more, I'm pretty sure I never want to know them. No, I meant that you have spent the most time by her side. You have listened to her speak. Looked into her eyes. So, tell me," he looked back at Ira, the firelight dancing odd flickering shapes across his eyes. "What do you think?"

Ira thought about making some quip to lighten the mood, but she could not think of any. She felt it then. She had felt it in that dungeon full of mold and darkness, and now in this room of warmth and light. Damian looked in his friends' eyes, waiting for her opinion, trusting in her loyalty. Because he had it. He had **owned** it for fifteen years, ever since the moment two children met in an empty kitchen. He had her, and he still did, but things were changing. Everything, once so sure, so solid, was shifting. The dreams of an old Faithful woman and a small girl with a newly healing brand, had suddenly, irretrievably, come to life. Things she had accepted, things she had grown accustomed, had passed and passed by. The day would come when she would be forced to choose between the life she had built and the life she had wished for since she could wish for anything. Those desperate hopes only seen behind closed eyes… until now.

Ira felt her heart squeeze, and her chest tighten defensively around it. She pushed the thought hastily aside. That time might come, but that time was not yet here.

"I think she's done a lot of good your majesty," Ira said, low but steady. "She's saved us. She's saved us more than once. She fought for us. Fought for us even after… all the history between her and the Four Kingdoms… her family and your own. She could have simply let us die, let the entire kingdom die. She fought for us because she saw that we are our own kingdom, our own people. We are not our forefathers… and maybe we should recognize that she is not her ancestors. I think it's time we fought for her."

Damian nodded, leaning back into his chair. "You're not the only one," he said, "And I don't mean the Faithful."

Ira nodded. There were many people, within the towns and still within the castle which had called for Kyana's pardon. Then again, there were the people who thought Kyana was responsible for the hirelings and the damage. A few proclaimed that she was, in fact, the Faithful Rainier himself, shrouded in some sort of disguise, and should be immediately put to death. The kingdom was torn between those who understood and those that *thought* they understood. The only problem was, those that did not understand seemed to shout the loudest.

"But people are still afraid," Damian said.

"They will know better… just give them time… and let them know her."

"You have more faith in people, than they deserve, my friend," Damian Lystad said with a smile.

"She won't hurt us," Ira insisted.

"So sure, are we?" he laughed, but it wasn't his usual boisterous sound. It was low and bitter and did not meet his eyes.

"You wouldn't have had me meet with her if you thought I wasn't." Ira pointed out.

"You asked me if you could meet with her, remember?"

"Because I was the only one with balls enough to speak with her face to face."

A smile twitched across Damian's face. "You were friends, Ira. Are you sure you're not letting your feelings for the girl cloud your—"

"Are you?" Ira cut in flatly.

Damian glanced up, but not for long.

"She won't hurt us," Ira said, softer this time. "She's not like that. She's not what they think she is, and she's not what history paints her as. And I think you know that. Or she'd be dead already."

"If my father was here… he would know what to do." Damian mused, reaching for the pitcher.

*Before or after he sobered up?* Ira wondered, watching the king pour himself another glass, but simply twirled it between his hands without another sip.

"Your father never dealt with anything like this before Damian."

"And that's the thing. No one has Ira," Damian jammed a palm into his tired eye, seemingly trying to grind away the weariness held there. "No one has ever been placed in the position I am now in. And I feel I have only made it worse. Should I have taken her to trial? Should I have just killed her?"

"If you had, the Faithful would have attacked, and we'd all be in a world of trouble," Ira said. The king snorted, setting down his goblet and grabbing a bright red apple off of the tray Ira had brought up earlier.

"Fight for her…" he said, eyes trailing towards the window, a window that was closed against the dark and bleak night, full of wind and uncertain showers that tempted from the hovering clouds but never quite fell. "And how do you suggest we do that when she doesn't even fight for herself?"

*Fight for herself.* The thought rolled around in Ira's mind like a leaf on wild waters. Twisting, spiraling, falling, until…

Ira blinked, and suddenly she knew. If Kyana wouldn't fight for her own life, if she felt like such a life was not worth fighting for… Ira thought she knew a different way. A different fight. She did not think her simple existence was enough to help the Faithful… well then perhaps…

"Perhaps…" Ira swallowed; mouth suddenly very dry. She took another long drink before continuing. "Perhaps, my lord, there is something else she *will* fight for."

"What do you mean?" Damian asked, eyes not leaving the window.

Ira swallowed, cleared her throat, and opened her mouth to speak the words she would never before have dragged from the deepest part of her heart and into the blinding light of reality.

"Amend the law," Ira said, barely believing her own lips were forming around those words. At that moment it felt like her hidden mark burned under her shirt sleeve. A mark that had been a gift, a gift given new meaning by the strangest of women. "Amend the laws against those that call themselves Faithful."

Damian looked around, eyebrows shooting up to his hairline, almost disappearing. At that moment, Ira was sure he knew. Sure, that her best friend, her king, had suddenly realized that she had been lying to him for fifteen years. In a moment of terrified mania, she almost saw her lord reaching for the sword that hung on his hip, but this was only in her imagination, for the sword had been sent out to be polished hours beforehand. Damian made no such moves and connected no such dots.

"You want me to make magic legal in Neira?" he asked as if Ira had just thrown a wad of horse dung in his face. "Are you *insane?*"

"No." Ira shook her head, never dreaming of reaching that far… or at least… not yet. "Not to practice. Just to be."

"You've lost me," Damian said, but his shoulders relaxed, and Ira let out a small breath she had not realized she had been holding.

"Keep the practice of magic illegal in Neira, but allow the presence of Faithful. No longer have it be treasonous to be a Faithful within the cities. Keep the law against the practice of magic. But to be a Faithful, you need not practice magic, it's not a requirement or anything." As a matter of fact, few were ever supposed to wield it. It was only the chosen few, handpicked by the dragons themselves, that were ever supposed to have access to magic at all. "One is an action. The other is simply a belief and a loyalty. A trust. A faith in a creature, and what that creature had to say. What they believe it stood for."

"A magical creature," Damian countered.

"That no longer exists," Ira answered.

"I'm sorry, did you go temporarily blind a few days ago or…"

"Yes, there is Kyana, but she is completely under your control, and therefore, so would any Faithful that choose to make her their new Docent."

"Docent?" The king blinked.

"It's what Faithful tended to call their clan's dragon. It's a title. Like their version of "my lord" or "king." Ira hurried on before Damian could wonder how she possibly knew such information. "These 'Rekindled' Faithful or whatever they call themselves. They just found a dragon, after so many years of waiting, and wishing, they will do anything to keep her alive and safe… even if that means following *your* orders. Following your rules. Your laws." Damian opened his mouth, only to close it again, dark brows knitting together in irritated confusion.

"Let them live here," Ira went on cautiously, "Let them live here, gods know they were doing so anyway, but let them live openly, without fear. Let the Faithful of Castle Lyist come home. Besides, none of them can actually practice magic without a relic. All you would have to do is make sure the relics are secured. Strengthen the Keepers. You must admit they've grown weak over the years."

"That I do," Damian mumbled, "It's run by old men and children. Their greatest strength is the gates, and that is not enough. Not anymore." It had been a tradition in Neira, that all Keepers were kept in a small generational group, passed down from father to son. When a Keeper had no children, they were allowed to hand pick a trusted replacement to serve after their demise. This tradition had been meant as a precaution against any runners from the shadow markets invading their ranks. Dragon relics cost a pretty penny, and many would kill to have access to the caverns kept by the Keepers. However, over the years, many of the Keepers passed on without lineage and many times without choosing an heir. The ranks had grown smaller and smaller as their trust in others grew less and less. They were a suspicious lot, the Keepers. Prone to seeing foes in shadows and cling to traditions like a drowning cat cling to the water's edge.

"So, break from tradition," Ira insisted eagerly. "Add more men, trustworthy men to secure each gate and protect the relics. Hell, bury all the relics! Gather them all up in the deepest chamber and fill it with dirt. Make them a non-issue. The citizens will still be safe from magic, the other kingdoms will hear that Castle Lyist holds the first dragon to be seen in centuries under its command, Neira will be strengthened, and Kyana... this will be her something to fight for."

"Thousands of Faithful," Damian mused, "Able to come out of the shadows."

"She may not fight for herself," Ira said, a smile playing around her wide lips. "But she's a sucker for a lost cause. And Faithful? Well, they're about as lost as anything could ever be."

Damian stood, silently, soaking in every word his friend spoke, saying nothing for a long time.

"And this will be enough?" he asked finally, blue eyes considering Ira. "This will be worth enough for her?"

Ira hesitated. Kyana was a dragon, but she was also the daughter of man. Just because she was a dragon did not mean she felt any particular responsibility for those that called themselves her Faithful. And she was a proud woman after all. Even with an amended law, she may still choose death over captivity. The thought broke Ira's heart, and she pushed it away with the hasty insistence of a child being told that fairies belonged only in books. Not wanting to know if that was the truth. Not wanting the truth if it was.

"I hope so," she said, quietly. "Gods, I hope so."

"This would outrage the other kingdoms."

Ira snorted. "Eryl Kingdom would probably applaud your progressive attitude. They haven't had a penalty against being a Faithful in their kingdom... well, ever. Not even after the Second War, they never made it a death sentence, just banishments for practicing magic. Even Kyar kingdom now has a city or two with Faithful factions allowed."

"Yes, a city or two. One or two." Damian said, lifting his fingers in demonstration, as if Ira may have forgotten what the numbers looked like. "Not the main city. Not the entire kingdom. Not as drastic as it would be here. And not with a dragon either."

"The fact that you have a dragon will be nothing but impressive, if not a frightening show of power, to the other kingdoms. Kyar and Eryl might think your extensive actions a little fast, and Sterlyn Kingdom might down right disprove but... what are they going to do about it?" Ira flashed a wide grin. "You've got a dragon."

"Who would, by this point, just as soon flee my kingdom then defend it from any other."

"They don't know that," Ira pressed.

"And if they ever call my bluff?" Damian asked coolly.

Ira hesitated. "Life is a gamble, my lord. You can only play the cards you were dealt in the best way that you can. The rest? It is to close your eyes and..."

"What? Have faith?"

"Essentially," Ira laughed. "Yes."

Damian sighed and rubbed his eyes.

"Gods, Ira... what days have we passed into?"

*Better days.* Ira thought, not daring to speak such words out loud. She had spent her arsenal of rash ideas for the day, perhaps for the rest of her lifetime. *Better days... if you allow them to come and not cling to the past.*

Damian thought, arms crossed, and eyes closed tight against distractions. Ira watched her friend in this stance that she had seen him in countless times before. The countless councils, meetings and hearings by his father's side and after he stood to make such decisions alone. Decisions that shaped his kingdom to be as it was today. As always, Ira waited, waited to see in what way the kingdom would be shaped. What would come with tomorrow.

When Damian opened his eyes, Ira saw their decision etched in blue stone. Relief flooded through her.

"Offer it to her. If she accepts, I will gather everyone once more. But," Damian's eyes grew cold and icy as he continued, "Ask her only once my friend and ask her only then. Let her know another chance will not come. She must decide. There is only so much... I can give."

Ira nodded and was about to get up when another question snuck its way past her lips.

"What do *you* want my lord?"

"Hum?" Damian asked, turning back. He had already made his way towards the large four poster bed at the other end of the room, looking haggard and ready to fall immediately to sleep.

"What do you want to happen?" Ira asked again, watching him yawn long and loud, showing a flash of white teeth.

"I already gave my orders, Ira," he said.

"I know your options and your orders," Ira said, leaning forward as she spoke. She wanted to know. She *needed* to know.

"What do *you want* to happen? Do you think Kyana... what do *you* want?"

"I want what's best for my people," Damian Lystad said automatically as if reading from an actor's script, written by, and for, someone else.

"That's not what I meant," Ira pressed.

"I know." Damian's eyes were back on the fire. Ira knew she would get nothing more out of her friend tonight. Ira stretched her cramping legs which popped and, with a groan, got to her feet.

"Well, goodnight Damian."

"Goodnight Ira," he answered. Ira was reaching for the door, when Damian asked, "Did she look afraid?"

"Your majesty?" Ira turned. The king's back was to her, once again facing the bed as he spoke.

"Kyana... did she seem afraid?"

Ira shook her head. "She did seem a little afraid... but Damian, we both know she is a lot tougher than she *seems*."

A smile twitched at the corners of Damian's mouth, but he only nodded. "Goodnight Ira."

"Goodnight, my lord." The door closed behind her with a soft click as the king sat on the bed. Despite his exhaustion, he did not fall asleep. He simply sat and continued to watch the flames dance in the hearth.

# CHAPTER 47

Ira returned the next morning as promised and told Kyana of all she and Damian had discussed the night before. She explained after much, hemming, and hawing, that earned her an exasperated sigh and rolling of green eyes, but finally everything was explained.

Kyana did not answer for a long time, letting the silence stretch and tremble to its very breaking point. For a terrifying, gut-wrenching moment, Ira thought she would still say no. That she would still choose death and leave the Faithful's to fight or flee as they wish. To leave all behind, to a fate that did not concern her any longer. She imagined Kyana's lips forming the last word on the matter, and the silence began to stretch her very sanity to the breaking point as well.

When she did finally look up from her clenched hands, Ira started in surprise.

"And they would live freely," she clarified, low and slow. "They would live without fear of attack or punishment."

Ira wanted to say yes immediately. She wanted to shout it, sooth the concern on Kyana's dirty and yet still lovely face. Wipe it away and give her exactly the answer she was looking for, but Ira could not do that. She could not lie to her.

"There would be an adjustment," Ira admitted. "Change is always an adjustment and such a sudden switch from outlawing to allowing Faithful… well, there will be troubled times. Some will be angry. Some may even lash out. All the more reason that we need you there," Ira said, leaning forward, unable to stop herself. "You will be ward to the kingdom, dragon of the court. You will have a title and influence; you can be the mediator between Faithful and non. You are the only one that can make such a change work, such a change last, with the least amount of damage done. And when time has passed by, you will have helped bring about a new age in the kingdom. An age of acceptance."

"Meager acceptance," Kyana corrected. "Partial at best."

"Every change must start somewhere," Ira insisted. "The very greatest of things, greatest of events, greatest of kingdoms, greatest of ages... started in one place, at one time, with one small act."

*Gods let this be one of those times.* Ira thought desperately. *Let it be now. Let us stand side by side and watch the old-world pass and pass by. For it is the old world now. You burned it down. Now let it die... and let the new age rise. On unsteady footing, yes, but let it rise all the same. It will stumble, but soon it will fly.*

Kyana sighed, eyes darting up to the ceiling that dripped green and gray water down around them in slow, plodding drops that splashed on the filthy ground. One drop broke against her sharp cheek, casting two little streams of green water down her face like tears to match her eyes.

"I am not what they need, Ira," she spoke so softly Ira barely heard her.

*You are everything I need.* Ira thought, and the truth of those words frightened her. She did not dare speak them. No, not yet.

"Perhaps," she said instead. "But you are *all* they have."

Kyana took one last deep breath.

"Fine." The word nearly made Ira cry. "Fine, damn you all, fine."

It was an answer that earned her another wide grin.

"Thank you," Ira said and reached out, taking Kyana's hands, dirty and chapped, and oh so warm, into her own. Ira surprised Kyana into wide green-eyed bewilderment when she bent down and kissed each. "Thank you."

Arrangements were quickly made. It took two more days for things to be ready. Kyana wondered what was taking so long but soon realized that they must be making her new dog collar. She tried not to give that idea too much thought. She was too preoccupied with self-pity and anger. A lifetime of imprisonment. A lifetime without her wings, for what? A jumbled mass of lost Faithful, who thought she was some sort of answer to their hopes? Faithful from different clans coming together for one last dragon? The age of The First

Peace was over, why dwell on it? Why not accept the new regime and have done with it? Death to dragons. Down with magic. Let it die. Let it burn and let the ashes blow away.

But Kyana knew Ira was right. These were people that thrived on their beliefs and tradition. It was their breath and the blood in their veins. There was no turning back. They were their beliefs, just as surely as Kyana was a dragon.

But what did she owe them? She had lost just as much as they. She had fought, just as hard as they. Harder even. What did she owe them, to be this chained dog in a kingdom of dragon killers?

And yet... her answer could be nothing but yes. Why? Was it the idea of stealing away an entire people... her people's... last hope? Was it the idea of causing such a wound... that pain that had been hurting her for so long, bleeding her dry for so long? Was it because she did not want to inflict that pain on others? Was it that little voice deep in her heart, with breath like fire and sounding of Kyaper, that whispered for patience that spurred her on?

Yes... but only partly. The rest of her reasons, fleeting or no, made its home in a blossoming warmth, and tear-streaked hazel eyes.

# CHAPTER 48

*Gods, she looks awful.*

This was Damian's first thought as Kyana was led into the room. Her usual full auburn hair hung in limp, sweaty, twines around her unusually pale face. She looked thin. Thin and tired with dark circles under her eyes, and more defined shadows accentuating her already sharp features. Her small lips held as little color as the rest of her and an unpleasant ripe scent of sweat and mold wafted in almost visible waves.

The next thought chased quickly after, and with far more impact. It ran headlong into his mind and hit with the force of a furious boar.

*Gods, if looks could kill.*

Her deep green eyes landed on him the moment she stepped through the door, and they landed with unmatched ferocity. Damian was reminded of a time when he was still but a child and first rode a stallion. There was a beautiful young horse in the king's stables that his father refused to let him ride. And for a good reason. The stud was not yet broken and fought against more experienced riders than Damian. He would toss them as quickly as a child could toss a straw doll. Damian however, being young, foolish, and with the pride and self-surety that comes only from lack of real experience, persisted.

After weeks of begging and whining, Damian, a shrewd young man of eleven, decided to wait until one afternoon when his father had particularly taken an interest in drink. When these days came, as they always did, his father was far more amenable about rules for his young son. Finally, Damian convinced his father to let him take a few turns around the training yards with the young horse. They had barely begun their first circle when Damian added a little more heal than the stallion liked.

Damian did not remember when the stallion began to buck. He only remembered what happened after. One moment he had been clutching happily to the smooth reins, watching the ground pass by between the stallions red ears at an astonishing rate, when suddenly he was airborne, reins were gone from his grasp. Everything gone from his grasp.

He remembered wondering, as he watched the sky rising closer before him, almost close enough to touch. He wondered if his father would be angry with him. Then he hit the ground. He had been lucky, all things considered. He was not trampled, he did not break any bones, but he had hit the dirt with enough force to expel every ounce of air in his lungs, leaving him gasping. He remembered the ache in his chest and arms, as he desperately tried to catch his breath. He watched the, quite literally breathtaking, stallion bound away with shining hooves still kicking angrily into the sky.

As Kyana's eyes glared, deep green tunnels of hate, Damian felt like he had hit the ground all over again and found himself praying for air.

He did not let this show. It was not his place to show weakness. Instead, he smiled kindly, as the woman… dragon, whatever the hell she was, came to a stop before the same small table they had used to meet with Temper.

The advisers and knights were gone, however. Today it was just him, Temper, and the guards that had brought Kyana. He had already discussed the situation with them all, had received various levels of reaction from mild-mannered encouragement to boisterous doubts. In Phobos's case, a great deal of outright defiance. At one-point Damian actually had to send the old adviser out of the room to gather himself. When he returned, the old man had been calm, but no more amenable to the idea. It did not much matter. Damian had made up his mind.

"Hello, Kyana," Damian Lystad said, glad to hear his voice was steady. "Please, let me introduce Temper Worsing." Temper stepped forward and dropped to one knee before her.

"Docent," he said, covering his mouth for a moment with his hand. He looked up from his place, and Damian saw the absolute wonder that pooled in his clear brown eyes. Damian glanced up to Kyana, who was watching the old man with obvious discomfort, but when she spoke, it was in a soft and kind tone.

"Stand Temper Worsing… and be well in any and all things."

Temper stood, a satisfied smile spreading his still glowing face.

"You remember the old ways?" he noticed approvingly.

"Better than you, I'd guess," she said, then her eyes trailed to the silver scales peeking out from the old man's collar. "… Or perhaps not." Her eyes moved back to his face. "Who was your dragon then Temper?"

"Little Stermay," Temper said, bowing his head in respect for the dead.

Damian's head darted up at this. This whole time he had thought Temper was a mere descendent of the Everhast Faithful. One that had those scales simply passed down through generations, as with the villager and his dragon claw. He realized, that was a ridiculous assumption, and instantly cursed his naivety. Damian was ignorant of many things having to do with Faithfuls, but he knew about the Main of dragons. He had also heard rumors that those claimed as a Main could live almost as long as the dragons that claimed them. Something about the dragon scales infusing them with longer lives. It was now so painfully apparent that Temper was one of these. Damian nearly laughed at his own idiocy. This feeling quickly faded as he looked back to Kyana. Such a young face… how many years had passed her by? How much time had floated through those deep green eyes, swallowed by them, until it finally drowned there?

"Stermar and Kyatta's foal?" Kyana was asking Temper, unaware of the king's eyes on her, or at least, pretending not to be aware.

"You knew them?"

"I knew her mother." Kyana smiled, and Damian watched her eyes slip into memories of years passed and passed by. "Not well, but I wish I had. She came to visit my clan when Kyaru was born and stayed for a few years after. She and Kyaper had spent many a happy year together in Aadya Castle, and I believe she wanted to be there to share his joy."

Temper nodded. "Kyatta was an amazing creature. Descendent of Kyara, just like you."

"What gave me away?" Kyana asked.

Temper reached up and tapped the corner of his ruined cheek, just below his eye. "It's hard to mistake those eyes." He seemed to hesitate before continuing. "Excuse my asking… but you are half human?"

"Clearly," Kyana said, but she said it with a playful tone. Damian watched her at this moment. Her back straight, her smile on, elegant even in chains and caked with dirt and sweat. There was a royal quality in her stance that he had never seen before. He wondered at it, watching every movement as if an enthralled viewer at a play. For that's what it was. A play. A part she was starting to perform. A role she was beginning to create.

Damian's heart sank at the thought, although he could not put his finger on why. This was the point, wasn't it? This was the agreement they had struck. She would play the ward to the kingdom that held her under control, and he would grant her a few liberties with the Faithful's and their charge. It was the truth of the matter. Then why was he having such a hard time swallowing it?

"I have many questions," Temper said, eyes lighting up with amazed curiosity.

"I'd be surprised if you didn't," she said, reaching up to brush back a strand of hair. The loud clatter and clinking made Temper's eyes drop for the first time, to the chains still connecting the girl's wrists and ankles. His gaze darkened as he turned back to Damian.

"Are those necessary?" he asked, coolly.

"No, of course." Damian nodded to one of the guards, who looked back at him as if he was insane but did his duty as bid. The guard unhooked the chain from around Kyana's ankles and wrists but left the thick looped shackles like chunky, inelegant bracelets. Kyana stretched her arms above her head, rolling her shoulders, letting a few loud popping sounds break the air. Damian winced.

Kyana gave a satisfied sigh.

"Better?" Temper asked.

"Much," she told him. "Thank you."

*No problem.* Damian thought ruefully. He kept this childish thought to himself and instead watched as Temper bowed his head to her.

"Any and all for you, Docent."

"Now," Kyana said, "I would love to answer all your questions, but we should get this out of the way first."

Damian had the sneaking suspicion that Kyana did not mean the official signing of the agreement between Kyana, the Rekindled Faithful and the Kingdom of Neira, but instead, the "this" in question was his own presence. Again, Damian let this thought slide by as easily as pulling closed a curtain.

All things eventually pass and pass by... even when they were incredibly annoying.

"Shall we?" he said, gesturing towards the table, where the papers were already spread out nice and neat beside the ink and quills.

The whole event, despite its genuinely monumental nature, a nature that would, with a few scratches of ink, change his kingdom and probably the known world, simply slipped by as quick and easy as a handmaid shaking out a floor mat. They reviewed the terms of the agreement, discussed in detail the parts played by Kyana, the Faithful, and the king himself. Kyana's conditional pardon, Tempers promise to disperse the Faithful, and the King of Neira taking the last remaining dragon as a ward under his kingdom. As long, of course, as that the dragon in question remained in the harmless form of a human unless directly ordered and allowed by the kingdom and its sovereign. Finally, the official alteration of the law regarding Faithfuls within the Kingdom and its major city, now allowed, with the stipulation that the use of magic itself was still outlawed by penalty of exile or death by the discretion of the king. Kyana's eyes had darted towards Damian at this point but said nothing. Other than that, her green gaze was strictly for Temper, and the papers in her hands.

When things were reviewed, and agreed upon anew, the quill was passed around the small table. The king went first, signing his name in the elegant looping scrawl that he had perfected over years of decrees, verdicts, and ceremonies.

*King Damian Lystad The Second*

Temper was next. His name appeared below Damian's, in short, sharp, almost hesitant scratches.

*Faithful Temper Louis Worsing*

Kyana was last. She stared at the paper for a long while, the quill twirling listlessly between her fingers, as her green eyes saw nothing. She was thinking, not reading, and they waited silently for her to come back from whatever dark thoughts she was obviously lost in. When she finally did, her green gaze drew up to Damian as slow and sharp as if it took physical effort to cut the air between them.

*How many times will you make me hit the ground?* Damian wondered as he met her eyes. There was a pause as the swirl of blue and endless green watched, waiting for one to blink, but neither did. To Damian, the world seemed swallowed around those eyes, drawn in, pulled in, like a strong wind through a tunnel. Those impossible eyes. The eyes of a dragon looking from the face of a woman.

*It's magic.* Damian thought, no fear, no discomfort rising to mar the pleasant smile he placed on his lips. *It's just magic. It always was.*

It was only a partial lie.

"Take it all then," Kyana said finally, in a voice so low Damian did not think it was meant for him at all. Kyana turned back to the paper and fixed the quill between her fingers. Her full name drew slow and steady onto the paper, in a signature befitting the last dragon of the known world.

*Docent Kyana Cara Castway*

With the last scratch of a quill, a kingdom was changed forever.

"Now," she said, turning her attention fully onto Temper as if Damian had simply vanished like some uninteresting trick of the light. "What would you like to know?"

# CHAPTER 49

The sun slowly crossed the sky, making the shadows stretch and churn over the floor and walls of the hall, filling the room with first a bright white, then dimming gold light. Kyana and Temper spent that time talking on many things. Kyana retold the story of how she was reborn, and Temper told her of his time serving Stermay and her clan.

He had been a young man of fourteen when he had become the small dragon's Main and had served her faithfully until her death. He had been there when Stermay was slain by a Libera from Sterlyn Kingdom and earned nothing but the deep cavernous scar on his face when he tried to save her. Stermay had been the last and her death had drawn an end to all dragon kind. Then eighteen-year-old Temper, with a still bleeding face, lead his clan into hiding. There, he and his scattered Faithful found others. They slowly built their own community in secret, traveling like nomads from place to place, never staying long and always out of reach of the Four Kingdoms. They had, over time, ventured farther and farther into the reaches of Neira Kingdom, which was risky, but lucky. If they had not, and if one of their own clan members had not been visiting a smaller, but rather affluent clan near the reaches of Castle Lyist, they would not have heard word of Kyana so quickly or been able to come with such haste.

Kyana and Temper spoke with a familiarity that neither had shared for far too long. They were both old creatures belonging to years passed by. They spoke the same language and saw things the same way. Both older than they appeared. Even the old man with his withering skin was older than imagined, his years spanning around three hundred. He had been kept alive so long by the remaining magic seeping through the silver dragon scales seared into his thin skin. He admitted to Kyana, with no small amount of shame, that he had taken to using other dragon relics to assist in extending his life, for the sake of his clan. Kyana had understood, and granted him pardon, which he took thankfully.

Kyana herself, face full of health and youth, had watched even more years pass by. Yet time had not sunk her features. Granted, many of her years had been spent in hibernation in the Caskcare Mountains, and age seemed far more timid to find dragons than it did humans.

King Damian Lystad sat by their side the entire time, but he had been completely forgotten. He did not mind. The young king was leaning forward, eyes wide, and mouth hanging open like an amazed child as he listened to them speak of things he had only read in history books or told through his father's bedtime tales. Unlike his father's tales, however, it was told from the side of the dragons. A side, Damian noticed, that had been forgotten through the histories.

At one-point Great Lawrence II was mentioned in a way very unlike how he was presented in the stories told to Damian by his father. In his tales, Lawrence II was a great man with a noble heart, who saved the world from the evils of magic that had grown too ambitious, and dragons that had taken down an entire kingdom in an afternoon.

He had been a great man, who had saved many, there was no doubting that, but when Kyana and Temper mention his name they said it as if they had sucked venom from a wound and quickly needed to spit it out before they swallowed it. Damian bristled for his namesake but did not try to counter their words, not yet. Instead, he listened. Listened to the weakly veiled disgust in their voices and recognized it. Recognized it for half of the story that it was, just as his image of the Great Lawrence II was only half. He listened and listened carefully. A young king trying to make whole a history, that had been for centuries, broken like two pieces of a single heart. And in his willingness, something began to beat. Slow and quiet, but steady.

# CHAPTER 50

What felt like days later, but was in actuality a single afternoon, judging by the procession of the sun and shadow, Kyana was led out of the hall. She had bid goodbye to Temper, who promised to see her on the morrow. The king had left a few hours previously, needing to attend to other kingly duties to be sure. He had issued orders for Kyana to be taken to her chambers after their conversation was through.

Kyana was led out by two of the guards, the third staying back to guide Temper out of the castle. He had been offered a room within Castle Lyist itself for the evening but refused it with a smile and a shake of his head. He wanted to go back to his people, tell them all that had passed, and join in their celebrations. Kyana understood, but she had been sad to see the old man leave. He had bowed to her, hand over mouth, and left her to be escorted away.

She followed glumly behind the guard's chestnut cloaks, watching as they wisped back and forth across the smooth stone floors. She thought absently of the moment she signed that piece of paper and signed away her freedom. She then pictured herself turning the quill and burying the delicate white and blue feather deep into her eye. She imagined the look of surprise on the king's face, to replace that smug smile he had been wearing all evening. Then everything would go mercifully dark. Death would hold more honor than whatever padded prison she was being led to.

The halls nearest to her room were completely empty. Probably ordered so until the feast, Kyana thought with equal glumness.

"A feast?" Kyana had asked Temper, dumbfounded when he had told her. "Why? How often do people feast in this city?"

"Well, the king believes that a celebratory ceremony will both appease the Faithful and also draw the still leery citizens to understand and accept the agreement," Temper explained, but an amused smile twitched the corner of his ancient smile.

*Silly boy,* that smile said, without a word.

"Yes," Kyana said, thinking of old men in purple robes and liver spots. "I'm sure there are many people who would rather see my head on a spike, then in a place at their table."

"True..." Temper nodded, "But there are many who remember how you saved their city... and are not likely to forget any time soon. The others just need time."

"And patience," Kyana added dully.

Temper smiled and blinked in a slow manner that reminded Kyana of Ira. He reached out and patted her hands, which rested on the table. They were warm hands. Warm, soft, and full of comfort and Kyana did not resist their touch.

"Things will ease their way through."

"Yes," Kyana smiled bitterly. "As it always has for our kind." Temper's smile faded then, but his hand only tightened around hers.

"Do not be afraid, my Docent," he said, in a voice as strong has his grip. "You are not alone. Not anymore. As you never will be again. We are with you. Through any and all." She looked into his warm brown eyes. Eyes so ancient, but time had not yet eaten away that spark of hope. Or perhaps that spark was new. Despite the bottomless pit that dug only deeper into her stomach, Kyana smiled at the kind old foolish man of hope.

"Through any and all," she answered, squeezing his wrinkled hands in hers.

So, there she was, being led down the empty hall by two guards who ushered her into the same room she had occupied only a few weeks previously as a guest. She noticed a few changes the instant she walked in. All the fire pokers, swords, and sharp ornaments were gone, replaced with soft, beautiful clothes, and decorative paintings, to cover their absence. There were also elegantly carved, but unmistakably strong, bars attached to her windows,

Yes. A very cushioned prison, indeed.

The guard had left the chains resting on the table in the hall, and now unhooked the metal loops around her wrists, but left the one around her neck. They did all of this without a word and left in silence. The lock slid closed behind with a ragged dragging sound. The light echo it left in the air made Kyana sure it was a new lock and one made of dragon iron.

She rubbed at the skin around her wrists, which had been worn thin and angry red by metal shackles. Her eyes then fell on the bed, to which she quickly launched herself. The thick cushions welcomed her, swallowed her, surrounding her in a soft fluffy cloud. She sighed, quickly chasing sleep. Nothing had been so soft. After sleeping on a cold, stinking, stone floor for weeks, there was nothing as comfortable as that bed. Kyana shifted onto her back and glanced up at the decorative brown and blue cloths that hung down from the canopy of elegantly carved flowers and twisted vines. Her gaze traveled down from the smooth redwood and found the dragon coat of arms hanging on the far wall. The coat of arms for the kingdom. The coat of arms of the Lystad.

Kyana scowled, got to her feet, and padded over to the wall on quiet toes. She reached up, taking the soft cloth between long, dirty fingers. She ripped the thing off the wall with one violent tug. She crumpled up the blue threaded dragon and tossed it into the far corner. She fell back on the bed, with her eyes squeezed closed, but sleep refused her. She could almost hear the laughter of denied dreams ringing in her ears as she pulled a pillow securely over her face and bit down hard.

# CHAPTER 51

Kyana was woken by the sound of little feet, scuffing the wooden floor of her room. There was a light click of dishes being set on the table, and the rustle of cloth being flipped open nearby. Kyana listened for a short time, not making any moves to get up, and instead tried to fall back asleep. She did not remember what she had been dreaming, but even in her disillusioned half-awake state, she knew it was better than her new reality. Sweet or not sweet, a dream she could understand, or even control if she put her mind to it. She had done it before, harnessing her consciousness under leagues of that heavy ocean of dream world, actually bending the imaginary universe to her will. It had been a long time, but she would have loved to give it another try. The shuffling sounds of someone in her room, however, was in no mood to allow her such luxury. Kyana regretfully opened her eyes.

The noisy intruder turned out to be a girl. Not Lilly but a different girl, a new girl.

Kyana wondered briefly, where Lilly might be. She quickly pushed that thought out of her mind with a rough force of someone who did not really want to know. She remembered the way the girl had looked at her during her trial. That fear she saw pooling in those watery eyes. That absolute terror. She did not want to think about how, Lilly herself, probably requested to be sent as far away from her as possible. Again, Kyana shoved away the thought and turned her mind back to the girl in her chambers.

The girl looked about thirteen years old, short, thin featured, with skin lightly tanned by the sun. Kyana could see her profile as she poured steaming water from a pitcher into a large wash bowl. Her nose was small and pointed with a slight upturn at the end, giving her a mousy look. Her mouth was also petite, but full and dark pink. Kyana could see a scar that curved down from her chin and out of sight under her jawline. Her light brown eyes were large and focused intently on the task at hand, which was proving to be complicated. The pitcher was so comically large and obviously hot. The girl's hands trembled around it, seemingly both with strain under its weight and also fear of being scalded.

She must have felt Kyana's eyes on her because her gaze darted away from the pitcher to meet them. The girl let out a little squeak, which was also very mouse-like, and dropped the pitcher in her surprise. Boiling water splashed out in all directions. The girl had sidestepped the steaming liquid, saving herself the almost certain burns in her haste. Kyana bit back a laugh as the girl quickly dropped to her knees and mopped up her mess with a nearby towel, face flushed with embarrassment. When the towel had soaked up as much of the water as it could, the girl straightened up and turned to Kyana. Her young face was seriously set, but a trace of pink blush was still visible under her ears.

"Docent," she said, falling to one knee, and putting her left hand to her mouth, which was customary during the First Peace when meeting a leader of a clan. Although it was supposed to be left knee and left hand, not right knee and left hand, Kyana decided not to mention that. It was a custom belonging to years long passed by and definitely did not belong to the girl before her.

"Don't do that," Kyana said, sitting up and flipping her legs over the edge. The girl's eyes seemed to widen twice their original size, as she looked up from the floor.

"M–My apologies Docent. Did I do it wrong? The elders showed me, but I've never—"

"No, you did it perfectly," Kyana lied, getting to her feet and lowering a hand to the girl. "I just don't want you to kneel for me." Kneeling before a prisoner, even if that was not her official "title." Ward of the Kingdom Neira and Castle Lyist, she supposed it was now. However, she was a prisoner none the less. The humiliation of kneeling before a prisoner was more shame than Kyana was willing to put on such a young girl.

The girl hesitated, eyeing her hand, before taking it and rising to her feet. Kyana saw the mark of the Faithful on the inside of her thin wrist, rippling delicately over the small veins there. Kyana blinked.

"Clan Bellway?" Kyana asked, recognizing the name that was burnt into the girl's skin. "You're a long way from home." The last Kyana heard, Clan Bellway held camp deep within Eryl Kingdom, where the homeland began to break off into their more populated islands.

*But,* Kyana mused, *that had been long ago.*

"That depends miss."

"On what?"

"On... on your definition of home," the girl said shyly.

Kyana looked down at her and caught her light brown gaze.

*One.* The girl had the most innocent eyes she had ever seen. Brown, but not muddy. Flecked with gold they were full, large, almost too large for her small rounded face.

*Two.* The girl's eyes seemed to widen farther, but she did not look away.

*Three.* The light blush seemed to run across the tops of her cheeks and over her nose. Kyana was instantly reminded of Ira and a smile tugged her lips.

By four, the girl blinked rapidly and looked back down to the floor, her blush growing dark and reaching her ears. Kyana reached out and tapped the bottom of the girl's chin, guiding her face back up.

"Please, call me Kyana," she said. "Forget the Docent business. And no kneeling. The floors here are hard and no good for kneeling."

The girl blinked a few times and smiled. "My name is Pennly. Pennly Graywater.... But my clan calls me Pen. I'm your new handmaid."

"Nice to meet you, Pen." Kyana nodded. "Welcome to Castle Lyist."

The young girl nodded, eyes darting around for something more to say.

"W–would you like to wash?" she asked, relaxing a little more under Kyana's smile. "I have some water here..." Her eyes fell onto the floor, where the water in question had slowly begun to dry. She looked back up hastily. "I can draw a bath if you like."

"Actually..." Kyana looked down at her state. She had spent the past week in a dark, filthy cell with no ability to clean herself and was in desperate need of some care. She could smell herself, ripe and sickly sweet, but she disliked the idea of having this girl draw her bath and clean her back. She had not liked it when it was Lilly, and she liked the idea even less now that it was some sweet girl sent into exile to care for the Lystad's new little bitch. Kyana had toyed with the idea of telling Temper just that when she saw him that day, and draw her own bath, but decided that would only serve in hurting the girl's feelings.

"Actually… a bath would be lovely. Thank you, Pen."

Pen practically beamed with joy.

"Of course, Doce- Kyana… miss…" She gave an awkward little curtsy before darting to the door and rapping lightly with her knuckles. The heavy lock slid back, and she flew out the door to retrieve more hot water, casting one last smile over her shoulder.

Kyana was not alone for long, which was good. Her thoughts were no friend to her today, and any distraction was welcome. Another knock came. Kyana realized the bolt was still drawn back, making the knock unnecessary. Someone was kindly waiting for her to answer.

"Come in," she called, and Ira entered with a box in her arms.

"Good morning!" Ira said, kicking the door closed behind her. She ignored the click of the lock sliding into place behind her, grin turned to Kyana. "How are you feeling?"

"Alive," she answered, after a moment's consideration.

Ira shrugged. "Well, better than feeling dead. You meet Pen?"

"Yes."

"What do you think? Sweet, huh? Think she'll do alright?"

"Yes, sweet… she deserves better than to serve a prisoner." Kyana shook her head in disgust. "Why would the Faithful shame her like this?"

"Oh, she asked to be sent here," Ira said, dropping the box onto her messy bed. "Her and about thirty other Faithful."

"Thirty?" Kyana glanced up, frowning.

"They don't see serving you as a shame Kyana… prisoner or no, you're a dragon. They decided Pen would be best, though. She's young, strong, shy, but intelligent. She is also young enough and lucky enough to be free of firsthand persecution by those against Faithful's. She's less angry, less resentful than most. It gives her a better chance of becoming happy here. Building a life."

*And what a life.* Kyana thought bitterly. *Behind bars.*

"What is that?" Kyana motioned to the box.

"Clothes," she answered, on odd spark in her hazel eyes.

"Clothes?" Kyana frowned. "I thought you were a kitchen hand? Why do they have you running errands like a common servant?"

"Oh, I volunteered to bring you these…"

"Why?" Kyana frowned, uncertainty rising in her belly like a dog raising its head to sniff at something unpleasant in the air.

"I wanted to see your face."

"Ira," Kyana warned. "What is it?"

"Well…" Ira said, her voice holding an odd warbling quality that made Kyana nervous. "The king and some of the… more agreeable members of the advising council, thought it would be best for you to have new clothes. An image to match your new title."

"What? A new set of chains?"

"No," Ira shook her head. "Ward of the kingdom. Last dragon and descendant of Kyara. Docent to the Rekindled Faithful." Ira had a curious grin as she looked down at the box. She seemed to be biting back laughter, and with difficulty. Her teeth were digging into her lower lip in a way that must have been painful. Kyana approached warily. She opened the box as if expecting to see a snake coiled and ready to strike. When she saw what had Ira damn near bursting with held back mirth, her jaw dropping in disbelief.

"No," she half groaned; half spat. "No. No way in the six blue hells."

"Ya…" Ira said, a squeak of laughter was quickly bitten back down. Kyana started to worry she'd grind her lower lip straight off her face. "I know."

"What the hell kind of nonsense is this?"

"Propaganda, my dear dragon," Ira said, eyebrows raised. "Pure, unabashed, unbridled, propaganda."

"This," Kyana said, eyes wide as she reached down to the fabric and pulling up a piece of the horribly gaudy material. "This is ludicrous."

"Ya…" Ira said, finally letting the laughter burst from her like water through broken damn, flooding the room. "That too!"

# CHAPTER 52

Kyana did not want to go. She stood, rigid and determined, a hair's breadth away from stomping her feet in protest. She knew she was acting like an impudent child, childish in a way she had never been before, even before childhood had left her. She did not care. She only knew she was being used. Toyed with, played with like a puppet or a doll and she did not like it. Not one bit.

*But that was the deal, wasn't it?* One of those damn voices hissed unpleasantly into her ear. Kyana tried to ignore it, but it slithered inside her mind, wriggling, satisfied in its "I told you so," fashion that made Kyana want to grab her long curls by the roots and pull. *That was the agreement when you signed your name so neatly, so **obediently**, below his. Well, here you are, little girl. Welcome to the consequences of your actions. Please enjoy your stay.*

Even so, it took both Ira and Pen a solid hour to convince her. The feast was for her, after all. It was to prove her acceptance as ward and to satisfy the Faithful that she was safe, while simultaneously convincing the kingdom that they were safe from her. A tremendous job for a single party, and a complete waste of time as far as Kyana was concerned, but the slinking, self-satisfied voice was right. She had signed her name, and now it was time to accept the consequences. No matter how bitter they tasted as they went down.

It took another hour for her to get dressed and ready. The ridiculous get up that was made especially for her, was so outrageous, Kyana had half a mind to set it on fire then and there. She could not, however, not with that shackle around her neck. She might be able to produce a little puff of dramatic smoke or even a spark from between her teeth, but for any real fire, anything that would genuinely burn, it would take at least some amount of change. The band around her neck was just snug enough to know that Kyana could make no such change without it burying deep into her skin, cutting off first her oxygen, and then her life. It was that thick and ugly piece of metal that Kyana though she would be wearing to the feast, but a stiff knock against her door came to prove her wrong.

A guard entered without a word or waiting for the bid to enter. He was holding a full set of keys in one hand and a small smooth wooden box in the other. He came in silence and stayed that way as he set the box and keys on the table.

"And hello to you too, Gerald," Ira said, finally.

Kyana glanced up to see a flash of annoyance in Ira's hazel eyes, which made her smile. Her gaze traveled to the girl's arm, whose sleeve was still covering the mark of the Faithful quite completely. Ira was willing to come to her defense… but she was not yet ready to give up her secret. At that very moment, with the new law in place, the Faithful's who had quit their houses within the castle to join the throng outside the city wall had begun trickling back to their homes. It was legal to live openly as a Faithful now, but Ira's situation was somewhat tricky. It made sense, she supposed, she still lived with her parents who were both avidly against Faithfuls. Revealing the fact that she had held onto her grandmother's stories, even after her parent's insistence that she abandon them, could lead them to throw her out. Ira had nowhere else to go. Besides, her best friend was the king after all. It would have meant telling the Lystad that she had been lying to him from the moment they met. Even a friendship built on so many years and so much affection may not last such a lie. Ira was obviously not ready to test either theory. That was alright with Kyana, but she could not help a small jolt of disappointment.

She turned her attention back to the guard, who opened the small wooden box to reveal a necklace. It was small, round, just large enough to wrap around her neck without choking her. The entire surface was coated with a thin layer of bronze, polished until it gleamed. Gold patterns twisted and swirled around its surface in elegant, almost fairy patterns. Little red gems dotted around the decorations, giving it a sparkling quality that Kyana could not deny was quite lovely. Underneath all the decorations, however, Kyana knew it was made of Dragon Iron.

The guard stepped up to Kyana.

"Turn," he said harshly. Ira frowned and Pen's eyes became so wide with astonishment that they almost swallowed her face whole. Kyana did not move.

"Turn... what?" The guard looked at her stupidly for a few minutes, before the exceedingly complicated thought locked into place.

"Turn, *please*," he said, in a tone tottering dangerously on sarcasm, but Kyana turned all the same. The guard clipped the necklace closed over the skin of her neck and checked that it was secure. He then used the keys to unlock the sizeable inelegant metal loop around her throat. It fell hard and heavy onto one of her color bones, and Kyana winced. The guard finished sliding it from around her neck and made to leave.

"And who has the key to this collar then?" Kyana called after him, tapping her new little decoration. She had noticed that the lock on the necklace was far too small for any of the keys the guard had on his ring. The guard turned and spoke in a disinterested tone.

"There is only one key to that lock, and it is in the safe possession of the king himself." He then turned and left without another word. Kyana held back the flurry of fire in her chest, her other self-flaring with indignation and frustration. If she tried to change now... if she ever tried to change again, she would be immediately decapitated. She had the judge, jury, and executioner wrapped ever so elegantly around her neck, and the one who held the key was of the same blood as those who helped to slay her entire family... both her families. Dragon and human. The idea made her ill.

# CHAPTER 53

The feast was just getting started, and Kyana could already hear the music, laughter, and lively buzz of conversation from the hall below. She gave her reflection one last mournful glance.

"You look lovely," Pen said. Kyana glanced up to see a look of awe on her new handmaid's face. Ira would undoubtedly have said the same, but she had already left for the kitchen to help with the feast.

*I look like a dressed-up puppet in a game I never wanted to play.* Kyana turned and made her way to the door. To her surprise, she found it unlocked. The guard who put on her new pretty collar must have left it open.

*Good dog. Here. Have a cookie.*

Kyana yanked the door open, and it slammed to the other wall with a loud bang, which made the decorative curtains sway violently. The two waiting guards jumped in surprise. Kyana swept out the door, Pen and the two guards falling into cautious step behind her. The halls were mostly empty, but not by some decree or order. Everyone was celebrating in the great hall. There were only a few stragglers here and there. Servants, going to and from various duties, and partygoers in brightly colored garb enjoying private conversations in quiet locations. A few doing a little more than talking.

Kyana passed a couple halfway hidden behind a statue of some long dead Libera, arms tangled around each other, lips never needing breath. The woman, whose black hair was already a tangled mess in the man's hands, glanced over as they passed. She made a squeaking noise like a rusty hinge and tried to shove the man away from her, but by the time he pulled back enough to see what his woman was shrieking about, Kyana and her followers had already passed by. Others scattered the hall, and all quieted and turned to watch with wide eyes as they went. A few whispered hastily behind their hands, but Kyana paid them little mind. However, a few whispering stragglers were not the only people she passed in the hall.

Augustine turned the corner just as Kyana and her followers made it to the edge, drawing Kyana face to face with the light eyed medic who had cared for her with such diligence. They stood, frozen for a moment. Augustine's eyes widened, looking down at Kyana. He surveyed her dress, saying nothing, until his eyes came back to her face.

"Augustine—" Kyana began but did not finish whatever explanation she may have started to form. She was drawn to a quick silence as the older man's eyes narrowed into gray slits and he spat directly into her face. Kyana's head jolted back, as if he had hit her. Pen gave a little gasp that she tried to capture behind her small hands. The guards did, and said, absolutely nothing. Kyana blinked the saliva out of her eyes, as Augustine leaned down towards her, so that his words would not be misheard.

"You should never have been allowed to live," he hissed. "I should have let the fever take you."

Kyana looked up at the man, spittle slipping down her cheek. The bemusement was gone, all hesitation from the throne room was out of his gray eyes. No, that moment had passed, and all that was left was anger… fear… and hate. He stepped passed her, broad shoulder brushing by hers, hard enough to knock her to the side. He moved away down the hall, but Kyana did not look around.

"Docent?" Pen asked, stepping delicately up to her, hand touching her elbow.

Kyana reached up and wiped the liquid from her face with her sleeve. She cleared her throat, gathered herself, and shoved the lump that had risen in her throat down deep. She turned to Pen and gave her a little smile.

"I'm alright," she answered, patting the girl's hands. "Let's go." She continued on her way, and the rest followed. She wanted to get this humiliation over with as quickly as possible. They continued swiftly to the end of the hall where two large double doors stood waiting. They were thrown open before her, and Kyana entered. Everyone near the doors stopped to turn and part out of her way.

Kyana honestly could not blame them for staring with such evident bemusement. She did look rather ridiculous. Her dress was made in the same slim pants and half skirt style as the last dress they made for her. These cloths, however, were made out of deep blood red and velvet black material. The thin, almost tight pants were black and so were the dragon claw-shaped clips that held it back on her hips. The skirt that curved back and tapered down to trail behind her was a deep red. The corset was also red but was patterned with a decorative dark gold string to emulate dragon scales. Black strings tied the corset in the back with crisscrossed patterns. The sleeves were black, half covered her shoulders, then dipped down to a half glove with a ring attached at the middle finger. Each ring was made of gold and decorated with a dragon head that's nose pointed into a nail. There were also golden cords that emulated dragon wings which took the place of a shawl. It swept from her left shoulder, curled around her back and attached again at her right hip. From there, it fell along with her dark skirts. The tips were pointed like claws and shone with triangular red stones. Her hair was curled in thick auburn locks which were then skillfully twisted into a loose bun by Pen and decorated with red and gold stones, and a thin black ribbon.

She was an absolute sight. Kyana knew it. An embarrassing, overdone, mockery of what she was. A show meant to interest, entertain, and sooth their fears of what scared them with humor. What frightened them was her.

Kyana slowed in her entry. She realized she had no idea what to do now. She stood there a moment, watching the dancing, eating, and feasting. Tables that lined the room were piled high with eyes which looked at her from all directions. She suddenly felt her face growing rather hot. Thankfully a voice called her name.

"Kyana!" Called a loud jovial, albeit slightly slurred voice from deep within the crowd. Neander broke through shortly; wide grin crossed his somewhat reddened face.

"There you are!" Neander bellowed in her ear, clapping an arm around her shoulders, pulling her in for a one-armed hug, his other hand occupied with a half-empty flagon of something very strong. "We were starting to worry where you got off to! Some people started checking for signs of fire!"

"All they needed to do was check my locked room to have their troubles soothed," Kyana answered stiffly.

"Oh, ya?" Neander asked, blinking at her, a small frown spreading his face. "I thought that would only be at night from today on. Well, unless we're feasting!"

Kyana watched as he took a long heavy drink and smacked his lips. "You seem pretty tense," he noted, squeezing her arm. "All the eyes, eh? Go on then" He held the goblet out to her. The smell made her nose wrinkle. "This is good stuff Kyana, you should really give it a try. Loosen you right up." He offered the drink again, but she declined.

"So, you can look me in the eye today?" she asked coolly. Bloodshot as they were, Neander's eyes had no trouble finding her gaze. She remembered how he could not even cast a glance in her direction the other day, standing before king and court.

"Oh, come now, don't be that way," Neander's face fell. "It was a trial. I had to be there, and I'm a knight, I have to go with whatever decision the crown and kingdom decides on… it's my obligation but… doesn't mean I wanted you to be harmed. Come angel, you know I don't wanna see you hurt, right? I mean, you may be a bit, uh, might have different wings than I originally expected, but you're still that same angel in the treetops, right?" Kyana nodded slowly.

"Well, then, I don't see the problem!" Neander said, leaning a little more of his weight on her as he took another swig. Kyana became very curious as to where Neander spent his younger years. He was most certainly not born in Castle Lyist or any of the larger cities of the Four Kingdoms. His easy acceptance of something so strange, so generally abhorrent, was clearly due to far less spoon-fed fears and fairytales full of prejudices. Perhaps one of the smaller villages, or cities that had broken away from the Four Kingdoms. Or perhaps even Eyrel Kingdom? She made a note to ask him about it later, but was currently caught off guard by how suddenly she accepted his words. His trust. It filled her with a small sense of relief, as if she had been holding dead air in her lungs and was finally able to let some out. Augustine may be lost to her… but Neander was still there.

"I don't think many share your feelings," Kyana noted, looking around the room to see many eyes quickly averting their glance.

"Some do!" Neander said. "And for the rest, damn their eyes and pay them no mind. They'll come around, eventually."

Kyana severely doubted it but felt no need to harsh Neander's high spirits. She glanced around, feeling the absence which was Pen. She and the guards had dispersed as soon as Neander wrapped his arm around her. The guards had gone to attend to other duties, and Kyana caught sight of Pen having what looked like a pleasant conversation with Ira. Pen smiled, and Ira waived. Kyana was about to wave back when Neander tightened his grip around her shoulder and started steering her towards the high table.

"Here, come, you should eat. And drink. And then drink some more."

"I don't think inebriation is going to help me here," Kyana said.

"Oh! I disagree!" Neander winked. "Inebriation helps everywhere! Besides, the speech is about to start."

"Speech?"

"Ya, the king has a whole to-do."

The king in question was not at the high table, which allowed Kyana some relief. There were, however, knights already seated and being served drinks, loaves of bread, and steaming vegetables whose salty scent made Kyana's mouth water. She was led to a seat, Neander taking the one beside her. This time, no one stood as she took her place. Familiar faces only staring as the bustle of conversation halted, seeming to trip and stumble over her presence. One knight shoved back from the table, making all the cups and pitchers rattle in surprise. He stood and left the hall entirely.

"Apologies for spoiling your fun," Kyana said hotly, to those who remained. But she felt a small blade like sensation digging into her gut. The knight who had left at the sight of her had been Everett. She could still see his tall, almost hulking frame, weaving in and out of the dancers to disappear out the double doors. Kyana knew as the doors slid closed behind him, and the dancers swept away the clear path he had carved through their distracted ranks, that his friendship had been burned away forever.

"No worries," piped up one of the knights after a long pause.

"Ya no worries at all," Neander said, snagging an unused goblet and filling it to the brim.

"Here," he said, and this time she took it without question, draining half of it in one gulp.

"Oh, easy there," Teller said, appearing at the table. He took the seat on the other side of Neander, leaning over the table, brown bearded face grinning to Kyana. "That is potent stuff right there. A girl like you should be careful."

"She's a fuckin dragon lady Teller," Neander said, rolling his eyes, "She can probably drink you under the table and then some."

"If her drinking capacity is anything like her bow skills, then you're probably right." Kyana looked up to her other side. Young Lionel had taken the empty seat Everett had left. He smiled at Kyana. It was a slightly nervous smile, but he looked her directly in the eyes as he spoke. "Good evening, Kyana." Kyana nodded, almost shyly.

"Oh, come off it." Teller shook his head. "So, she's a dragon. She can breathe fire like a dragon, doesn't mean she can drink like one."

"Shall we wager?" Neander grinned, leaning in.

"Neander, do not enlist me in your drunken competitions," Kyana said, but she was smiling now. She smiled not because she could win the wager. No, actually, dragon or not, she had very minimal capacity for drink. She was smiling because of them. The three knights sitting by her, talking to her, actually joking with her. They were not running. Not vying for her blood. They were not scorning her for what she was. They were teasing her, but with no ill intent... they teased her just as if she was simply Kyana of the woods, the girl they had known before. This amazed and filled her with a swell of overwhelming gratitude that made her eyes sting with unfallen tears. Those three... those three knights and Ira. They knew what she was, and they still saw her for *who* she was... at least to a point.

Kyana fingered the collar around her neck. It was a step, though. She was not dead. A few did not hate her. It was small. But a start. But a start to what? Acceptance? Trust? Would that... *could* that ever be the case? Or would Kyana only ever be the little pet of the kingdom? *Good girl. Drink your drink. Wear your collar.* Kyana swallowed the rest of her cup.

Their conversation seemed to be drawing more attention. A few passersby slowed to listen. A few other knights that Kyana had seen before, but did not know, joined in.

"Nah, Nah, I bet she would be down after one glass."

"Screw off, Wayne. She's already down one glass and she's still perfectly sober."

"I'll bet four down, and she's passed out."

"Ten, and she'll just be getting started."

Truth be told Kyana's head was already feeling fuzzy as she was handed her second glass. She looked up to see who was giving it to her.

"Ira," she smiled wide. The knights went quiet in their debate and then burst out laughing.

"Why does she like you so much more than us?" Neander asked Ira in a mockery of anger. He banged his hand against the table, nearly toppling his glass and its contents everywhere.

"Well, because I'm just so much better looking," Ira said with a wink.

"Well, that's just not true," Neander said brushing back a lock of hair with a dramatic flick of his wrist. Another volley of laughter followed.

*Perhaps this is a prison.* Kyana thought, watching Neander try to pelt Ira with a bread bun, and Ira ducking behind Lionel's chair to evade it. *But... it is a very... cheerful prison.*

She had missed the sound. The clanking of cups, the talk, the music, such noise. As soothing the sound of silence is... the woods did get... excessively still. Exceedingly empty.

Ira leaned in to fill her goblet once more.

"Call me if you need anything," she said.

"Thank you," she said, meeting her bright eyes.

"Pen is around also... and eager to please." Ira's hint was so heavy it nearly broke the table as it dropped. Kyana glanced up to see Pen standing off to the side, looking nervous but smiling all the same. Kyana waived a little. Pen seemed startled at the friendly gesture and hesitantly waved back.

"Not what she expected me to be?" Kyana asked under her breath.

"No," Ira whispered. "I don't think she minds though. She looked a little afraid when I first saw her coming in this morning. Skittish, truly."

"Oh?"

"Ya," Ira grinned wider. "Seems quite taken now though."

"Taken?"

"She likes you."

"She never saw a dragon before in her life," Kyana said, watching Pen exchanging her weight from one foot to another, infrequently chatting with passing servants. "She was expecting a monster with fangs and claws."

"You do have fangs and claws," Ira pointed out.

"Not all the time." Kyana shrugged, taking another long swig.

"That's three!" Neander called happily, not paying attention to Kyana and Ira's conversation, far more intent on the betting as coins actually began to exchange hands.

"Why is she just standing in a corner?" Kyana asked under her breath. "She looks very uncomfortable. Why doesn't she eat, sit, dance, do... something?"

"She's a handmaid... she's the one who is supposed to be serving, not being served."

"Then why is she—"

"She's your personal handmaid. She's a Faithful. She only serves you."

Kyana suddenly realized the full depths of Pen's situation. A Faithful girl, in a strange place, with her only purpose being to serve someone who did not want to give her orders. The thought of making Pen fetch her food, water, made her uncomfortable. And yet...

Kyana motioned for her to come over. Pen nearly tripped over herself with her eagerness.

"Can I do something for you Docent- Kyana, mam... um, mistress...?"

"Breathe girl, you're gonna hurt yourself," Teller said, patting Pen on the shoulder.

"It's okay, Pen," Kyana said in a tone as soothing as possible. She could already hear a slight slur at the end of her words as her tongue started to grow loose in her mouth. She corrected it as well as she could.

"Can I do something for you?" Pen asked, trying to straighten up a bit.

"Yes, please," Kyana said. "Grab that chair over there." She motioned to an abandoned seat off to the side. Pen did so immediately. "Sit."

"Mistress?" Pen looked at her like she was speaking in a foreign language.

"Sit with me," Kyana said. The knights stared at her, utterly bemused.

"But..." Pen's eyes darted around her. "Mistress I..."

"Don't call me Mistress... and also, have a seat... please."

"But Kyana, miss... I don't believe it is customary for a handmaiden to..." Pen trailed off slowly.

"Customs be damned!" Neander bellowed loudly, scooting his chair so that Pen could take a place at the high table. "We have a dragon in our midst. What is customary anymore? Besides, you don't follow the typical servant's code of the kingdom. You follow hers... right?"

"Please sit, Pen," Kyana smiled. "That is what I would like you to do. If I think of anything else... you will be close by. Makes it easier for me to tell you." Pen sat slowly, as if waiting for Kyana to change her mind and send her away. She did neither, and the conversation started in full force once more.

"Unfortunately, I don't work for you," Ira said. "I've got to get back to it." She gave Pen a little wink, before moving back down the tables.

"Here." Kyana handed Pen her half-empty goblet. "Drink. You'll feel better." Pen took it timidly, took a sip, and then coughed. The knights laughed, and Neander pattered her on the back. Pen smiled.

*That's better.* Kyana thought, watching Pen chatting timidly with Neander. *Smile. That is much better.*

"Ah!" Teller straightened up in his seat. "There he is."

Kyana looked up, and her stomach dropped. She knew he would be here. Obviously, he would be there, but for some reason, it still hit her like a fist in her chest. He stepped through the double doors, two guards to his right, and Temper on his left. They were speaking with smiles and made no moves to interrupt the feast with their arrival. The crowd parted before them in any case, allowing them a clear path to the high table.

Kyana watched the king's blue eyes crinkle as he laughed at something Temper said. Two people coming to an amicable agreement. Two people as different as it was possible to be. One old, with a face withered by time and robes of humble blue fabric. The other tall, young, full of life and virility, draped in rich golds and browns, screaming of the power given to those born into it. Side by side they walked; smiles painted on their faces like so much art on the walls. Everyone stood as the king reached the high table. Everyone but Kyana who was instantly set upon by Temper.

"Docent," he said, falling momentarily to his knee, putting his hand up to cover his mouth. "It is an absolute pleasure to see you again. You look lovely tonight."

"Thank you," she said, watching him rise, purposefully ignoring the king's gaze. "Are you staying for the feast, Temper?"

"I'm afraid I had to decline the king's kind request," Temper said regretfully. "I have matters needing attending to with your Faithful. After the toast, I'll be returning to them. Much work to be done."

Must scatter the Faithful. Keep to the agreement. They do not want those pesky heathens blocking their gates any longer than necessary. Then there are those that might choose to stay. How many would that be, Kyana wondered. If they had any true thoughts in their heads, they would all go and go quickly. Perhaps it was legal to be a Faithful in Castle Lyist, but she could not imagine it would be a comfortable life. Not for a few decades at the very least. Maybe a few centuries.

"I'm sorry to hear that," Kyana said, with utter honesty. She had enjoyed talking to the old man. Sharing stories with him had been like a letter from home. Her real home, of years ago. A time of war... but also the time of her life when she had family, friends, and her dragons. When the world was crazy and violent, and out of its gods damn mind, but hers, all hers.

Temper smiled kindly as he spoke.

"I will be back in three months' time, my lady," he said. "I must see home those of my former clan, back to their villages and their families... but then I will return to you and yours. I promise you this."

"It has been a pleasure, sir," Kyana said, still not looking at the king, though she could feel his eyes on her, searching her face.

Temper bowed his head. "The pleasure, dearest woman, it has been all mine."

"Shall we?" the Lystad finally said, gesturing to the two remaining seats at the head of the table. Temper nodded, gave Kyana another bow, and shot Pen a warm smile, before moving down the rows to take his seat. Kyana turned to the plate of food which had been slipped before her when she was not looking. It sent wafts of steam into the air along with the sweet scent of sugar and gravy, but Kyana ignored it. She had lost her apatite. Instead, she pulled her goblet close, as if a child searching for comfort in a familiar plaything, and gulped down the contents hastily.

"You feeling alright?" Pen asked, leaning in beside her and lowering her voice. "You look pale." Kyana was about to answer when someone banged their goblet on the long table and called for silence. Kyana looked up to see the king getting to his feet as the great hall quickly hushed and soon fell silent. Every eye was turned towards the king who stood, goblet in hand. His blue eyes seemed to watch the table before him for a moment, seeming to gather his thoughts. He then looked up, and that mix of light and dark blue shown, and a smile broke his face. He began to speak.

"Today... today marks a new day. A beginning. The beginning of something ancient and something revolutionary. The day of new friendships," Lystad looked over to Temper who inclined his head. "The day of burying old hates."

Kyana snorted softly to herself. Everyone either did not notice or at least pretended not to, eyes and ears for no one but their precious king.

*Oh, that hate did not die.* So far from being buried six feet under. She knew six feet under, she had dug it herself, and this was not it. That hate, that fear, in that kingdom and all the kingdoms against dragons, had developed over centuries of squabbles, massacres, and stories of the past and passed by. No, it was far from dead. It was alive and kicking. More than that, it was skipping, dancing, on the graves of dragons. Or at least, it would be, if the kingdoms had not denied to give them any sort of burial, and not just dumped them in the trash heap like steaming dung. A few signatures would not change that. A few choice words in a pretty, pretty speech would not heal the wounds on either side. But yes. By all means, let's put on our parties, our best smiles, our false, false, good natures and say all is better. All is *fixed.* Put away your wounds, there are healed! Praise the gods, dragon fire, and saintly royal Lystad! King of peace through imprisonment! Bringer of false good faith! Bringer of the temporary reprieve! All hail his majesty!

The Lystad continued.

"Today we begin a new age for Neira. We begin an age of understanding. An age of cooperation, and although magic is still outlawed in our lands, and for good reason… on this day we welcome someone… someone who has saved our castle, our way of life, our lives themselves… a thing of ancient times, and a woman of magic. And if you don't know who I'm speaking of by this point… well, I'm truly curious…. What rock has your head been buried under the past few weeks?" A great laugh erupted from the crowd but quitted quickly as the Lystad continued.

"We thought her kind was gone. Dead and gone for centuries, but she proved us wrong. You all still have many questions I am sure… we all do… and we will have plenty of time to ask every single one because today we welcome her into our home." The king of Castle Lyist, lord of Neira, son of Jeromy Lystad and decedent of Great Lawrence II, donned in all his glittering royal glory, turned to raise his glass to Kyana.

"To Kyana Castway, Reborn in dragons breathe. Descendent of Kyara. Soul remaining heir to Clan Pastenfair, and Docent to Rekindled Faithful. And, as of today, ward of Neira Kingdom."

"To Kyana!" the entire hall called with a bravado that echoed off every wall. All goblets were raised, tipped and drunk. Neander gulped down the whole drink before dropping his cup to the table with a heavy, satisfied, "thunk" that made several people jump then laugh nervously.

"Well," the Lystad said, smiling out at the crowd after a few moments of silence. "Get back to your fun. Go. Go. This is a celebration after all." He shooed them on with his hand, and everyone laughed as the music started up again with a quick whine of strings. Kyana felt sick but reached for her goblet, anyway.

"You look ill, beautiful," Neander whispered, leaning in to fill her goblet to the brim.

"Well, I feel ill," she answered, putting the cool edge of the goblet to her lips.

"That'll help with that." Neander grinned, leaning in to clink his cup against hers, sloshing a bit of wine as he did so. "Always does for me."

Kyana tipped back the goblet and downed the entire thing in three gulps. She put the cup down to see Neander beaming with humor and excitement.

"Alright, then," she said, flashing a smile and licking stray drops from her lips. "Let the healing begin."

# CHAPTER 54

Temper had visited Kyana one more time before leaving the great hall to return to the Faithful outside the city walls. He had knelt before her, and that time Kyana had not scrunched her little brows in discomfort. Instead, she had smiled, cheeks bright pink, but not from a soft blush of embarrassment. That was four glasses of mead ago.

Damian had been watching her the whole night, counted each glass the girl put to her lips, watched her face growing pinker, her laughter growing louder, with each raise of her arm, and tilt of a cup. It was not a peal of happy laughter, not really. It was the sound of distraction, nothing more. No comfort or contentment in the sound. Damian should know. He had watched his father do the same thing since he was seven years old. That false laughter that was not truly his. Damian heard Kyana laugh only a few times, but he had memorized every lilt, every breath, and this was a false mockery of the music it once was.

It looked like she and Neander had started a competition to see who could drink a certain number of goblets in the least amount of time, which Neander had won easily. After all, he was an experienced drinker, and it became more and more evident with every passing second, that Kyana was not. Her movements were becoming sloppy, and a soft glaze dimmed her green eyes. She nearly tipped her last two cups with an absent sweep of her arm and would have spilled over the table if either Neander or Ira had not been there to catch it. Needless to say, Neander owed Teller a lot of money.

Damian wanted to walk over there. He wanted to snatch the cup out of her long fingers. He wanted to tip the pitcher over, spread it across the floor for the maids to clean instead. To have those green eyes, which had been avoiding him all evening, land on him. In surprise, or even in anger, Damian did not care. Anything was better than this. Watching her drink as if to drown herself with red wine, thick mead, and false laughter.

The third time she succeeded in tipping her cup. It clattered to the table, sending a stream of wine spattering down the long wooden surface, staining the white tablecloth a dark red. This was followed by the whooping laughter of Teller, Neander, and Lionel, who had been cheering on Kyana's continued spiral into the world of irretrievable intoxication.

"I guess that's my cue for bed then," Kyana laughed to Neander's groaning disappointment and Damian's great relief.

"I'll go ready your room then miss!" Pen said, jumping to her feet, elated to finally have something to do. Kyana smiled to the girl, thanked her, and watched with gleaming eyes as she darted up and wove her way through the remaining dancers on the floor. The feast had been going on for hours and had just begun to slow. People began retiring for the evening, slipping out in singles or in pairs, but the room was still active and loud. Damian supposed it would continue for at least a few hours more. He, however, had no interest in staying. He got to his feet, slapped Sir Arbor on the shoulder as he went, and downed the rest of his goblet.

"It's about that time for me as well."

"No! Not you too!" Neander groaned unhappily, but Damian saw Kyana stiffen as he made his way closer.

"Would the lady allow me to escort her back to her room?" Damian said with a smile that did not break the cold gaze she leveled on him. He half expected her to say, "There is no lady here," but she did not. Instead, she thought a moment, eyes narrowing ever so slightly, lips pressed tight together. Her eyes darted to the onlookers, of which there were many. Not only were Teller, Lionel, and Neander watching their interaction with rapt attention, but a few of the dancers had stopped mid-step, eyes on them, waiting to see what the dragon lady would say to their king. She looked over them all, until her gaze crawled unwillingly back to him. A tight smile pulled her mouth.

"The lady would be honored," she said, in a voice that sounded anything but honored.

Damian blinked, realization spreading sickeningly fast, like a splash of water from an ice-cold river in his face. She was playing the part again. That part he had seen with Temper when she stood in chains. The glimpse he had caught during his speech when she sat tall and elegant in her gown so gaudily made for her and inspired by his advisers, all of which he would like thrown in the Caskcare falls for dressing her like such a fool. Like such a toy. And there she was. Playing the role they forced her to play. *He* forced her to play. The part they both needed. Him to keep his kingdom safe and gain recognition from his sister kingdoms. Her, to simply survive. He knew it all and felt disgusted. It made him want to lean over the long high table and let out his supper on the stone floor in a most unkingly manner.

Instead, Damian held out his arm to the dragon lady, and she took it without hesitation. They left the hall side by side. People moved out of their way as they passed, eyes following them until the massive doors closed behind them with a creak and a thud.

The instant the musician's mewling bows and lyre was muffled behind wooden doors, Kyana pulled her arm from his grip. No, "pull" is the wrong description. She jerked it away, yanking it hard and fast as if it had been in a vat of fire and she was only now able to retrieve it from its tortured place. No, not fire either. She was a dragon, after all. Ice, then.

"There is no need to take me all the way back … *your* majesty." Kyana said, without looking at him. "I know my way well enough."

Damian noticed the slur in her voice, that was no longer slight. It hung the edges of her mouth in awkward angles and her usually sharp eyes were dull, red and glassy. Her step was also tilted, edging her sideways towards the stone wall. She was able to compensate for the moment… but moments had a way of passing by after a few glasses of Cabot's favorite mead.

"I think it would be better if I did," Damian insisted, but kindly.

"Well if you think so… then it must be true." Kyana snapped, the last word slurring until it came out as "ru". She continued down the hall, Damian following at her side. He noticed one guard at the double doors beginning to trail behind them and waived him off with a smile. The guard only nodded, before replacing himself by the hall entrance, leaving Kyana and Damian to continue down the hall alone.

"Not afraid to be alone with me?" She asked after a few moments.

"Why? Should I be?" Damian asked.

Kyana snorted. "No, I suppose not," she answered, and Damian saw her trail a long finger across the decorative necklace around her throat. He was glad at least to find it had been made to his specifications. The result, as lovely as intended. He had to check in with the smith several times to keep him on track. The smith was not lazy, Damian did not tolerate the lazy, but dragon egg, or dragon iron as it was named, was no easy thing to mold, shape, and even more difficult to decorate. Most stones, gold, gems and paints did not want to stay and took far more effort and time to fashion. There were several failed attempts with a few diamonds, sapphires and other precious stones that Damian had found pleasing to the ladies of the courts on the extremely rare occasions he had spent his leisure time in one or another of their company. Not to mention the one misguided time he had tried to give such things to Ira.

This had been back when Damian was still a pimply boy of sixteen and had developed a brief but intense infatuation with his best friend. He had presented the gems to her with all the panache and grace of a boar breaking through a wooden gate. Yet, Ira had not recognized the gesture for what it was, or at least, she tactfully pretended she did not. She oohed and aahed over them, and then promptly gave them back with a smile and a 'thank you' for allowing her to look at them. That was the end of the matter. She had never been interested in him. It hurt the young boy's feelings, how could it not, but Damian had also been grateful. Even if she had shared his interest, such a relationship would never have lasted. For him, for both of them, their friendship was important and made all the stronger for never trying, or ever truly wanting, to make it anything more than what it was. Damian quickly realized that it was enough. It was more than enough. But his times of giving away shiny trinkets had been far from over.

Damian's father had continued to introduce him to various daughters of the nobleman and lords, to which he had been polite, but had little interest. They were proper – lovely but also uptight, formal, and always appeared to have a stick shoved somewhere quite unpleasant.

Damian had been willing to put that aside occasionally, for the sake of his father's wishes, and performed such present baring rituals as was customary for courting fine ladies. He distinctly remembered one girl in particular. Giuliana. A daughter of the third prince to Sterlyn Kingdom. A royalty of a lower order, like himself. Elegant and beautiful with flowing black hair and sharp silver eyes. They would make quite a pair, his father had told him, and so Damian had courted her, but not for long. He noticed things in her short stay at Castle Lyist. Noticed the way she treated the servants and her own handmaids. At court, and to all the lords and nobles, Giuliana was the picture of beauty, grace, and intellect. The dream of any man. To the servants, however, she ignored their existence. She allowed her eyes to pass through them as if they were beneath her ability to even see as living, breathing, things in the room. Damian did not like that, not at all.

"You can tell a lot about a person by the way they treat those beneath them… and she was telling a great deal that I did not like," he had explained to his father after his father had questioned him. The king had not been upset with Damian. In fact, he had been proud of his son's character. Besides, what did it matter if Damian ever married? He was not the heir after all… or at least, he had not been at the time.

As pleasing as the young Giuliana had found such expensive jewels, the dragon iron was not so taken. All of them had fallen out of their setting, or in the case of the diamond, splintered into slivered shards as if in protest. They gave up on such and turned instead to older, less typical stones, ones that had been in the royal collection for some time. These stones had little value themselves, but they were pretty things. They had been pulled from the Caskcare mountains decades before, and seemed quite at home inlaid within the band of dragon iron. In the end, it had come out quite beautifully, but as he watched Kyana's face… he knew it was still just a shackle. No amount of paint, no glitter, no gems would change that. Again, that sinking feeling.

"That's not what I…" Damian trailed off. Kyana was not listening anyway. She had stopped part way down the hall, eyes fixed on the floor, swaying slightly. "Kyana?"

"Yes," she said, completely clear, as if she had never touched a drink a day in her life.

"Are you alright?" he asked, stepping up and ducking his head to look at her face. It was still pink, and her glazed green eyes were watching the floor with an intensity to break glass.

"I? I am fine," Kyana said, blinking a little. "Your floor, however, needs some work."

"Oh?" he said, looking down to the space a few inches from her feet, not noticing anything out of the ordinary except some stray clumps of dirt tracked in by the feet of the guests. "What's wrong with it?"

"It keeps spinning," she said, in a voice that teetered on the edge of humor. "You should have that looked into."

Damian bit back a laugh with effort.

"I'll get right on that," he said. "In the meantime, I find it helpful to hold on to the wall as you go... just as a guide."

"That'll stop the spinning?" she asked, eyes darting up to him for a brief moment before going back to the offending floor.

"No," Damian admitted. "But it'll help."

Kyana moved, reaching out her right hand, and began to drag it along the stone wall as she went. She walked towards the staircase with a more direct track, but she still stumbled every few feet. He wanted to take her other arm, help steady her step, but he knew that would upset her, so he left it alone at her side, and watched every inelegant stride with cautious eyes, ready to step in when the moment called. At least this time she was not bleeding all over the place.

"I don't believe I told you how lovely you looked tonight," Damian said, eyes still waiting for a stumble too large for her to compensate.

Kyana snorted.

"I look ridiculous," she answered, tugging at her skirt with her free hand, while still keeping a firm grip on the wall with the other.

Damian bit back another laugh. "Yes, I have to admit, the designers went a little over the top."

"A little," Kyana looked over her shoulder to him, eyes wide and for a moment the anger was gone. For a brief breath, all the ice melted. She was just Kyana. "My dress has claws. Did you see the claws?"

"Yes, I saw the claws," Damian said grimacing. "They just thought... you're a dragon and well..."

"My clothes should state it... nice and loud?" Kyana finished for him, turning back to watch her step.

"I didn't think they would go that far with it." Damian's voice held a note of apology.

Kyana gave a little grunt of recognition as they reached the staircase. She stood before it for a moment, face blank and staring as if forgetting how stairs worked. Damian was about to ask her if she needed help when she stepped forward and began the ascent.

"So, how are you?" Damian started breaking the most complete and uncomfortable silence he had ever known. He had to, another moment and he would suffocate under it.

"What?" Kyana asked as they stepped out onto her floor and they continued down the hall.

"How are you? How's your room, is it satisfactory, or is there anything you need?" Damian said as they stepped up to Kyana's doorway and she turned to stare at him with glazed, distrustful eyes. "I'll have a word with your dressmaker, have them tone down the whole… you know…" He gestured with a hand to the dragon claw clips and wing-shaped shawl. "Just, well, *all* of that. But is there anything else you need to make your stay more comfortable?"

Kyana frowned at him, glazed eyes half squinted. "My stay?" She suddenly burst into laughter. A laughter that made Damian cringe. High, false, and sickening laugh. It was a mockery of joy. The bastardization of happiness, raped by an unmistakable, underlying, despair.

"We're alone Lystad," she said, laughter cut short, green eyes going dark as a sneer slipped her face like a pacing cat trapped in a cage. All ice returned. "You don't have to pretend here."

"Excuse me, what?" Damian tilted his head in that way he never noticed he had. In a way that always made his father smile with true joy. He frowned at her.

"You don't have to pretend here," she said, raising her hands and glancing around the empty hallway. "There is no one here to put on a show for. Let's not pretend when we don't have to, it's exhausting."

"I don't understand," Damian said, but he did. He saw it in the deep endlessness of those eyes. That distrust. That disgust. And it hurt him.

"Let's not pretend this is anything but temporary, shall we?" Kyana's false laugh cut the air like a knife through hot butter, and Damian just stood there in stunned silence. "I will not be here long. You have what you wanted. You have it all. You took it all, as is your way. You have your kingdom, the Faithful pacified. Soon you'll have your gates back up, and your men at the ready, and you will have no use for some petty truce between your great power and some scattered, pathetic, powerless Faithful." Damian took every word in stunned, eye-widening silence. He felt that pit in his stomach growing heavier and heavier with every word that spilled from her lips. They struck like teeth and burned like poison. "Then I'll just be a dangerous inconvenience, as all dragons were. And just like Great Lawrence II, in time you'll see... it's better if I'm just not here to cause trouble. Beautiful dog collar or no. So, let's not pretend I'll be breathing air for much longer, let alone giving a gods damn whether my room is prettied up enough." Kyana pushed through the door, and moved to close it, but did not get the chance. Damian's hand shot out and slammed hard into the heavy door, holding it open. Kyana looked up, eyes widening in surprise.

"Is that what you think of me?" Damian felt the anger thundering in his chest, battering against his ribs. This was not *fair*. After everything. After all of it. All the effort, all the time, the grappling with his inner demons. After listening to hours of Phobos's bitching. After all the sleepless nights, which had been plenty. Which had been most since this woman, that now looked on him with such insolence and anger, quite literally dropped into his life. And he was tired. Oh, so *tired*. He was tired and frustrated because this was the last of it. This was simply unfair.

Damian was never the sort to pout, or rage, or throw a tantrum like a child. No, he was better than that, had been raised better than that. But at that moment, with that woman standing before him, that infuriating, unbelievable woman who had put him through so much in such a short time, glared at him and spat those unfair accusations, and with weariness battered at the inside of his mind like a smith at his hammer, driving him deeper into exhaustion, Damian finally broke.

"Is that who you think I am? Some petty... petty *liar*, who says only what is convenient to him at the moment?"

"I..." Kyana trailed off, taking a step back as Damian shoved the door wide, and stepped into the room after her. It banged against the opposite wall, making Kyana jump, eyes widening until they could go no further.

"Is that what you think?" Damian's voice rose, swept up on the wave of fury that spilled to every inch of his skin, every corner of his being. After everything. After all the god's damn effort it took to convince them all. Phobos, Carver, Pently, Thysman, all those sniveling, cowardice idiots that this was a good idea. And before all that! After the battle. After the woods. After fighting side by side, after all that time, after the hall... After all that, she thinks... "You think I saved you out of sheer convenience? *Convenience*?!" Damian ran a hand over his face, grinding his fingers into closed, tired, eyes, trying to clear them of this sudden blinding rage. "It would have been far more *convenient* to let them kill you. Have you executed right then and there."

"But the Faithful—"

"That fucking ragtag group of women and old men?" Damian laughed. "Yes, sure, there was a lot of um... but seriously Kyana. Them against Castle Lyist's trained army... who the hell do you think would win that fight? Even with the gates down, who do you think stood a chance? Because I have a pretty solid guess myself. And you think I'd simply go back *on my word?*" He leveled his glare on her once more. Kyana did not shrink from it, on the contrary, she leaned forward, eyes narrowing, green gaze darting around for either an exit or something with which to defend herself. But he saw it there, something he had only seen in those eyes once before. Not since that long-ago time when she was standing surrounded in a courtyard by what she thought had been demons.

*Fear.*

Damian stepped back, breathing heavily, reeling himself in, ashamed of his outburst. He waited a few moments for his temper to subside. Kyana watched him, on edge and ready.

"I do not give my word lightly Kyana Castway. I never have, and I never will," he said, voice calm. He turned to leave the room when he heard her speak.

"But do you always keep your promises Damian Lystad?" He turned back. She was standing where he had left her, hands resting by her sides, and face turned half away, as if not interested in his answer.

"Would you believe me if I said I did?" he asked, a small bitter smile cast over his lips like a shadow.

She looked at him then, deep green eyes nearly black in the half darkness of her room, which was lit by candles Pen had left for her mistress before heading off to sleep herself. The room was shadow and firelight and flickered around Kyana in a way that was past strange and into... magical. Kyana in her red and black dragons dress, auburn hair falling from its place... she had never looked so odd and yet so... right.

"No," she answered.

Damian nodded and turned to leave.

"Then I suppose you'll just have to wait and see." The door closed behind him with a soft click. He looked up to see a guard standing awkwardly in the hall, waiting to take his place outside Kyana's door for the night. As was agreed.

Damian nodded to the guard.

"Goodnight, Killian." Killian bowed low as he passed but said nothing.

King Lystad of Neira moved away down the hall of Castle Lyist, his shoes clicking against stone as he went. He glanced over at the shield on the wall and took in the dark two-headed dragon carved into its wooden surface. He stopped a moment there, watching the paint shine and gleam in the flickering light from the lamp which hung beside it. Shadows fought against the light, twisting and swirling in an odd dance for dominance. Damian thought it looked like a battle between two sides. Light and dark with the midnight dragon caught in the middle. He remembered the look of fear in Kyana's eyes and wondered suddenly, which side he was on. Or if either side was worth choosing.

Damian sighed, shaking away the absent thought. For now, everything was a mess, but all new things tended to be. Children were not born clean, no, they were born in slime. They were born bloody and crying. All new things, even good things, came at a price. But for now, everyone was safe and, in time, all would be fine. All things eventually pass and pass by. As all things must.

# CHAPTER 55

Kyana moved, every step like walking through a distorted dream. She tried to blink away the twisting room, but it refused to go. The floor continued to shift defiantly beneath her feet, and she stumbled. She caught herself on the large wooden table, which rattled beneath her weight. She looked with blurry eyes to find a tray laden with bread, fruit, and a pitcher of water waiting for her, and she thanked the gods for Pen of Clan Bellway. Kyana reached out with an arm that shifted in unison with the room. It took three missed attempts, but she finally caught the goblet and filled it with water. She drank three glasses before stopping for breath.

*Gods, that was bad.* Kyana thought, pouring herself another glass and putting it shakily to her lips. She had pushed it way too far. She had pissed him off, had seen the anger in those eyes, and if he had let it fly, Kyana would have been powerless to stop it. She reached up and fingered the noose around her neck. Kyana did not have her secret escape anymore, no last resort. She could fight, she was a good fighter, but not when she was like this, not when she was slopping drunk, and trussed up in this flaunting death trap of cloth. No more. Not again.

Kyana drank the glass of water and poured another, promising herself that she would never again be so powerless. She would never again drink herself into such vulnerability.

*But do you keep your promises Kyana of the woods?*

Kyana gave a crackling laugh that broke like a twig in flame. The laughter did not just break. It burned away. Kyana blinked her blurry eyes and found that drink was not the only thing twisting her vision. She reached up with a trembling hand and hastily whipped away the tears before they could slip down her face.

*Like a child.* She thought, grinding the tears under her palm, but they refused to stop. They tumbled and dripped from her cheeks and hands in an unstoppable stream, and her shoulders shuddered. She leaned against the table, trying to gather herself, reaching for every scattered piece with her mind, but they were too far and wide. She gasped for air, tears tumbling faster.

"Miss?"

Kyana jerked around to see Pen standing there, a pitcher of hot water in one hand and a towel in the other. Her sweet eyes were wide, eyebrows knitting together.

"Pen?" Kyana straightened up, wiping her face on her sleeve. "I didn't hear you come in."

"No, sorry, I thought you might be asleep so I..." Pen set the pitcher and the towel on the table and looked at Kyana. "Miss, are you alright?" Kyana opened her mouth to say yes, she was perfectly fine, just too much wine. To say she was wonderful, thank you very much. She opened her mouth to say just that, but her words had other plans.

"No," she whispered, a smile twitching her lips. Pen stepped forward, and before Kyana knew what was happening, had wrapped her arms around the taller woman. Kyana hesitated, feeling Pen's small arms tighten around her, then returned the hug, pulling the younger girl close.

"I'm so sorry, Pen," Kyana mumbled into the girl's hair.

"For what, miss?" she asked. Kyana broke another laugh.

"I'm sorry that you're here."

"I'm not, miss."

"You deserve better than this. You deserve better than me. I'm no dragon." Pen pulled back and looked into Kyana's eyes. A sweet but earnest smile met Kyana.

"I think you're wrong, miss. I think we don't deserve you." Kyana blinked at the girl's words, confusion searching through the fog of wine and mead. "I mean," Pen continued, shaking her head. "We've known of you for... what... a week? Look what we've already done to you. Look what we've turned you into." She looked down at Kyana's skirts, a mimicry of dragonhood, and grimaced. "You were fine before, alone in the forest. Temper told me everything. Then we found you. Humanity found you. You save us from our own shadows. You have given us hope... and for that I thank you... but in return we twist you, we dress you up, we make you do things... things you don't..." The girl looked back up, and now there were tears in her large eyes, making them glisten. "Look what we've done to you." Pen shook her head again. "We don't deserve you, miss. Not the other way around."

Kyana stood stunned, words coming and going from her lips, not making a sound, because nothing could compare. Nothing could touch. Instead, she pulled the girl to her once more, clinging to her for dear life, and Pen made no protest.

*Stupid, stupid, deluded girl.* Kyana thought. But she also knew she would kill for that stupid girl. She would kill, and die, and suffer any dress, manipulation, punishment, and injustice. As long as a stupid, silly, beautiful girl like this believed in such a beautiful illusion as herself. She would protect that innocent dream at all costs. She would do it all. Because that was what it was all about. Not Lilly's view of anger, of hate, of chances to kill and taking them. Not legends of burning kingdoms and desires for power. Not of revenge and fury. No, that was all too *human.*

It was about this moment. This embrace between strangers that were suddenly family. Because they were family now, as sure as day churned into night, and night back into day. As days passed by without return, and as inevitable as the passing of time itself, this was what it meant to be a Faithful. It was about his connection, this comfort found in the arms of another. This belief in better days, and devotion to creatures and things not quite understood. Perhaps never fully understood, and that was okay. One need not understand to believe. One does not need proof to hold hope, and Kyana would not take it from this girl. She refused to burn it away.

Together they wept and comforted, and when they fell asleep, it was side by side as sisters. For the first time in over three hundred long years, encircled in innocent arms, Kyana Castway began to remember.

# CHAPTER 56

"What?" Ellis did not feel the word form on his lips, nor intended to speak it. It just blossomed on its own, blooming out from him in an involuntary parting of his lips. Rainier watched him calm and patient. Ellis felt like the tall man could see the squirrel of thoughts chasing circles around his mind, and he was quite content to watch its panicked scampering.

"You need to go back to Castle Lyist," he repeated simply.

"But, but, general, sir," Ellis's words tumbled from him now. "I-I can't go back. I can't. I've been gone for over a week, they will be suspicious."

"Tell them you were afraid when the attack came," Rainier said, leaning back in his seat on the flat stone, hands crossing over his lap, long fingers laced together. "Tell them you were one of the first to evacuate. That you hid in the woods. It wouldn't even be a lie."

They were far past the stretch of woods separating Castle Lyist and the meadows to the South. Ellis had followed the general for hours on foot, he was panting by the end, but the general never seemed to tire. They walked out of the dimming forest with darkening shadows, and into the open rolling meadow filled with moonlight and the smell of grass and flower pollen. It was deep into the night before the general had reached his destination. A small creek broke the otherwise uninterrupted sprawling meadow. It drizzled almost unnoticeably beneath tall dancing grass, marked only by long and flat gray stones that scatted around its edge. The sound of water bubbled in the soft autumn night. Here, beside the creek, they had buried the dragon skull, marking it with one of those large and flat rocks. It was here, after putting down the last bit of soft dirt, that the tall man had torn his eyes from the starry sky and told Ellis the news that made his blood run icy and his eyes blur with fear.

"But the skull is missing!" Ellis said, eyes wide, fingers opening and closing by his sides in an unconscious gesture of panic. "They will know it's missing soon, and that's... that's..."

"The skull is not going back," Rainier's voice was soft, but held a warning edge. Ellis heeded and went quiet. Rainier's eyes were on him, those eyes of dark, never-ending silence. That insane silence.

"She is finally at rest. I will not send her back to that horrid place. Never again."

Ellis could not find his voice. He seemed to have lost it somewhere in those empty eyes. He nodded slowly.

"But you, my dear boy," He stood, brushing at his cloak. "You must go back."

"For what purpose?" Ellis asked after he found his voice. Even then, it was barely above a whisper.

"Isn't it obvious?" The Faithful turned to him, eyebrow raised, and small smile traveling from one side of his face to the other.

"But the dragon... the lady.... The dragon lady will be out of my reach." Ellis said. "I was just a Keeper. I don't have accesses to the dungeons, which I assume is where she is now if she hasn't been executed already."

"She lives," Rainier said, eyes traveling towards Castle Lyist, although the ability to see it had passed by miles and miles ago. "... I can feel it... I can... I can feel her..." He closed his eyes, and that smile widened on his face, almost breaking open, and Ellis prepared himself for sharp fangs that did not come. "Oh, gods, I can feel her... it's been so long." He opened his eyes and looked back down at Ellis. "And as for you reaching her... all in good time."

"I'm just a Keeper," Ellis said. *If they believe my story and take me back* "It'll be impossible." *Especially if I've been executed for treason and murder.*

"We just saw a dragon rise out of the inner walls of Castle Lyist for the first time in centuries Ellis..." the general's eyes sparkled, "Nothing is impossible anymore."

"But I... but I... but I killed Patryk!" Ellis burst out, hands running through his hair, tugging at the roots as if they were the source of his problem. As if he just tugged a little harder, it could release the rampaging squirrel in his mind.

"Yes, that was a bit... unexpected, wasn't it?" Rainier was still smiling, completely unfazed until he saw the tears welling in the boy's eyes. "Oh, my dear child..." He moved forward, took Ellis's hand from its desperate tugging at his hair, and squeezed it. "It is alright." He said, dark eyes softening. "You did only what needed to be done. You had no other choice. It is not your fault. Everything will be alright."

"But if they haven't found him by now, they will soon," Ellis mumbled, the warmth of the strange man's hand softening his panic. The squirrel slowed a little. "And I've been gone so long... they'll suspect me if they find him."

"We will think of something," the man soothed, reaching out to pat his shoulder. "With the skull... with the body... we will think of something. It will work itself out... I have a plan." A light breeze rustled the boy's hair, and he breathed slow. The fresh grass and smell of dirt filled him, and he drank it in, steading himself, gathering his nerves. Readying himself for what came next.

"... What will we do?" Ellis asked.

"We get your situation settled back in the castle... and after that... I will contact you and tell you what we must do."

Ellis licked his lips. He could not believe this was happening. He could not believe he was about to do this. Return to the place where he had just committed so much betrayal. Back where they would have hated him before he killed Patryk and would kill him if they found out he had. And Patryk! What was he to do with him? Lying under rocks and dung, slowly roasting in those heated caverns for days now. The smell of his rotting flesh mixing with the thick stink in the air. How was he supposed to move the body without raising suspicion, or without getting caught?

*We will think of something. It will all work itself out.*

Easy for him to say. He did not have to do it. But Ellis did. And he would. There was no denying it, there was no, 'oh sorry my general, sir, I can't do it.' Ellis could see it in those endless black eyes. There was no turning back now. The puppy was barking, and Ellis had to take care of it. As he always did. As he always would.

The sister moons spilled their light over them both, filling the air with an eerie silver sheen. It cast across Ellis, sending his shadow out, long and dark behind him, stretching like a man on a rack. Every passing second pulling him to his breaking point, but for the shadow, there was no breaking. It stretched and stretched across the cool dirt and waving grass. It may not break, Ellis thought, but if it had a voice, it would scream.

"Any and all for you, general, sir," he spoke in a steady voice that surprised even him. The Faithful smiled that long travailing smile.

"That's my boy," Rainier barely whispered. A light breeze rippled through the grass, decorating the soft browns and greens with spirals and waves like water. They swept in and out of existence. There one moment, gone the next. "That's my boy…" He leaned forward and squeezed his shoulder with reassurance. The moon caught in his black eyes, filling the emptiness with silver light. "And in return… I will bring you a gift."

"A gift?" he asked, curious, heart thumping. "What gift?"

The man blinked, and in those hollow eyes, something moved. No, not just moved. It crawled. It stalked forward into the light of the moon, awakening from a deep slumber.

"Something to sooth those bad, bad, dreams. Something you've wanted for a long, long, time." He leaned in as if to impart the most precious of secrets. "You have done very, very well, and it's time you had your darkest wish." Ellis felt warm as the man pulled away. As if the hand on his shoulder had sent its own heat into Ellis, filling him until salty sweat trickled down from the bottom of his hairline.

"You mean… him?" was all he managed to say around the violent thudding of his heart in his throat. Rainier smiled and nodded eagerly.

"Yes, child. I told you I would, and I told you truly. What would you say to a little family reunion?" As Rainier watched, a smile slid slow and steady across the boy's face. From one side to the other. With it, the Faithful was oh, so pleased. "Now then…" he stood and held out a hand to the boy and helped him to his feet. "Shall we begin?"

# ABOUT THE AUTHOR

Lydia R. Outland graduated from California State University, Sacramento with a bachelor's degree in philosophy. Because she struggled with significant dyslexia, it was not until high school that the endless universe of books was opened to her. Her dream is to open that same world to another person, even one other. Lydia is active in animal disaster rescue and lives in Amador County, California with her family and numerous animals.

# NOTE FROM THE AUTHOR

Word-of-mouth is crucial for any author to succeed. If you enjoyed *The Strangest Woman*, please leave a review online—anywhere you are able. Even if it's just a sentence or two. It would make all the difference and would be very much appreciated.

Thanks!
Lydia

Thank you so much for reading one of our **Fantasy** novels.

If you enjoyed our book, please check out our recommendation for your next great read!

*War of the Staffs* by Steve Stephenson & Kathryn M. Tedrick

"Offers an enjoyable romp for high fantasy fans."

*-Kirkus Reviews*